BROTHER RED

the sudden stillness, all of us focused on the child, I felt
like a gossamer skin on every particle of air and tree,
flower and body. Sillindar. Sillindar was here not many years
past, within the life span of the woman before us. Then she
brought the knife down. The baby didn't make a sound. I
threw forward my arms, the dust of creation from my hands,
a moment too late. The air spun savagely, my thought made
material, a force to tear the knife from her fingers. But she'd
stabbed herself in the gut, the force I'd applied pulling the
up through her stomach instead of into the air.

By Adrian Selby

Snakewood
The Winter Road
Brother Red

BROTHER
RED

ADRIAN SELBY

www.orbitbooks.net

ORBIT

First published in Great Britain in 2021 by Orbit

1 3 5 7 9 10 8 6 4 2

A CIP catalogue record for this book is
available from the British Library.

ISBN 978-0-356-50844-3

Typeset in Apollo MT Std by Palimpsest Book Production Limited,
Falkirk, Stirlingshire
Printed and bound in Great Britain by Clays Ltd, Elcograf, S.p.A.

Papers used by Orbit are from well-managed forests
and other responsible sources.

MIX
Paper from
responsible sources
FSC® C104740
www.fsc.org

Orbit
An imprint of
Little, Brown Book Group
Carmelite House
50 Victoria Embankment
London EC4Y 0DZ

An Hachette UK Company
www.hachette.co.uk

www.orbitbooks.net

For Mum

"Now I'm old enough to understand the iron of a mother's love. Too common and too profound for poets, this love."

Brother Red

Our breath, our colour do each of us keep,
On lonely trails, in mountains cold.
I mix your brews, you guard my sleep,
It's our blood, my brothers, protects their gold.
And if I die far from the fields of my home,
Take up my cloak, Brother Red,
For my tally's to claim in our fieldsman's name
that my love and my kin shall be fed.
So honour the Creed and drink to the dead,
And fear not if that be your fate,
For you'll find there's a room at the Old House,
I'll stand at the window and wait.

Chapter 1

The Magist

She's been more brave, more resistant to the torture than any of the humans.

"I'll say his name again. Lorom Haluim."

Behind her stands one of her own people, an Ososi, a giant of their kind. Some of the slaves here hail him as a brother, proclaiming that they have been changed from ordinary humans to immortal Ososi soldiers. Full of pride they show me their glistening brains and the artless ruin they've become under the knives of these drudhas who removed the tops of their skulls and experimented with flowers and roots, poisons and herbs in that quivering, warm clay.

She watches me as all the elderly Ososi have in the time since I have served the Accord, as I take their hands, transmit this shivering dust and let what I taste evolve their pain. They look at me with all the contempt a mortal lifetime confers. "It is just power" speak their eyes. Between her cries of pain she hums a handful of cracked notes, a childhood song, I think, for it is a song I heard also the Oskoro children put into harmonies, the Ososi's distant kin that once lived far across the Sar sea

1

in the Citadels. She sings one note in a minor key here, and I marvel at the depth of the change it makes to the lullaby, a note that remakes the song as though she's sending it backwards to the girl she once was.

Then I catch a word – the dust has unlocked something in her, the name of a river, and hearing it sends a rare shiver of happiness through me. In her delirium, mumbling, chasing a memory that must have followed her song, she has given me a clue to where the rest of her tribe may live. I look up at the giant Ososi behind her, known to all in these lands as Scar. Many years ago he had been capped, the top of his skull removed to leave the braegnloc ready to receive the Flower of Fates. It would have made him the tribe's chief. The work done on his skull had only just been completed when the elders of his tribe learned he was not worthy of the honour of leading them. He carved the skin from their faces, cut their own skulls to pieces and stitched both to cover his head again. He is my finest hunter. He knows of the river this old woman's pain has revealed. I'll join his crew and we will find the children belonging to her tribe. I will hope too for that wisp of disorientation, that lurch in the belly if it's close, the power of another magist, of Lorom Haluim, the one I have been tasked to find, to lead the Accord to.

"Thank you." She frowns, not realising I'm speaking to Scar, ordering her execution. His hands go to her head and chin, a smooth, fast twist breaking her neck.

Scar drags her body past me and out of the tent. We've had some quiet while the drudhas have been spooning out the droop to the prisoners, stupefying them for a while. Many are in persistent agony as a result of our work, the price of progress on any frontier.

A cold wind enters the tent as Scar leaves. This camp is high in the Sathanti Peaks, away from the scrutiny of all but the wretched tribes that live in these heights. The drudhas make good progress for they are working with living slaves that I have provided them. The soldiers they will soon learn to make from these slaves will be more than a match for any army this world could muster. The Lord Yeismic Marghoster has been as generous in the provision of slaves as his word. It took very little to fix the deformities of his younger daughter and his gratitude has been predictably ample. I recall he wept and kissed my feet as she ran about us for the first time in her life. Who alive, after all, has met a magist such as I? Their myths make us out to be gods, understandable given their limitations. His wife, more sensibly, screamed, a horrified suspicion on her. For some time she thought it must have been a trick, some potion that would wear off. I wish I could feel as these people do; their mortality generates such heat.

As I ate and nodded where required at a feast to celebrate the miracle of her straightened bones, Marghoster shared his fears for the prospects of his oldest daughter, a potential marriage to the heir to the throne of Farlsgrad, young Prince Moryc Hildmir. As I told him how little the Hildmirs would soon matter I felt his wife next to me grow more disturbed by my proximity, shifting in her seat, sweating. Yeismic would not have approved of some of her thoughts. She suffered the memories that come unbidden while in proximity to a magist for two whole courses of our dinner before excusing herself, tears streaming from her eyes. We agreed that the joy of seeing a crippled child cured could be overwhelming to a woman's more sensitive disposition.

Scar returns, giving a short grunt as he forces his huge frame through the flap of the tent. He stands once more, silent, eyes following me as I wipe the Ososi woman's piss off the only chair here.

"I don't like this place. I wish I could return home." I don't expect a reply but I need, sometimes, to say it out loud. I unstopper the wine flask and pour a cup. Taste is the second most interesting thing about taking the form of a human.

"I hope we'll find those escaped Oskoro with that old woman's tribe." Scar remains silent, watches me drink. I see a subtle shift in his eyes, a tenth of a smirk, a mote of annoyance. We had tried to capture or kill the Oskoro that lived across the sea in Citadel Hillfast. Bigger than the Ososi, an older race, all of their kind are as dangerous as Scar, and their chief, the Master of Flowers, far more so. With Scar's crew we butchered all the Oskoro we could find, for they could not withstand me. They cried out for Lorom Haluim, even his master, Sillindar, one that I dared not hope would appear. Sillindar is the Accord's great enemy and the reason for my search for Haluim, who has made his home on this world. I quelled as many Oskoro as I could, my dust taking their strength so they could be tied up. But a handful of them saw their chance, aided by the Master of Flowers, drawing in and killing two of our mercenaries, wounding even Scar. The Master, a drudha and five others fled. Worse was still to come, for as we threw lime bombs into the houses that remained, one of the women came out holding a great prize in her arm, a baby girl, her skull newly cut, the skin sewn back and a seed in her skull – clearly marking her as their future leader, the next Master of Flowers. Her mother saw us, saw me and raised a knife. I raised my arms up, a supplicating gesture, waving to instruct my men to stay back. In the sudden stillness, all of us focused on the child, I felt it, like a gossamer skin on every particle of air and tree, flower and body. Sillindar. Sillindar was here not many years past, within the life span of the woman before us. Then she brought the knife down. The baby didn't make a sound. I threw forward my arms, the dust of creation from my hands, a moment too

4

late. The air spun savagely, my thought made material, a force to tear the knife from her fingers. But she'd stabbed herself in the gut, the force I'd applied pulling the knife up through her stomach instead of into the air. She fell to her knees gasping, letting her baby fall to the ground. Scar rushed forwards to it, kicking her back. He took the baby up in an arm while the other reached for a pouch, a salve that hissed hot on the tiny body. He hummed and shushed her as he did so. I ran to them, smoothing my dust over the hole in her chest but she was already dead. Reversing death is beyond me. I attempted it nevertheless. I always do.

The wind scuffs and kicks at the tent flap. I stand and take a fur from the desk nearby. Scar remains still. He's elsewhere, eyes vacant.

"You'll leave tomorrow. Tell your soldiers. I will return to Farlsgrad's capital, Autumn's Gate. The High Red, Yblas, has returned from the Old Kingdoms. I must be at his administrator's side."

Chapter 2

Driwna

I look over at Cal as we ride at the head of the caravan, my best friend in all the world. He's started singing an old ballad I taught him, "At The Willow", and looks over at me with a wink, for my mun would sing it when I was a child, a song from my homeland that we were cast out of.

"You go well together, Driwna, you and Cal. You're quiet, he's always singing. He's going to sing me to sleep in my furs tonight, in't you Cal?"

Leis this is, on the lead wagon, poking her tongue out of the gap where she used to have front teeth so she can lick her lips.

"He could slide it in there without you moving your jaws, Leis," shouts one of the crew further back.

"Sure he could. Long as he sings me "Away To The Corn" I'll go down easy."

Cal's singing breaks up at this, he's laughing.

A horse canters up behind us, its rider, my captain, clears his throat. "Driwna, it's getting late, ride on with Cal and find us a spot we can pull the wagons around."

Garn this is, Vanguard, as the captain of a caravan's called. He runs the Post's sheds in Lindur as well, the settlement I've called home these last few summers. He's easy to respect, old man been in the field some ten years, lost an arm, but as reds guarding the lots on vans such as this that's far from a steep price for the coin he's made.

"Yes, Vanguard," I say. "I've seen some whitebark up on the slopes; we should do some cutting once we're settled. Laurel might like this earth and all; I'll scout for it." Laurel and whitebark are always welcome in our fieldbelts; they grind well for "scabbard sauce", the poisons our blades soak in.

"Good idea, Driwna. Not seen much but the firs. Head off with Cal while the wagons are rounded off and there's still some light; you're our best sniffers for plant."

"Let's go then, Driw, I'm keen for a few pipes tonight." Cal this is.

Trail's been cut and shored up now we're nearing Lindur, a blessing as we've been making good ground and looking forward to getting back to our sheds there in a few days. Border with the Roan Province has been quiet, must have had a purge on as we heard they were losing vans on Cruck's Road. Did fuck all about our vans getting taken, mind, but it was crossroads coin for this van, meaning we were paid the same purse as those on runs that were a risk to their lives. This run didn't look to be taking us through bandit country, but I couldn't pass that kind of coin up anyway with the shit my pa's been in at the kurch. Long story.

Clouds are coming in, air's got a lick of ice to it as I nudge my horse into the yampa and sedgegrass. I turn to look back at Cal riding after me. He's away in the clouds, humming and taking in the view.

"Beautiful as it all is here," I say, "I need your eyes between

7

the yampa around us and the stands of pine we're heading into. You see any dung or hoof from horses, I need to know."

"Sorry, Driw." He stops his humming.

"Are you going to put her out of her misery and fuck Leis before we tally up at Lindur?" I ask. He smiles, knows I'm fluffing him.

"She's a bit thin for me. It's like she's been chipped out of flint and her colour doesn't help. It's turning us all from whatever colour we've had to this cold grey, this fightbrew they've been training us on. We look like we're dead already. You know I need a bit more than a handful in the furs anyway."

"I do."

I'll say it now, upfront. I wanted a go at his handful, years back at Epny, and he wanted a go at mine, not long after we became friends at the academy there. He's a beautiful man, with a smile that fills his big brown eyes and brings the sun out. I was mad to kiss him first time I saw him. There were a few of us had a bet on getting in his leggings, for along with his look he was the son of a wild and disgraced Rulger, noble blood, while his singing could put a dog in season. Back then, same as now, I had bad blood with my pa, for the Rulgers had fucked my family as immigrants on their land long after the Marghosters had betrayed us out of our own. Well, we got mashed one night, too many cups and kannab, and I fancied I'd do something I knew would upset Pa. So I got into Cal's furs and after some kissing where I bit his tongue and his elbow smacked me good in the nose as he tried to get up on me and collapsed, there came a sort of stillness with the moment when he finally got it in. We looked at each other properly, clearly. You don't look at someone that sort of clearly when you're body's rising to it and we both felt it. I remember we smiled at the same time, shrugged at the same time and laughed all the more for how we matched those gestures. It wasn't what we really wanted from each other. We held each other till we fell asleep, him telling me how lucky he was to have met me. Me the same. We've been on the same crews ever since.

We use sign lingo while scouting, talking with our hands as we nudge the horses through a few rare oaks. Beyond them there's a bit of a rise in the land that'd give us a decent lookout. We dismount to check it a bit more closely, sniff the air.

This looks right, Cal signs.

I shiver then, put my hand up to still his moving about. I flick my head over to our left, roughly in the direction we'd come from. I hear the low whoop of a grey grouse's mating call. I tap my finger in the air in time with the whooping, to single out the sound for him. He nods.

It's not mating season, I sign.

Fuck.

Mount casual, turn, juice eyes in cover of trees.

The juice'd sharpen our eyes fierce, help us to pick out who might be thinking of an ambush. I follow him, try to flatten off my breathing. It's cold, they'll see me blow and know we've cracked them.

As we walk the horses into the oaks we get our bilberry thumb-bags out and squeeze juice into our eyes. I grit my teeth with the pain of it, listening best I can while my eyes burn. Other calls I hear then, the grouse again, brown robins but not sweet or clear enough, mouthpieces not up to the mimicry. They're between us and where the wagons would be.

We kick the horses to a canter.

Dayers, signs Cal, meaning the mix that gives you a touch of the strength and speed a full fightbrew can give without paying the awful price after.

Agree. We take a slug. A sword rings in the distance,

at the van. We kick up to a gallop, my heart thumping and I feel sick. Now the juice has got in and the itching's worn itself down a bit I see them, bandits it must be, moving through the pines near the van. Horn blows as they're spotted, but there won't be anyone on a full brew and no time to flatten one and get up on it. I hope to Sillindar that these are bandits too poor to have a real brew. Cal rattles his sword in its scabbard to freshen the sauce before pulling the blade free. I do the same and we ride in. Our vanners have been caught cold really, bandits chose a good time after a long day and no guard or defences set. I can hear Garn, our Vanguard; he's calling in Farlsgrad field lingo for the crew to gather up and push to the trees, towards our coming, for he's rightly assumed we've got wind of the fighting. It's dusk though, and hard to see what's going on. Cal gallops away right to run down two that are trying to put arrows into those of our van who are crouching among the wagons. The wagon-horses are stamping and neighing in fear and two break right, taking their wagon off along the path. One's been hit with an arrow to the gaskin; he's frenzied. Garn's near the head of the van where I'm riding in at. He sees me.

"They're brewed, Driw! Get Cal, get to Lindur, there's no hope! It's over!"

"Get on, Garn!"

"Not the Vanguard's purse, Driw, you know that." He's taking mouthfuls of a full fightbrew. It's a stupid thing to do without being able to prep himself for it, but he's going to die anyway. I can hardly believe what he's saying, the last time I'll see him and it's come now, out of nothing. But now I've closed on the wagons I see the massacre. Garn's horse is dead. The van is fucked. I can't see one of our crew alive. The shouting and screeching is of a victory, not a fight. I see one of the bandits leap high and far from a wagon and run for Garn then; he's hot with his brew, fast and savage as a wolf.

"Garn! To me! Please!" But I know he won't.

"Get Cal, girl, you're not dying here!" He hasn't looked back as he's said it. He's standing ready with his two-hander as the bandit runs at him, frighteningly quick on a brew. I look for Cal. He's off his horse, against a tree. He looks to me for sight as I can see past the tree he's behind. No one. He must have killed one or both of the archers. I ride for him.

Garn dies shortly, as anyone would without being risen on a brew to match the soldier they face.

Cal breaks from the trees and runs towards me. The bandit that's killed Garn comes charging after us. I don't trust I'll get an arrow off so I keep for Cal. Two more bandits burst out of the trees behind him. They're closing. Cal's laughing, the mad fucker. He gets like that when death's about. I can't lose him.

"Drop right!" I shout. He knows. I'm grateful for my horse, Anilly; she's calm as a cow as she heads at him. He leaps out of my way as I whip past him, and the two chasing him, only fifteen yards from him then, see too late what I've done as Anilly hammers into the first of them and my sword's out and I swing at the other as he tries to fall out of my way. I've done enough to buy us time. I lead Anilly about, kick up back to Cal, who's standing, sword out as Garn's killer closes. He won't make it. Cal gets my arm, swings up and behind me and we're away up the trail as horns of triumph sound, the van lost.

We ride until we're sure there's none following. Cal puts his arms around me from behind.

"Glad you're alive, Driw. Those poor bastards."

I put a hand over his. There's nothing to say to that. One

11

moment we're flushed with the prospect of a flask and a few pipes, the next our crew's dead. "Worried I lost you as well for a moment, Rulger filth." He gives me a squeeze.

I pull the horse up and we dismount. I give her a snivet and a kiss for she's saved our lives. We're in a stand of pines, up a slope that looks back across the grasses we've just ridden. Cal goes to the edge of the trees to look out.

"Anything, love?"

He shakes his head, wraps his cloak about him.

"Fuck this life," he says.

"It was a good van. But it was the purse too, Cal, not an easy run. Garn was a good Vanguard, made leadership look easy. The Post's going to miss him. Fuck it, I'm going to miss him."

"Led seventeen runs out, he told me," says Cal. "Weren't meant to be bandits on this stretch, for all that we got paid some more coin."

There's a quiet moment then. I am angry with myself for not being enough. Much as Garn led well, we were close enough to Lindur we made mistakes, complacent, and a shade of that shit out here gets you killed and I didn't see it, didn't call it as Garn's second.

"How many did you see, Cal?"

"Bandits?" He turns to me. "You're going to say something stupid."

"They caught us cold, full fightbrews to none. They'll be paying colour soon enough." Paying colour is what we call it when the fightbrew wears off and leaves you in pieces, helpless. It's a heavy price we pay for a strength and speed not even cougars can match.

"I saw eight, ten? Heard more. There'll be twenty or more wherever they're camped. Driw, leave it go. Didn't think you were the sort got their blood up for revenge. I like you cold, we live longer." He comes over to me, knowing I was filling up, sad and angry. He puts his hands on my shoulders. "Go on then, girl. Say your piece."

I lift forward the edge of my cloak, the red cloak that the Post gives all who take its purse after passing their training. I wipe the sweat and tears from my face.

"I want to get that van back. For us, Garn, all of that crew's final tallies, and because we're Post. I took the red because of what it means, never mind that no other fucker excepting yourself seemed to care about it beyond what purse they could earn. Amaris, our teacher, it's like we were the only two listened to her stories as she taught us all the idea of what the Post should be. We both fell in love with that woman. It's another family, she said, and one that's for some good in the world; no slaves, no more politics than it takes to keep itself strong. She talked of a creed that she's fighting to have us all swear on. Help the helpless, peace through trade, remember?"

"I do, love."

"I believe it, seen it enough on our purses. You know what it means to put this cloak on, how people look at us, trust us not to fuck them over and see us respect their ways when we're in their kurches, their towns and hams. These cunts, paying colour, they won't believe two Post with one horse will take them on."

He smiles. "Marghoster filth."

"Rulger filth."

He's quiet a moment.

"You don't seem set on it, Cal, and I won't, can't, do it alone." I think I sensed in him a question about what I was saying we should do. Of course it's hard to go risking your life if not for kurch or country, but Cal knew well enough why I held the Post so close; it was as close to a kurch as I had now, for I could no longer stand to see what had become of my own kurch, the Bridche.

"Driw, you have a way of getting at what's right even when it's telling a man he should go die with you for some kegs of ale and salt. I just needed a moment to accept what I already knew. Fuck it, I fancy us on a brew and all. We'll have a song about us, how we gave our lives for a kurchman's salt."

We ride back to where the wagons had been attacked, seeing none lingering. My horse, Anilly, we have to leave and hope she remembers her training and waits.

We have a strong brew, being Post. "The Amo" it's called and I have no idea why. Normally a drudha'd bind us up once we swallowed it to stop us bringing it back up. We just have to manage out here and hold each other's mouths shut. Cal calls it "Riding the Boar", and he sings as he fights. I don't know what to call feeling like my body's being ripped open by a tree from the inside, for you grow on a brew; sinew and muscle, all senses are much multiplied and you sense what many have called the Song of the Earth, a feeling like you are dissolving, flour blown into the air. Something more than you've ever been.

The stolen wagons had been led up into a wide valley that forked as it rose, cliffs all about us. Easy to defend. We string our bows and go over our fieldbelts before moving in, making sure the mixes we'd need – powders, spores and poisons – are in good order. I scale an outcrop of rocks to get a view ahead.

Dogs. Six, I sign back to him

Below me Cal preps a pepperbag for them.

Two guard. Twenty more. Paying colour. Drinking. I sign the spots and yards to each.

Three guard, Cal signs back, pointing higher up, and as he does so, the one I'd missed above us belches. Unprepared.

My kill. I'll cover you. Join up on count of thirty.

He salutes me. I doubt he'd start singing but he's done some stupid things in his time.

I find some more handholds to get higher and get a shot at the guard that's above us. Our bilberry mix is good in this darkness, though it's less good with fire. He's absorbed with fletching an arrow, winding thread around feather and shaft. It keeps him still and my shot's good, through the side of his head so no chance to alert the camp. I scale to his position and sign Cal to move in.

He slings in the bag that contains spores and pepper to send the dogs mad, a savage throw smashing it open against a tree near them before he runs in to the guards. They get to their feet just as I put an arrow in one of them, centre of his chest and Cal cuts the other guard's arm off, running him through before he can make his move. I put two arrow-bags down into the camp among the tents there as the dogs start howling and sneezing with our powders. The count of thirty now up I run down the path from the lookout into the camp. We work fast, no panicking on the brew, working always to keep it under control. I've seen soldiers pull out their eyes when they lose it on a fightbrew.

I put two quick stabs into all the bodies I can see; in bedrolls, crawling out of tents in their woollens, those who are paying colour and all, writhing in troubled dreams as I stick them. It is silent work until I hear swords clash. We'd missed some, still risen a bit from their earlier brew, or they'd taken dayers that were starting to work. I sheathe my sword, take up my bow. A bandit rounds a tree to the side of Cal where he's engaging another; must have come from the far side of the valley.

I shoot her just as she looses her own arrow, a moment's difference that saves Cal's life, for seeing me fucks with her stance and her arrow hits Cal in his thigh. My arrow finds her true enough, shoulder only, but they have nothing for our poison. She cries out as it begins spreading, starts going through her belts but the only counter we know of doesn't grow in these parts. The bandit on Cal moves in when he sees him hit, knocks Cal's sword out, for he's got no form with the arrow in his leg. Bandit's on Cal in a moment, punches him before he can raise his other arm and then gets him round the throat, getting himself behind Cal, using him as a shield against me.

"Drop the bow you ugly red cocksucker." He puts the tip of his sword to Cal's ribs. Cal chokes, tries to move his weight, but for all his strength on the brew, the arrow has him hobbling and he goes still when the point of the sword digs into his side, the threat accepted.

I have the sight, bow fully drawn. It's too much ground to make up. The bandit is leaning on the notion I'd not risk the shot for killing Cal.

"Easy to see you're wet for him, woman. We can all live this out." The dogs have gone, a distant howling and yelping in the trees about us as they run blind and without a sense of smell. The archer I'd shot finally hits the ground, bleeding from her mouth. I remain still, bow fully drawn.

He hears her hit the ground, looks behind me, around us, hoping someone is still alive. "I count three and—"

I let fly before he could finish. Cal saw me wink the moment the soldier's eyes left mine, was quick enough on our fightbrew he would see the arrow in flight. He drops a shoulder, moving his head sideways. The arrow shaves Cal's neck, hits the bandit in the mouth and passes through him. He chokes, clawing at the arrow's shaft as he drops.

"Cal!" Blood pours from his neck. He falls to his knees and the arrow in his thigh snaps, sending him into a spasm.

I unstopper a vial as I run to him, kneeling. "Move your hand!" Blood is pouring between his fingers as he presses the cut, moaning and shaking. "Move it, Rulger!" I tear his hand away, put my knee on his chest to flatten him down and empty the powders onto the slice in his neck. He throws up over me, bucking about under my knee as the powders soak to a jelly and then a wax. I take a strip of gummed linen, press down on the cut, lean over him.

"Cal, look at me!" He does, but only for a moment. I'm losing him; his heart is wild as he loses the brew and it's drawing the arrow's poison in. There's no talking him back. I dig out a couple of thumbs of betony and sugar, put them on his gums and he falls still. He hates betony, we all do, for it's easy to crave and cows the strongest men into an addiction to last to the end of their days. Right now, it'll save his life.

I cut the arrow out of his leg, the brew giving my hands strength, precision. I clean the wound, press the feathery plugweed into it, chew and gum some bark to bind the skin about it and let the fightbrew fight out the poison in peace. There's no more I can do for him now.

I stand and go about the camp. All of the bandits are dead. I hack about at a couple of bodies to get the rage out of me, for I had nearly killed him with my shot. Half an inch to the left he'd be dead. They train us not to think like that and I know that if I had spent a moment thinking then he, or both of us, would be dead for sure. On a brew you can't think, only act.

Act.

The cold blue of dawn seeps west, the valley here still mostly dark. I've mixed what I can to help with paying the colour but I'm falling hard. There's no choice now. If we've missed even one of them we're dead. Cal hasn't woken, his heart's faint and slow. I've built up the fire to help us and brought the horses from the wagons a bit closer before paying the colour got too much for me, giving them some food and setting some ankle breakers and lines about. They'll only stop the careless.

I wake with a start. An eagle screeches above us. Afternoon, but this time of year the sun's not high enough and the valley's dark. I turn to look at Cal. He's moved at some point but is sleeping again. I'm sweating pins, bitter sharp, and it hurts so much I look at my hand expecting the skin to have been flayed. I begin crying, happy Cal's not dead and sad because I'm not dead. Then I smell it, feel it on my legs. I've shit myself. I can't move myself, my arms, I can only watch them twitch as I pay the colour. My legs spasm, it feels like my heart stops and starts, chest pains and blackouts.

I manage to get a finger of betony and rub it in my gums. It isn't wise, but my wisdom's crouched up in a tree looking down on me with pity. I sing, something to help the horses, something to pass the time. I can thank Sillindar there's been no wolves, but this amount of dead bodies and tied-up horses will bring something into the valley sooner or later.

A few hours later Cal begins mumbling. The burning and shaking quieten enough I can bring my knees up to reach my boots and begin the attempt to get my leathers and leggings off. I get half of them off but my strength gives out.

The betony's worn off Cal now, but he's still spasmic, the poison prolonging his paying the colour. I try again to wriggle out of my woollens, feel the icy wind on my arse and thighs. I'm crying again, I feel so weak. "Kill me before I come to this in my old age, Cal." He doesn't hear me. He's dreaming. He's shouting at his pa, living in a memory, fretting about their arguing. I said he was son of a disgraced lord, Barolt

Rulger. Rulgers were one of the noble families in Farlsgrad, they even ruled once in times past. Barolt Rulger was one of two brothers; the other, Edral, is Lord now. Barolt was as handsome as Cal, hair black and shining as the night sea, his lusts and his wit as sharp as a fillet knife. At Autumn's Gate and the Hillfast Tourney he gave parties that even Amaris, our mentor and long a feared assassin, blushed at the recall of. But betony and brandy ground him into a bore and a gambler. He lost everything, and left Farlsgrad. Nobody saw him again. Cal's mun, Soenka, was merchant-born but beautiful, ended up being cared for by Edral, Barolt's younger brother. Edral had not been invited to his older brother's parties. Quieter, less striking and with no lechery or lust for drink in him, pitied perhaps, he turned to his letters and made the most of the coin their father gave him. Cal had to be disinherited, of course, paid a stipend to stay away, for Edral had no children of his own and Cal might have a claim to his wealth as the next man in the line of their father. Despite Edral having his own keep, what they call a "wife" in the Old Kingdoms, it was clear to Cal that Edral lusted after his mother. Who's to say if it was real, or just the desire to take some kind of revenge on his brother for being their pa's favourite.

"Driw, why can I see your arse?"

"What? Oh fuck, Cal, close your eyes. I haven't had the strength to clean myself up."

His voice cracks as he tries to laugh but he coughs and yelps with the pain it causes him. The air's changed, the light. I've slept again.

"Didn't think you'd wake till tomorrow, if today's the day we killed all these," I say. "I've lost track of time."

He looks about us as best he can. "Don't know how long

19

I've been out, love. That one there, head hanging off, she's about your size, bit of meat on her. Her woollens'll fit you."

He's right. "How are you, Cal?" I crawl over to him, lie down next to him. He takes my hand.

"Thank you, Driw, saving my life again."

"You keep there while I get something to put on and put this fire together again. These bodies'll be drawing some interest from wolves and the like. I need to light the place up and bring the horses in." I squeeze his hand. "I think we should crack open a keg when I'm done. Say it got lost in the attack."

He nods, his eyes heavy.

The bandits had a supply of logs cut, kindling I find in a tent. It takes a long time, I'm weak as a baby. I find a mouthpiece that helps with singing the horses into camp.

Two fires set and a keg rolled up to our fire, I kick Cal awake.

"Smoke?" I ask him. "There's a bit of bacca here, sign of the Irkre Brothers on the wrapping."

"Irkre are the big guild over in Ullavir. One of their runners said they'd had a van hit south of here. Might be this crew that did it."

"Well, there's enough we can sell a bit off I think. If you're on your feet tomorrow you can help me go through the tents and look for their stashes. Here's the manifest for the lots." Cal takes them and starts looking through.

"Get that keg open then, girl. Help me sit up."

"Yes sir, Rulger sir." I find some furs and bags to prop him up against so he can sit upright. He's quiet. He was speaking soft, throat had swelled. I think he's worried about his voice.

"No spigot so I'll have to knock a hole in the top and lean it over." I stand the barrel up on an end and I feel something inside, something solid in the ale that bumps faintly at the staves.

I find a spike for setting tents and a hammer, make a hole in a stave just below the head hoop. The smell hits us quickly.

"What the fuck is that, Driw? That's not right."

"Alka and something. Vinegar?" I put my nose nearer the hole in the barrel and my eyes water. "Vinegar, and there's something in it, I felt it."

"Nothing on the manifest but ale, Driw."

"I know. Haven't got the strength to set about this barrel tonight though, Cal; need to look at the horses."

"I know, love. Let me keep an eye out while you get some rest; you look done. I'll give you a kick if I hear anything."

He kicked me as the birds signalled a dawn that wouldn't reach us for a few hours. I gave him a few hours' sleep in return but I was feeling a bit better so got up to go through this camp properly.

A pipe helps lift me; I found a pouch of kannab, another gift from the Irkre Brothers. Flies are setting about the dead fierce now. We'd make a good bit of silver off the plant and some fine copper necklaces and rings. I find too what they'd looted off our dead crew, and I'm pleased to find their cloaks unspoiled, for it'll help confirm their final tally as it's called, the Post paying to the dead's kin two silver pieces. The wagons hadn't even been unloaded as we'd only run from their attack a few hours before we returned.

When Cal wakes again it's to some fried eggs and a few mushrooms I found. He lets me feed him and see to him. His neck's set fine, the wound looking no worse, and I'm pleased, though he needs scrubbing down. His thigh's not so good but no infection I can see, nothing that won't respond to a mix.

"We'll need to get you in a wagon. I think I can rope this van in line and lead it back to Lindur Post."

"Opened the keg yet, Driw?"

"No, needed a bit to eat and a rest. Been readying things, foraging these fuckers."

"Go on then, let's find out what's being hidden inside it."

I'm pleased to see him use his arms to move himself a bit for a better look. I have another go at the keg, this time with the hammer, knock a few holes together into one in the hood of the keg near the edge I'd opened so I can get my arm in. Even with a mask the vinegar and alka has me choking.

I reach around inside the keg and I feel something soft, small, the size of a carrot. As I grasp it properly, I feel fingers, a fist. A tiny one.

"Driw?" He's seen me close my eyes as I hold this tiny hand in mine.

"Driw? What is it love?"

I wipe a tear away with my other hand and then reach in with it, find the armpits, pull her out, a baby girl. As I do, and I'm not quite looking because I can't, Cal cusses, shocked. I open my eyes proper and then feel the baby's head against my arm, see her head, the skin cut back from the crown and folded neatly and sewed like a ridge of pastry around her braegnloc, the top of the skull missing. I twitch, a moment of horror and I want to drop her, before pulling her altogether out of her dark tomb and into my arms.

"Oh Cal, Oh Sillindar."

"Driw, she's Ososi, In her braegnloc, look, the stem, the leaf, a Flower of Fates."

Hard enough, I think, to describe how an Ososi looks. Can't imagine more than a hundred people in the whole kingdom of Farlsgrad have ever seen one. They might have been like us once, the songs and tales might tell it different, but here, in my arms, is a baby girl that looks much like any, but for her head being open, the flower sprouting in what is now the pickled braegn, the bone cut and removed for the flower itself to thrive. The Ososi, as they grow, have plants that grow in them, vines that wrap about the arms, over and under the skin. Some grow moss, mushrooms and other plants on their bodies, mostly their limbs and heads, to impart whatever qualities they possess into their own senses. This girl is the first I've ever seen that's had her head opened. The buds of what must be the start of her vines are making lumps under her skin. This girl would have been the chief of her people, her blood containing the violent power of the Flower of Fates, the most potent of all plants. It's fatal to the rest of us, so violently growing and changing a soldier in thought and sinew that a man can withstand an army alone, if only for a short time before the Flower kills him.

I put my hand to the back of her head to support it as I hold her out in front of me. Her chest's been sewn up, a stab wound only a pale line. The flower in her braegn is still only a shoot, black stem and roots and thick red leaves darkened by the vinegar.

I hold her close again – an instinct, a stupid, necessary one, that I could warm her up a bit, that she'd been alone for too long.

"What the fucking hell is she doing on our wagons, Cal?"

"Garn must've known it."

"No, not Garn, he was straight as a spear, loved the Post." I crouch down and take up one of my furs, put it over her.

I find myself rocking the little body in my arms, for my own sake. Cal says nothing to it. "She won't go in the earth here, Cal. We'll get her out of this valley first, somewhere higher I think."

He's still then, finding some words. "Driw, I reckon we should put her back in the barrel."

"What?"

"Hear me through. If we get the van back to Lindur, somebody's expecting her to be in a barrel, aren't they? They see that she isn't and we won't know any more about who did this to her. Nothing'll be said."

He's right. I don't want her to hear it. I don't want to let her go.

"I fucked the keg right up, haven't I?"

"No choice, love. Give me a hand up, let's look at the wagon."

"You can't walk, Cal."

"Put her down, help me."

I lay her down carefully in the fur I'd put round her, on my bedroll. Then I get hold of Cal and pull him up onto his one good leg. Using me for balance he hobbles with me over to the wagon the kegs were on.

"There's tools here," I say, "carpenters' bits, I'm sure. We put her back in, find a saw and fuck up one of the other keg's heads and nail this one down, we'll say it got damaged and we tried to fix it with one was beyond repair."

"Manifest says the kegs are due to a Brask & Son. Roan ale in these," says Cal.

"Third quarter shed in Lindur they have, wine and bacca mostly. They've been the Marghoster wine merchants for a lifetime."

"Who imports ale from Roan? It don't travel that well."

"I know. The Brasks have had a shed for sixty years, not sure I ever saw such imported," I say.

"Where else, Driw?"

"Their sheds? Other than Caracsas where we set out from, not sure – they don't put much with the Post. Marghoster's always had a problem with the Post, like most of the noble families of Farlsgrad have." It stops me then.

"What, Driw?"

"Now I think on it, they have been doing more with us through Lindur. Usually from their sheds on the wharf of Ullavir, and it's to Caracsas or it's bacca out into the Sathanti."

"From when?"

"Don't know, hadn't given it much thought beyond seeing their name on the contracts and manifests a bit more often."

We break one of the other kegs open, and thankfully it's ale and we have a good couple of flasks while the sun climbs its way to the mid-day. I give this baby girl a kiss and put her back in the keg, though I'm crying all the while. Taking some wood from the ale keg's head I manage to nail a piece over the hole and gum it with some mashed guira. It's a shit job really, and we have to hope they'll buy the lie about it being damaged.

It's early afternoon we head out from the valley. My whistling piece eventually brings Anilly to us and I'm delighted to see her again. Cal's lying on one of the wagons, horses have had a bit of grazing and some water, and I lead them back onto the trails, slow with how weak I still am from paying the colour, and I'm asking Sillindar to spare us any more need for a brew.

There's no proper Posthouse at Lindur, by which I mean a proper walled compound on the standard layout. The nearest is north at the Spike. The Posthouse here is a few sheds taken at favourable rates, joining up the kingdom of Farlsgrad and the Roan Province ports that we've had an interest in for almost as long as the Post's been going.

Lindur itself is a fort against troubles in times gone by, still with a garrison of around seventy, forty horse, for it watches two borders, that of Roan and Sathanti. A settlement has grown up around it, as they always do, emporia that Sathanti kurches, what are called clans in Farlsgrad and the Old Kingdoms, come to for trade and to pass on news. The Post itself does good trade on what it brings in from everywhere and we have a contract to supply the garrison's needs here. Unlike the Spike further north it has wooden walls and sentry posts, the dyke long dried out and the red clay in these parts made for orange mudbricks that have come to smell of home when warmed on a summer's day.

I lead the van through a dell and out onto rising lands that are growing barley along with runs of plant that are behind strong fences and guarded, mainly avent's root and golden seal, valuable crops for both fightbrews and the mixes that aid the recovery from them.

A horn sounds up at the fort; we're seen and must have been missed for how much later we are than expected.

A couple of Post ride out to us, only one in the red of the Post, cloak blowing out behind him and it's a welcome sight.

As he closes I see it's our senior cleark here, Atko, local born, skin like lard for he prefers candlelight by day. I see, as he approaches, that he's looking down the line, frowning, for there should be more of us. He pulls up his horse next to me.

"Second Marghoster, good to see you. Report."

"Atko, you're a welcome sight. Need a drudhan, got a Post wounded — Cal, three wagons back. Rest of us, Vanguard Garn too, didn't make it. I'm signing in the caravan Lindur Twelve as its Second, cloaks present for their final tally."

"You look like shit." The other rider this is, a lad surely no more than fifteen summers and stunted somewhat.

Atko puts out his arm and I clasp it before he dismounts and gives the lad his reins. He takes a moment then to look

26

down the line of wagons, the absence of so many reds we both loved.

"Thank you, Driwna. High Cleark Rogus is down from the Gate. He's nuts deep in my rolls and tallies and we were facing a big claim on loss of manifest. It's like Sillindar sent you back himself. The Post finds a way, eh, Driwna? Welcome back. Morril was worried sick for you."

It's not in me to draw comparison with our own travails. I'm tired. "Sorry to hear that, Atko. Cal and I will report to Rogus but he needs work on his leg and I need to see this manifest signed off."

"As do I, so let's get you up to the gates and we'll get some help to get the wagons into the shed. Trid, go back, tell Rogus Lindur Twelve is here, tell the crew to come out to the common so we can bring her in."

"Cleark." He canters off, putting to his mouth a heavy pipe that seems as at home there as it would in a beak.

By the time we lead the van in, there's most of the Posthouse out for us, High Cleark Rogus to the fore, a rich red robe under his cloak, crossed quills in gold stitched to the robe at his breast. He wears no beard, hair shaved, a shadow of grey on a surprisingly weathered head that speaks of a life in the field. I hear my name then as we approach, my friend Morril shouts it out and it's followed by a cheer. She knew to fill the silence of our loss, for many about me loved Garn, Leis and the others and put their arms around each other for comfort when they see just me and Cal alone with the wagons. I blow Morril a kiss.

"Do you have their cloaks, Driw?" Another of our crew shouts this.

"All of them, Grogg." They cheer at this, that they'll see those families get their tally without argument or complaint.

"Third wagon. Cal Rulger." Atko this is, telling the drudhan who takes one of our soldiers along to get Cal off the wagon. Cal gets a cheer as well of course, another one of us alive and he's much loved.

"You are a welcome sight, Second Marghoster." Rogus this is, stepping forward to clasp arms.

"As is Lindur, High Cleark." It's the noise of people I have missed. The wild is full, night and day, of a chorus unconcerned for us.

"Amaris will be pleased you both made it. We shall write the report up over a proper roast."

"Thank you, High Cleark. The Post finds a way. How is Amaris? Is she still in Farlsgrad?"

"She is, keeping old and young reds honest wherever she goes, appearing and disappearing about our offices and sheds as suddenly as the coins of a conjurer. I try to hide from our politics in the hope that our politics will not find me, but she is never so lucky."

"Yet you work for Administrator Stroff, do you not?"

He smiles, though as I hand him the satchel containing the manifest I'm watching the wagon with the kegs on it come past us, through the pavilions and mudbrick hovels outside the dyke and into the outer bailey of the fort and main settlement.

"Marghoster filth." Cal this is, on a stretcher as he's carried past me. He blows me a kiss and points at the wagon ahead of him. I nod. Morril, seeing me with Rogus, joins those carrying Cal and starts making a fuss of him.

"Great to see you, Cal." Rogus this is, calling over to him.

"Thank you, High Cleark. The Post finds a way."

"It does. You do. Once more."

I step forward to give Rogus his cue that we should get into the bailey after the wagons.

"How are things at Autumn's Gate, High Cleark?"

"Our capital is not where Administrator Stroff's concerns are. They're here and along the border. I'm pleased that Lindur Twelve is not another tragedy we have to explain to our principal investors, the Main Tens, along with the other purses. But out west is getting worse. Over the Folly and the Lakes three vans this autumn vanished into the mountains, all Post lost. Two vans in the summer. North at Nailer's Road we have five vans on which I had the foresight to double the guard, and all but one fought off bandits or tribesmen. Coin is down at the Spike and I don't believe all of it's a loss of contracts. Worst year in a long while."

"Are we making it easy on ourselves there? Garn was our reeve as well as the Vanguard here in Lindur and he made a difference here since I came with Cal. He proved a capable ally to the villages and farms alike, settling disputes and keeping us honest."

"You are far too modest, Driwna. He gave you much of the credit in dispatches. Many in the lands about here noted how Garn and yourself spent time with our drudhan visiting the farms and hamlets after last summer's blight on the crops. A few in our offices in Autumn's Gate saw a waste of time and effort, but you rightly saw an investment, a goodwill that is repaying us with interest."

He knew nothing of what those same hams, as my people call hamlets, did to my kurch when we tried to make a settle in these parts back when I was a young girl. I help those with children mostly because I care nothing for their pas or greatpas, men my pa wanted revenge on.

"Look, Driwna, regarding the west and these other troubles, something's wrong, something's changed out there, I just can't find out what. I don't think it's our reeves becoming corrupt or causing trouble, not on so wide a scale so suddenly."

I'm about to ask him more of it but I see that the two

with the keg wagon are talking with a cleark; must be a Brask man.

"Rogus, could I have that roast with you later? I see one of our purses there, Brask & Son, and I'd like to make sure they're satisfied. I would also talk with you about the Spike. I think Cal and I could make a difference there." He wasn't getting the real reason.

"Of course. You anticipate my own thoughts. I've put my bedroll in the sheds, no reason to take a room. I was a deckhand for long enough I can't sleep without the sound of farting and snoring nearby. I'll see you there around sunset."

It's the first time I've met him and I like him. I'm pleased Amaris has good people about her up at Autumn's Gate. It's well known that she doesn't get on with Stroff.

The Brask cleark looks over at me approaching. "Driwna Marghoster?"

"Just Driwna is fine." He offered nothing more. "Normally more of you Brasks here for the wine. This lot is ale. Does it travel well?"

"One damaged keg, one lost. Didn't drink it did you, Driwna?" He winks. I feel a flush of anger, a prickling of tears and all. But I have a sense, hard to pin on, that he doesn't know anything about the baby. He's familiar to my crew here, a moth-bitten look about him, cheeks collapsed without any teeth to sit on, no guile in his eyes.

"Can I help you back with the wagon? Sorry, I don't even know your name."

"Oh, it's Iglin. Yes, happy for you to walk along; would help my senior as he always seems to have more questions than I have answers and he'll have a lot of questions about this."

"Will he?"

"Told me that Marghoster paid a fine sum for this ale, for a great feast we'll never see the door of too, I expect."

"Always the way with the likes of us eh, Iglin?"

"You got it here, they should be happy. You lost good people. But you Post don't give up, do you?"

"We did lose good people. My Vanguard was true. He saved my life and so saved the van."

He holds the bridle of the wagon's horse and we walk it onto the flagstone path that runs up from the main bailey gates to the inner bailey. There's a lot of sheds and stalls, pavilions and stables; an autumn here of harvest trade, noisy and stinking and a delight as it has been all the years we've drunk to Haluim on Winter's Eve. Haluim's the magist that first taught us to tame the ox and speak with the horse and gave us the mouthpiece and forms that also gives us command of them. Sathanti Lakelanders are here with their gold nuggets and plant, always looking for iron and oil. There's Roan herders in the paddocks and fields of the cattle markets. Always I've put the smell of dung and good living together, heartened at seeing so many that might be at war instead smoking and sharing cups. I look back briefly and see the plain bright red flag of the Post at our shed, higher than all others here, and it makes me proud.

"This ale bound for the Marghoster estate then? You'll roll it up to the Spike?" I say. We're approaching the Brask shed and pavilion.

"Who knows, the last wagons . . ."

"Iglin." A strange, soft voice, like the hiss of sand over desert stone, comes from behind me and above me. I turn about. He's within two feet of me, impossible I should not have felt his approach. He's nearly seven feet tall, broad as a draught horse and a hood and his leathers hide all but his nose and mouth. The colouring's yellow and black and I cannot believe I'm the only one here knows he is Ososi, for none move as they do, with the silent grace of a cat. I know

31

us soldiers' skin becomes coloured with the brews we take and the rubs we use, but none have a texture like this, following the veins, and those veins prominent in the skin, more black than blue.

I look at Iglin and then the others in the shed; clearks, their cooper, the shed-hands. All have slowed or stopped at his approach. He's not one of them. They are scared for their lives.

"Go." He says this to me, no more than a soft, high breath, then steps closer to me, a gesture for Iglin to move the wagon on.

I look up at him, and I expect to see some sort of conviction in his eyes, that his will is being realised as he looks down at me, but his eyes are closed. The moment, for him, has already ended. There is the Ososi stillness about him now; when they choose to rest they do not seem to breathe, they become still as stone. The leathers, buckles, the salt stains, cuts and stitches tell their own story of a life in the field; leather on the pouches is worn to a shine, the drawstrings knotted neatly, all of it waxed. His fieldbelts carry twice the plant I could manage a fight in. There are knives about him, a fine but plain sword that would be a two-hander for anyone else.

"Peace to you, Iglin. And you, my giant friend."

He doesn't answer. I know the Brask's senior cleark. It's him we'll need to get our answers from about the keg, if anyone.

I step back from this Ososi and walk back towards our shed. I look back and see he's already turned to watch me. I stop, look past him briefly to the wagon, then think better of it.

Back at our shed I whistle, two long notes and two short. It brings Livvie out of some hidden corner. She runs up to me and puts her arms around me. Fourteen summers now she is, blue ribbons threaded through the matted locks of her hair, one eye the white of milk.

"I cried when I thought you were dead, Driwna."

"Morril knows you'd have my final tally, Livvie. And she knows you'd spend it all on a dress." She leans back to look up at me though she's not far off as tall as I am.

"Not any more Driwna. I'm not a girl. I'd pay to get my letters and be the best cleark in all the borders, like you were."

"Who gave you all this wisdom since we last spoke?"

She glances a moment to someone behind me; her eyes fall, embarrassed.

I hear his voice – it's Conti, apprentice to our farrier. I reach forward then and pull bits of straw out of her knotted clumps of hair.

"He could do worse than you." She can't look up at him as he passes, puts her head into my neck instead. I hear a slowing of his step behind me, stretching the moment, hoping to catch her eye. We've all done it.

"I'm too young," she says. This once he's passed by.

"You are right now, but when you get your letters he'll have to join a line of boys if he wants do the work you'll make him do for a kiss." Her blushing is a delight. "First of all, though, you can watch a wagon for me. I can't trust anyone to do it better without being caught."

"What sort of wagon?"

I describe it to her and with a kiss she leaves me. She was brought in by Garn on a van last year. She'd got away from gangers she'd been sold to, so there's little more I need to say about her life up to that point. I know I was seventeen summers when I left our kurch, and I've not told many people either the why of it. She's asked me to keep her secrets and I will, but the Post took us both in when we needed help.

I pass through the shed to where we have our timber huts about a communal firepit. Our drudha, Gennic, is working on Cal's wounds. He's about ten summers older than Morril and I, sleeves rolled back on his woollen shirt, strong arms, using some gut to stitch up a line of bark mash into Cal's neck. He has a magnificent beard, but he's hairy and stocky as a chimp generally.

"Before he passed out he said you were the one shot him in the neck." He cuts the gut after tying it and stands straight, gives me a wink.

"An inch to the left and I wouldn't have to put up with shit like this," I say. He shakes his head, a smile on him.

"Makes a change from pulling teeth and looking at fuck-sores," he says. "This is proper work for a cooker."

"You're no cooker, Gen, you're better than that." Cooker's the name for someone who hasn't trained properly in how to prepare brews and mixes using plant.

"Not a proper drudha yet either. I'm shining the wrong palms with silver."

Morril's mixing up a paste for Gennic. She's been on my side since I first came to Lindur; we've looked out for each other. She's tall, lean like Cal.

"Glad you're home, love," she says. She hands Gennic the mortar and comes over.

"I'll get another pail, wash you down. You look ready to pass out."

"He's going to be well?" I say.

"He is. Won't walk right for a while with that leg. No fieldwork, but that's for you to say now, isn't it, Reeve Driwna."

"Yes, I . . . I haven't thought through any of it." She's right. I could drop asleep at a pinch. The number of duties I ought now to assume command of, to see are done, hits me like a wave. I was Garn's second, so I'd be running it all now.

"I'm proud of you, Driwna. You've come a long way from

that girl I bunked with, became our quartermaster and then went on to Epny to pay the colour. Your mun and your pa would be proud."

"Would he really be proud?" I say. "Tell me he's asked after me since I left for Epny, after all the contracts we put his way for the plant and eels when I was quarter here, enough to get me in trouble with Stroff at Autumn's Gate for paying more than the going rate." She nods, keeps quiet.

"Sorry, Morril love. Sorry." I take her hand. "I've had enough of the last few days. I'm feeling so sick about Garn, about us living and all the rest dying out there. I will have that wash down if you'll do me. In here's fine, Cal's seen it all before, as has Gennic. I'm meeting with Rogus in a few hours. I need my wits for the high cleark."

My leathers are salty, bloody and stinking from the field and the fighting we'd done. Gennic strips my fieldbelt down while Cal sleeps, and makes note of the plant that will need replacing. Morril strips me down, a pail of cold water, some alka, grit and a brush to scour off the filth and the rubs – the ones we need to protect us from poisons, and the ones that thicken the blood if we're cut.

It hurts, for I'm not fully over paying the colour and I feel sensitive like I've been burned. The pain wakes me. She sings to me then, Morril, and I hum along to "Two Cold Crowns".

"I'll fetch you a dress and your summer boots, Driw," says Gennic. He cups my right cheek with a hand as he passes, kisses the other and leaves us.

"Has he got any brandy in his chests over there?" I ask Morril. All drudhas have a stash and it's cold in here with naught on.

"You can warm up in my bedroll tonight after you've met with Rogus. Haven't had you in a while and this is reminding me of many pleasant hours."

"I'll only fall asleep on you the moment the furs go over me. I'm empty, Mo. I'll share a pipe with you, if you'll still have me. I'm more for getting out of this body that's paying the colour than I am having it stoked up with your tongue."

"I'll take that as an order, Reeve."

I give her a clip to the back of her head as she scrubs at my legs.

"Things going well with Rogus so far?" I say.

"Well enough he thinks my help is needed elsewhere. You know Atko's been with him through his whole visit, letting him know how well he's managing it all."

"It's the Spike that Rogus is talking about."

She stands up straight before me then, her scrub done.

"It is, and sorry as I'll be to see you go, if you get made reeve at the Spike it's no more than you deserve and I'm surprised he hasn't already asked. Right, you're clean enough."

"Crejda's the name on the rolls; she's reeve of the Spike."

"Maybe they think she's not cutting? Don't know, love."

I kiss her, just as Gennic returns, the smell of the fire outside promising a good broth.

"Put her down, Morril, she's reeve now. She's got work to do putting word in at the Gate I'm ready for the Academy, haven't you, Driw?"

"It'll be my first signed roll in the morning, Gen." He throws me a dress along with a shirt and leggings to keep me a bit warmer. "Sillindar bless you. I want someone with Cal tonight, one of your juniors at least."

"Already planned," says Gennic.

"I'm famished," I say.

"Whatever you need, Driw," he says, "just let me know over the next few days. You'll have much to fathom with the lots and the contract rolls that'll need signing for the next van. You should make Atko earn his keep showing you the knots in it all; nothing else will get his tongue out of Rogus's arsehole."

Rogus is at the firepit sharing pipes with the rest of the crew when I leave the drudha's tent and come over. They all stand when they see me.

"To the Vanguard!" shouts Krajic, our smith.

They all cheer. I take the cup Krajic holds out to me.

"To Garn, Leis, Runy, Ulic, Seic, Mac, Elic, Ibrul and Luce. We loved those fuckers."

"Have you managed to get their *uilest*?" This is the tradition most of the peoples in and about Farlsgrad honour still, from a time before kings. The uilest is a palm's worth of plant to put on the fire they are remembered before, that will find them and aid them in the far country. It's not a Sathanti tradition, though I like it as well as our songs, and having heard so many different beliefs about the dead held as fervently as my own, I'm surprised there aren't more doubters about the truth of any one of them. I hold up the pouch of euca leaves, and we drink a measure for each pinch I put on the fire.

Rogus knows well enough I need to share a few cups with the crew now I'm reeve. He picks a moment after we've settled and leads me away from the tents and the sheds, stables and workshops, into the inner bailey. I can't see well enough the Brask sheds, but he's sharp enough he knows something's wrong.

"What's got you on needles, Driw? You followed that wagon earlier, couldn't take your eyes off it when we talked, then put your girl Livvie onto it. And now, on our way to a well-earned roast, you're drawn to it like a wasp to honey."

"We don't run bodies or slaves now and nobody's told me, do we, High Cleark?" The Post has never worked with

37

slavers since it was founded, nor has it shipped bodies such as drudhas would use for their research, not that a reeve knew of anyway.

"No." He slows his walk a little. "Let's take the air a little longer." He leads us off the path up to the inner bailey's walls and the north gate that leads out into the plant runs that Lindur controls. There's nobody out here now the farmers are finished for the day.

"What's on the wagon besides Brask's kegs?" he asks.

"One of them kegs got a baby inside it – an Ososi, Flower of Fates already taken root in her braegnloc." I give him a run through of what happened to the van and our recovery of it. He's stopped walking and has taken out his pipe, a mellow bacca and kannab mix that doesn't do my tiredness any favours to be breathing. He's listened closely.

"I share your view, Driwna, that the soldier who stopped you knows what's in the kegs, or the one of them, and is here to protect the shipment as it moves on."

"I need to follow it. I have to know who the baby is for."

"You need to know where it's from, how it got on our van and whether there's anything else we don't know."

"There's rolls that will have recorded all that, High Cleark. But they can mask, as we both well know, the true intent of a trade." I can't tell him that I can't abandon her, give up on her.

We stop at a fence that follows the bailey's walls and now gives us a view of the sunset west, clouds the colour of strawberries and gold. Rogus seems to be sorting through his thoughts, deciding which to pick.

"I need you to come to Autumn's Gate. You and Cal Rulger."

It's an order, given his rank.

"High Cleark, that baby . . ." I understand why he looks surprised as my eyes fill up. How do I tell him she's far from home and all those who loved her? He waits as I look up and around, seeking some self-control.

"You would follow the keg, see where it goes?"

"Yes, we have to."

"Well, now, if you were moving a baby Ososi and a chief at that, and you'd noticed the keg had been opened, what would you do?"

"Move it out, quick, under guard."

"I'd run decoys as well; for the price she'd fetch I wouldn't spare the expense. But can we spare you, or any good Post, to follow two or more vans who knows where? When there'll be those on the van that know what they're carrying? There'll be no knowing where she is once she leaves Brask's sheds and plenty would kill any looking to find out."

"Fuck!"

He puts a hand on my shoulder. "I'm sorry, Driwna. It is a very strange and worrying thing to find on a Post van. We don't have the crew, in number or skill, to support the tracking of a well-guarded van, especially if it goes west, or anywhere off the Wheel.

"Right now, bringing home Lindur Twelve is good news that's sorely needed with our High Red, Yblas, convening a gathering of the administrators at Autumn's Gate. I'd like to see you commended, with Cal of course, for what you've done. You've inspired the crew, bringing home the cloaks and the van. Others were watching, other crews and clearks. I'll be surprised if we have trouble manning our next vans and more so if we don't have one soldier or cleark want to take the red. Driw, I've not seen such cheer in a single Posthouse on the Wheel in many months, and that despite the loss of a man such as Garn."

The Wheel he speaks of is a network of roads that run out from the capital like spokes of a wheel; stone roads, wide, ditched and well kept, that help soldiers and all others travelling cover far more ground than they could on trails or open country. We have Posthouses along them all, as do many other merchant companies and guilds.

"You'll forgive me if, on my return, I look to find out more regarding the vans we've run and the rolls," I say. "In my bones I can't believe this is the work of a single trade, that there isn't more to it."

He smiles, pipe clenched in his teeth. "If you return as reeve to the Lindur sheds, you will execute your responsibilities fully. What you then do cannot put the Post at risk, or our reputation."

I couldn't have expected any other answer. Sillindar only knows what field of spears Rogus must dance across every day to help keep the Post honest.

"Come, Driwna, let's get something good to eat and some fine salted beef for Cal. We'll leave for Autumn's Gate tomorrow. Morril will, I believe, manage well enough as reeve while you're gone."

"I'll leave once I've given out the final tallies. Atko wasn't in the field with them, he won't have the words." This is true of course, but I need to delay him a little longer to find out from Livvie if the Brasks have moved the wagon.

Chapter 3

Driwna

Our road to Autumn's Gate was swift. A little more than two weeks from Lindur with fresh steeds ready at Posthouses along the way.

I've not travelled to the Old Kingdoms across the sea. The Old Hall Inn where Cal and I are lodged would grace any of their fabled cities. Citadel Hillfast is the furthest I've been, over the Sardanna Strait, the north end of the Sar sea. Posthouse Epny is there, the academy where I trained and learned to pay the colour, the terrible and beautiful way it changes you. It is the Post's beating heart. Farlsgrad was the first kingdom outside of Hillfast that the Post secured its presence in, strengthening here ever since.

Posthouse Amondsen takes up what was once the grand hall of the Marghosters and that has pleased me each time I've been here. The villas for the nobles and the Post sit high in the hills that the port is built against. Autumn's Gate was once known as the Jewel in the North, a name that for me stank of Old Kingdoms arrogance, as though there was little else of beauty and value in these lands except what those

41

kingdoms could make profit from. Farlsgrad's wealth lies in its farlswood forests, its plant and its proximity to the northern seas and the whales. From this balcony at the inn, Cal and I can look far below us to the ships that crowd the wharfs and anchor in the bay; the navy cutters, barges and square-sailed cogs from the gulf. The wealth presents itself in subtler ways, with all but the poorest alleys paved with good stone and cess troughs cut along most of them. It is a fine sight, these thousands that live below and about us, all in some way in service of the trade that flows through the Gate. Few of any that live and work in the markets or on the docks find their way much beyond their warrens and alleys, fewer still have business among the Four Stairs, great roads that wind their way up the hills to these fine villas and the high plains beyond. Here in their great halls the rich look down on the rest of us as they have always desired to do.

"I could get used to this." Cal this is, and two weeks on since we arrived he's had the care of our best drudha here and is able to limp about with a staff. We've been given the best room the Old Hall has. The pot I shat in was better than anything my family have ever owned. We have been garlanded by the great and good of the Post for Lindur Twelve just two days past and I'm glad it's all over.

"What do you make of his letter?" he asks. Yblas, the High Red, the man at the very top of the Post, had sent a Post agent to meet us this morning, bearing a satchel that contained a letter from him and a leather rollcase inside which were a number of much, much older letters. Over a pie and some tea we'd read these letters, artefacts of the Post's history, written by the woman Autumn Gate's Posthouse was named after, Teyr Amondsen. The agent stands at the door to our rooms, guarding us on account of the letters' very

42

great value to Yblas. His own note made mention of a tribe that were considered cousins to the Ososi, the Oskoro, and it suggested they had somehow vanished. I realise now that it is possible the baby girl was Oskoro, but as I'd not seen even an Ososi clearly, I had no way of scrying the difference. The Ososi are forest-dwellers that live in the wilds of the Sathanti Peaks, widely respected and feared for they have experimented with plant in their bodies for generations and many are as much plant as they are man or woman.

"It feels like Yblas knows something of the Oskoro, but is limiting what he would otherwise say. He's too clever for this not to be some acknowledgement of the body we found, Cal. At least now I understand why our brew's called the Amo."

"First I heard of the Oskoro. They must be blood with the Ososi, a different clan that worships and uses plant in the same way."

"Didn't you hear talk of the Oskoro coming from the Almet forest over in Hillfast, when we were training at Epny to the north-west of it?"

"I heard talk of 'creepy tree fuckers' and bandits and beggars selling mixes on Mosa's Road, but no more. Thought it was some sort of clan had taken root in the forest there."

"Singing us girls into your leggings seemed to be all you had a mind for outside of the studies and the forms."

"I was young, what can I say? But why's Yblas sharing this with us, Driw? He's pleased with what we did bringing the van home, though I couldn't give a fuck for all those administrators banging their cups in support of us while whispering to their runners and lackeys." By this he meant the bit of ceremony held for us while the eight administrators were meeting together from all corners of the Post's empire.

43

"Stroff at least yawned openly as Amaris gave us our scroll and our purse."

"He did, the sour prick. Fuck him. The coin's what matters." I'd sent the silver I'd earned with the promotion back with a messenger bound for the Rulger's fort and they'd see it on from there to my pa and our kurch.

"She seemed like a good woman, Amondsen," I say.

"You're like her. Left your family but wanting well for them, she became a soldier, too, well, a merc. Least you could do now is become the High Red like she did, then we'd be living like this and I could show my mun I'd done something, become something she could be proud of." I hear his voice crack a bit as he says it and I leave the balcony to sit next to him, put my hand in his.

"You talk some shit. You should write to your mun, tell her you got this commendation, send her something – have something made, there's craftsmen can do fine work here."

"Edral wouldn't let it get anywhere near her if he thought it had come from me."

"We should ride there, when you're back on both feet."

"You know I can't, that's the fucking deal I made."

There's a knock at the door then. The agent opens it, nods and lets her in; Amaris, a legend across the Post, an unmatched assassin until the colour demanded its price. Fifty-two summers now, she keeps what's left of her grey hair shaved, most of her head and face is either bark or scars, but I'd have her in my furs in a heartbeat. Her eyes could make all of us at Epny tremble with lust or fear – the yellow of a panther, they can silence kings. Us two she watched over, Cal because of what they did for each other, which is its own tale before he came to the Post, and me because she said I cared about the Post as much as she did, and too few went through the academy with the right sort of pride as far as she was concerned.

"Agent, how are our two wonderful guests?" she asks.

"They've had no visitors, my lady. It's been quiet."

Agents are the Post's most fearsome killers and among the very finest at arms. She clasps his forearm, approvingly, for he rightly gave no indication he'd listened to anything we might have said, utterly discreet and loyal to both her and Yblas.

Cal does his best to stand upon seeing her and she doesn't shush him down into his seat again until we've all embraced.

"I'm so proud of you both. I'm sorry I couldn't be there for your commendations. Yblas wishes you to join him at the Posthouse. I'm here to ensure you and our satchel arrive safely."

She takes up the satchel from the table, lifts it to her nose to smell it.

"You know, Yblas lets me read those letters from time to time, whenever I'm at Amondsen's house with him in Hillfast. It's called the Old House, and nobody knows of it. Not even you." She gives us a wink. "Amondsen was the greatest woman who ever lived, yet none now know it."

"'On our sisters' silent bones rests this world of men.'" Cal this is, a saying he'd learned from an old Cassican deckhand we'd shared brandy with on our voyage back from Hillfast, both of us meek and restless in the long shadow of earning the colour and our bodies paying the price of our first fightbrews at Epny.

"We're both honoured to have read the letters," I say. "I cannot imagine what she endured, that Mosa's Road was the start of it all, and her dead son's shirt the one Yblas swears his oaths on."

"You both have her spirit and desire for the Post to stand for something other than pure greed. Haluim knows how boundless the greed of the administrators can be."

45

"Your creed," says Cal, "Driwna and I recall it, it guides us. The one you taught all of us at the academy."

"The one they kept asking you not to teach," I say.

She smiles at this. "I know it guides you. It might yet guide us all." She follows this with a ripple in her lips of a smile only partly leashed.

"I'd have been happier taking the commendation from you than any one of them," I say.

"We both would," says Cal.

"It couldn't be helped. I've been with Rogus, as concerned as he for the borders west. I need your eyes and ears open when you return to Lindur. Any Sathanti you find there you should speak to, ply with wine, do whatever you can to garner news from the kurches there."

"Who else is to meet with Yblas today?" I ask.

"Nobody. Just the both of you. Come."

I'd like to think that it might be good tidings that keep us here at the request of the High Red himself. I had yet to meet him, a formidable man by all accounts, as easily a friend with his arm about you as a pitiless judge and jailer. The stories we'd heard over the years were hard to pin to one man, so different was his behaviour in them. Yblas was renowned for what he could remember, the smallest details of conversations years past, the price of a point block of shiel in any one of a hundred ports. It's what the Post needs, a High Red who could run it on his own if he didn't have to sleep. Trouble is, it also means he'll be able to recall the things I did wrong when I first became Post.

Amaris helps Cal up onto her horse, surprising us both with the ease of it, and we follow a hill path past a few grand villas until we come to the hard, grey stone of the Posthouse walls, a flag catching a weak breeze above the red gates.

She leads us, as she did to our commendation ceremony, through the vast courtyard and the workshops there to the patio. The courtyards are busy and many huts have been built to extend the offices of the clearks. Servants walk about with pots most likely full of tea and caffin extract, proffering them to all our visitors; all the more pennies for Stroff to count. There are two vans being prepped for the field, the drudha and his apprentices, the drudhans, doing final checks on the vanners' belts. The vanners break into a raw and lusty song when they see Amaris, who dips her head in acknowledgement as she leads us inside the huge main house.

Stroff runs an orderly office. Floors are swept, candles lit and no wax about the floor beneath them. I pity whoever has that awful and wasteful task. The robes of his clearks are clean, with only their stained black fingers and inkwraps giving away their work.

Rooms to our left and right hold rows of desks and walls covered in the boxholes for rollcases. Ledgers are ordered on desks with obsessive precision. Stroff has beaten clearks on the raised patio outside in full view of all who come here for leaving any ledgers open while away from their desk.

We pass through unacknowledged and Amaris makes a game of these timid scratchers, greeting each cleark by name, offering a compliment, purely to watch them glance up a moment from their errand and hurry on lest Stroff leaps from under some desk nearby. I take a bit of pride in seeing her remember the names of all about, from the highest to lowest standing. She taught me the importance of that.

For all the dark stone walls and slate-tiled roof on the outside, Rakinic Marghoster, father of the current lord, Yeismic, had the walls inside lined with white marble, and the staircase had been carved from blocks of the same marble brought from kurches north-west of my homeland, above

Kristuc's Folly. The cloaks and robes of former administrators hang from the walls, while Stroff has had commissioned busts in a similar marble of both predecessors and favoured clearks. Prick.

The stairs split left and right near the top and we ascend to the quieter hallway above. We didn't get to come up here when Yblas gave us our commendations. Amaris knocks on and then opens a heavy farlswood door on the left side of the staircase. A marschal answers, standing to block the doorway, full leathers, the same grey as the agents and double belt. He clasps arms with Amaris, a hint of nervousness in his eyes that reminds me as well how formidable a killer she used to be. He stands aside to let us into a huge room, a library. Along the walls, floor to ceiling, are bound rolls, bound vellum, parchments, and other skins. Our noses are full with the smell of leather and oil. Carved onto narrow tin plates nailed to the shelves are the categories for these records, by region mainly. A farlswood desk fills the middle of the room, polished so it glows. It has to be Stroff's room that Yblas is using, for there are carpets littering the floorboards woven to depict maps of all parts of Farlsgrad. There is nothing of the man here, only the administrator.

"A purity of purpose intended to elicit trust. A high seriousness. This is what we feel when the administrator rises to greet us, his robes and his desk luxurious. This is the Post, eh Amaris? This is tenure, history, status."

Yblas this is, rising from Stroff's chair behind the desk, dressed only in plain grey woollens, a simple grey wool tunic. A brooch, the skull of a crow fashioned from white gold with a diamond and a piece of jet for eyes, hangs on his chest on a plain silver chain. It is the High Red's brooch, the only indication Yblas is wearing of his status, the same he wore at the ceremony though there it rested against a far finer robe. He was distant then, a cold formality during the various and dreary commendations. Now, close up, I confess Cal and I are somewhat wide-eyed at his gentle mockery of Stroff, his infectious smile. His beard is cropped, along with his hair, mostly grey and standing stark against his colour, a murky blue, paler in places, and as we clasp arms I realise he's strong still, knuckles of a fighter, hands scarred by work and poisons. Not a lick of fat on him either, a lean face, though his nose had been broken long ago and he must have lost a few teeth. His first years were spent in a workhouse. No kin-name he can recall. I try a kind of half-bow, unsure how to behave before the man who is responsible for all us thousands spread across the many more thousands of leagues of land and sea. How is he so, well, peaceful? He bows in turn, a smirk that does not mock my attempted deference and I retreat quickly. Cal does the same. For Amaris he breathes deeply, walks around the desk to her, holding his arms out. She embraces him, a lingering fondness between them. They've been inseparable down the years, a great frustration to the administrators who would attempt to place one of their own with him, render him a player of the political games they seem to enjoy. She gives him the satchel containing Amondsen's letters, which he puts on the floor next to his feet.

"You'll be walking in a week or so our drudha says. But a few months before any more fieldwork, Rulger, yes?"

"Yes, my Red," says Cal. Yblas gestures him into one of the fine-looking chairs before the desk and a glance behind us tells the marschal to leave.

He's already moved to a cabinet between the shelves, above which shutters are open to the day and the echo of gulls. He pours from a jug, brandy it must be, into cups the like of which I've not seen before, for they are made of glass but clear as spring water. He lifts the glasses up before us.

"We have two cogs returning from the Dust Coast, I hope, laden with these and tiles of the same. I've seen horn used in a lead window frame, I'd like to see if this glass can be used similarly. Winter daylight without the cold. Not even the wealthy Juans of the Old Kingdoms know yet the compound. Stroff, of course, uses these glasses to good effect. Your father used to collect glass, did he not?" He's speaking to Cal, who smiles at this.

"He did," says Cal. "Hets'qavarian urns, blue and green, the colour of the southern seas. Faience jewellery as well, my mun always drew comment with her eardrops and amulets." He didn't need to add that his pa would have lost all of it gambling or to pay the debts of his dice.

"How is your mun getting along?"

"Not seen her in a while. My stipend depends on me not showing up at Edral's. He's the lord now."

"Yes. I understand." Yblas serves us our brandy and bids us sit in the two remaining chairs facing the desk. I'm moved by this and it is also instructive. He waits on us and remembers the details of Cal's life as though they were sometime friends. Cal, both of us, are made to feel at ease with him. I have to confess an attraction to him and I will be far from the first.

"You'll excuse me, young Yblas, if I sit in Stroff's chair. When he arrives it'll infuriate him." Amaris this is, rounding the desk and easing herself down into his chair, putting her well-worn boots up on his immaculate desk.

"You're right, Cal, that your uncle is now the Lord Rulger." Yblas this is. "I shared cups with him three weeks ago. We share some Main Tens and his blisterweed farms serve all our drudhas from here to Khasgal's Landing. But it seems that he's suffering lately with the operations of a well-organised network of bandits. Gangers, more accurately, accosting vans in and around the southern Rulger territory and the border with Roan. The worst is the Rethic Fens and Aehrsmet. What struck me most was how much worse his own vans were preyed upon than the Post's. He noticed that when he hired Post crews to guard his vans they were more likely to get through, with bribes or without."

He takes a sip of his brandy. He's looking at me of course. I swallow, for here is the first glint of his steel.

"My Red?" I feel flushed with shame.

"This is an opportunity to open your hand for me, Driwna Bridche, that I may see it is clean." Though he called Cal by his family name, he addressed me by my own, for he knew of the purpose of our being called Marghoster, the shame that went with it.

"I made mistakes, my Red."

"You did. You began buying our cattle, hides, fens plant and peat blocks from your kurch and at a reduced profit, much to the annoyance of Reeve Garn, who had since made you his second. You showed favouritism to your family back then and the Post's name was sullied by it. But you also exposed punitive taxes to your kurch family made by the Rulger militia captain your pa wished you would be made the keep of." To be made someone's keep is to be wed, as it's said in King's Common. "I trust there's more than one straight quill at Lindur now?"

I want to tell him they killed my brun and nobody has paid the blood. They killed a lot more of us, all of them about Lindur got our blood on their hands. Thinking of my brun gets my own blood up.

"I hope there is, my Red," I say.

"How do we tell your pa, Dreis, he needs to keep his nose clean?"

There's no telling my pa, for he's the most stubborn fucker I know, and I'm at a loss for what to say to Yblas.

"If it is your wish I can visit my kurch?"

"He'll not listen to you treat with him as a reeve. I've had an agent there for nearly a year, working for the Adibric twins. He believes their banditry is directed somehow by your father, for he is, what do you call it? *Daith-ru*? Lord over his affiliated kurches?" The Adibric were one of the kurches that had survived the journey from our homeland before the Marghosters fucked us. My pa and the heads of the four kurches that survived where thirteen set out, there's bonds there as good as blood, strong as steel. What I couldn't tell Yblas, for those too were bonds I held dear, was that any easing off of the Post's vans was not on my account. I'm as keen to know more as he is.

"I've not told him anything of our routes, my Red. I don't speak to him."

"Yet he finds out the routes somehow."

Fuck you, I think to myself. "I don't speak to him, my Red." I look over at Amaris. She's staring at me, reading me. My eyes are stinging with tears, anger mostly. It suffocates me to think the High Red, and worse, Amaris doubt my loyalty.

"You have made oaths, Driwna." Yblas this is, a seriousness about him then, chilling the room. "Had I the Bloody Shirt I'd hear you make them again before me now."

"There's a suffering, a remembering of the refugee's hunger and fear in Driw's marrow, isn't that right, love? I expect you'd know something of it, my Red." Cal this is, putting his hand on top of mine as I clench and ease my grip on the arm of my chair. "We make mistakes when we are young and we hope to be forgiven. She knows her oaths, she wouldn't have a dog question them in all these winters since Epny." His lips tighten at the inference, ready for Yblas to explode. His defence of me fills my heart for it was instinctive.

Yblas finishes his brandy in a mouthful. He looks out of the shutters a moment before looking back at the pair of us. Then he laughs suddenly, heartily, muster-bell loud and twice as happy.

"Well said, Master Rulger, very well said. Too few of us who sit in rooms such as these deciding the lives of hundreds, too few have cried with the cramps of starvation or the bruises and cuts from fists and boots. And I speak of the suffering of children, not those that come with a purse. You both shone like stars in our academy at Epny. Amaris has seen you take on the colour, exemplary with horse, spear, bow and even, Driwna, some drudhanry. The Post is lucky to have such a reeve and her second." He refills all our glasses and comes to sit before us on the edge of the desk.

"I care to punish those who take our pay, the best there is to be had among all the guilds and merchants of this world, and then choose to take more besides. But I cannot have your kurches prey upon our vans, or those of Edral Rulger. Cal will visit his uncle and see his mother before he arrives back at Lindur. A letter and my seal will clear it as it will the other business I have for him. I'll have my cleark sign one out for you to present at our Posthouses along the way.

"Yes, my Red." Yblas and I both see his eyes light up, but he's curious too. I'm thrilled for him, for he misses his mun badly.

"Good. Lord Rulger will better describe the routes his vans take, where they were most likely to have been raided. Cal, you'll then need parley with Driwna's family. We have to know who's passing them knowledge of our routes and manifests. You'll have a persuasive purse to take with you, and my approval to strike a contract for whatever reasonable requests they might have in respect of plant, food or weapons, if such a deal loosens Dreis Bridche's tongue."

He takes a moment to look behind him at Amaris, in case she has anything to add. She simply shrugs, and unhooks the top catches of her leathers to cool herself a touch. It doesn't cool me.

"We don't have long before Stroff returns," says Yblas, "for there's news I've asked him to come here for. What I don't want to discuss before him is what Rogus said you'd found. The baby."

"Your letter to Cal and I at the inn suggested an interest in it. We're grateful to have been able to read the letters of Teyr Amondsen. Thank you. I would know where this baby was headed, but I did not think Ososi came from Roan or further south to have been hidden on our van."

"I have more than a passing interest. The baby was Oskoro, however. I've met the Ososi Master of Flowers. The Ososi cut the skin away from the braegnloc when they plant their seeds, not fold and sew it. That is an Oskoro practice. I've spent time in Hillfast. Few know that while I was on the crew for a van taking Mosa's Road to Stockson, shortly after my own training at Epny, I left the van as it passed the Almet forest and went in, though many said it was forbidden. I'd heard the stories of the Oskoro from the clans that lived and worked about the Almet Posthouse. Only after I'd read the letters in that satchel did I realise the Oskoro were responsible for many of the recipes that have given the Post an edge to all its trade in hostile lands. If we put more guards to every van than other guilds it is mainly because we must guard the fieldbelts themselves. Each one lost could potentially mean a recipe of ours is learned and shared. How much worse would the assaults on our vans be if those who knew of the Oskoro or Ososi thought we bore mixes and brews that they had invented? Nobody outside of this room knows of these letters, of the origin of our brews. You might wonder why I've shared their secret, but it will become clear shortly.

"Driwna, we owe the Oskoro everything, as did Teyr Amondsen. That baby is priceless and I doubt she was killed through accident or ignorance. She's come over the Sar from Hillfast and is being moved west out of Farlsgrad, presumably to somewhere in the Sathanti Peaks. I have no idea why and that pains me more than that it was our van she was put on. We are complicit, some cleark or docker, some ganger, some soldier of ours. Before I return to the Old Kingdoms I will go to Hillfast, to see what I can uncover."

"If I may, my Red," I say, "the Brasks put the kegs on a wagon, her inside it, perhaps at the port of Ullavir, for if she's come over from Hillfast with a view to her journey catching fewer eyes then Ullavir's where I'd bring her in, and the Post don't open kegs or crates belonging to others without good reason."

"A fair point, Driwna. Still, there is something more at work here. This is a child intended to be the Oskoro Master of Flowers. I fear for the Oskoro now. I've sent an agent to the Almet Posthouse for news."

His frown was one we shared the mood of, for the Sathanti we know, the Sathanti I recognise, respect the Ososi utterly.

"Will we send Farlsgrad's Marschal?" asks Amaris. "Discretion and a lack of ties to our crews there would be wise."

He softens his voice. "Marschal Latimer's keep was a guest of Sir Jayut Stalder at their hall here on the fourth day of Crutma just gone. Her dress was embroidered silk, a fine golden necklace, plain but well worked. Latimer is paid well for his skills, but he could not buy that dress.

55

That he looked like a chicken awaiting the pot all that evening suggested that he was none too happy with the stir the dress had created. He's Stroff's man, not mine. Stroff may well think I am too busy to notice his patronage, but I notice it all."

"You don't trust Administrator Stroff?" I ask.

Amaris clears her throat. Yblas pauses for it. She might as well just have said "fillet as thin a truth as you can".

"There are rifts, Driwna, quite serious factions in the administration of the Post. Our ambitions in the south, in the Old Kingdoms, are all the grander now for the efforts of my predecessor, Jenniek. Our power and influence there have indirectly caused this rift, north and south. Administrators are ambitious men, whom talent and our power have raised up so that they now share cups with kings and lords. I see it. I am from nothing. Like Jenniek I was chosen because I was the least controversial High Red, one over whom these men could gain a domination. But we both had Amaris to guide us as she has guided you both in turn. Jenniek and I were both clay in the hands of these would-be lords, but Amaris fired the clay and saved us."

I look past him to her as she slouches in Stroff's chair. She seems lost in thought. Twenty winters or more putting up with all these games of men. What a High Red she would have made.

"Stroff and Heikk, our administrator in the Citadels, once in command of the Post's natural heartlands, now both find themselves sidelined. Their ambitions, their proposals, are being passed over in favour of our pursuit of contracts and influence in the Old Kingdoms. It cannot be helped, for that trade brings us far closer to Amondsen's ambition than their best efforts could yield. We already have the north. Stroff has little love for me. I have to hope he's not involved in any harm to the Oskoro, but the smuggling of this baby's body is not the work of copper-penny thugs."

Just then there's a knock from outside.

"How perfect," says Yblas. "Come in, Stroff!"

Cal and I stand and turn to the door.

"Litko?" Yblas this is.

"Stroff will be along shortly, my Red. He and Heikk are with some scribes below."

Litko's colour is that of the Farlsgrad brews, the grey spread over more of his skin than on Cal or I, the dull burgundy colouring of the skin rubs less prominent. It must be some time since he's taken a brew. Like Stroff and Rogus, though ten summers younger perhaps, he keeps a smart beard, with only a ring of stubble around a bald crown. Litko strikes a strong figure in his red leather jerkin and leggings. He looks at Amaris then, at the filthy soles of her boots perched on the desk.

"Might you remove your boots from the desk, Amaris? It's not a becoming gesture."

She rubs her eye and yawns, crossing her legs over. I shiver, blink, as though cold air blows over my eyeballs. Yblas stands up from the edge of the desk and clears his throat. Amaris leans forward, bringing her boots off the desk to sit upright and cough. A smile plays over Litko's face.

"Brandy, Litko?" asks Yblas.

"No, my Red. Who might we have before us?"

"They're from our Lindur Posthouse, here for a commendation for their recovery of the Lindur Twelve van from bandits. This is Driwna Marghoster and Cal Rulger."

He's used the name I am known by in the Post. It was too much to hope he would use my own kurchname more formally, for all that it would be unfamiliar to them.

"I see. Very good." I'm about to introduce myself but

Litko keeps his hands clasped behind his back and looks down at his boots instead. Cal and I share a glance, his eyebrow delivers a *fuck him* shrug beautifully and I have to suppress a smile.

Just then Stroff arrives, and with him Heikk, who I recognise from our ceremony. Cal and I step back from the desk so as to be able to face all in the room. Litko steps aside for Stroff and Heikk to pass. There's a strange moment where Heikk attempts to move quickly to the other side of Stroff from Litko, knocking his shoulder as he steps around him. Stroff, beard as precise as his ledgers, head shaved, is a man that used to be much more the size of Heikk, but now his face sags around the chin.

Stroff clasps arms with Yblas weakly, distracted by Amaris sitting in his chair. She rises last.

"Thank you all for coming," says Yblas. "Litko, you should congratulate our new reeve at Lindur, Driwna Marghoster. She reports to you now."

"I expect the good work at Lindur to continue, Reeve Marghoster," he says, with all the interest of a man addressing a fly.

"We all do. Though I ought to tell you I have other plans for Driwna, making this the shortest tenure of any reeve in the Post's history." Yblas this is, and he says it with a smile and a clap of his hands. Amaris stands and moves to the side of Stroff's desk, and he's caught in two minds as to whether to move around her to take his chair or not. I'm grateful to be spared of such trivial and subtle acts that weigh so heavily with insult and purpose. Stroff then makes his mind up, moving around to his chair, allowing Litko to come around too. Amaris moves to stand next to me, leaning into me a moment for reassurance.

"Do tell us more, my Red." Stroff this is, easing himself

into his chair. "Will she not, then, be the reeve we need in Lindur?"

"You'll remember, or maybe you won't, under my predecessor Jenniek, that Amaris proposed a role and a creed that is more important now than ever. Our recent assembly and the tallies of our high clerks have all revealed a growth in our contracts, our trades, but not the expected growth in our vaults. Corruption and greed is a plague and all here despise it. We need the best of us, astute judges of character, hardened to the field, versed in the rolls and free to call to account any and all of us not upholding the principles of our Good Company."

"This is Amaris's treasured 'fieldsman' and her Farlsgrad Creed?" says Stroff. "Are you here to tell me that this time you have enough votes to overturn our previous good reason regarding this sinister distrust of those who serve you?"

"Yes, this vote was narrowly won. If I'd known how persuasive Amaris is, I'd have given her the chamber before the first vote. I'll remind you, Stroff, that Fidruin, the third High Red, created agents to fulfil just this role, only now they work as killers. They were once our fieldsmen.

"Besides, I have reason to distrust those who serve when I consider the discrepancy between our trade and our tallies. I hope you aren't forgetting that we all serve each other, Administrator." He waits for Stroff to acknowledge this, asserting his authority. "Why else are you so severe with your clerks for their errors, genuine or otherwise? You recognise as keenly as I the avarice that abounds where such wealth as ours accumulates. I worry that in the hinterlands, at our outposts, we are not quite as pure of heart."

"What are reeves for, and agents, if not this, my Red?" says Stroff.

"Can a reeve speak truth to a corrupt high clerk or their

own corrupt high reeve? And if one of my administrators were, Sillindar forbid, themselves corrupt, what then?"

"You'd have the fieldsmen report directly to yourself, my Red? Do they not have clearks and hands to command?" Heikk this is, neck wobbling around under his damp face, his belly his king and master. Neither he nor Stroff ever paid colour, and it wouldn't help with a lot of crews that they haven't, but when would administrators ever be seen dockside except when there's something wrong?

"The fieldsmen will work alone. A fieldsman solves their own problems and must be able to call on all in the Post to assist them. How else can they call all to account?"

"How might we establish the corrupt and the clean among your administrators, my Red, when they are confirmed by you?" Litko this is.

"No administrator begins their tenure corrupted," says Yblas. "None are above the very natural failings that ague us all. Bad decisions are made for what would seem to be good reasons, and these decisions may be hidden for what may seem also to be good reasons. A fieldsmen might shine a light in every corner."

"Every corner?" says Stroff, his meaning clear.

"Every corner, Stroff," says Yblas. "If a fieldsman finds me to be corrupt and can present that to the Assembly, the majority may oust me. I welcome such scrutiny."

"Might I ask why we are discussing this creed and the notion of a fieldsman before these two?" asks Litko.

"Because it is Driwna here that Amaris and I believe would make an ideal fieldsman."

"What?" Litko this is. Heikk looks over at me, frowning. Their low opinion of Yblas's decision is obvious, and I don't doubt it's intended to be so. At the same time I can't hide my own surprise, I grab Cal's hand instinctively and he now

leans in, putting his other hand on my shoulder in congratulations.

"We have excellent marschals who would be due equal
consideration, do we not?" asks Stroff.

"I'm sure Driwna is flattered by your congratulations on
her new role, Administrator Stroff, especially as she has
excelled under your command," says Amaris.

Cal clears his throat at this.

"Amaris has overseen Driwna Bridche since her time at
the academy" says Yblas. "As you know she excelled there
and, while her time as a quartermaster beforehand showed
something of a bias to the survivors of her tribe in the Rethic
Fens, she's acted in good faith since as Reeve Garn's second."

"Marschal Latimer would best her in sword and spear,
many more years in the field besides. Yet she'll outrank him,"
says Stroff.

"You misunderstand the role of fieldsman, Administrator.
It requires knowledge of the way we work as clearks and
quarters, our work on vans, our rolls, drudhanry and indeed
a good measure of skill in arms. Driwna has all of these, and,
crucially, has won hearts and minds wherever she's been.
She is also, as we saw with Lindur Twelve, willing to risk
life and limb to uphold what we stand for, what the Farlsgrad
Creed represents. This creed will be drawn up on vellum for
every Posthouse and shed we own, from Cassica to Coldbay.
There will be other fieldsmen, but they will not be known
to the Administration. Amaris will find them, so you'll be
free of her guidance for some time, Administrator. As always,
you run Farlsgrad excellently without me."

Another delicate thrust, an insult I can't quite taste,
although Litko's lips tighten, his eyes briefly flashing with
anger, something only I seem to notice.

"Cal Rulger here will become second to a new reeve at

Lindur, Morril Eidenrich. Rulger fills me with confidence, wouldn't you`agree, Administrator?"

Stroff nods. "A fine choice. Rogus will make up the necessary rolls for Morril Eidenrich. And, Marghoster, it is indeed an honour that the first fieldsman will come from Farlsgrad, well, close enough, eh. We shall enjoy a fine partnership bringing further order to our realm. In what way would you have me support her, my Red? Let it not be said I would resist an objective eye on our work." I had expected he'd refuse to call me Bridche, but it annoys me all the same.

"Your objective eye is most needed here at Autumn's Gate, Administrator. King Hildmir complains of being cheated out of taxes, he's raised our tithes twice this last year on our lands and crops, while berths and the sheds all now cost us more. The merchants lobby against us and the agreements we have worked hard to maintain since Crusica Hildmir signed them off with Brekeuel's mentor Thornsen a century or more ago. With Reeve Crejda's reports from the Spike of the border tribes acting up and how much more dangerous it's suddenly become to move vans through to the Lakes, I believe Fieldsman Marghoster can help ease Crejda's worries and investigate freely their causes while you maintain a view on all that goes on in and around court and the guilds. Rogus will see Driwna is provided with the best of fieldbelts, horse, leathers and chain. Rolls will also be dispatched with the Farlsgrad Creed that shall inform all of her seal and authority. We can talk more of Hildmir shortly." He leans over and clasps arms with me, then looks about at all of us in the room as he says these words:

"Help the helpless. Honour the purse. Peace through trade. This is the Creed."

I clasp arms with all there, Amaris, Stroff, Heikk and Litko. As I raise my glass for a cheer, I feel suddenly sick, empty, plunged into a memory – myself as a young girl standing before the bodies of a family I've long forgotten, swinging from trees, naked and blackened, misshapen by beatings. It's a memory so alive I feel the cold of that dawn, my breath misting in my convulsing panic, for such cold must be a trick of my senses in this room.

"Driwna?" says Cal. He limps to me, puts his arm around my shoulder.

"Sorry, I wasn't expecting this. Thank you, all."

"I'd say you and Cal should find your way back to the Old Hall Inn," says Yblas. "Rogus will call on you in the morning."

Yblas clasps his hands behind his back, our cue to leave. I glance at Amaris. She's smiling, but her eyes have filled up with her age, the battles of her duty against the endless tide of men and their arrogance. I get a flicker of a wink before she attends to her brandy and in a moment we're being led by an agent along the corridor to the stairs.

We walk in silence, out of the courtyard, finding our way between the wagons that are making ready to leave, their guards undergoing inspection. A Post van this, all the wagons ours, red sideboards and covers, the wood varnished, covers new, unpatched, unweathered.

"Where are you bound?" I ask the Guard as we come level with the top of the van.

"The Third, Throag." It is a border town, like the Spike, but to the north-west, Hildmir lands. By "The Third" he meant the third road of the wheel.

"Peace through trade," I say.

He looks puzzled.

"Sillindar with you," says Cal.

"Sillindar with you," he says back, turning to his second, who's packing a pipe.

"What do you think of it, Cal?"

"The Creed? It's right. Simple words, easy to recall, easy to be held to. I prefer fine words, verse that lifts. You know me."

We follow the stone road's fork into a slope down towards the top of the Stairs and the Old Hall Inn. The van will take the other fork, into the highlands.

"I was talking about me, you cock, being made fieldsman. It's unsettled me. Something has. I couldn't wait to leave that room, to get into the sun, but I feel like I'm standing at the bottom of the ocean and my air's fading out of my chest."

He takes my arm and halts us on the verge of the road as it rolls down, criss-crossing the hill we're on. It's all square stone houses here, verandahs looking over the views, well-kept tiled roofs in blue and green, their own plant runs and stables, like inns but only families with the run of them.

"Take your time, Driwna. We've only got the Old Hall's cellar to get through and half a day to do it in and I'm not walking right."

"Rulger filth. You're too tall for me to support you properly. And you're not limping that badly."

"Wasn't far wrong, was I, Marghoster filth? I said you should be the High Red, sounds like you've got the seal for the next best thing."

"I don't understand what I have to do, except I'm to do as I please in his service."

"It isn't that hard to understand, you daft sow. You snoop on people and earn a purse for it the likes of which us common Post will never see, Lady Fieldsman."

"You can fuck off Cal before I take that walking stick and shove it in you."

"Tempting."

"Behave. He's clever, isn't he, Yblas? He knows what I'll choose to do and he's freed me up to do it."

"Aye. You can only go after the baby if you've not got other duties. He's given me freedom to strike a deal with your family and all, whether or not your pa's been raiding my uncle's vans. There's a reason he's the High Red. More than all that, Driw, you deserve it. I just wish I was going with you, if only because you seem to need someone to wipe your arse while you're paying colour."

He gets my elbow in his gut for that.

It's a fine view out to the horizon. My head's settling a bit. I take a deep breath and hold it before reaching for his hand.

"You're going east where the baby Oskoro's come from, I'm going west, to where she's headed. We'll tie it together Cal. I hope Morril's managed to get something out of Livvie, some idea of where I'm going."

"Yblas wants you in the Spike, Driw. I think he knows you won't find her van now, you have to look for what follows, seek the pattern in the rolls and tallies; the reds and whoever else is deceiving us and using our vans, they're what'll tell you her destination.

"Have you met Crejda?" I ask.

He begins singing "Pay The Master No Mind", gesturing to the view before us down into the port, the single long note normally used to call a chorus to order. It's his way of bringing me out of my thinking ahead to this moment that I'm meant to be enjoying. His voice has softened, grainy with the wound I caused him. To me it seems improved for being less pure, if that makes sense, his singing the more moving for its flaws. If it upsets him he hasn't shown it. There's a clapping from children and travellers alike sharing the road with us, taken up with verses that he carries over the houses here, as he leans against me and limps in time with the song as we head for the inn.

65

Chapter 4

The Magist

"When does that cunt sail?"

Administrator Heikk is brooding. He doesn't speak so freely before Litko, my usual form, so I have taken Stroff's form – the refo is a familiar one now, useful. Stroff will wait in my quarters as always while I assume his visage.

"Yblas sails tomorrow, Thesselday," I say.

Yblas and Amaris had taken their leave of us once we'd agreed with them a proposal to assist in King Hildmir's border preparations. In response to the trouble in the Sathanti Peaks, Hildmir is strengthening the garrisons at his forts along that border while showing no interest in assisting trade along that frontier. The merchants suffering this loss of trade bemoan the greed of their van crews' demands for higher pay, though they do so over roasted beef, sweetcane jellies and Mount Hope wine.

We'll meet with the other merchant guilds tomorrow. Yblas thinks they've been lobbying against the Post's interests and it is useful that he believes that. A number of these merchants have loved ones in need of my help, in exchange for the means to secure a substantial number of mercenaries without Yblas or the Post's ledgers being involved. Along with Lord Marghoster we have Lord Ullavir. His family of merchants had long forgone a presence at Hildmir's court in favour of commerce and have been quietly recruiting for hands to work with their shipwrights. A quiet harbour in the Ulaf forest that edges their coast now has four war galleys with three more nearing completion. Ullavir's wife has recovered completely from a growing deafness and I've rejuvenated her in other ways that should work as well as any of my words in securing his loyalty for what's to come.

"I recall no waverers on the previous vote for that ridiculous creed and the fieldsman role," says Heikk. "Why has the Administration folded now?"

"You'd do well to consider what Yblas offered to whom to secure their vote. The way he talks about the south suggests something big is afoot and it's the Old Kingdoms administrators that will benefit from it. He's been there most of this year, we've seen farlswood and stone from the Citadels and Farlsgrad sent down at almost triple the volumes. Do you have no spies there?" I know the answer, as does he, for he says nothing, pouring instead more brandy into his glass.

"Heikk, you'll put two of your agents on a ship, two that might do what our new fieldsman is meant to do – sniff out answers, integrate into the offices of Administrator Lachaz at Jua and Troost at Issana."

"Yes, Stroff. We've a cog on its ballast leg awaiting the tide, I'll have one of my hands take a roll to Hillfast."

"Good."

He stands, his arm moves out briefly to clasp mine, but it won't do for me to touch him. Not until he returns and I can put time into preparing him for patterning, for the recovery from refo is long and painful, especially when it's a new subject.

"Should we worry about this fieldsman, this Marghoster girl?" he asks.

"I would have said no, seeing her as we just have, but the fact Yblas and Amaris back her, and that boy with her, tells me she's unignorable, quite apart from her now having the same rank as ours."

"Ridiculous. Yblas might just as well have had us on our knees at his cock."

"Heikk, don't annoy me. You're subverting his goals every single day you're an administrator. Now, do you know anything about her?"

"No."

"We need leverage, on both her and Cal. He's soft on her, the boy, that was obvious. She's leverage against him. Reeve Crejda's mine, she's been ten years at the Spike and she's sharp as a butcher's knife. Has to be down there, it's as corrupt a shithole as you'd find anywhere. Ideally Driwna'll have an accident," I say. "I'm going to Lindur to find out a little more about her and the boy Cal."

"Is Crejda involved in our work?" asks Heikk.

"Yes. But I'll need to give her some guidance directly. We both know what's running off the ledgers there. Our work is not yet done in the Peaks."

I know Crejda indulges her crew too much, which means they're loyal but are likely skimming off coin and using the Post for their own operations. Such things are as common as grass. Still, if she's half as capable as she ought to be running the Post operations at the Spike, she should ensure this Marghoster girl is given the run-around while I make the final preparations for the end of Farlsgrad's monarchy.

"Will Hildmir's fortification of border garrisons be a problem?"

"No, Heikk. No garrison will withstand us."

Chapter 5

Driwna

The Spike is a cesspit.

For a bit of history, it's a fort built up on the ruins of a vast old stone fortress that has been here since before anybody can remember, thick walls of a strange stone white as snow but hard as the blue granite that completes them. The mix of foreign and native stone has left the towers looking mottled, almost sickly except for the high tower itself, at the top of the hill, that stands unblemished and shines in the sun, its conical roof tapering like a charger's lance. The contrast between its beauty and the corruption orchestrated by its castellan makes it all the sadder to see. The layout of the old bailey is fenced in with proper farlswood now, patched-up stone towers for lookouts and archers. These are empty as Cal and I approach, pointless too given the town has burst the lines of the fence and spread wide about it. The castellan, Gruslatic, has made the Spike a fief of his own and rules with a subtle and clever violence.

The land here is all hills and vales. North-west the mountains fill the horizon, snow capping the distant peaks as the month of Crutma ends and Norva begins. Winter soon enough. The Spike sits on a hill that looks down upon the River Iblar, the main vein of trade from the Bouskill Lakes and Sathanti mountains to the Spike before it cuts south and feeds the marshes over Lindur and, I don't doubt, the fens my kurch now lives on many leagues to the east.

A town of hovels and tents squats outside the stone buildings that fill the flats and slopes about the fort, following the lines of the old foundations and spanning the river as we come in on the great road of the Wheel known as the Fifth. Our horses pick their way through the muddy runs between the tents and huts. There's families gathering around common fires, duts crying for milk, arguments, laughter, pots bubbling, smells of mint and fat frying, a flute somewhere, all within a spit of us. A few watch us from their fires and doorways and a wake of children spreads behind us with well-rehearsed tales of their troubles. Cal throws some coppers about, for we're in our red, and despite the Creed now making its way in the saddlebags of messengers and on boats to all our interests, Cal and I know already how well kindness repays itself.

The Post sheds are easy to see for the red flags amid the other sheds and their own colours. Post has five sheds, only three less than Autumn's Gate itself, more than any other guild here. The Posthouse is walled up enough it can be laid out something like the Posthouses across the rest of the world.

We see a big tavern called the Doris; two storeys, its walls proper stone, a patchwork of the foreign white and local blue granites sat amid the sheds, a hive of drinkers inside and out, the square leather patch hanging at the door shows they welcome mercs, which these days is also a sign that betony might be found inside if you know how to go about asking.

"Sure you won't stop over tonight and have a few cups with me?" I ask.

"I'd enjoy that," says Cal, "but we both need me back at Lindur helping Morril and getting out east to my mun and your kurch. I'll let Morril know a bit of what we're up to. Our promotions will give us an excuse to get in among the rolls and I can snoop a bit more about Brasks."

"I'm going to miss your singing." I want to say I'll miss him just being a lift for me, a man who could bring the sun out when I'm getting over my paying the colour or some killing we've done.

"Marghoster filth. You can't be a Rulger so you want the next best thing."

"You're not a real Rulger anyway."

He's about to give it back when a red steps out in front of us, recognising the colour of our cloaks. "What's your business, reds?" We've come to the Post sheds, there's tracks leading off to each of them from this main run that snakes on through to the edge of the Spike, throwing trails and cord runs out to the river stages through row after row of workshops, market and cattle stalls.

"I'm Driwna Marghoster, this is Cal Rulger. You should have had word sent of the Creed, and of anyone bearing the Fieldsman's Seal."

"We had word, yes. The High Red won't be happy 'less each of us has a spy to ourselves." He's old, this one, fifty or more summers and his hands, one holding a pike and the other a pipe, are trembling. Betony withdrawal I'd wager, paying the colour's yellowed his eyes and he's gone to fat, skin the colour of ash, must have taken to drink to keep the betony at bay. He's got a leather jerkin on, no belt, no vadse from the look of him, which isn't right for anyone guarding one of our gates, for vadse sticks are better than caffin for

71

keeping alert. The other red that's with him is a boy, thirteen summers at best, and he's asleep, his apprentice cloak filthy.

"I'm your new spy, Fieldsman Driwna Marghoster." I hold out the seal, a treated leather strip stamped with the Creed in Farlsgrad field lingo one side, Post field lingo the other and oiled with a filweed juice mix that turns water a dark red when it's splashed on, proof enough the seal is genuine given the rarity of the mix.

He takes it, recognises the lingo from his eyes tracing it – must have served in Hildmir's army at some point past.

"You'll be wantin' Crejda then. She's in shed two, keeps an office with her ledgers there. Fine horse you got, miss. Four or five years I'd say an' she likes you a lot." His hand to her nose was easy, a few clicks practised without mouthpiece but a way of sizing her up that showed me he loves horses and is good with them. He looks up at me, a smudge of approval in his eyes, before stepping back to allow us to walk in.

"Stable's past the far shed, behind the two wagons with red covers stood together. Odivric is master there."

"Thank you. What's your name, red?"

"Bray."

"Would you take our horses to Odivric for us?"

"Can you keep mine saddled," says Cal, "just give her water and some grain. I'm moving on."

"Aye. Lad, wake up!" He gives the sleeping boy a kick and he wakes with a start, falling off the stool he's using.

We dismount and leave Bray to fuss over the horses. He leads them easily through the crews that are about; some are standing and smoking, others must have been put to work in the shops about, wheels getting their bands, repairs to running boards and harnesses going on about us. It's noisy with the hammering and laughing. A few look at us as we walk through, some nod, others simply watch, for my leathers

72

and belts are new, well worked and grey, unlike the brown and black that's the usual for Post soldiers. The armourer at Farlsgrad had also stitched a thick, dark red leather pauldron about my lead shoulder and on the facepiece that hangs loose at the side of my cap until needed.

"Eyes on you, Marghoster filth." Cal this is, speaking quietly next to me.

"It's the leathers, they're piecing me together with the Creed that has come through I expect."

"Except the one to your right who's got his hands cupping like he's got your babs."

I look right – the man's hands drop to his side quick and the three others with him laugh but he keeps my eye as I walk past, though it's no more than the look of a boy caught out.

Second shed's the biggest, stone walls towering over the other Post sheds, beams and slate tiles covering it all and the track we're on, pillars supporting the roof either side of the track so wagons can be unloaded out of the rain.

I'm glad to see proper flagstones have been set inside the shed. Braziers are lit inside, plenty, giving a fair light. On the left as we walk in there's a raised stand and a few steps to a wooden dais on which stands three tables and shelves of rolls, I expect as a protection against flooding.

Crejda stands as we enter, must be forty summers, the grey colour of our brews but a softness about her that tells me she's been off Guard duty for a year at least, finding the shape of her chair as Cal might say. Her hair too is finding its grey from a deep red and she's wearing it about her shoulders, lucky that she hadn't got any mixes in it over the years or it would be shaved like mine.

"Welcome. By the looks of you, you must be Driwna and Cal."

"Reeve Crejda," I say.

She steps down to the ground from her table and we clasp arms.

"How was the Fifth?"

"We made good ground."

She introduces us to her clearks and those of her crew near enough about before Cal tells her of his need to get out on the river and south to Lindur.

"We have our own stage on the river. I can put a couple of us onto a three-hander and get you on the river to the Lindway." The Lindway was the nearest the river passed by the Lindur fort.

"That'll do me, Reeve. Thank you."

"Fayrn, get over to stage two, Lairkic and Crunnetch should be caulking the new skiff. Tell them to ready Runner Four for the Lindway, then find Bray here, tell him to lead Second Rulger's horse to the Runner."

"Reeve." Fayrn runs off ahead of us as Crejda leads us out and across the track, opening a cattle gate back across the main run and onto a lane heading between more rows of hovels, a few droop joints filling our noses with their luscious decay. Some of the doorways have blue curtains hanging across them, embroidered with roses – the sign of whores, some of whom are on their steps, in their pipes or sewing, waiting for dusk.

"You lost a good man down at Lindur. I was sorry to hear about it. I'd met Reeve Garn many times. He'd bring the wet ones up here to blood them a bit and show them how much easier their lives were going to be than in this huge fucksore of a fort."

"He always spoke well of you," I say. She nods at this, happy to accept the compliment. He'd spoken well of her once, but there we are.

74

"And you, Fieldsman? I'm looking forward to being able to share a plate and a few cups. The Creed has everyone here yapping like puppies and I've told them we're expecting you here as your first assignment."

"Like you said, Reeve, it's a fucksore here, a border fort, lot of trade, lot of Farlsgrad, kurch-kin from Sathanti, mercenaries, slavers and beggars. You've sent reports to Farlsgrad, to Administrator Stroff, regarding border issues. The Hidzucs are a problem?"

"They're never a problem – their kurchmen come in and tell us that plant rights are being violated and buffalo herds attacked for meat but it's all the usual. There's less trade because of troubles that I think are further west. They care only for getting their hands on kannab and bacca when they're here anyway."

"That is a problem for our leather trade, nonetheless; their buffalo leather's better than anything south of the Sathanti."

The Hidzuc confederacy of kurches, just over the border from the Spike, now live on land that belonged to my own kurch's confederacy once, the Bridche. I know the Hidzucs aren't a problem directly, for they're as besotted with the Marghosters as my pa once was, closer to Farlsgrad than they are to their own Sathanti brothers, softened with its luxuries and especially its kannab. Fuck all good such ties did us when Marghoster sold us out, but the leather from those old herds of ours is too good for any in Farlsgrad to risk their ire.

"I'm here to help," I say.

We come to the river, eighty yards wide here. Longboats, skiffs and even a few cogs crowd at the thirty or so stages. There's a lot of Farlsgrad militia about, for there's good tithes to be made from so many and the Hildmir purse clearly can't afford to miss it from what I heard back at Stroff's library. Crejda turns to Cal.

"Cal, Sillindar follow you south. Please wish Reeve Morril well for me. Fieldsman, you will have passed a busy tavern near the sheds – I'll see you there, I'm keen for a few cups."

Crejda leaves us.

"A fucking soak for a Reeve?" says Cal.

"I don't think so, but one drooper and a boy barely old enough to have any cockfluff fast asleep on guard is a concern. She's soft for sure."

Cal smiles and takes my arm in his as we watch the two Post get the runner in order. I glance at him and there's a sheen to his eyes.

"I'm going to miss you, Marghoster filth," he says. "We've not been parted, have we?" I nudge him because seeing him upset has upset me. He's right. We've been together since the academy; pipes and cups, paying colour, and for me, just listening to him sing, the most beautiful voice I've ever heard. He can silence a tavern full of soldiers, but it's no surprise as us soldiers are as prone to the high feeling of love and grief as the greatest poets, for who knows the colour and the agony of it better, the visions of land and sea hidden to the normal bounds of our senses.

"I'll miss you, Rulger. We use our cyca for the letters; it won't do for any to read what we say while we work out who we can trust." There's none but us know our cyca, the shapes we use instead of King's Common or Farlsgrad lingo to crypt words from spies.

"Have you anything to say to your mun or pa?"

"Just that I love them. You'll say the rest. Mun will be pleased to see you again. And tell Morril I love her too, and I'm proud of her becoming Reeve. We can trust her, I think we'll need her. My rank's going to sew up a lot of mouths."

"I know. Driw, take good care of yourself, love."

76

Bray walks up to us, Cal's horse with him, alert and nuzzling him for some more of a snivet he'd given her.

"Here's the lass, Second Rulger. Sillindar follow you." Bray steps forward and throws a couple of sacks he'd had over the mare's back onto the mainboards of the Runner. "Rations, plant and grain in 'em."

Cal nods, takes my face in his hands and kisses my head and nose. There's little fuss from his mare as she boards, which impresses Bray I can see, but we've been given two of the finest horses the Post had at Autumn's Gate.

Lairkic and Crunnetch push the boat off. Bray stands with me as Cal and I wave each other away, Crunnetch getting the small sail up, Lairkic and then Cal helping to pole and oar themselves into the main current.

I turn to Bray. He's standing behind me, looking at the boards of the river stage we're on, his hands still trembling, lost in thought. He's only a bit taller than me. I see he's lost his hair, angry scars on his head, some dirty grey tufts of hair he's not bothered to shave that are tinged yellow with bacca. Like his belly with ale, his fingers are swollen, hands spotted with old skin damage and his jerkin is a disgrace to the Post, more food and ale soaked in it than the oil it needs.

"How are you, Bray?"

He looks up, his twitching getting a touch worse. Nervous.

"Fine, miss. Fuck, Fieldsman." He looks to his feet again, a soft shake of his head, hoping I'll let him go. Instead I take his hand so I can hook my arm in his. I sense him stiffen to this unexpected familiarity and he looks at me warily.

"This miss needs a cup or two to wash the dust out of her throat. Will you join me?"

"Yes, Fieldsman." He's pinioned to his rank and duty, one advantage of these leathers and this seal I'm bearing.

"Is there anything you want to ask me?" I say.

77

"No."

"Why not?"

We've started walking and I've slowed it to the pace of lovers. He looks at me more directly then, frowning.

"No business o' mine, your doin's."

"No? I'm here to help you, all of you at the Spike."

"Same's what the Administrator spoke, to the reeve. Crew's feelin' a lack of trust Crejda don't deserve."

"He's been here recently, Stroff?"

"Not sheds, miss. That lad I be sorry to say was sleepin' earlier, he was late that mornin' and . . ."

"Where was Stroff?" I say, hurrying his account along.

"Sorry miss, Kietr, the boy, was late in an' said he was passin' the keep when he sees Crejda comin' out of the tower itself, Administrator with her."

"Did she say why he was here?" I'm trying to keep a lid on. Stroff cannot have made that distance more quickly than me and Cal riding the Fifth unless he never slept and took messenger horses all the way here. The questions pile up in my teeth.

"Crejda's not said fuck – I mean, eff to us, miss."

"No need. All ledgers and tallies, our administrator. He has little to do with vanners and crews."

"You work for him an' all then? Stroff?"

"I report straight and only to the High Red."

"Fu . . . right, yes, Fieldsman." He looks at me again. I guess at his thinking.

"I sense you think I'm young for it."

His eyes drop again, he shrugs. "Red says you're good, you're good enough. Red's no dut. I shook his hand, marschal he was then. Said I did us proud." His jaw clenches. There's a nub of pride in there, a wagon-load of regret and self-pity perched on it.

"You're midlands-sounding. Redfields?" He nods. "Where'd you serve?"

"Post or Farlsgrad? Done both when I was clear o' this shakin' and shiverin'. Fuckin' colour. Apologies."

"You served King Hildmir?"

"In Egrodor. Four campaigns."

"You meet the Goose?"

"He was my captain, two year."

"He was your captain? Those are hard fuckers, the Egrodor. We learned this at the academy. They named Goose Warrens after him. A hundred miles into a land no Farlsgrad soldier walked since before the Orange Empire."

"None better than 'im, miss."

"You were on that campaign, the making of Goose Warrens?"

"Aye, miss."

That shuts me up a moment, for Cal knows at least five songs sung of the crew that went out there and the three that came back; Moon, Lady Death and the Weeper.

"I was called the Weeper once, as you're thinking on it. Bit more weepin' done since then an' it give no purse as you know."

"How come?" I was about to say more, trying to place how a soldier who should be a legend to many here ends up with the life wrung out of him. "You have a keep hereabouts?"

"You jokin', miss. Not the worth of a good woman's love, I be. Might have been different if . . . It don't matter. The cups have me, the betony before it, and before that, well, what we done out there, what I done, I . . ." And he stops a moment then, looking at me. He smiles, only six teeth left I can see, but it's a moment when, talking of the Grey Goose, a crew any soldier would be proud to have served with, he straightens an inch or so, and he's threaded my questions. I

79

see a man ten summers younger, a flicker of fire long kept soaked.

"You're one o' those, like the reeve. Soften a man up like butter with takin' an interest in him so's he'll obey you easier. No offence, miss, you're good at it. I saw it on the boy. He'd follow you to the end."

"Your wit hasn't soaked out just yet, Bray. It's a privilege to meet you. Cal will kick himself he missed his chance to hail the man 'of knife and whispers'." He shrugs at this. It's a man he's not looked back on, I'd guess, a Bray long banished. No noke – by which I mean someone who's not ever paid the colour like a soldier – could understand why we would admire what Goose and his crew had to do. He must have kept it quiet since joining up here, perhaps had kept it quiet for years.

"Nobody'll hear any more of this from me," I say. It shouldn't quite need saying but I want him to be sure of me.

"I know."

That makes me smile.

We walk back past the Post sheds and stand outside the tavern Cal and I saw earlier.

"You'll come in for a cup?"

"On duty still, reeve's in there, you're here to make yourself known proper."

"I could order you to take a cup with me, Bray, but really I'm just a soldier wants to say she's had a few cups with the Weeper and lived to talk about it."

He smirks, but his eyes flit between the reeve he can see inside and the gates where the boy stands alone, wondering what's going on with us.

"I won't be talkin' about how Goose died. That's my promise to him."

"I know."

He's stone-still for that moment, caught in the memory of it.

"I don't want to cause you trouble, Bray. You should get back to guarding our sheds, we can't leave that boy to it. Just tell me something. Can I trust Crejda?"

"She been good to all, miss. All us crew have love for her. She put up with my . . . habits when I went wrong. Din't have to."

"Thank you, Bray."

"Miss."

He walks back, his step a bit quicker, perhaps relieved not to start so early into cups.

There's good heavy smoke in the tavern; kannab, some different baccas, smell of frying meat, hops. Must be a hundred in the big main common room and two rooms I can see off at either end. Long serving table's at one side, two militia keeping an eye. The barkeep's there, leather apron and a club at his waist, filling some tin mugs from a keg. A couple of girls and a boy are standing to the side of the long table, made up for looking at, cheeks rosied with powder, shirts a little too tight and all have filled them well. Crejda's standing with an older man from one of the other sheds, crest sewn on his sleeve for another guild. She squeezes his arm for a farewell as she sees me enter, bids me follow her into the back room across from the doorway.

Back here's a lower ceiling, thicker still with bacca smoke, five booths, two with curtains across them. I can smell betony pipes here, the sweet, vile smell coming from a doorway leading up some steps. There's two more militia there, for good money's to be made off those needing the betony.

She bids me sit in one of the booths first, must have been reserved for her, and she sits opposite me. A girl brings a candle and proper glass bottle, a soft nose of blackcurrant suggesting red wine.

"I have some bottles put away here," Crejda says. "Booth is paid for from our profits, good for managing a conversation and warming up a trade."

"I agree. Let me toast your health, Reeve, and that of your crew here. Not an easy posting, the Spike."

"The High Red has made this your first call."

"He has. What did Stroff tell you?"

There's a moment's hesitation. I'm not sure what to make of it.

"He'd come with a messenger, the High Red's concern is Stroff's. Might be vans go west to the Lakes regularly enough but it's wilds there and the kurches are only ever one succession away from a leader with his braegnloc and his cock swapped out where reason's needed."

I'm still distracted with figuring Stroff's speed at arriving here before Cal and I. Not even I could manage the messenger runs, for they go hard between our outposts, with horses prepped for swapping out and vadse and caffin mixes that push them through the nights on highways such as the Wheel. I can't say anything just yet. Something's not right with it.

"I've been sent here to find out what might be going on out west."

"Have you been out to the Lakes, up to the Folly? In recent months anyway?"

"No, been south in Roan, vanning to Lindur."

"The Hidzucs would be glad of knowing the Post cares for their trade. Further west? There's little civilisation there, just nomads, useful for hides, mountain laurel and pokeweed. We can't forage out there, but what lots the Hidzucs could manage of that plant no longer comes back here."

"Have we found a way to mask the pokeweed yet? It could be a boon to some of our mixes."

"No, and if the Hidzucs have learned, they're not telling us. If you do have any reason to go west, you might take a recipe for barter as it would be worth it." Crejda leans towards me. "Have I wronged Administrator Stroff or the High Red in some way, that you're here?"

"No. I'd say that any wrong being done here is being done without our being aware."

"In my sheds? Are you looking also for corruption?"

"I hope not, but not everything we van comes through our sheds. Do you trust your clearks?"

"Utterly." The word was a blade. "There's not one on my crew I doubt. Isn't that the way at Lindur? Did Garn have the loyalty of all he worked for?"

"Apparently not, though he believed he had. Some lots had been tampered with." I let that hang a moment. "At Lindur we don't check what's in each chest, keg or crate we van. Do you?" I ask.

"I see. And we now must? We'll lose much trust and opportunity if we start demanding this from the guilds, farmers and craftsmen who use us."

"Better that than traffic bodies without our knowing." She's taken aback by that, but no more, as far as I can read, than any reeve might be that carries responsibility for the vans.

"All here know the Post won't move people, dead or alive."

"That's reassuring. Do we have any vans due to go west?"

"No. There's some unrest out there. Since Harud, so, two months ago, we've had few wishing to put a wagon with us. News of the loss of vans travels quickly along the border, and north in the Tongue there's also been Sathanti trouble. Our promise to find a way comes at too great a price now to be worth the profit on whatever's being waggoned."

"It has?"

"It's doubled to eight silver pennies each lot."

"Eight over the standard van fee? This sounds somewhat worse than I'm hearing."

"Finding a vanguard better than Gallic, who knows the trails through Ilkashun land as well as he does, would cost me three times his purse. I've got nobody else I can trust to see a van there and back again. The vanners here know it."

"You've got no vans out there now, not even wagons with the Brasks or the Cottic?"

"No, just river work at the moment. Why did you speak of the vanning of bodies?"

"One was found, in a Lindur van. I need your help with any trade we do from hereon in. If somebody's moving bodies for drudhas without our knowing, somebody's making good coin and using our crews to do it."

"You have my word."

"Excellent. This is fine wine." I take a good mouthful, warming to my next words. "I'd like to take Bray into the field with me, west to the Hidzucs."

"Bray?" I might as well have farted. "He's a poor choice. Hasn't had a fightbrew in years, fat, drinks too much. It's pity that sees him draw coin from us; he's worn the red for years and does well enough at our gates but I wouldn't trust him to saddle my horse."

"I'd hate to take away anyone more capable or more involved in your operations."

She knows it's an order. She holds my eyes a moment then, looking for my purpose.

"I hope you can bring him back stronger and a bit happier. He's a miserable shit, walks about with a face like a dog chewing a wasp."

I ask her a few questions about the Spike, the others that

84

trade here, and some more about our crew. I get all the right answers and no wrong ones. And that bothers me. She finishes a second cup and excuses herself, leaving me to finish my own and promising me a room where Stroff had recently stayed.

I'm cross with myself for trying to score a point in mentioning the body. She's loyal, has the trust of her crew, and that's fine. What am I missing?

I fold a stalk of vadse into the side of my mouth and head back into the main room, filling even more now with evening on the way. I take a stool that a butcher leaves and one of the fine-looking girls swaps coins for a few mugs of their ale. It's shit ale of course, for the tavern's too convenient with no competition besides to worry about providing better, but it buys me time to listen, the vadse sharpening what's said in even the far corners of the room.

I learn more than I need to regarding what could be done with the girls and boy serving us. Marghoster's tithes are up and he has collectors in the lands about making more of a nuisance of themselves than they have for a long time. I see five mercenaries, deep colour, are talking low, and it's some lingo, some King's Common. Hard to make out more than that they were waiting for someone from the fort to bring news of the purses going there.

I'm halfway into my second cup when Bray walks in, a waxed rollcase in his hand.

"Fieldsman. Messenger's just ridden in from Lindur. For you. Crejda signed. Messenger was bein' sent to Autumn's Gate. Makes sense they might not have known you bein' sent here."

"Thank you, Bray. Would you stay while I read it, in case I'm required to respond by return?"

"Miss."

"Hail, Bray my handsome, will you have a cup?" One of the serving girls this is, long brown hair and heavy babs drawing the eyes of all about as she clears cups and some bowls from the table I'm sitting near. Bray looks irritated – no, conflicted. He's not paying her or her babs any mind, and it saddens me, for it reveals the extent of his troubles with ale and the like.

"What's your name, girl?" I ask. She sees me properly then, sees the quality of the leathers and belt, sees the coin.

"I'm Alaqua, miss. Is there anything you'd like?" If her name's really Alaqua, mine's Stroff.

"You've got a lot I'd like, but for now there's just a question about soldiers, those with colour." I put two silver pennies on the edge of the tray she's carrying. Bray raises an eyebrow. Alaqua is rather more excited.

"What would you like to know, my lovely?"

"Have you seen a lot more of them, last few months?"

"Oh I have. Come in off the boats, don't they, Bray? He's here every night, still working up the courage to take me upstairs, in't you, handsome? They asks for the boards, where the clearks put out the purses they want done. But they don't tip like you, miss. Not even your reeve does, and she can afford to."

"You've got a dut to feed, Alaqua. I imagine that's not easy with you having to work."

"Oh, miss," she frowns, "what you been spying on me for?"

"Alaqua, my girl, I see on your shirt there's faint marks about those fine nips. Bit of milk leaking would do it, if you were feeding."

She looks down, pulls the neck of her shirt to lift it and see for herself.

"I had terrible trouble, miss, would hear a dut cry and

86

I'd be wet with milk, and him," she points over at the barkeep, "he was moaning about it for he has half the tips and there's no man wants to see milk where he's thinking he'd want his own mouth."

"So there's more soldiers coming through, Farlsgrad militia as well?"

"No, just mercenaries, no more militia than we usually get in here of a night. They speaks all kinds of lingo, these mercenaries, looking from their features and the way they're inked like they're from away south or over the Sar somewhere."

"Thank you, Alaqua. Bray'll have a cup of brandy, he's sitting with me."

She puts a hand to his arm and looks at me. "He don't paw me, don't dirty his tongue with saying what he'd do to me. He's a good man this one." She goes then to the serving table for what must be Bray's usual cup.

"Sit down, Bray. Tell me what you know about these mercenaries coming through the Spike, once I'm done reading this roll you've brought."

I look closely at the wax that seals the cap to the case. It's not been tampered with. I use my nail to crack through the wax and open out the roll that's inside:

For Driwna Marghoster,
Posthouse Amondsen
Autumn's Gate

Driwna,
 The moment you arrive at the Spike I would ask you to ask Crejda to spare a crew or put a purse up for any that would go into the Sathanti. We put out a van the day after you and Cal left. Gennic went as

Vanguard, seven of our reds along with four keeping
guard of wagons belonging to Fegredic & Wallen. We
expected a missive back from Hidzuc at least to tell us
they're on their way home, but nothing. I've put a purse
with five mercs said they knew the Hidzucs and the
Ilkashun trails enough they could find them.

Livvie misses you. I'm not as free with the honeyed
apples I fear! She says she saw the wagon you asked
her about get taken with a van going to the Hidzucs. I
found out as much when I followed up with Iglin but
he wasn't saying if the van was going further on.

Give my love to Cal. Would it kill you to let us
have the benefit of him until we discover where Gennic
and our crew might be?

Reeve Morril
16 Crutma 574OE
Lindur Outpost

"Good news don't ever get put on messengers. Am I right,
miss?" says Bray.

"You are." Alaqua's put his brandy down at our table and
he's doing his best not to drink it down. His shakes make it
difficult for him to even hold the cup comfortably.

"You take kannab at all to help with your hands?"

"I don't, miss. Not been paid much, none of us have.
Reeve won't be rid of us even though contracts are down.
We all agreed to take less an' hope for trade to pick up."

"You weren't tempted to go where the pay might be better,
man of your experience?"

"Pay's bad all about the Spike, miss. A few I used to
have cups with tried movin' on, two of 'em were found
dead in Little Lanes, you come through there from Fifth.
Awful shit. Gangers must've had them for coin owed. They

get rich when you's poor enough an' stupid enough to borrow from 'em."

"Where do you live, Bray?"

"I keeps a mat in the sheds, and I gets a few more pennies for guardin' them than a dog would an' I don't piss everywhere there's a leg." He laughs, causing him to cough, and what he spits up I can see needs treating.

"I need someone to ride with me. Hidzuc lands."

"Aaah, no miss, please. I's out o' breath havin' a shit. I can't go in the field no more."

"I have plant'll do well for that chest, Bray, and more of what ails you besides."

Like all old soldiers, talk of plant, anything that can heal or help, pricks up the ears.

"I's tried most things and found 'em wantin'."

"I've got a bindweed recipe and a decoction of Lady's Bedstraw."

"Bedstraw? I heard of it – for bleedin' though. Guts, mostly."

"It's more than that, and I'm not saying you'll appreciate what I have to do, but I can give you your breath back and you can thank the man we're headed out to the Sathanti Peaks to find. If you'll agree to come with me."

"An' you're a soldier'd deny another their breath 'less a bargain's made?"

"No, Bray. But you'll want to do me a favour in return, won't you?"

"Don't ask me that, miss."

"Let's see how you feel after we're done."

4 Norva 5740E
Administrator Stroff
Post House Amondsen
Autumn's Gate

The Fieldsman has left for the Hidzuc lands. She's taken one of my crew with her. A roll arrived from Lindur shortly after she arrived and she left within a week. She would not say what spurred her departure. I know Reeve Morril requested of the messenger he hand it straight to her. Would you know more of it?

In her time here she has asked a thousand questions of me and my clearks. Your warning was welcome but our ledgers are clear of our other work, as they must be for the tax collectors of Marghoster. My crew are well drilled in respect of the ledgers. They appreciate the gifts sent. As does Castellan Gruslatic. He has agreed that we can hire a small crew he retains to see to our friend. They will then move on to the mountains.

Peace through trade!

Reeve Crejda

Chapter 6

Driwna

It took Bray two days before he could speak and two more before he would speak to me. I took a room at the Doris to take care of him while I healed him.

Gennic's recipe for the Lady's Bedstraw decoction called for a drowning, of sorts. Couldn't use betony to get Bray calm and soft enough he'd take me drowning him a moment, but a few pipes of kannab helped to get him sleepy enough he'd struggled to fight when I put his head in a pail of water infused with the bedstraw extract.

Bindweed vapours were easier to manage the following day and helped lift what water was left out of his chest once the bedstraw had healed the bleeding.

He needed rest for two more days and in that time I got into all the corners I could of our sheds and learned what I could about our work at the Spike. I found nothing. Which is a problem. Everywhere I've been there's been some bit of trade kept off the books, some mistakes in the tallies. Not here. It wasn't just because Stroff was such a fucker about the tallies that they would have to be perfect. The clearks

91

knew more than any cleark I worked with about the ledgers. Like they'd been drilled. Our wagons that ran on other vans were something I couldn't check directly without some more time. Sad to think I had little faith in Crejda looking into the trade the Marghosters were doing. I tried to fluff her up a bit with reminding her how well she knew the other reeves and the castellan of the Spike himself, one of Lord Marghoster's cousins. I could say little of all this to Bray, who's done well by her and so is, rightly, loyal.

Besides what Morril had asked, I left the Spike sharply with Bray when he was well enough to get about because of what I learned from the boat crews and vanners that ran Gethme's Tongue. The Tongue was the big hill trail that, through Haluim's great working in centuries past, runs north south almost unnaturally straight between the Frithmet Vale where the Spike is and Happy Valley and its fort north of the great range. Legend has it he could melt the stone away with his hands and so fashion the trail wide enough for two wagons through rock and ravine.

All these crews were yapping about a Council being formed of the Sathanti chiefs, that there's kurches in the mountains speaking of family being taken, and only the young and strong of them. There's been bloodshed among the kurches in those cold heights, and it made the least sense of all as they were always tightest bonded on all Council matters. Surviving there, amid the fickle shifts in storms and the land's own treachery, left little time for the nurturing of offence. Saving a life there would earn a seat at a kurch's table for a lifetime in gratitude of it. No, it all spoke of something wrong. And if a council was called, it was rarely for anything other than a war. Nothing's happened like it since before I drew breath.

Looking back on those days at the Spike I should have

let up with my questions as soon as my suspicions were inflamed. It made it harder to win Crejda's crew over and it was already hard. I realise now how much I depended on Cal, not that I didn't tell him. The way he is with folk, knowing their songs, for he was a keen scholar of that if nothing else, he can get them blabbing everything about their life and it bonds them to him. I miss him. This fucking seal, these leathers, they're putting walls up like they would an administrator.

The last few days waiting for Bray to heal had been hard. Crejda suggested I should head out alone, but I'd be mad to ride into the wild without someone who knows its rhythms. You can't prep for the field alone and it's been years since I walked the lands of our elders, now claimed by the Hidzucs.

We're four days over the border, in the Sathanti Peaks. We're riding west. North of us the ranges form a forbidding skirt of grey fangs, legions of savage peaks I find myself still proud to say had never been conquered.

The end of autumn bites into the trees now, as though a whetstone's been taken to the air itself, keen and clear, perfected by a cold wind from the north. I had to buy furs and paid also for Bray to have his leathers mended, patches sewn in that he might move more easily in them now his belly had gone to fat. He hadn't forgotten how to saddle a horse, or talk to one, but he admitted his arse was no longer leathery from the field. I was glad of my instinct in choosing him, for as the plant runs gave way to the trails and the country could begin to manage itself, he had remembered it all well enough, and sniffed well enough; fresh whitecap belets, some fine and rare black cohosh he'd heard could be found in these near Hidzuc lands, that would help better than my own mixes with his chest. He reminded me of the usefulness of juniper ash, something I'd only ever heard my mun talk of, and there was plenty out here. He told me it was why I had better teeth than most of my fellow reds, and that observation alone surprised me, for he had not appeared to take notice of much at all. He saw also wolf and bear tracks quicker than I did and he explained to me something of how he looked at the land, how it guided his eye to these things, as it would guide the eyes and nose of such animals. I'm not the first to curse how many good people the droop takes.

I had hoped that being out in the land would lift him, give him some peace. I think instead, despite his chatter about plant and tracks and despite the joy of seeing wild fields of cranesbill fill our eyes with a searing purple almost painful to look at, there were many hours where he was lost in himself. Alert only at the sight of others on horse, or hearing the horns and bells of herders echoing over the hills, he found much to grumble about.

He's got over the drowning, I think, and I'm pleased to hear his breathing improved. Each morning he's stripped to his waist at the embers of our fire and he's taking instruction on his forms. It's a sorry sight if I'm honest: he's got the belly of a drinker, shakes of a drooper and the grim focus of a man remembering he once had neither. It puts him in a bad mood. His head, heart and shame's woken and burning by my dragging him away from his tavern, by how little his body can now do. He's refused even a tot of the brandy I'd thought to bring to help with his mood.

"Crejda was sayin' these was your family lands once, your kurches? Never could tell if your kurch was your land or your people or what."

"The word covers both, Bray. Land and people are one with us."

"There's I thinkin' you was a full Marghoster, a rich miss paid her way to her belt and leathers, and turns out your kurch as you call it surrendered it all to old Rakinic Marghoster."

"They were our lands, Bray. Kurch Culchle Oak, that was here where we're camped, sworn to my own kurch, the Bridche and part of our confederacy. We swore loyalty to Marghoster, but didn't take his name. That was forced on us later. The Culchle had a good herd my pa said, they were our eastern neighbours and respected always our marking stones and thicket flags."

"All Hidzucs now. None seems to have been 'venged upon by your ghosts an' tall men." He meant the poles we carved showing our stories and our ancestors that were meant to defend our lands with us.

"Aye, all Hidzucs now. Ghosts aren't so good against steel, for all the bleating my pa did about the kurch-fod, which is our history and our stories of the heroes that made us Bridche."

"How did they come to take your land?"

"Fuckers had the fens at Lake Alderuc, over west of our own kurchpoles and always were thieving plant and poaching, making claims on our lands they said was theirs. Farlsgrad, through Rakinic Marghoster, won our land and spared our lives if we swore to him. But Rakinic wouldn't follow the king's son, who was thirsty for more conquest of Sathanti land. Rakinic knew the hilltribes better and knew the cost of it would be too great. His army didn't join the prince's when called upon. The betrayal cost him and the Marghosters dear ever since. He gave up our lands to the Hidzucs to forge the treaty the Sathanti demanded of the prince after his conquest failed, for we were seen as his own people because of the oath he made us swear. The Bridche name was taken from us and we were called Marghosters for shame and were made to leave our lands, and my pa says our ghosts left them also for the shame and wander still until we find a way to take these lands back."

"Expect it kills you to have to see Post dealin' with 'em for the leathers an' plant these lands and herds give."

"No, Bray. For one, I was too young to remember these lands when we had them taken from us, though I remember too well what we suffered after. For another, I'm sworn to the Post."

"Sworn to the Post? What a lot o' shit. You swear to blood, not cunts gettin' fat off you, havin' you riskin' your life for their furs an' their coffers. Well, expect you're in for a fine penny or two now you're made to this fieldsman."

"You get paid well enough for what you do, Bray, or you'd be guarding another shed."

"True, I's this fine cloak an' a few more cups. Not worth havin' to go back to the field for. What they payin' you, Fieldsman?"

"What good would it do telling you? We're here now, I'll see you right when you get back to the Spike."

"What does that mean? Heard a lot o' promises like that, 'we had a good season, here's a bit for your hard work', an' then there's twenty coppers put in I's hand and I thinks about that mountain o' gold Stroff has in a big chest somewhere. What's the use of it?"

"It doesn't all go into chests. Takes a lot of coin to run the Post as we do. The Creed you will have read in its own way is going to cost coin if I have anything to do with it."

"Not enough coin then to give all the reds fancy leathers an' belts like you have."

"I'm not happy about the belts and leathers, Bray; makes crews believe I might think I'm better than they are. It helps

96

people see who they're dealing with and saves a bit of fuss over anyone looking for who can decide something. The same with captains and generals leading armies, it needs to be clear who's who."

"Interestin' way of puttin' it. Post has the biggest army there is, for a merchants'."

"Folk will only say of us that we find a way if we have the coin to give to soldiers like us can actually find that way. If I was the High Red maybe I would find a bit more coin for everyone, but when's it ever enough? People have enough for ale, they want wine, enough for broth, they want beef. And still people clip off some coins of any deal struck in every Posthouse I've been to except, it seems, the Spike. Those ledgers have been bathed in alka."

He's quiet for a while, not pleased with the thrust of my point but saying nothing to it. We're leading our horses to a stream running off the Iblar to the north of us.

"When did you last see Hidzucs at the Spike?" I ask.

"We in Norva now, must've been Silva, two month ago. Chief come in. On his way to see our Lord Marghoster."

"Name?"

"Eirakh Hidzuc."

"What did you make of him?"

"Not happy like most kurchmen comin' in to the Spike, was he. Most Hidzuc wants the bacca an' kannab an' they get in their cups fierce, but he's not used to the stink an' the people. Him an' his crew o' fluffers stopped in for a few hours but I's busy shiftin' sacks about. They all looks stupid in their armour an' spears an' bows. As if a fight's goin' to break out among a lot o' nokes."

"They not lost any land, as you can recall?"

He frowns, a bit unsure of why I might be asking. "Not as I know of. Marghoster would settle a dispute here, miss.

97

They might not be his lands but he's got Hidzucs spread an' ready for the trade he puts by 'em."

If he meant an insult by it he wasn't saying and he didn't have the look of someone after a rise.

"I was asking because if the Hidzucs had bad relations at their western borders it might explain why a van or two would be had by those they're at odds with."

"Sure he'll gab about it when he sees your fine leathers an' thinks you're there to do somethin' about it."

I smile, because I can't let him see that these last few days he's done well at wearing down my determination to put some fire in his eyes.

"If I recall, this be Crackell's Run. Kurchpole'll be in sight tomorrow. It be the run your kurch would've taken when seen off. There's packed stone just over that span, stone laid before your kin put anyone in the ground here. Expect the scholars at the Gate have rolls tellin' of who put it down."

My pa told me of Crackell's Run. He'd spit when he spoke of it.

"Many people got slaughtered here when we were run off this land for Marghoster's betrayal of Kristuc Hildmir. There were twelve kurches that were kin to our own, Confederacy of Bridche we were. We had nowhere to go when Kristuc and Marghoster had us run out by the Hidzucs. Must have been six, seven hundred of us. One of our kin-kurches, the Kiplic, they'd come from south-west of here. We had already begun moving for the border, towards the Spike. Pa had agreed with their chief where they should meet up with us. Perhaps they didn't move fast enough, perhaps the Hidzuc saw them as trouble, or taking plant they now saw as their own. They saw enemies, traitors to the Sathanti and traitors that were stealing all their valuables; recipes, plant, coin. My pa says he came back when they hadn't met with us at the border. He rode back with the other chiefs, saw what had been done to the Kiplic, left in a pile to burn, to the last child, here at Crackell's Run."

I know a lot's shaped my pa to the life he has now, the wrong he does, but he wasn't always this man. He had a choice.

"I'm sorry for it," says Bray, who picks up from how his horse's ears move to look behind him. I follow his eyes to the trail we left to water the horses. There's five riders, got arms about them, sword, axe, bows. Hard to make out they have colour in the fading light until they come level with us. Don't recognise them, neither does Bray from the lack of acknowledgement, though these five'll be twenty years his junior it looks like. There's a nod from one as they pass on and over the stone span that fords this small river.

"Travelling belts, six or eight pouch. Not heading into or out of trouble," I say.

"Headin' for Hidzuc, must be. Only settle for leagues about. Third lot o' mercs we seen since leavin' the Spike. Be war out here?" Over the past few days we'd been riding they'd come past us in pairs or small groups, either not wanting to miss out on a purse must have gone up on the boards in border hams, or because there's more trouble than we thought out here.

"You have first watch, Bray. I'll take the darkwatch, a vadse should help."

"We find a spot we can 'tropnet part of, we's safer. None o' them looked trouble though, miss. Mercs rarely is, less there's a purse." By 'tropnet he meant a fishing net that had been adapted with some seasoned caltrops. There were leaves enough about it could be hidden well and used to cover a path into the camp we'd set up.

After we prepped camp, Bray set down for his first cup

of brandy since we left the Spike, gave me the flask back to remove temptation from himself. I looked about at these lands that I might once have lived in. Good earth here, a strong river running, stands of firs and juniper thick and ink-black already. I think of the marshes and woods we'd hide in, the wretched hunger and the screaming of those taken away, burned alive as we ran with what we could carry and fuck all else, and I blink away some tears for it, for those things killed the girl I was.

Next day we saw the Hidzuc's kurchpole on the side of Crackell's Run, marking out their boundaries. Didn't look cared for as it should, not oiled or cleaned in months I'd guess. Such things speak strongly of a kurch in my view. Bray knew to tell me of the respect we still had to pay the pole, symbolic of our wishing to show no ill intent towards the Hidzuc and their land. It made me sick to do it, for who was watching? He said only that the faces carved on the pole were watching but they were enough. It was strange to me that he understood and seemed to really believe that the ancestors judged us by our open arms and our saying of the oath. The dead are dead and no magist's shown it wrong.

We saw more wagons and soldiers that paid colour coming in from all around, though these were kurch-kin, not Farlsgrad. A group of eight daith-wa, the Sathanti name for drudhas, were also together riding in from their kurch runs. Out here we Sathanti share our recipes with our kin-kurches, and our daith-wa, even down on the fens where we live now, travel about the kurches to heal and replenish plant stocks as the seasons bring and take the plant that keeps us alive. It's still unusual to see so many together.

Plant-croppers are out as we reach the runs that mark out the borders of the main Hidzuc camp. Some are just turning soil, others among the plant that can be farmed year-round, guira and amony are most of it, but potatoes and other veg are there. There's worksongs going and their breath rises about them like a field of ghosts hovering in the still air. Bray knows these songs, follows snatches of their chorus.

"I's cropped runs for a time, miss," he says. "Couldn't make a belly like this wi' what coin they give and the work they wanted. Days was simple an' I miss 'em. Times was I'd look up an' see the likes of us ridin' through an' wish I could ride out of there on horseback. Not so sure now, if that makes sense."

"You had time to worry up some ambition, you had choices beyond hoe and plough, dice and cups when you first paid colour and took a purse. I expect you had to think too about how to spend that coin because you had more than what put a roof over your mat."

"Life and death then, in't it, miss. Life and death at every corner." He keeps on whistling and as we crest a hill we see the camps, must be a hundred or more tents about the Hidzuc lodge and its barns. The Hidzuc colours, weavings of red and blue squares set inside each other, hang about the lodge and between the two giant bloodstones below which the firepit is dug.

"It be bloodstones we go to first, miss, say the oath as we did at kurchpole," says Bray.

"Thank you, Bray."

"Most who's visitin' won't, but it puts us above 'em in the hearts o' the kurch-folk about."

Our own bloodstones would have been here. My pa told me they pulled them down and broke them as our kurches left. Our dead would serve their dead was his belief, as their bloodstones were raised over the bones of the Bridche chiefs past.

Smaller fires have started up about the tents, a lot of soldiers here, mercs and kurch-folk. They don't mix, the kurch-folk clustering in a big group near the lodge, where the Hidzucs are passing out what must be bilt, like the cured meat we have on vans, filling cups with whatever's in the pots these men and women are carrying about. As Bray had said, most of the Hidzucs, even the older children, have pipes, and the smell of kannab is sweet and heavy here.

As we pass through the camp the cookers for the various crews or kurch-folk are at the fires, pots hanging from frames, and what's bubbling in them all about us makes it hard to breathe. About us too, amid the whispering of their talk, there's the *ssshhh* of whetstones, and some are sewing field-belts and armour. Traders that must have known of this gathering have made some fine coin from the wood we see piled about the tents of the mercs for their fires.

We're wearing the red so we get a few looks as we lead our horses among the tents. I don't recognise any here, no other Post I can see, no marked wagons. The daith-wa, head to foot in earth-brown robes and heavy packs, are among the Hidzucs that are in their kin groups about the firepit, treating those who need it. There's a handful of children then come shouting at us to take our horses into their care while we're here. I see a few paddocks about, must be used for the daith-nu, the chiefs of each kurch, when they visit for their councils with the Hidzuc chief.

"Our coin and horses go to whoever of you can guess where this woman was born," says Bray.

That hushes them for a few moments as they stare at me. I give Bray a look and he's got a shade of a smile, so I smile back at him, for it's a question isn't going to put any of these Hidzucs at ease. The moment I smile one of them says, "Ilkashun. She's a fucking Ilkashun." He spits at me. Ilkashun are the confederacy at their western border. I hadn't thought they'd ever had bad relations, but I shouldn't be surprised now given these rumours we're chasing down along with my Oskoro girl. A couple of the others take a moment to think about what the boy said, before a girl says, "She's Post," the rest then meaning nothing to me, spoken in some Hidzuc lingo I can't get hold of.

"That's close enough," says Bray, repeating it in her lingo. I look at him for understanding. "She thinks you're sad. The way you look at the bloodstones, she thinks you ran from your kurch, that you're a Hidzuc in exile." The girl looks at me, perhaps for my confirmation.

"Close enough," I say.

She takes the reins of our horses and we take from them our fieldbelts and swords. We both know not to wear either, just sling the belts over our shoulders and hold the swords in their scabbards point up, balanced against the shoulder.

We approach their bloodstones and we're stopped by a woman in chain, an axe held casually.

"Oath?" she asks, in our lingo. I nod.

"Bray, tell her I'm an emissary for the High Red, I wish to speak to Eirakh Hidzuc."

She listens, looks at me in a way of telling me she's unimpressed, before heading off, after gesturing us forward to the bloodstones where we speak the oath. I wish I could say that I felt something wrong with them, that they didn't belong in this land I've heard all my life was mine. But I don't.

There's eyes on us, then on Eirakh as he approaches. As with my pa many years ago, his hair is fashioned up with gum and wound about a tall crown of oiled sisters' oak, fashioned as pale grey interlocking fingers. His keep is with him, her hair shorn, as it would have been at their ceremony so it could be woven with his when his hair was first shaped to the crown. He wears the Daith-nu's knife, the only knife that can cut a keep's hair.

"You make the oath and you are welcome." He's used to speaking Farlsgrad lingo. "Daith-ru," he says, half turning.

His keep steps forward. She catches the eye of all about, a button of a nose and wide, expressive eyes. There's warmth for her, respect. That he brings her forward tells me they are strong and she is strong.

"Daith-nu Hidzuc, Daith-ru, I come from the High Red," I say.

"So my guard tells me. Have you replaced the administrator, Stroff?"

"No. I am made fieldsman, to hold all who wear the red to account according to those things we stand for. We have a new creed we must abide by."

"What is creed?" The Daith-ru this is.

"Help the helpless. Honour the purse. Peace through trade. This is the Farlsgrad Creed and all the Post will be bound to it."

"You will need many fieldsmen." Eirakh this is, and he laughs with it. Bray bows his head, hoping I won't see him smile in response, but I understand why. Like many before them, they underestimate how much it means to me.

"You may be right, Daith-nu Hidzuc. We have some fine words on the one hand and thousands of reds spread over thousands of leagues, both sides of the Sar, on the other. I have no answers for this puzzle, except that I do what I can to embody the virtues of our founders. We seek news of a Post van coming through from Lindur, bound for the Ilkashun."

"You are, I think, Sathanti?" asks Eirakh.

"I am Bridche."

They both cannot help but take a moment. The Daith-ru gives me a slight bow, at the same time as he glances to the bloodstones. I've done right by them, done as the Post demands. Still, when I speak my kurchname, my skin prickles, the sight of my pa by the light of a fire talking of our people with tears in his eyes comes to me.

"There's been no Post van through."

"No reds? No word of trouble west?" I flick my head back, a gesture to the camps behind me.

"There's trouble west. Ilkashun confederacy."

"What benefit would causing trouble bring to the Ilkashun?" I say.

"Survival of his lodge," says Eirakh. "Their chief is desperate, his kin-kurches are restless. He has no heir. He will want to appear strong. If peace and trade are important to you, his actions are against the Post's interests. Ours are not."

"What have they done?"

"The Lord Marghoster has lost two vans, bound for the Lakes and not returned. It is the work of the Ilkashun."

"How do you know this?"

"You and your man should stay clear of Ilkashun lands, for I cannot ensure you will be safe and we do not wish to lose the goodwill of the Post. My daith-ru will fill your pipes, pour your cups and serve you tuika. Your horses will be ready at dawn." He raises his fingertips to his lips and forward to us both, a farewell.

He leaves us with his keep. I need an ally here.

"May I ask your name Daith-ru? I am Driwna. This is Bray."

"Leusla. Come." She leads us the few steps to the firepit, puts her hand on the shoulder of an old woman who, like the others, turns to her and smiles. The woman puts her hand over Leusla's and pats it. Leusla gestures to us and speaks in her lingo. The old woman finds two wooden bowls, carved modestly, an apprentice's work but not wasted on that account. She forks and cuts strips from the breast of the nearest tuika fragrant with sage, skewered over the coals. With it we're given a spoon of wild rice. Leusla leans over her to cut and pull off one of its wings for herself and licks her fingers with pleasure after eating it.

A girl, eight or so summers, unstoppers a clay bottle and pours us what I'd have called cornmash gutrot in any other circumstances. Leusla whispers something to her and she giggles before giving Leusla a cup. We've had to lodge our scabbards under our armpits to hold both cup and bowl. Leusla then leads us to a patch of ground outside the lodge. A privileged position that draws comment.

From a large pocket sewn to the front of her dress, one she must wear for helping with the work of the camp, she pulls out a large bacca pouch. The smell tells me its threaded with kannab."

"Will you take some?"

It's tempting, but I need to keep my wits. "I do not get on well with kannab, it upsets my gut." It's bullshit, but there we are. Bray shakes his head as well, relieved, I think, he doesn't have to show good manners and accept the offer. She has a typically delicate pipe, letters I can't read faintly incised about the bowl and stem. Soon enough she's packed the bowl, lit it and taken a good draw on it. She leans back to blow the smoke upwards before returning her gaze to me. She seems to approve.

"It is good for woman to have trust of so much." She runs a hand over my leathers and knows well enough to avoid touching the fieldbelt's pouches and pockets, for they are coated with poison I and very few others would be immune to.

106

"The Post values trade with the Hidzucs. It keeps peace."

"Bridche and Hidzuc. I believe you. You honour us with oath. Please, sit."

We put our belts and swords on the ground and sit, enjoy our rice and tuika; the hot white meat has its crispy skin still on it.

"Do you know what Marghoster has lost? What was on the vans?"

"Slaves, plant. Very big caravan. A hundred of them."

"Fine bit o' coin in all that." Bray this is, wiping his mouth on his sleeve. He's right, not the kind of coin anyone would write off without some trouble.

"Hidzucs will go with these mercenaries to the Ilkashun?"

"Lord Marghoster has given ingots, iron tools, guira and alka for our brews. We go . . ." She takes a moment to find the phrase, and that troubles me, for it suggests these are not her words she is being careful to say. "We go to bring order, to protect interest, our lives."

"Have you seen any reds in the last month?"

"The Daith-nu has answered your question."

"He has, I'm sorry, but I'm so worried for them. You do the Daith-nu much respect, you are much in love I think." I sought her answer in the nuance of her face and she lowered her eyes and the corners of her mouth twitched, a brief smile suppressed with another draw on her pipe.

"Marghoster was a fine ally to the Bridche for a time," I say. "My mun was the best stamper and cutter of leather in all the Bridche kurches and my pa made her his daith-ru for it. He made saddles and fieldbelts. She graced them with illustrations and patterns I have found no equal for to this day. And when Yeismic Marghoster came to visit us, my pa made him a gift of a saddle, the finest work my mun had done. Marghoster has this saddle today."

"Your mun made this for him? I have seen it. Driwna, it takes the breath from me."

"We would have done anything for Marghoster, my pa was proud of it. But you know our story. It is all around you. Marghoster will do as Marghoster must do. He is happy to use you as he used us. I hope he better honours you and the Daith-nu."

"Much wrong was done to Bridche confederacy. Some Hidzuc kurchmen brought shame to us. I wish it was different." She puts her hand on my arm instinctively. She speaks of the fires.

I know what I want to say, and Bray doesn't need to clear his throat to confirm to me it's on my face. Yet she has surprised me.

"You do me great honour, Daith-ru Leusla, both with your words and with your service to us. We must be keeping you from your duties to those kin who have travelled from all over these lands. You must be with them."

"Thank you, Driwna. I hope we meet again."

She leans across to Bray and clasps arms with him as soldiers do, then does the same to me. She is strong for a noke. I wish I could hate her – and all these Hidzucs who occupy my kurch's old lands – but I don't feel it. She stands and walks to a group of her kin.

"Riskin' a lot for Farlsgrad, they are, as Sathanti. Goin' against their own in't they, with Ilkashun?"

"They are. Their blood's cheaply bought if it's just for iron and plant. Who goes to war only for that?" And that bothered me. Iron and plant don't bind on their own, it takes blood, shared or spilled.

"We be goin' to the Ilkashun then, miss?"

"We are. Not since us Bridche were run out of here have I heard of a confederacy attacking another one without the

108

Council having had its say. They're intending a massacre with this many soldiers and if it's driven by Marghoster there's a world more trouble beyond."

"Not readyin' for war tonight, miss. We leave early, go east half a day before runnin' a wide line back an' west is my advice. We be ahead of 'em."

"We will have to be."

Chapter 7

Driwna

Six soldiers have been sent to kill us. An ambush. Not that I can tell there's six at first. I smell one, then two more, their leathers, breath, like I might see motes of dust in sunlight. Then I see movement of another two, from trunk to trunk finding their way to our camp, downwind. Bird calls come from left and right, as I'd expect if there was an ambush, the only calls they must know, for they're pheasants, and I haven't heard any in this land up until now. A sixth call I hear further off, their leader perhaps. It's night, me and Bray camped on a slope in a thick stand of pines on hills overlooking the distant edge of the first of the great lakes, Lake Fildric. My horse confirms the ambush, I hear her move, huff, enough to still those approaching. I have two flasks at my feet where I'm squatting. Behind me the fire is still warm, but I'm facing away, luta juice in my eyes to help them see clearly in the dark. One flask is water, shredded vadse, the other a dayer, packed with fresh amony. It won't match a fightbrew. My heart picks up as I breathe in and lazily take up the dayer. A swig, no more or less than I've been taking this last hour. I yawn to hide the trembling, the need to reject the foul, peaty curd. I risk another mouthful. Bray's horse stamps, ears prick up. The moment's here, for I don't know if I've convinced them I haven't been alerted, don't know if my body's given me away somehow. If they're on a fightbrew they'll know.

Next to the flasks is a limebag, size of my head. I flick it into the fire, use my knife to drive it into the glowing, charred wood, tear open the gummed mash of wood pulp. Feathers and lime catch on the flames and throw up smoke. I hear a whistle. They've lost a line on us for their arrows, a sure shot.

"Bray," I hiss.

He's awake in a moment, was in the field too long to let himself sleep fully. I get to the ground, harder to target, loosen bags, get my bow and arrows. Bray is already rubbing his eyes with the luta mix and has his dayer ready. The fightbrew is too much prep, too long in the rise.

Arrows whip through the smoke, pulling wisps of it after them, giving their positions away. Our horses are hit then, so the fuckers are mercenaries. Bandits or clansmen don't kill horses, they're too valuable. They whinny, scream, pull at their ropes as the poison works in. Bray is on his knees and moving to a nearby pine higher on the slope. I stand to cover him; I have to trust I'm too quick in that moment for them to get a line on me. Then I'm after him. It's the only way out of the camp; the other paths in are 'tropped and there's ankle breakers been dug about as well. What I'd learned as good camp prep in the academy Bray had learned with the Grey Goose. He taught me more setting up camp in the field the last two nights than I learned in the two years I was at Posthouse Epny. One mercenary, must have been one of those had come from downhill that I'd seen moving in, he finds the 'trops and cusses loud. The others are wise enough not to react and give away their own positions. His breathing quickens, so something of what the 'trops are coated in has got into him. He might live, but he won't be able to fight. I ready an arrow and lean around the trunk I'm against. The smoke's filling the air well; I see it darken, a shape within it, another merc, bow ready. He checks the position of one of his crew, a look to his right. I'm lucky, leaning out when I did, for it's a moment I can raise my bow and shoot. I hit him high in the chest I think, it's hard to be clear, but the way he breathes out tells me I've hit him in his pipes and he falls to his knees. His crew again make no sound or respond to this. Four at least left, hopefully four at most.

I look back at Bray and I'm about to signal for him to put his mask on when I hear the bowstrings. He drops, as do I a fraction later. He's got his mask ready to put on but hasn't had a chance to tie it. An arrow hits the tree above his head, as it was meant to. It had a sporebag tied over the soft iron point. It explodes and powdered spores blow out over us both. I'm masked, it's unlikely to hurt me, I've got my helm on, but he's bare-necked, half his face and his head exposed. As he's reaching for his bag of alka to kill and wash off the spores I hear another merc hit a breaker; he stumbles, he's close. I step away from the tree I'm leaning against and see him look up just as I level my bow. He manages a "No—" before the arrow's through his face. I find a sporebag of my own and roll it carefully over the end of a bag-arrow. They know where we are so I have to put bags around us to hedge them, control the yards about us. Then Bray vomits up his dayer; his hand, holding his mask to his mouth, comes away as he bends and lets go. He's gasping, his skin is swelling with whatever mix was in the bag. He's not in the fight. I

112

can't see or sense the others now I've pulled my mask up over my nose. He is calm, coughing and giving us up, but keeping at the alka, some powders in his nose and mouth as his breathing gets louder; his throat must be swelling. He draws his sword while pouring the alka over him. There's a crack of a branch nearby and two mercs are at us, one coming for me, the other the far side of us going for Bray, and they're brewed up enough to bellow with the bloodlust that's in them. I know enough to jump at Bray, shoving him out of the way to meet the merc that's moving calmly in, ready to fight. Then the sixth whistles, higher up the hill from us, sharp commands, rolling notes and short chirps with a mouth-piece. I block the young merc but he steps back, confident, goes to take out a sporebag from his belt. A glance to the knot betrays his youth, gives me a moment to pull a knife from my belt, throw it. He's so fast on his brew he almost gets out of its way, but it lodges in his arm. I don't press, for he's as good as dead, the knife coated with a Juan henbane mix, the rarest of poisons. It should be in every red's belt, not just mine. My skin's starting to burn with their mix, a powder I've not smelled before. My eyes are itching, blurring with tears. As the boy before me convulses I pull a powder block from my satchel, squeeze it in my fist until the hard-sugar cracks and throw it behind me, past Bray, at the feet of the merc closing on him. She instinctively flinches, an older woman, can't see how two ambushed reds with their dayers taking hold can match her. She doesn't know Bray's bluffing at least some of his sickness, I don't either. Bray leaps forward. She's strong enough she can parry him, but Bray hadn't intended to catch her with his sword, it just gives him a moment to flick an egg into her face, the gummed shell smashes, mustard powders. No mask can close out so much so close, and she hasn't already been holding her breath.

113

Her training's sound enough she stabs Bray in his gut before the mustard sends her into a frenzy and she drops back holding her face. He growls in dismay but doesn't miss then, running her through. He falls to his knees, wheezing. I take up my bow, wait, listen as best I can above his grunts. He's dying, but if I help him I'll get an arrow, I'm sure of it. I hear the crack of twigs, a scrambling, receding. Is this a trick? I can't wait any longer as Bray clutches at his throat, his breathing shallow, rapid. I drop to his side and I squeeze out some paste that'll help with my eyes, the better to help him. Each moment I'm expecting an arrow and I'm fucking itching, skin feels like its burning, it's driving me mad. I rub the paste over my eyes.

My training, remember it, heal myself to heal others.

Heal myself to heal others.

Heal myself to heal others.

Flask of an alka mix for spores. I splash it onto a rag, wipe my face. Alka on his head, a soaked rag in his eyes while my fingers feel for the blood, the heat of his gut wound. Third pouch left strap, sticky bark.

"Go miss, save your life." His voice is curdled with the damage from the spores he's breathed.

"Fuck you, Bray. You live, stone it."

Pouch five, gummed linen.

"Another's out there. I's not worth you, miss, not worth it."

My eyes are weeping, clearing out the mix so I can open them. Smoke about us. No arrow yet. Not a crossroads purse for whoever's out there, by which I mean a life-or-death purse. I risk a glance up now my sight's a bit better, the dayer sharpening my senses. Nothing.

"Need to drown you again, Bray." I'm losing him, his skin's blistered about his face and head; it'll be blistered inside him and all.

114

"Crejda, she's . . ."

Don't betray her, Bray, I sign. *Let me work.*

I have chosen to save his life over my own. It isn't wise. He's right to tell me to leave him, it isn't good field practice. I have a sense the other merc sent in at us has gone. Too much smoke, too many 'trops and spores. He's weighed the odds and the coin isn't up to it.

I straddle Bray, he's keening a bit, the pain must be awful. Once more I'm putting the mix in him that'll fill his chest and pipes. I put the rag over his mouth and nose after pouring it in. My knees have his arms pinned, his body's frenzied spasms don't have the strength to buck me as the mix froths in his throat and chest. I count to ten. He snorts out a black bubbling dribble of the mix, the look in his eyes I've seen before, that death is inevitable. I roll off him and he jerks onto his side, convulsing. He retches up some of the mix. I slap his back as he coughs and retches more fluid. I hope it's done its work in there before the spores did too much damage to his pipes.

He's still on his side, wheezing again, breath slowing. He holds out a hand, which I take. He squeezes it, signs with his other hand that he wished he could have enjoyed me on top of him a little more. I laugh out loud at this and he lets go of me to cry. I get up, the air rich and clear now on this dayer. I leave him and creep away from the camp, trunk to trunk towards the spot I heard the sixth merc's commands. The prints of leather socks are in the soil, pine needles helping me read his steps away up the bank into darkness. In an hour he'll be on his back paying the colour. He's no more of a threat, but chasing him down in that hour is a risk with Bray so close to dying. I walk back to him and lie down against his back, put my arm around him and hold him until he's done crying. He falls asleep soon after and I use the strength

115

the dayer's given me to clean myself up, get the rubs off me, treat my skin where the spores caught, treat his too as he sleeps. Using an alka rag to clean off the poison, I go through the belts of the dead mercs around us. I don't recognise them and they've got nothing on them to link them to their purse, as I'd expect. Still, someone's occasionally that stupid.

They've got some fair plant, little or no food, but I'm delighted to find two honey blocks. I take a few bites from one, thrilling to its taste. It's good for healing throats and I don't see it enough in field spreads. I heard a story of the Dust Coast, far to the west, far from even the Post. It was said the emperor there kept bees like we keep our pets and could fill a river course with honey. It would be a fine boon for any lord or king.

I begin to make out more of the woods about us as dawn comes. Bray deserves a couple of hours of stillness, it'll help the mix to work, won't do to cough too much of it up with walking. I walk over to our horses. Always moves me to see dead horses and I was very fond of mine, though I hadn't known her long. Anilly I'd left at the Gate and I'm glad this wasn't her fate. This one's head and flank's sprayed with spit from her thrashing around on the floor with the poison before it took her. I smooth her cheek and kiss her neck. The mercs wouldn't have had a chance to get at the saddle-bags, so I get to work freeing up the bags and flasks, two extra quivers that'll be welcome if we get more trouble. I doubt we'll trouble anyone in return, but arrows are always good for hunting if nothing else. So much will have to be left here it pains me. The bilt, some rope and kindling I take. I don't hear or smell the horses they'll have followed us on. Their survivor will have taken them all with him.

I wake Bray as the sun rises and holds the trees still in a pale orange light, fierce to look upon with the bit of luta juice still in my eyes. Bray sits himself up and nods his appreciation as he takes and sucks on the honey block. He needs help standing. He folds some bilt into his mouth and, without speaking or asking, he wipes himself down, drinks some water, checks his belts, bow and sword, freshening the paste in his scabbard. He looks half dead, but he's standing and waiting for orders.

"Thank you for saving my life," I say. "I learned a lot from you earlier. Your mind's sharper than your forms it seems."

He clears his throat, tests his voice, though it's thick with muke and my mix. "You asked I not to betray Crejda, miss. Don't know why not, but I respects you for it."

"You owe her a lot, she's been good to you. I wouldn't want you feeling you'd let her down."

"There is work that's off the ledgers, miss."

"Bray . . ."

"No, miss, it's right you should know. I wasn't sure o' you of course, but I see what you're made of now. She's been movin' plant, a lot of it, ingots, arrows, supplies that'd be o' use to the Hidzucs with what we saw there, though much of it was in service o' the Marghosters."

"You think we have something to do with what the Hidzucs are planning?"

"Might be, miss."

"Reason enough to want me dead, if she thinks I'm sniffing about her ledgers, as I have been."

"I don't think so, miss. She had to have expected it when you come to the Spike. She don't kill Post though, she's made the Post her keep, as the sayin' goes."

"Who knew we were out here, Bray? Lot of mercs at the Hidzuc lodge, none knew of our intention to come out this way, past the Hidzuc kurchpoles anyway. We did what Eirakh bid us not to do."

He's looking out through the trees, thinking it through.

"Crejda din't know we'd come out past the Hidzuc poles either."

"The two must go together, this trade of hers and the threat she thinks I pose to it all. I don't understand how it is Crejda would be putting trade out here if she knew anything of the mercs and the trouble that's brewing here. She told me there was trouble north."

"The kidnappings?"

"Kidnappings?"

He frowns. "She not told you about them?"

"I heard crews yapping about it when I was at the Spike, but not more than that. What else do you know of the trouble?"

"Only the rope bridges and high mountain shelters about the Tongue have been cut off. The kurches in the mountains want no Farlsgrad there and I guess it's on account o' their kurchmen goin' missin'."

"Fuck me, Bray. Crejda didn't think to tell me this?" Something doesn't add up. Any reeve along the border would be concerned about their trails and roads into the Sathanti, and might have told their own about it before they headed out here.

"I needs a pipe, miss. Bit o' bacca might help clear the rest of this out. Bit o' kannab might ease the worry you're causin' I an' all."

I loosen some loops on my leathers to get at my pipe that I keep in my shirt. A small clay I'm fond of that my mun carved for my brother and gave me last time I was home.

"They gave me some fine weed when they gave me this fieldbelt. Reminds me of how an orange tastes. You should pack some and try it."

"You sure, miss?"

"The drudha working for Stroff told me it's good for a sore throat in particular."

He takes the pipe and my jumpcrick bones, packs and lights it.

"Let's see how far I can walk," he says.

It's a cloudless day, the sun's warmth a pleasure as we move into scrubland. We have to stop a lot, as I'd expected. It's pride driving him on; he's gone within himself so I let him have some peace. I put a sniffer's mix in my nose to better sense what's about us, but can't get anything on the wind, very little plant worth having and no smell of horse or soldiers. As we crest a steep rise we're rewarded with a view of sunlight shimmering on Lake Fildric, first of the Bouskill Lakes.

"We're spotted." Bray points to a bird high up, hovering, then banking and diving away to the lake.

"What?"

"Ilkashun have Sathanti Greys, miss." I'd heard of these birds – pabagoy, or parrots in King's Common – that could speak, even remember conversations and repeat them to their masters.

"Which kurch's land are we on, now we're in the Ilkashun confederacy?"

"This be Canendrigh kurch, miss. Ilkashun's own land be further west."

"Pa told me this was Bridche land in generations past. Well, the pabagoy warning will bring them to us and save some time exploring."

He's sweating heavily, blowing too. He's pushing himself too hard, but I think I just need to wait for him to tell me he's overdone it. Except he doesn't.

He begins to descend the slope when he stumbles. I see his leg give way, a spasm; I think he'd fallen asleep, as he was walking. He just about keeps his balance.

119

"Bray?"

"Leave it, miss. Don't need any more shame than I gives to myself." He's holding his belly where he was stabbed.

"Pigshit, Bray. You been ambushed, took a fair old wound, been doing your forms, watches. Field finds you out, you know the saying. Let me look at the wound and your throat." I catch up with him as he drops to one knee. He's done for the day.

"Kind enough words, but field's makin' I ashamed. Were your pigshit idea to bring I out an' who knows what you was fuckin' hopin' to achieve by it. Here I be, miss, a burden to you an' fuckin' everyone. I see it in Crejda's eyes, don't think I don't. Pity in 'em as she says 'well done' to me, but all I's doin' is holdin' a pike an' standing about. Not even the fuckin' whores . . . Fuck, what am I tellin' you for. That's pitiful right here."

"Bray, you're right. You're fat, tired, haven't paid in for years, got a look that says you're beaten and that's the way it should be. But your camp prep did for half those mercs and your wiles did for one more, even as you are. I saw the man the Grey Goose must've seen; field discipline, a wisdom I wouldn't have found in anyone else at the Spike. It's not your body I need out here, Bray, it's your wit, your tasting of the wild. You've lost none of that. You're a good man, Bray. If you're not careful I'll start expecting a bit more from you, then you'll be fucked."

He looks up at me, a bitterness in there and I think an acknowledging too. I kneel next to him and put my arm round his shoulders. He's trying to manage the pain, deep breaths.

"I'm what I am, you're what you are." I slap my head and slap his gut. "Both of us are thick in our own way. We keep our discipline out here, you keep working on your breathing and your forms, keep on with the pipe." I look up, he does too, we can feel the hooves, then we hear the dogs breaking out of the barley runs and heading for us, whistles now, shrill, commands. I stand before Bray and draw my sword. I doubt I could take four dogs. Six horse follow them. Ilkashun, two moving to flank us, bows in hand. The dogs reach us first and, thankfully, are whistled to stop. I quickly move my hand to hold my sword by its blade, hilt up in the air.

The riders close and stop twenty or so yards from us. The dogs' ears are back, listening, panting and hackles up.

"*Ukr il matiship a fe Bray, a fe Driwna. Sitee bostl mori a Ilkashun.*" Bray this is. "I said we're no threat to 'em, miss. I can't stand yet."

"You did. And you're right." Their leader this is. A tall, strong and very handsome man dismounts from a fine night-black charger. The leathers he wears are thick, ragged and rough-stitched, a heavy coat and skirt to his knees. He looks altogether in need of unwinding, like we're yet another problem after a long day of them. In any other circumstance I'd help him with that gladly. I notice then his beard plait, forked and hooped. He's their chief.

"Farlsgrad lingo, Daith-nu Ilkashun?" I say.

"If you have no Ilkashun." He claps his hands and holds them palm outwards, a sign of peace and welcome when proximity has not been confirmed safe. He smiles as he sees me look him over.

"I am Driwna, Bridche kurch. Now I am Post."

"I am Yicre, this is Ufra, daughter of the etza-Ososi." By "etza-Ososi" he means chief of all the Ososi. Bray stands, elbows my arm and draws my attention to the woman dismounting next to Yicre. She does not raise her eyes. Bray explains later that the Ososi will not do so until they feel a measure of respectfulness.

121

Her skin is a smooth sandy yellow where it hasn't been sliced with bark or cut for plant. She wears a sleeveless woollen vest, for her arms and neck bear much of the plant work they have done. Ribbons of vines, like seaweed, run along under her skin, red tips of thorns breaking through along it. One thumb has in its place a stem of some sort, fibres trailing from it. From somewhere under her vest appears the spiralling grey weed that must live in her skin, thorns along its length as it curls around her ear and to her cheek. She runs her tongue along her lips. She looks only as far as our feet, no doubt tasting the air and drawing a sense of us from it. Her lips are a marvel, full and soft, edges of her mouth turned up slightly under a small, flat nose. Her skull is intact, but her hair's been razored close where the skin hasn't been sliced and worked back with bark.

I'm at a loss for words as I look at her. I yearn to see her eyes, to have her look upon me.

"You've not seen an Ososi woman before." Yicre this is, quite aware of the woman's effect on me.

"No, Daith-nu Ilkashun. It is a privilege and," I feel myself blushing, "you are a joy to look upon, Ufra."

He smiles. I can't believe I just said that. She looks up at me, quickly, then back at the ground. She waves her hand before her, the plant fibres from its thumb giving her a sense of us.

Yicre whistles and the dogs turn tail, relaxing but padding about among the horses, ears flicking towards us as they sniff about.

"You are Post. You seek your van. It is safe," he says.

"I come from Yblas the High Red. If our crew is safe know that Yblas will pay well for their return. I would know what causes you to risk the wrath of Farlsgrad, for other vans are missing."

"They also are with us and safe as well. We expect parley with those kannab puffers the Hidzucs and their lords at Farlsgrad. These slaves are bound for the same place our own and the Ososi's own are taken."

"Your people, and Ososi, are being kidnapped?"

He hesitates. "We find no bodies. I am at this border with my kurch-kin at all the poles, guarding them, for we will not have any crossing our land without our saying so." A fine but unconvincing sentiment when borders in the Sathanti are not hardened with war into lines on vellum and forts with garrisons. They have only their kurchpoles, staked against agreed landmarks few and far between.

"This is Sathanti, Daith-nu. Farlsgrad can have no interest or land in the mountains without going to war."

"You know not of such things?" Ufra this is. Hers is a deeper voice than I expected, a gravelly character, as of someone older, a pipe smoker. The plant might have altered it as it had with the huge Ososi back in Lindur, but in Ufra it is as though her voice is warmed by a fire.

"No, I would tell you if I did. The Post does not go to war or join war with anyone."

"Beggin' your pardon, Daith-nu, but you have no contact wi' the kurches north?" Bray this is. "The Bugroz? Cargamun?"

"I heard from crews working vans along the Tongue that there might be a Council forming. Have you had word?" I ask.

"We have seen nobody," says Yicre. "Maybe they too lose their people. Nobody can stop Scar."

"Who?"

"Scar," says Ufra. "He is of my kind. Ososi."

"Is he very big?" I gesture the size and massive shape of the Ososi I encountered in Lindur.

"Yes. He hunts us. Takes our elders and our children."

Her own lingo has coloured her voice and her words to a buttery flow.

"Not your soldiers, your strongest?" Bray this is.

"No."

"Yet he leaves our oldest, takes all others." Yicre this is.

Bray hisses, buckles over. He hasn't stood properly upright since they arrived. He holds his belly where he was stabbed.

"We were attacked," I say. "He took a wound. I've done my best. Are any of you a drudha?"

"All Ososi are drudha to us." Yicre this is, looking kindly upon Ufra.

She breathes in, then looks straight at me. I feel stripped before her. Her bright green eyes, as though made of luta itself, sparkle like the sun on coral. She is seeing me in a way nobody has ever seen me and I shiver, unable to keep her gaze. My own eyes spring tears but I feel thrilled, nervous, young again, bubbling like broth in a pot. She goes to Bray, kneels, her hand under his chin so he must look up to her. He is held still as stone by her, his breathing shallows, a spark of fear, for she is not like us, her kind the horror in the rhymes of the ignorant. Then she lies him back to the ground, her hand at the back of his neck, and with a gesture for him to relax she begins humming a song, the sound rich and smoky as a winter fire. The bark of my old wounds itches and tingle with it. I have the strange thought that the plant in me is responding to her song, but I don't see how it can be. He makes no move to stop her as she moves belts and pouches aside, unbuckles the leathers and gets under his woollen shirt to the wound I'd worked. It's leaking, I had no time to chew and set the bark as I would have liked. She takes the bag slung across her chest and puts it on the ground, takes a flask, pours it on the wound, humming still, her tongue making a kind of dry clicking sound. Her brow furrows and relaxes as she works, then she looks at Bray, half a smile breaking open. Bray smiles with me at the heat of it. There are flecks of something in the oil she's poured from the flask. They move. She puts her strange thumb about the bark I mashed into the wound, the tendrils brushing over it.

"You have been trained well, Driwna," she says.

She takes a knife with her other hand and eases the bark out, pours more of the oil under it before taking a mix of her own, more like a mud. She presses it into the hole and over the skin about it. Bray doesn't flinch; something in the oil must have numbed it all entirely.

"Put your hand here." She takes my hand in hers. The stem of plant that is her thumb feels warm, the tendrils tickle and prick me slightly, seeking purchase of their own accord. She puts her palm on my hand to give me the measure of the pressure she wants me to maintain. I don't want her to let go. She doesn't for a few moments. Her fingers trail up the back of mine before she lifts her hand. I feel flushed, hot. I take a breath and tell Bray to hold still, not knowing how else to hide myself in the silence as Yicre and his men watch her work.

"Somethin's ticklin' in there," says Bray.

"It needs an hour," she says.

"He'll have my horse to ride back to the lodge. Lucz, Beildrun, stay with him. We'll walk back." Yicre this is.

"I have to warn you," I say, "the Hidzucs mean to attack you, over these stolen vans."

"I do not think so, for these are not their vans. They will come to parley, as I said. They will be welcome."

"I have seen soldiers, many of them."

He thinks on this a moment.

"Perhaps they mean only to prevent further kidnappings.

125

It is a long time since any on those lands bore arms for Farlsgrad." His meaning is obvious, a subtle insult aimed at my own kin, a test of my temperament that's easy to pass.

Yicre's keep isn't with him. She's back at the main lodge for the confederacy further west, on the banks of Lake Ilkashun itself, a week or so's ride distant. We ride up to his temporary lodge, a wooden frame and skins for the walls. This is the land of the Canendrigh, an Ilkashun kin-kurch that is led by his keep's brother, Lodre Canendrigh. Twenty could fit inside this makeshift lodge. There are other pavilions about it; one keeps the pabagoy and pigeons, others house kennels, chickens, craftsmen and their stores, outside of which is the firepit doing the work of feeding the camp. Two hundred he brought to the border, and a hundred are out along it, many leagues north and south. I look about us for the wagons of all the hijacked vans and see that they are clustered into two camps, one for the Post, one for the two Marghoster vans, a hundred yards from this lodge and its own tents. There's much moaning and crying coming from the slaves in the Marghoster camp, all chained and sitting or lying about in the grass. Most of Yicre's soldiers are about the camp's perimeter in threes and fours. The soldiers belonging to the vans are keeping a more casual watch of their own, and true to Yicre's word they seem unharmed and appear to have been given wood for their fires, even tuikas I see being plucked and prepared.

The sun is setting, the fire's stoked up and great pots are on stands over it. We are gathered outside Yicre's pavilion.

"I would see Gennic, the Post drudha and the Vanguards of the Marghoster vans."

"You will, Driwna of the Bridche." Yicre this is. "You won't go alone. There's much unrest among those Farlsgrad people and we have only just met. I would be sure of your purpose."

"As you wish, Daith-nu Ilkashun."

Ufra dismounts from her horse and I feel those around us slowing or stopping to look upon her. I want to say something to her, and I'm about to when I see her walking straight up to me.

"Come," she says. Gennic can wait. After I dismount she hooks her arm through mine and leads me past the lodge and along the bank of the lake away from its tents and the wagons of the caravans further off. She splays the fingers of her free hand and holds her hand out slightly as she walks, reading the air I expect. She leans into me as we weave through reeds and shrubs, furtive glances up at me that tell me she's aware of how flustered I'm feeling and she's enjoying it. My flush redoubles. With a hint of pressure from her arm she stops us walking. Her eyes lose their focus, as though she's listening. Then she giggles, as if somebody had spoken. Laughter echoes back from a tent at the lakeside. An Ososi stands up from long grass nearby, still smiling, his arms also out before him. He shakes them, she releases my arm and shakes hers. After a moment he looks at me. His colouring is more brown than Ufra's yellow, he wears no tunic or vest, his chest is misshapen by bark that spreads up around his shoulder, its rough edges silver-tinted with a fine fungus.

"Welcome. You make Ufra happy, Sathanti child." I taste then the spores that they must have released with their shaking, a damp mist, a hint of dark soil on my tongue.

"The Master of Flowers wishes to see you," he says.

"Your father, Ufra?"

"No, this is the Oskoro Master." The Ososi turns from us and claps his hands and from the nearby tent steps the most remarkable man I will ever see. I am struck still with awe as he pushes through the flaps and stands upright. He is as big as Scar. He moves forwards awkwardly, bringing to mind a bear that is choosing to stand on its hind legs. He wears nothing except plant, ropes of mandrake root, longer than I've ever seen, sprout and hang from his chest, belly and legs, mixed with vines I don't recognise. One arm's skin has been replaced entirely with a soft, leathery black bark, ants scuttling across it. But growing from his skull is the largest, most perfect Flower of Fates I've ever seen, its leaves of red and purple, a black stem, black roots running thickly from his braegnloc, down about his neck and shoulders as hair might have grown. At the heart of it, the flower itself, an orange so violent it almost hurts the eyes, soft, the bulb almost a fruit, latticed with yellow stamen. It shines with strength, as if it contains its own candle within; the price of a kingdom and power of an army behind his eyes, filling his veins. His head, as I come closer, is stitched, and I recall the baby girl. He is Oskoro, not Ososi, for as Yblas told me, the Ososi do not stitch the skin into a ridge around the braegnloc, they remove it. Fast as a spider he comes at me then, I'm shocked by it, for he is the size of a gorilla. I have heard of the Flower being used in battle, the untouchable supremacy of Grmodzic, the drudharch of the tales, who achieved the sundering of the old Farlsgrad empire with just one of these flowers. This is the chief of the Oskoro, in exile he must be. How Yblas would yearn to know he lives. He stands close to me. In the encroaching darkness I cannot tell his colouring, but his eyes, like Ufra's, shine green. I feel frail as I look upon his great chest and arms.

"Your hands." His voice is clear and loud as a dockside bell, beyond any normal man's breath to carry so strongly in the air. I put my hands up to his and he pulls me close, puts his cheek to mine and he breathes deeply of me, cavernous lungs, like a horse's. There is a web, no, a substance of some sort, on his skin, of his skin, warming my cheek, the warmth spreading, a surge like the tide through to my core, stilling my thoughts. My muscles loosen, like my bones have been summoned away, and I fall to my knees though my hands are still in his. There's a buzzing about me, but I know it not as a sound but as smells of apples, dung, cooked chestnut. My breathing makes it all louder.

"Where is the girl you held to your breast? Who killed her?" I have no idea if he even spoke this question, but, perhaps compelled by him in some unfathomable way, I bring my arms up to rock her, look down on her, convinced he can see her lying there, asleep in the sun once more.

"How do you know? It's been so long since I held her."

"There is more to alkaest, what you call the Flower of Fates, than you can sense. I feel it like an ache, here." His fingertips brush the leaves of the flower in his head.

"I seek her," I say. "I would know how she came to die. I didn't want to put her back, back in the keg, in the dark. She is in the Sathanti Peaks somewhere. Someone moves her in secret."

I turn then, to look over at the vans behind us.

"She cannot be there," I say, though I realise this is something he would already know.

"Scar has her," says Ufra.

Something is whispered by many voices at the mention of his name. I look about us and see, though I don't know how I could have missed them approaching from the grasses about us, ten or fifteen more Ososi, three more Oskoro.

"Scar killed her, killed us all. Scar and one other." The Master looks over my head, suddenly, alerted to something. He breathes deeply, then looks away from the lodge of the Ilkashun and the caravans beyond it, out into the fields east.

129

"Riders come, dogs. The lodge is in danger."

"What?" As I say it I hear barking, then distant horns on the wind. "This must be the Hidzucs. Ufra, they mean to kill Yicre and his Ilkashun!"

"If we are to defend ourselves, defend the Ilkashun, you must cut me and drink!" I'm confused for a moment as the Ososi and Oskoro about us rush up to him. I gasp as Ufra takes her knife and runs it across his upper arm. He pulls me up off my knees and I find my strength has returned, as though I'd merely forgotten it. He holds the back of my neck, starts to bring me to the cut Ufra made. Instinctively I tense, try to stop him. His eyes lock on mine, they hold me still on their own. "Drink, Driwna, alkaest will defend us." Tentatively I drink from the cut that is now flowing slowly with whatever he has for blood. I know something's wrong, his smell has changed, a dark sweetness to it that I would swear has drawn the others to him, their knives drawn and ready. The mouthful of his blood I get is hot as pepper seeds. Then I scream. Other impulses are in me, other imperatives invading with the blood, rivers of will converging. As the Oskoro and Ososi cut him to drink his blood this chief of the Oskoro holds me upright as I shake, for I can't bear it, the night is like daylight, pale blue roaring out of the black. I look up at him, surrounded by those drinking from him. Their heat and spores, their scent is thick as smoke in my nose. I see his breath, giving life to the air, curtains of orange and green rippling outwards, waves on a mighty tide. They all step back from him, exultant, draw clubs, knives, bows; some are weeping, some laughing. They turn and run for the camp. I'm fighting to control my breathing, I can't take in enough air.

"Run, Driwna, it will help." Ufra this is, her skin shining as though varnished. But she did not speak. Her purpose is as my own thought. It is my purpose. She takes my hand, draws her sword and we run. My first step is huge, my thighs growing stronger with each footfall, all of me is growing, sharpening and hardening, my lungs bellows of great power. My sword no longer seems to weigh anything. Then the sky lights up, fire arrows shot towards the Ilkashun camp from the fields beyond, away to our left. The trails are almost still, long streaks in the dusk air that seem painted into it. Invisible to the screaming and shouting Ilkashun are sporebags, slung with the arrows, iron caltrops in among the powders. I can see them by the trails of the air itself, whorls of brown, the exploded bags blackening the silver grass, billowing out from the ground or tents struck. Mothers gather children, fierce in their haste. Ilkashun soldiers take slugs of their fightbrews and there's no time to stone it and get it under control with each other as they mask up and fight to get their belts on. It will be the death of some of them. The Ososi running ahead of us move as a flock, five splitting and heading out into the fields where Hidzuc's soldiers must be, five more to our right to the Ilkashun lodge, where they begin tending to those coughing and crying out, the spores in them. I look out to the fields, to see what force it is we face. There are flickers of breath like embers out in the blue, Hidzuc's soldiers all gathered there, clear and sharp to my eye as needles, all alight with their fightbrews. I see the silhouette of Eirakh Hidzuc's crown, then the flash of fire in a line as arrows are lit and another volley launched. Now I hear the dogs more clearly, fifty or more, ravenous, cutting through the grass from the Hidzuc line towards the Ilkashun lodge.

"Ufra, we need Gennic and his crew to help defend these people."

I run through the Ilkashun tents and along the riverbank

to where the caravans are camped. Ufra is with me. Despite the dark this blood I've drunk has given me the sight of an eagle. I see our flags, see Gennic has gathered his crew up, is already masked, strapping up their belts as they start stoning their brews.

"Gennic!"

He turns at my voice, stares in shock at me.

"I, I . . .' He shies from me, he's not seen me risen on a brew, let alone one such as this. He sees Ufra. The crew draw swords, thinking themselves attacked, panicked by our speed, the noise the Song of the Earth makes with us, that thrilling sense of each other's presence as soldiers on brews come close, the story of our bodies and our power told in the air between us.

"Dogs are coming, Gennic, get your crew among the people, ready powders and pepper."

He nods, accepts the order in a moment. I leap to and off a wagon, land running. This is the world the Master sees, so much more than we can know. I run among the wagons of the Marghoster vans, find their crew in a small clearing at the heart of their camp facing what must be one of the Vanguards.

"To arms!" I shout. "Vanguard, your soldiers are needed, the Hidzucs are attacking the lodge." For a moment I am pleased to see they too are ready to fight, leathers to belts and brewed.

"Good," he says. Two of them turn and raise their bows at me. I realise, slower than Ufra, that they were too ready, being already risen, their fightbrews stoned and under control. They knew this attack was coming. Ufra throws her knife at one of the bowmen, he spins away and the other's bow is knocked and his arrow flies off to my left, a breath of cold iron.

A shout from their vanguard, not a lingo I know. It's taken up by others on the far side of the Marghoster camp, who begin running for the Ilkashun lodge. Most of the Ilkashun guarding these caravans have already gone to the lodge and the tents for their loved ones. They think the threat has only come from the east and the Hidzucs.

Never before have I been so quick. These Marghoster vanners before us might as well be carcasses hanging from hooks for all the resistance they're capable of. Attempts at binding with my blade I smash away, breaking their grip or their wrists. I barely feel my sword work. I can see the colours of their intentions, see the tapestry of their tactics unfold and the shrill flares of fear in their last moments. Eight, ten dead, Ufra with a spear now has five dead at her feet.

"I have to tell Gennic, these Marghosters are fucking traitors."

No sooner have I said it, I hear him shout, his cry taken up from the direction of the Post van's camp.

"He knows, Driwna, our Ososi in the camp will take care of them. We must stop the spore arrows, the Hidzucs."

She says no more, leads us out of the Marghoster camp and into the fields. I care nothing for my own life now, seeing the dogs race into the camp, some hit with powders and frenzied, the others finding the desperate arms of mothers defending their children as fire rains down among them all. Ososi are shooting the dogs wherever they get sight of them, though among the tents they get little sight before it's too late. Screams echo across the fields, flesh is burning, the world about us livid with fire and the bloodlust and terror of all us beasts. I follow Ufra, sprinting hard, revelling in how tireless I feel. I suffer no indecision, I trust the Ososi and Gennic to do what they can, but only five Ososi have gone out into the field, at the lines of soldiers that wait for their plant, fires and dogs to take the fight out of the Ilkashun. There is no time to seek horses; they are either tied up in terror, dead or long gone. So we run. The Ososi ahead of us have been spotted and a horn sounds the commands. Twenty or so riders have broken out from the Hidzuc ranks. They exchange shots with the Ososi. Then we are both seen and their archers draw and the arrows fly, sporebags on them. I reach for my mask but Ufra shouts at me. I look at her and she smiles, shaking her head. We won't need them. She slows and stops, unshoulders her bow, throws me her spear. She looses an arrow, two, three, four smooth draws, keeps going through her quiver. Two hit their mark, the other two are aimed at the cluster of horsemen about Eirakh Hidzuc, forcing them to scatter. Two more hit horses and unseat their riders in the confusion. We were judged too far away to be a threat to him directly. Another horn and eight of their riders come out at us, looking to run us down, spreading out. Ufra moves a step to the side from the one arrow that might have hit her. I lean to my right, reading the air's movement as another flies at me. I have time enough to see the grain of the wood as it whips past my cheek and I would yell with the joy of it if I could forget what I saw their spores and dogs are doing to the innocent. The spore arrows land about us, fuzzy plumes of dust kicking up. I breathe and taste the spores, they settle on my skin but I feel nothing.

The horses close on us, Ufra's last four arrows find their mark. Four horse only are left. I run at them as they approach, moving to try and split them, giving Ufra moments that I know will be enough. Two come at me, two at her. The first at me levels his spear. I have mine held as anyone would to withstand a charge. They are within yards when I change the grip to throw it. I stop running, too late for them to react, throw the spear with a thrilling power into the breast of one horse. It collapses forward, its rider pulling hard left on the reins, pulling its weight back into the other horse. I leap out of the way as their bodies roll past me like thunder, bones breaking, horses and the one living man bellowing with pain. I turn to see Ufra jump aside from those charging her, whipping a powderbag from her belt and throwing it at the head of the nearest horse. It rears up in pain, throws its rider and Ufra is on him, stabbing. The other rider takes a few moments to get his steed under control and I run at him, force him to charge me. I have only a sword now. Spear levelled he knows he has no choice, a desperate fear and hope in him that he can run me down. But I can see each hoof land, see his hands, his knees, his intent. I knock the spear up as I drop beneath its point, spin and bury my sword in the horse's thigh. It shrieks and falls, thrashing onto its side. I finish him as he tries to free his leg trapped under it. I stab the horse through its head, end its pain. I draw breath, look for Eirakh Hidzuc. He's readying to charge, but not at us. I feel the drums of hooves in the earth behind me. Ilkashun horses charging at the Hidzucs. There is fury in what I feel, rippling through soil and stone, it tugs me after it. I begin running. Ufra will follow me. Eirakh's horsemen form a line and they charge forward themselves, Eirakh among them. There are far more of them than us, I can feel it before the Ilkashun horses overtake me to my left. This blood I've drunk holds me to the moment, sinks me, leaves only bodies and movement, smell, taste, a world without memory or plan. The horses hit each other with a force that stills the sky. Every Hidzuc or mercenary focused on the Ilkashun before them I move to and stab, for I am too quick and quiet for them to react to my approach. One cut or stab will be enough with my poison. I find a bow and some arrows on a mercenary that was thrown from her horse, a hole in her chest from a spear. I have to turn her, pull the bow from her shoulders, arrows from the quiver, three snapped, five still good. It is easy to draw with this strength, easy to see with sight like Sillindar's own. Four I choose and four I kill. The fifth arrow, as I rest it against finger and bow, I know I must keep for Eirakh Hidzuc. *You are Bridche*, the grasses whisper. *You are home*. Ufra runs past me, takes up a spear from one of the fallen and is in among the fighting. The Hidzuc falter. It's in their song. I see then Eirakh's crown, he's still riding, two mounted spearmen his guard and support. They see someone, Yicre it must be for they spur forward as one, riding towards the heart of the line of fighting. Then I see Yicre, alone, dark with blood, his reins held into his chest, protecting a wound. He means to die, all reason has been burned away by his grief at the slaughter in the camp. I raise the bow, draw. Yicre hits the rider shielding Hidzuc from my line of sight, driving him back off his horse as Yicre passes. He caught Yicre too at his collarbone, dismounting him.

And I have a clear shot.

Eirakh Hidzuc pulls hard on his reins to turn his horse about, his eyes following the falling Yicre until he sees me. He knows instantly he's going to die, the earth sings it, the ghosts boiling in the ground around us fill the clay and roots with Bridche lingo. These fields are deep with our bones, rich and black with our blood from before my pa's time. Eirakh doesn't belong. He knows. My fingers roll off the string and the arrow bows and shimmies as it makes the distance in a blink, hitting Eirakh in his chest. He doesn't move, just one sharp breath, his final note. His foot slips from a stirrup and he falls off his horse twisted, hanging from the other stirrup a moment before hitting the ground.

An Ilkashun runs him through before running on to seek some other to kill. Some of their mercenaries ride off, routed. When the other mercs see their wisdom, themselves on foot with no way of escape, they throw down their weapons. It is done.

I turn and walk away from the carnage, look back to the burning camp and lodge. There are no cries of battle there, just the howling of dogs and mothers and fathers. Now I feel the torment of the Flower of Fates; the vastness of the plains, the weight of the lake. There is no end to the thirst of all life, all stone and flesh, wood and leaf. The dead here will be drunk dry in their turn and the land will still take more. I can't bear this truth. I smell Ufra, then, as she approaches, her heat. The thorns in her skin have grown longer. I can't stop my tears before her and she smiles before kissing the tears as they fall, her lips wet and warm as butter. I embrace her, kiss her back. She puts her arms around me, gently pressing her thorns against my leathers, seeking my answer. I press myself into her, her thorns sinking deep into my skin, binding me to her. I hiss as they enter me, then gasp as her heat fills me from each thorn's invasion, and I'm so giddy with need I press myself harder still into her arms, feeling more thorns enter me, demanding her plant and blood, to have its seed in my own. She breathes heavily, trembles and moves her lips up to my nose and then my head, easing me down to her neck. I kiss the vine there and she shivers more, breath quickening as I run my lips along it. She squeezes me harder as I do it and the pain of the thorns across my arms and chest sharpens and I feel it coming, in both of us, our songs joining and all of me dissolving. I can barely say her name before the ecstasy takes us, sudden and savage. The fist about my whole body slowly unclenches and I release my breath. She holds me as I begin to cry, knows I need to be held. We are vulnerable to each other and cannot let go until we have found the faces we make for the world. Another Ososi runs over to us. I don't understand what he says, the sounds he's making. Ufra speaks in the same way. He leaves us.

"We all have healing to do." She whispers this. "Driwna, the blood fades. Vadse and kannab will help for these coming days when you are once more returned from the heart of the Song. Be among friends, be with me."

"I would be your friend, Ufra."

She lifts my chin, kisses me again. "I would like that, Driwna of the Post."

I remember that it would be selfish to stay here, that we must go to the camp and heal who we can.

"Let's see what we can do for these poor Ilkashun," I say.

The world darkens as the Oskoro's blood runs its course. I lose the clear glory of the Song, a fog shrouding my senses when really they're only returning to what they were. I think of Bray and Gennic, don't know if Bray even made it back to the camp before the Hidzucs came. The horror becomes clearer, this the curse and favour of losing the Song. I pass Ososi, Hidzuc and Ilkashun soldiers, all dead, pass the dead dogs, dead horses all around us. Then, as I approach the tents, the smell brings fresh tears to my eyes, the smell and the first of the children. Most are covered in bedrolls or canvas. I pick up a small arm that had been bitten off, put it under one of the rolls with the body there. There must have been bodies in many of the tents now burned and collapsed. A man sits on the ground with his wife lying across his lap in his arms. He cleans the weeping blisters on her face and neck though she's dead, and he's singing to her. Others there are in the depths of their unbearable grief; what good does it do to list them all? The Oskoro Master is here, he kneels at the side of a woman, humming to her in a way that makes me feel sleepy as he works an ointment into her blisters and what must be an arrow wound in her belly. Those not already dead will be saved. There is drudhanry of great power here, and I would watch them work, the Ososi and Oskoro, but I must find my own people. I shout Gennic's name.

"He's with the slaves, miss."

"Bray?" His voice came from one of the few tents left. I pull aside the flap. There's room only for three or four at most in here. Bray is kneeling over a young man who's shivering and moaning. I see from the bite wounds about his left shin that his leg needs to go at the knee.

"Need some help, miss, been a while since I done one."

I lean down to kiss his head. "I'm glad you're alive."

"You too, miss. Here, lad, drink." He takes a few mouthfuls, this brown-haired boy with the first soft wisps of beard beginning to show. He looks up at me, then Bray, strangers to him. I kneel and find his hand, hold it in mine. His eyes close. If he wakes at all he'll wake a different man and who knows if his spirit will thrive or break on a crutch?

I tie up his thigh, wash his knee with alka and ready the bark, gummed linen and slippery elm. Bray goes to work and he does a better job than I could have, though I shouldn't be surprised, given what he must have seen and done in that other life. Another sorrow to think what he could have been without the droop.

Soon as he's through the leg I'm cleaning the skin he's left me, folding and stitching it over the bark and bandaging it over the linen that'll keep the bark in place and let it breathe a bit. All the while I'm doing it he's stroking the boy's head with slick, blood-soaked hands.

"There's a girl I loved once," he says. "Prettier'n you, miss, if you can believe it. Kasyr. I would have had a boy an' girl with her but my brother took her because I loved

139

her an' he was the one would get the herd after our pa passed. Her pa, her hamost, or hamlet as you'd call it in Common, was poor an' Pa's herd was famous in Urdris, so she had to be my brother's keep, din't she, him bein' heir. Wonder if a girl'll take pity on this one now he won't become a man o' means."

"You did a fine job with his leg, Bray. There's little you can do for his resolve. Will you stay with him till he wakes? And can you give him a finger of this betony and not take it yourself?"

"Course I won't, miss. I's not in love with that stuff no more."

"Good. I'm going to see Gennic, see what's happened to Yicre and those fucking Marghoster vanners."

"Most dead, the rest might be dyin' slowly if these kurchmen get their way."

There's shouting outside now, yelling for Ososi. Then I hear his name, Yicre.

Outside the tent there's Ilkashun men and women about a sled that's been used to carry Yicre's body from the field back to the lodge. It's pulled past me, into the camp towards the firepit. I see him stir and I thank Sillindar he's alive. There's an Ososi and what must be Yicre's guard or captain that's pulled the sled in. His guard collapses in pain, paying the colour. I'm about to step forward, not seeing the Ilkashun drudha, when Ufra appears at my side. Like Bray, she is soaked in the blood of the wounded.

"Ufra!" calls the Ososi, continuing with noises I don't understand.

"Come," she says to me.

As she walks through the Ilkashun they step back from their chief; they know Ososi drudhanry is his best hope.

Yicre's breathing is fast and shallow; he gasps as Ufra

kneels and pulls his hand away from the wound he was protecting on his horse. There's a fierce cut on his other shoulder. The spear must have sliced through and then caught in his leathers, to have driven him from his horse. Two other Ososi join her, kneeling across from her. The rest of his kurch gather around us. He opens his eyes, looks up. He manages a brief smile.

"The Post." He lifts an arm, points at my red cloak. "Our brothers in red, you fought Hidzuc and Marghoster with us. We are grateful."

"I've not a cock the last time I looked, Daith-nu, but you're kind to say it," I say. He smiles at my correction, gestures his apology. "The Post would not stand by and watch a slaughter. I wish we could have saved more of your kurch-kin." For a moment I'm not sure if I should have said this, but Yblas has given me free rein to speak for the Post and I'll use it until I'm told otherwise. One of her Ososi treats Yicre's shoulder while Ufra treats the stab wound in his side. As with Bray's wound, something shivering in jelly is thumbed into the cut and he cries out.

"Calm yourself, etza-Ilkashun." Ufra this is. "Betony, Driwna," she says. "Our plant takes to him better if he's calm."

I get a smear of it on the end of my finger and push it into the corner of his mouth. The betony they gave me with these belts back at the Gate has white honey mixed in, a sweetness as seducing as the betony itself. His breathing settles as it takes hold of him. Ufra begins stitching up his wound. She glances up at me a moment and smiles. It is a delight, that smile, and the many holes that her thorns made tingle a moment, adding to the pleasure of it.

"He will be strong again, your chief," says Ufra, standing up now and speaking to all those about us. "We will help put your people in the land. Then we take our own back to feed our people, make louder the Song that you would one day all hear it."

The first of what she says warms the crowd about us, the second not so much. I stand with her and she leads me away from the firepit, towards where some of the Ilkashun have begun putting a pile of the bodies.

"I must speak to my Vanguard," I say to her.

She holds my hands together, squeezes them. "We will drink later, at dawn."

I watch her for a moment, talking with the Ososi and some of the Oskoro that I saw earlier, though there is no sign of the Oskoro chief, the Master of Flowers. They hang upon her words. She could lead the Ososi even without a flower in her braegnloc.

I make my way to the camps at the lakeside where the Ilkashun kept the Post and Marghoster slaver vans they'd kidnapped. There's eight men and women, stripped of armour and belts, kneeling in a cluster. Two reds stand with them. A few of those kneeling are battered and bruised, one's crying, young he is. The reds see me.

"Driwna?" I recognise the voice, then see his big heavy pipe.

"Trid?" This was one of my old Lindur crew, on the missing van Morril asked me to find.

"It's me. Come to beat these fuckers again?"

"Sillindar, no, Trid! That's not our way. They took up arms against us and they paid for it. They've surrendered now."

"These Marghoster fuckers, no offence to you, killed two o' those mercs Reeve Morril sent after us and two of us reds, Ladruk and Calicz." He turns about to the nearest of them, an old man. "Got some back din't you, fucker." He goes to punch him and the man flinches; his eyes are swollen already and he's shivering, for he's in his woollen shirt only.

"I'm sore sorry to hear it, Trid. There's enough suffering tonight, we'll have no more. And you should know, both of you, to treat them as they treat us is to be no better than them."

I can't say he's happy to hear this, being a boy still and burning in the fire of a boy's feelings. I step past them to the man on his knees.

"What's your name?"

I can barely hear it, his lip's split badly. "Thelg." He's got some colour, but not recently; his fighting days were years ago, probably made it through on dayers for runs that might expect little or no trouble.

"Thelg, you'll get no more beatings. Do you want water? A cloak?"

He glances up at me, then at Trid.

"I'm in charge here Thelg. None higher."

"Be grateful for that, lady."

"Trid, where's Gennic?"

"With all the slaves, feedin' 'em," says Trid. "Droop round, keep 'em sleepy."

"Get him."

"Yes, Vanguard."

"It's not Vanguard any more Trid, I'm Fieldsman."

"Sorry, Fieldsman."

"Stand up, all of you," I say to the prisoners.

Their heads are down, standing is difficult for some of them.

"If you got a beating from a red here I'm sorry. On a brew and in a battle nobody's thinking straight. I'll have words with them."

"Can't think why Farlsgrad folk'd be beating on their own

143

when we're surrounded by cannibals and these Ilkashun mud-fishers that's giving them their own to eat." Thelg this is, and there's a few murmurs of agreement.

"It's a poor vanner don't open their eyes to see what's true for themselves. You think you're taking slaves from Farlsgrad into the Sathanti to be eaten? Because there's eating costs less coin than that. Now, I'll see that you get my drudha to look over your wounds and whatever else you need. I'll see you also get some food and water. It's not dependent on you answering me, but you could return the goodwill by telling me where those slaves were bound for."

There's the predictable looking about anywhere but at me and I see that a few of them are looking at Thelg at the same time. So he's their leader.

"Thelg, your Vanguard's dead?"

"Yes, lady."

"My name's Driwna. Your crew's looking at you like you might be in charge at the moment."

He looks behind him at the others, but they don't meet his eyes.

"Nobody else is stepping up, so why not."

"Where were you taking the slaves?"

"We're not told. We meet a van comes from the mountains north of Lake Ilkashun. They get taken north from there, we get paid and go back to Farlsgrad."

"What else goes with them? There are many lots here."

"Fifty-five lots food and plant, ten lots of arrows, ten more hides and ale."

"Is it a Marghoster van that takes them?"

"Don't know."

"You fucking know, Thelg; don't do this."

He looks up at me then, I don't see guile in him. "We're told nothing."

"He'd fucking kill us to a man." Another of them this is, woman about my age, cheek swollen, good colour and strong looking but one arm hanging limp.

"Who would?"

"Scar."

"He's on these runs?"

"Some," she says.

"Ososi cunt," spits another.

"You'll have an Ososi look at your cuts and they'll fix them well. Don't mix bad people with good on account of their tribe," I say. "How many runs have there been?"

"Least four for us," says Thelg.

"How many slaves?"

"Eighty, this run is."

Fucking Sillindar. Three hundred slaves. Scar being part of this proves the Oskoro baby's part of it too. She was being taken to the mountains.

"What's in the mountains?"

Nobody says anything. Of course I'm tempted to cut it out of them. I have to find another way.

"We might say that this is something Marghoster's doing. This, tonight, is Marghoster's doing. He's starting a war. And that means Farlsgrad's starting a war, with the Sathanti Peaks confederacies. Or Marghoster's against the king. Being part of what Marghoster's doing will, I expect, be of interest to the king. I'd see it as necessary, for the Post to maintain its relations in Farlsgrad, that I bring you, safely, to Autumn's Gate to tell your king all about it."

"Lady . . . Driwna, we don't know what's in the mountains. It's why our run ends in the plains. Might be it's Marghoster as you say, but Scar's not anything to do with him."

"Is he not? Is Marghoster not using slaves far beyond his own borders for some reason none of us can guess?"

145

"You know how wrong that sounds, lady. What need does Marghoster have for slaves out here more than at home on his lands?"

"You're the living proof Marghoster has brought war to the Sathanti. We're going to take good care of you. You'd best hope the king shows as much mercy if he's not aware of all this."

"Driwna Marghoster!" Gennic this is, returning with Trid. He's got his arm about Trid's shoulder. Paying the colour or wounded. He doesn't look well.

"You're a Marghoster?" says Thelg.

"No, Bridche, Sathanti. I'd explain it to you but I can't be fucked." I tease Gennic's arm from Trid's and embrace him.

"You're a welcome sight, Gennic. Couldn't have borne losing you." He's trembling. There's a sharp, vile smell of guts and poison strong on his hands and arms. I doubt I smell any better.

"As are you, Driwna, though I don't understand how you've come by such a fine belt and leathers."

"You'll have missed the rolls sent out across the Post, then. I've had a promotion."

"Marschal? Do I bow? Get on my knees and suck you off?"

"Something like that. Trid, see these vanners get water and something to eat. From our van if need be, I'll understand if the Ilkashun won't feed them. Lay one glove or boot on any of them and you're no longer a red." He isn't happy about it but gets about the order.

I put my arm around Gennic to help him along.

"I'm going to need to lie down, Driw."

"Gennic, do you know if this is Marghoster's doing?"

"Seems his crews knew what to expect. I heard their

146

vanguard holler something, saw them go for the Ilkashun, and us. We killed those didn't surrender. The mercenaries that had been sent to help us by Morril, they were in the Hidzuc camp briefly, other mercs there said they'd been paid a purse by the crown, Hildmir."

"No. That can't be right."

"And I saw Bray'd been stabbed. You were attacked on your way out here?"

I can feel the tears behind my eyes. I'd had little time to think of it since arriving here.

"We were. I need some time to piece things together."

"You should rest somewhere, put me to sleep and lie down yourself. The world will wait."

"I need to see the slaves and the manifest. It'll tell us if the vans that the slaves were meant for are also Marghoster's."

"There's no manifest," says Gennic. "I expect it was ruined the moment they were ambushed by Yicre's kurchmen."

"Fuck it. I know it's him in my gut."

"I've tended to the slaves. Only two were close enough to the spores to get the blisters. Thirty are droopers that'll want to stay slaves to whoever keeps feeding it to them, the rest might want their freedom, I haven't asked. Personally I'd love to see all that coin of Marghoster's lost, if it's Marghoster's."

I can't see how Marghoster is allied to Hildmir. There's a lot more I can't see; what Crejda is doing trying to kill me, who might have brought the Oskoro girl over from the Almet to the Brasks, why Hidzucs and Marghosters are trying to start a war among the Sathanti, why the mountain tribes along Gethme's Tongue are cutting bridges that have been in use for generations. It's in the mountains I'll have the answers.

"Driwna." Gennic eases himself to the earth, holding his guts. He's going to pay heavy, I can tell.

147

I kneel next to him, finger betony into his gums, take off my cloak and put it over him. There's arguments going on at the lodge and back in the vans and a tiredness hits me so hard and fast I'm dizzy with it, falling back on my arse on the earth next to Gennic.

He begins smiling as the betony gets into him; stops twitching. I pull him over onto his side, save him drowning in his own sick should that happen.

I need a drink of something.

"Driwna, miss?"

I open my eyes with a start. Bray's standing over me.

"Sit down and get some rest, Bray. I'm keeping a watch on Gennic while he pays colour. How's that boy?"

"Sleeping still. Mun was killed by a dog, his pa burned bad and din't make it."

I've got no words for that.

"Not much use wi' this wound. Speared a dog, was about it. Heard you killed the Hidzuc chief."

"I did."

"Your own'll breathe again in those fields an' forests. You did your kurch proud."

I expect he means our dead, our elders. I won't lie, I'd like to be able to tell my pa, see what he'd say, but it wouldn't be enough for him. Too far gone in his new life.

"You be payin' colour soon I expect," he says.

"I – I'm not sure. I took whatever the Ososi have for a brew. They said it'll make me sad, and I certainly want to cry, can hardly stop myself. Not felt anything like it. But I don't think I'll be paying this colour, I got none of the sickness that comes with it."

"Colour looks fresh on your skin, miss; that grey's almost silver. What's all those holes in your leathers? Darts?"

"No, thorns." I smile and it confuses him.

148

"Reckon they'll give us their brew, then? Not havin' to pay colour for a fightbrew'd change the world."

He's right. "I don't think so, 'less you like drinking blood."

"Can't taste half as bad a brew as the Amo."

"That's true."

Gennic is sleeping. The camp about us is alive now dawn's come and the dead are being taken to be buried, the sorrowful singing that calls their ancestors to witness the burials, each singer finding the harmony that's started and filling it.

"I need to see Yicre. This assault by the Hidzucs and mercenaries from Farlsgrad could lead to a war." I need a measure of Yicre's character.

I've nearly got Bray killed twice now, but there's a bit of light in his eyes, I think.

"Would you rather be on the gate to our sheds in the Spike still?" I ask him.

"Forgot what war stinks like. Feel a bit more like I's awake, miss, and that's honest. Don't think I'll thank you fer it, though, not just yet." He leans into me by way of a nudge. "Best go an' save the world."

"Depends on whether Yicre and his Ilkashun kurches can listen to a woman telling them what's needed."

I stand and yawn. Ufra was right regarding this feeling I have now the blood's gone through me. My skin is tender where her thorns have been, makes me shiver and itch. At least I won't feel like sleeping.

Most of the Ilkashun have left Yicre with his guards and with Ufra. His keep's brother, Lodre Canendrigh, sits with him. He is leaner than Yicre, even in his leathers, a cold anger in his face. Yicre is awake now and furs have been rolled up to put under his shoulders and neck to prop him up. Unlike Lodre he has been crying, his eyes full, his cheeks soaked.

"They strengthen your lands with their blood, Daith-nu Ilkashun," I say.

It is what is said. They all repeat the saying. I look over at Ufra. She pats the ground next to her.

"Sit with us, Brother Red," says Yicre with a weak smile, "and forgive me for speaking only of brothers earlier. It is the way in the Sathanti as you know."

"I would see the Post be a brother to all Sathanti, even a sister. It is good to see you awake. I don't doubt you will need time to heal, even with Ufra's care. I hope I may offer counsel as a brother, for then no forgiveness is needed."

"You have the ear of the High Red himself," says Yicre. "All will listen to what you must say."

I sit next to Ufra. I am careful only to glance at her, to keep my crossed legs from leaning against hers, for I worry what might be obvious in my disposition, my desire to have her hold my hand, to touch her in some way. She ignores such considerations and takes my hand in hers anyway. I speak quickly, to take the focus away from us.

"I would first hear what you think, Daith-nu Ilkashun. This is your land, your blood that's been shed."

"I will have the land of the Hidzucs. The council would back me against his kin-kurches. They will put our heron at the top of their poles." The heron is the Ilkashun's chosen mark, the ruling kurch's mark sits above all others on the kurchpoles that mark out the lands. "As brothers, the Post could benefit from this. Your High Red would not disagree."

"As Bridche you are for this." Lodre this is. "Our kurch-poles, those of even the Hidzuc, show Bridche and Canendrigh marks together. Not as low down as all that, either. We all lost much to Farlsgrad and it's Farlsgrad whose bidding Eirakh and his kannab puffers did."

"Forgive me, Chief Lodre, for they might say it is the

caravans you have here that forced their hand," I say. "You taking them in protest at the loss of your people has given them an excuse to come into your lands for them. You might have expected parley, but your act might tell a different story to some, for they don't see the desperation that's driven you to it."

He's young for a chief, no older than me, and he's lost many of his family here. I have to assume his own keep must have died some time past, for she is not introduced or mourned here. I should have known he'd not react well, for all he speaks truly.

"Forgive me, Brother Red, for standing no more for our people being taken, my sib-daughter taken in Marta, three more of this kurch in the months of Iuna and Ulyn, two more again in Silva, sons of our daith-wa, and himself then killed trying to save them. There is too little colour here to defend those without it."

"You did not kill or injure, until tonight, any of these vans, nor take from the lots. If I could bring these vans back to Farlsgrad, to the Post, with what slaves choose to remain at the droop, it will go well for your claim, for Farlsgrad can have no reason then to hold to revenge."

"Those van crew your reds now have prisoner, the slavers, they cannot go free. There's our dead being buried and you expect us to watch you take them home? Keeping these wagons and working that crew to death is justice. It is the least we must have. The slaves you can take, for they won't respect the land in our way."

I can't help thinking that's a bad idea, that the wagons are of enough value to be the reason to take some Sathanti land.

"What do you say, Daith-nu Ilkashun?" I ask.

"I will have parley with the Hidzuc heir. This is no matter for Farlsgrad. The vans may go back."

"Daith-nu, no!" Lodre this is. He stands slowly. "This is weakness. No daith-nu takes orders from a merchant's runner, no daith-nu takes orders from Farlsgrad about who they can and cannot kill on their own land. On my land. They attacked us, these crews on the Marghoster vans, just as the Hidzucs came, and for punishment they get to leave as they are?"

"Hear me, Lodre. We are Ilkashun. Our revenge is land for our children. We will take it and so deny them. Revenge is a winter flower, it thrives in the cold."

"We cannot grow salt and iron, farlswood or plant."

"You might have let me finish. There would be more of these vans, if we prove our intent. The Post I hope would find reason to trade with us at least, if Driwna here has the ear of the High Red, but the wagons from Lindur and the Spike do not come if their masters believe we might steal the lots and horses, kill the crews."

Lodre is restless now, looking out to where his people have taken their dead. He knows well enough not to argue with the Daith-nu, his sib-brother.

"Chief Lodre," I say, "allow me to take these vans back, as the Daith-nu advises. I can speak for you, prove there is goodwill by sending more Post vans this way. Marghoster would hate to see the Post gain a route for itself and at his expense. We can give you the trade you value, help you and your people. Your plant is prized among Post drudhas." His hands clench and unclench, he's doing his best to put his grief aside. It does him credit.

"Strong words, Brother Red, but you killed Eirakh Hidzuc, and I cannot spare soldiers to protect you on your journey back to the Spike to fulfil this promise. The Hidzucs may well take their revenge," says Lodre.

There's a murmur at this, a few here not sure who Eirakh's killer was until now.

"I must hope the master of these caravans we're taking back, being, it seems, a master too over the Hidzuc, wishes safe passage for us. I succeed all the more if I take Hidzuc's body back to his land for this to happen. I will give it to his Daith-ru to bury."

There's a crying out at this, the guards and Lodre shocked, looking to Yicre for his dismay. Yicre looks at me, weighing up my intent. I hope he understands how necessary it is.

"They'll kill you," he says.

"The chiefs will hear of this, Yicre," says Lodre. "I'll have my finest stags sent to Driwna's wagon as a further gift for the Hidzuc bastards to enjoy, shall I? Why stop at his body, master's wagons and crew. Excuse me, Brother Red, I must join what's left of my people preparing to bury our dead." Lodre spits into the firepit and leaves, his two guards with him.

I speak quickly to quash any reflection on Lodre's insults. "I've met Eirakh Hidzuc's keep, she's no fool. If I'm not run through I'll tell them of what you've said, how right it is that at a Council they would suffer what comes of a break of laws. I'll have ten or so who've paid colour with me. They may not have that many after this massacre; she'll hear me out. I will make a parley for all of us, Hidzuc, Ilkashun and Farlsgrad, and I will bring Marghoster to answer for what is in the mountains. Daith-ru Hidzuc will agree to the parley for we have brought back Eirakh, the Marghosters will agree because we have brought back the vans."

Yicre looks to Ufra. "What is your counsel, Ufra?"

"I trust Driwna. I feel the Song strongly in her. But she has enemies. A parley shows goodwill from us, but we prepare with strength in case she fails. I must return to my father, Ushnor, and speak of what happened last night. You, etza-Ilkashun, must summon your chiefs to your lodge. We cannot

153

let them shed blood until we hear from Driwna. It is Zemna, we shall wait for midwinter, the beginning of Jenna, for word from Driwna to go east. Our father cannot bear the hunting down of our people any more, we suffer as you do. He looks for a reckoning, as does Chief Lodre. We must parley before that, for I cannot bear more to die for something so shallow as pride. If Driwna fails, then we will have our revenge."

I look for disagreement in the eyes of those gathered, for she commanded us all with her words. We are silent. My heart beats faster to look upon her, I feel foolish and happy all at once and I curse that we must part now.

"Your father should be proud of you, Ufra," says Yicre, "as proud as we are all grateful for your drudhanry and kinship. Let us make sure both Ufra and Driwna have what they need."

He gestures to one of the guards present, who stands, waiting for us to rise and follow.

"Midwinter, Daith-nu Ilkashun. I will do my best to get word to you," I say. "Sillindar follow you."

"And you, Brother Red."

Ufra and I walk towards the vans. Most of the Ilkashun are together a league or so from the lodge, away from the water's edge, many digging, others singing, the breath of all of them rising in the morning's clear chilly air.

"How are you feeling, Driwna? The Song is so quiet without the blood."

"I am not myself. I feel somehow nervous. You . . . I feel as though your thorns have left something of you in me, I can't describe it. I want . . . I can't say what I want, can't understand how I've known you a day and . . ." She smiles and steps towards me.

"Driwna, the sting of my thorns is not so innocent. I am

careful who I hold, all Ososi are, for a binding begins and . . ."
She stops, unsure how to frame what further consequence
there would be. "Maybe the Oskoro blood quickened what
my eyes found pleasing, what my own plant and body judged
to be strong and beautiful. Forgive me, Driwna, for how
quickly I chose you. The heat in your skin will pass and
you'll feel more yourself. There's more I can give you, to
know the bond we could have in sharing blood and plant.
If you want it from me."

"The blood of the Master of Flowers, it made the world
clearer than I've ever seen it, and you even clearer within
it," I say. "You won't get verse or fine words comparing you
to the sun and the white moon, but you are the most beautiful woman I have laid eyes on and I saw the good in you,
the flow of the Song had no edges with you. If only people
could see each other in the Song more clearly."

"Words only point and command with breath and ink. It
is the curse of you Umansk, you who are not Ososi. We don't
need words." She steps closer, I cannot hold her gaze but
her intensity is thrilling.

"That's good. I cannot find them. I . . ." I cannot finish
what I want to say. It doesn't matter. I don't know if it's only
the echo of the Song of the Earth that filled us as we killed,
or if I need to feel the pain of those thorns over my arms
and belly. For a moment I wonder if they cover her body
entirely. I move my hand to the back of her hand as she lifts
it to meet mine. My thumb circles around the skin, a thorn.
I push my thumb onto it, shock myself with the suddenness
of my desire, my choice. She catches her breath, brings her
other hand on top of my thumb, presses it down hard, a
thrilling pain before letting me go. A pearl of blood blossoms
and then dribbles along my hand. She brings it to her lips,
pressing the blood to them before kissing it away, moving

my hand so it lies flat against my chest. My breathing quickens, the only sound I can hear, and I force a slow and deep breath, embarrassed. I look at my feet, feel sorry for the transgression. I can't meet her eyes.

"Ufra, I had no right."

"It is the plant and it is our blood." She lifts my chin so I must look at her again. "Midwinter, Driwna of the Post. I will look for your red cloak against the snow."

After leaving the Canendrigh lodge I told Gennic and the other vans to move on to Lindur so as not to risk their lives should it go badly with my returning Eirakh's body to the Hidzuc lodge. Their scouts found me first and some ran ahead to tell them of my coming. As we approached the lodge and the tents croweded about it, mothers and keeps dropped their baskets to run to me, for they waited as did all those at the lodge for word of the battle. By the time I rode the wagon into the camp, all of Eirakh's own kurch had lined the trail to the bloodstone. They were numb with shock, for nobody else had returned. Leusla it was stepped forward to greet me again as she'd done only days before that. I wore the red of the Post, to discourage any from thinking me Ilkashun. She gestured for two of her guards to take Eirakh's body off the wagon. Her eyes stayed on him the whole time. I could only wait in silence with my crew, who, like me, had disarmed themselves to affirm our peaceful intent. Once his body was on the ground she kneeled over him, opened his eyelids. I sensed relief. Then she wept and held him. Others took up wailing with her as is custom. I could think only of how many I had seen crying over broken or mutilated bodies, bodies from our kin-kurches of those that had gone missing, cloudy with flies, burned bodies that had me retching as soon as I got anywhere near, the awful snapping of bones

156

as they were clutched and held by men or women insensible to the awfulness of the charred bones; frail, exhausted puppets in their embrace.

I'd been lost grieving in such memories and had not noticed Leusla stand and come towards me. She stood close and searched my eyes; I believe she searched for my guilt. I felt my cheeks flush. I could not hold her gaze and looked at my boots. She must have known I had killed him. I was about to speak, to confirm it, when she took my hands in hers, kissed both my cheeks, left tears on them. "Thank you for bring him home unspoiled. He guide us with his fathers." By unspoiled she had meant his eyes, for it is a terrible thing out here to deprive the dead of their eyes, that they might not see where best to guide their children to the fruits of the land and away from its dangers.

It may sound strange to say that at the feast in his honour, when I was asked of how well he died, I found myself recounting it truly, that it was an Ososi and I that killed him. It is as it is with the Sathanti. Had Leusla condemned me I would have died there and then. But she had known the moment she kissed me. Instead she passed me her cup, and I drank from it. My pa would have cut his own throat to have seen such an honour given me, but I took no pleasure in that.

Chapter 8

Driwna

"Miss, wake up! Miss, what's wrong?"

A purple sky, dead Ososi underfoot, as far as I can see. I step on them and they hiss and writhe. I try to keep my balance, for I'm holding the girl, the baby. She's crying. I look down at her, to shush her. The Ososi pull at my legs, I lose my footing, my arms fly out instinctively, letting her go. I scream until a shake and a kick wake me. Bray it is.

"They seen the van," he says. "Scouts from the Spike, sendin' horses."

We were about eight or nine hours from the Spike when we pitched camp, thinking to arrive fresh. I expect word got ahead of us, after our stopping at the Hidzuc lodge.

I manage to get my leather surcoat on, but it's unbuckled still as the Spike's castellan rides up with Marghoster's reeve, Lighroz, and Crejda. I really want a pipe and all.

Crejda has the nerve to smile and I look over at Bray, who looks like he's bitten through a lemon.

The castellan, Gruslatic, dismounts and stands before us; a nasty, powerful animal that I heard was kicked out of the

158

Farlsgrad army for what he did to prisoners and his own soldiers. One killed herself after a tour with him, and she being the daughter of one of the king's clearks, it led to him being moved to the Spike, where he was charged with getting hold of the corruption here. Which he did, killing most of the gangers and running the rest. Tithes returned to what the high cleark required and the rest I imagine Gruslatic enjoys. He's one that's been eating rocks, as we used to say at Epny, lifting stones and logs for strength more than most soldiers. He's not wearing armour, just a thick woollen robe over leggings and shirts. Couldn't be mistaken for a scholar, bald scarred head, and one scar giving his lip a sneer, a white hook of skin in an otherwise dirty, knotted black beard.

"My girl Crejda says you're a fieldsman? Some new spy for Yblas while he's away south living easy." He looks behind me, to the wagons and those remaining of the crews getting them all harnessed, horses brushed and fed.

"Bray? How's Goose's old sword doing. Wooded this filly yet?" Gruslatic walks up to Bray, who's standing to my left, clasps arms. He slaps Bray's belly then. "Fieldwork's helping this anyway, thought you was getting fat watching carts. Might be he'll want to work for me now, Crejda; can't smell betony on him at all."

Bray clasps arms with him strongly enough, but he struggles to meet the castellan's eyes. I mistake it for fear, but only for a moment.

"I's been put straight by her. She's bringing these vans home, helped I with the droop an' nearly got I killed a few times. You're lookin' well, Grus." He glances over at Crejda, who's dismounted. I wonder if she'll read into it what he meant.

Being close to me now, Gruslatic looks me up and down. He makes a point of staring at my babs a bit longer than the rest, then the leathers get his attention more.

159

"You don't report to Stroff then?"

"No."

"Good man, Stroff, gets things done. Should've been the High Red long ago. That right, Crejda?" He's smiling, making his mischief.

"Yblas is a capable High Red. We are not diminished in Farlsgrad, as you say, thanks to the diligence of Administrator Stroff." She might think herself clever with that, but why waste breath answering such a question. It should be beneath her, unless he has some hold over her or she's humouring him. I'm beginning to think the clearks and reeves of all the guilds in the Spike are running it for themselves and Gruslatic, not their guildmasters. He's another problem I don't need. He at least has some power over me, as he does everyone here, and I doubt a scruple ever turned a hair of his grey.

"I heard you killed the Hidzuc chief, Fieldsman," says Gruslatic.

"I did. There's trouble in the Sathanti Peaks and we'd be wise to have parley with the Ilkashun and Hidzucs. We must—"

He holds a hand up. "Are we to expect a few hundred Sathanti herders and farmers to bring war to Farlsgrad, mightiest of all the kingdoms in the north? Eh? Well, we might if we have merchants going about killing their leaders." He puts his hands on his hips, turns his back on me, shakes his head like a player of dramas would. There's some polite laughter from the handful of crews belonging to the vans that are around us. He continues speaking with his back to me. "Or do you mean by parley that we must stop them from killing themselves? With Eirakh Hidzuc out of the way, I will enjoy making new terms with his widow. She is in a delicate position with her confederacy and needs our strength." I take a breath rather than remind him he's talking a bit too freely of such things.

160

"How many lots do we sell into the Sathanti confederacies south of the range every year?" I say. "Without parley we may sell none."

"The Hidzuc will still treat with us, as the castellan says." Crejda this is. "They must have their kannab after all."

"Reeve Crejda, the Ilkashun mean to bring their confederacy down on the Hidzuc lodge and take everything. Is that what Marghoster wants, now arming Hidzuc has failed so spectacularly? Or was that his plan?"

No, it wasn't a wise thing to say before the Marghoster cleark, not wise to bait Crejda either. But as I learned at Posthouse Amondsen with Yblas and Stroff, these pricks are obsessed with status and if I'm a fieldsman I can't have her lining up against me with a ganger in all but name, regardless of how badly she or whoever owns her wants me dead.

Gruslatic turns back to face me.

"While I decide whether or not you're being treasonous, I'll remind you who runs the Spike and who owns you while you're on its lands. Me, Fieldsman. Here and now isn't right for talking the politics of it all, I can see this van need drink, a good bath and likely a good fuck and I'll make sure they all get it before nightfall. Can't have been much fun on this sour bitch's watch, can it, Thelg?"

He looks over my shoulder to where Thelg must have now made himself seen.

"I'll be glad of a bath and of seeing my keep again, I know that, master Castellan."

"Maybe the legendary Weeper will make a tour of my brothel with me?"

"Betony takes your wood wi' everythin' else, Grus. I needs a bed is all."

"More for me an' a few o' the Marghoster crewmen then. Driwna, you, Crejda and Lighroz will come to my quarters

161

at the tower tomorrow morning. There I'll have your field report and inform you of what I plan to do."

"Yes, Castellan," says Crejda.

"Yes, Castellan," I say, desperate to see him back on his horse and off.

Crejda walks up then, as Gruslatic mounts and leaves us be. Lighroz walks past us to Thelg to see what's what with the vans.

"Yes, Lighroz, I am also gratified to see these crews safely back," I say as he walks past. Ignorant fucker.

I'd hoped I could work out what to say to Crejda before seeing her, but she's here so that's done.

"Fieldsman, well done on bringing the vans back from the Sathanti Peaks. Morril will be delighted. Did we lose many of the crew out there?"

"Two, and two mercs Morril sent after the van. Gennic and the others are fine, they left us two days back, should be at Lindur in a day or two if the trails have been kept."

"I'll be glad of a report ahead of our visit to the tower tomorrow."

"We can expect a boost to our trade with the Ilkashun if the parley is approved. You're in good standing with Gruslatic, I trust you'll back me if only for the boost to our trade here."

"Of course, Fieldsman. That's excellent." She's said it reflexively, stumped for something to add to that. I expect the meaning of all those mercs and the Hidzuc aggression could lead a bit too close to how I was attacked. I'll save her the embarrassment for now, and she'll know I'm doing it and all.

"Let me lead these vans in, Reeve, find myself a bath and some time to clean and treat these leathers and my belts, then I'll be with you at the sheds. Thank you for releasing Bray to ride with me. He's an excellent man to have in the field." He's close enough he can hear this of course. "I doubt he'll want to go back to guarding the sheds and we mustn't lose him to another guild. There's none know these confederacies and their ways like him."

"Thank you, Fieldsman. Thank you, Bray, you've done our Posthouse proud."

"Reeve," he says.

They clasp arms, then she has the fucking nerve to offer her arm to me. I take it. "See you tonight, Reeve," I say.

The moment she's ridden off and Lighroz, with a conciliatory nod, follows her, Bray joins me on the lead wagon.

"Can't believe she took I's arm after tryin' to have us killed, miss."

"What else could she have done?"

"You din't challenge her on it."

"No, not here, not now. Not you that's wanted dead, and I hope you don't feel bad with how that sounds. I can't prove it wasn't some bandits or mercs trying their luck on two travellers."

"Happy to be o' no consequence an' breathin' a few year longer."

"Glad to hear it."

"Watch that castellan, miss. Not a right bone in 'im."

"I know."

A bit of snow, not cold enough to settle, sees us into the Spike. Though it's still busy on the river, all the harvest trade has died back. Thelg and those left alive of the Marghoster vans point us to the Marghoster sheds where Lighroz is waiting, along with some family of those both alive and dead. At first there's a cheer to see the vans, as much from the crews about the sheds as those that have come to find out if their loved ones have come home. Then they see how few are with us and they have a right go at Lighroz,

163

asking that they get coin for their loss and one at least is reminding him that the Post sees the family of their dead right and that it's a disgrace that Marghoster don't. This makes me happy. A few guards appear then to threaten the women wanting some coin for what happened, for they're pushing Lighroz about and he's as sturdy as a young willow and there's one just screaming at him. Hard to blame her, for how will she eat now with winter here?

Thelg's keep comes up to us then, as his crew have come forward from the wagons they were driving and are finding keeps, sons, daughters, muns and pas.

"You're safe," she says to him. She seems worn with work herself. She has their son with her, ten or twelve summers to look at. He puts his arms round his pa and Thelg looks over at me.

"Thank you, Fieldsman." First he's said it.

"Was her, was it?" his keep asks. "Got you home?"

"They'd have killed us all if not for her; she persuaded their chief to let us come home."

"You're a red. You don't work with my Thelg?"

"No, miss. We had a van lost too, I went out there to help. Thelg might explain better than me why so many died there."

I'm glad he's alive, but fuck him. He can tell her how they tried to kill the Ilkashun nokes while their warriors were fighting in the fields against Hidzucs.

"He's home for midwinter and I'm grateful," she says. "Now, Thelg, you make sure that drip of a cleark Lighroz sees you right for coin. Don't let him twist you up with his words like he always does. You'll go looking to work with this one and the Post if he don't put things right." With this she puts her arms around him and his face into her neck. She's been fearing the worst, the way she's shaking, the relief burning off her.

164

Me and Bray leave their sheds and the scritching going on there to find a bath and some hot food.

"Think they'll have a room with a bath in the Doris, Bray?"

"Might be lucky, most who can afford it goes to the tower. The rooms are worked by the whores usually."

"Might Alaqua be working?"

He shakes his head, knowing what I was meaning by it. "She's lovely, miss, but she can't make her patter genuine enough I'd think she has an interest. Besides, she in't one o' the whores, though she was a while back."

"Might be worth giving her a few pennies extra, if it don't bother you either way. I said I'd settle with you for your help and it'll be a good purse, a lot more than you'd have earned watching that gate. Might be she's looking for a man not given to taking whores and who's got himself clean."

"She'll think it's a jump I's after. I can't . . ."

I put my arm around him. "I know, you said. I'm sorry. I confess I'm wondering whether it's really the droop any more now you're off it or whether it's a bit more about your pride."

He twitches, pulls slightly from my arm. "You tryin' to fix I? Not seen this in your creed, taking pity on old soaks. It say that in there?"

I've misjudged us a bit. "Sorry, Bray. No, you don't need fixing. No, you don't need a jump and you haven't talked about it or even tried it with me. How you conducted yourself in the field, and saved my life, well, it makes me give a shit about you and I'm sorry for that."

"Sorry, miss. Course if I's pennies to spare she'd be a good way to spend 'em. Seen her a couple o' times when she's not workin'. When she is, think her mun has the dut, and her mun's a bit old for such caring. Can barely lift the thing, last I saw when I be running messages up to the tower. Alaqua could do better than I, though."

165

"I doubt it, from what I know of men. Look, I got coin to spare, Bray, I have a purse given me for furthering the Post's interests. Won't hurt to have someone watching and listening in the Doris anyway. If I can get a room and a bath there, you make sure to get us some food and suggest to Alaqua that she could make some serious coin letting you know what's being said and done in there, plant as well for those she loves. Won't do if she's seen speaking to me."

"Will do, miss. She'll appreciate it, her and the dut I's sure."

"About time we got you some new boots, leggings and a jerkin and all. You've lost some fat out in the Peaks."

He smiles then, briefly, knowing that I'm doing it to goad him.

Inside the Doris I'm told there's a bath in its own room I can use that's shared by whoever takes one of their cots, there being only two other rooms and four cots in each. It's Alaqua that I hear making the fire and putting a pot of water over it to warm. She drops me in a brush, pail of water and a flask of alka that I'll use to wash the rubs off my skin and feel clean for a day or two I hope.

I get out of my leathers and give them a wipe down with water and alka, then get my needle and gut, gum and patches and wax. There's holes from Ufra's thorns need sealing up and I'm glad to have the cleaning and repairs to concentrate on, for the thought of her, the memory of her holding me, kissing me, has me staring off to nowhere.

I hear then, outside the door, footsteps and a musical humming, followed by a drum of fingers on the door and it takes me a moment to place where I've heard it before.

"Cal!"

He opens the door, not entering yet.

"Driw?"

"Stay there a moment. Let me get my shirt back on."

"Entertaining?"

"Fuck off."

"Saving it for me I hope?"

"I'll never let a Rulger have it."

He laughs.

"Come in."

He's not field ready, no belts or leathers, just a robe, leggings and a cloak, all dirty from travel. He looks about the room at all my things over the floor. "How's anyone else going to get a few hours' sleep if they can't get to their cot because of your shit?" He can't hide from his eyes that he's pleased to see me and it makes me glad.

I stand and throw my arms around him. He's looking worn out and stinks, but there's his smell with it all, the comfort of him being alive and returned to me.

"I couldn't hope you'd be here, Driw, but I'll have your news and you can have mine, what you haven't picked up already. There won't be anyone else in this room, I paid enough for that."

He kisses my cheek, keeps holding me. The small scars of Ufra's itch. She's not wrong about something being in my blood, for I miss her even with Cal here.

"I missed you, Driw," he says. "I heard you nearly lost your life out there. Hidzucs sent an army."

"Not that many, but enough that half of the Canendrigh kurch, one of the Ilkashun kin-kurches, was killed. Cal, there's a lot going on, a lot of trouble."

"You don't need to tell me."

"Sit with me. We can bathe when the water's hot." I lean back from the embrace, kiss him and clear some of my kit away from the cot.

"No need, Driw, got a room with a bath at the tower; Yblas's

167

purse was a heavy one for the work he asked me for. Sillindar knows what you're doing in this fleapit. I can even see fleas on the bloody mat." He nearly gets me to turn around to see where he's pointing, and gets a dig in his shoulder for the joke.

"I get to feed some fleas for more interesting conversation, I hope. It's the crews come in here from all the sheds about and they gab after a few cups."

"Fair. How was Gennic and the crew?"

"We lost Ladruk and Calicz. Those cunts working for Marghoster turned on us and the Ilkashun when the horns blew and the Hidzucs came at the lodge, like they knew there would be an attack. Gennic and the rest came through well, the van's gone back to Lindur."

"Morril was worried sick I'll bet. I saw Bray downstairs, that guard from our sheds with that feast of a barmaid. You took him with you I heard. Hope he was more use to you than he is with her; she's giving him the fluttering eyes, pawing him a bit."

"Turns out he's the Weeper, the Grey Goose's man."

"What? The Weeper? Fuck off is he."

"True, love. He helped me take on six with fightbrews in them and us only on dayers. Crafty fucker and only a sliver of the kind of health and strength you need in the field. Can't imagine how he was in his prime. I learned a lot from him."

"Where's my ink and quill; here's a song, 'The Weeper and the Woman Who Made Him Cry Again'."

He gets another dig for that.

"I have to meet him, all these years I've been singing songs of him. But Driw, look at him, I thought he'd be . . . well, *more*."

"Betony."

"Ah fuck."

"The bar girl, Alaqua . . ."

168

"Alaq-what?"

"Don't, I know. He's giving her some coin to keep her eyes and ears open. Might be why she's all flirty. Tell me what's happened with you since I last saw you."

"Wish I could give you some good news, Driw, but your pa's dealing in slaves by the look of it."

I know my pa had hardened in his ways once we'd settled on Rulger land, I know as well he's a ganger, but slave-trading is something different, for Sathanti don't hold with slaves. It breaks my heart.

"Worse is your ma isn't good either. Got the wasting I think. Her voice, she can hardly speak and struggles to swallow. I think you should go back and see her." He puts his hand on my knee, squeezes it. It's upset him for he's met them before and my mun especially loves him.

"It upset me to see her so. And your da has to be taking it badly, and not just being a cunt to me because I'm there from Yblas to ask him about raiding vans and the like. All the while he's mouthing off she's waiting on us. He's got his gangers in there with him and she's waiting on them when it's him that should be waiting on her. Sorry, Driw."

"What did he have to say for himself?"

"Couldn't deny it, for I'd found where the slaves were being kept by accident. I was looking for somewhere in among some trees to rest up once I'd got among the fens. There were tracks leading to what I thought must have been a farm, but it's a barn, and guarded. From the sounds I could tell there was people inside, but then I saw the slave wagons and managed to sneak up to them. From Ullavir they were, names on the wagons painted over or scratched out, but from the bits of letters I saw I think I know the merchant who they belonged to, so they've either had them stolen by your pa or they're part of it, and that'll be easy to find out.

"In the main room of the house there's all the trappings of a ganger, lot of barrels stacked up, boxes, weapons and arrows enough for a big crew. If any of the king's militia walked in there they'd have him before a reeve in no time. He's still talking about how they're treated as refugees, how the collectors are always at his door and the tithes going up, still getting abuse at the Rethic markets and never seeing any militia or reeves giving them justice. Before I got there I stopped by some roadcamps, shared plant and coin, and it seems your pa's lands are often avoided now, and the militia don't go there much. Some are saying he's got an agreement with militia, so he might well be lying to me."

"What did you offer him?"

"To back off? Everything I had. More than I had. Made out with my coming from Yblas that nothing would be too much trouble, the seal doing its bit to confirm it. He said there's nothing the Post could give him."

I reach about for my pipe, Cal finds it in my pack, along with my bacca and my jumpcrick bones for making a spark.

"I need to see my mun then." I can't hide from him how upset I am. "She didn't look too bad last I was home." Though this was a few years before, when I'd had word I was to go to the academy at Posthouse Epny over in Citadel Hillfast to become a red. The kurches that survived the wandering we did from Sathanti to Lindur, then Rulger land, had finally found a settle in the Rethic Fens. By then my pa and his crew of chiefs and others that had paid some colour had pillaged as they needed to keep us alive. Only a few kurches with a few families in each had made it to the fens. There's where I lost my brun, Leif, killed for nothing in jail. It was the same with a few other sons of our confederacy. All the while since I had joined the Post, as Yblas had said, I was making sure I could send back what I could and give them contracts for whatever they could sell. Mun would send notes for me along with our crews that passed by the fens, but Pa wouldn't. She'd talk about how things were with Eli my younger brun, and how my pa was doing well from our trade, though what trade she wrote of was far more than I could have given them. I said nothing on it, for had the Rulgers, whose vans he had been raiding, not killed my brun, their son?

Mun never once complained of her own problems.

"Want me to get your grit and give you a scrub, Driw? Might make you feel better to wash the trail off you and get into something a bit cleaner. That's if you have anything besides what you're wearing." He kisses the top of my head and lets me gather myself.

"That would be good; need to get these rubs off me before I get more problems. How's your ma, Cal? Tell me while we sort me out a bath."

He goes through to the room with the bath in and I hear him and Alaqua share a word as she brings more water up. There's a giggle, and I can't be sure it's hers, before he returns.

"She's nearly done with the water; another couple of pots on the fire and it'll be ready."

"You'll wait until you're back at the tower? You're not exactly smelling of perfume."

"Aye, I'll wait, love. Be a bit too cosy for us both, that tub. My ma, well it was lovely to see her. More lovely to show my uncle Edral's guards my seal from Yblas and then see his face as he has to invite me into the castle. He tried to tell me she was away and was about to usher me into his gatehouse, but she saw me from a window and came downstairs. Makes me sick him wanting that; told me later it was to spare her the upset of being reminded of me. Cunt.

"So she insists we have some tea, for Edral has some fine leaves brought in from Cassica, strong and all. I could have run back here from his estate after a few cups and they livened my ma up wonderful, full of stories she was about her and Barolt and none of the moping and sorrow that he brought us before he left. These were stories of them younger, and the look on Edral's face as she said a few things a son doesn't want to hear, never mind a brother-in-law that wants in her skirts. I loved her for it. I doubt it's always as merry there, and she's got some grey in her hair now, younger than she'd hoped she'd be when it turned; said her ma didn't go grey till she was more than fifty summers. Not many gets longer than that, do they." It bites him, this last thought, for without the seal of Yblas he might not see her again, such was the agreement signed and witnessed. I hold his hand then.

"I would have loved to see her, Cal."

"She asked after you of course, and it was my business anyway to tell Edral that you've been made fieldsman. Shocked, he was, and she was delighted, clapped her hands and was saying "my Driwna a fieldsman", and asking me to make you my keep for there's no other I can speak of that's in line for it."

"You are getting on a bit now, Cal."

"You can wash your own grit off, Marghoster filth."

"And Edral's not up to anything with his vans?"

"Not as I can tell. He listed the vans he's lost and some near enough to the fens that your pa's heading for trouble if he keeps it up. One thing Edral rarely does is slaves, and he's had no trade I can tell to or from Hillfast, so I don't think he's running any vans knowingly carrying Oskoro."

"Edral's one quality is how straight he is," I say. "But it makes me worry for what my pa might be involved in if he's raiding. Can't see why Rulger, on his own land, hasn't got militia going in there to root our kurches out."

"Those roadcamps were tight-lipped about the fensmen for the most part," says Cal. "It was those not planning to return that were willing to talk to me for some coin. Those that make a living near there were saying nothing. Your pa's a serious ganger, and if he's moving slaves, then he's working with some big guilds, maybe even rivals of a merchant such as Edral. Might explain how he knows of the Rulger vans, if he's working with some gangers out of Ullavir."

"Ullavir's where she's come in, our baby girl. The Ullavir family gave up seeking a lordship at court and mind their own over on the coast, pay their dues from the port and appear generous doing it according to Lindur's reeve. But they can barely manage with the number of boats coming through. Flies about shit I reckon."

"Driw, we can't know our own aren't lining their pockets or getting involved in whatever's coming through on some wharf or other jetty hidden along the coves south of the port."

"I know." I close my eyes, take a breath. I'm struggling to work out what to do.

"Come on, let's get you in that bath. I'm sick of seeing your bare arse."

What many don't get when a soldier says that you can't prepare for war alone is that it means, as often as not, working in the skin rubs to protect against spores and cuts and poison, as well as giving each other the luta or bilberry, and the fightbrews of course. It's common enough then that in a camp, as in this small but now warm room with the bath, a soldier has to stand naked while the alka and grit are worked in with a brush, and never a soft ladies' hairbrush, more a horse's brush. Fuck it hurts, and Cal's thorough, as he must be. Leave rubs on too long and the skin goes bad. He doesn't have to do as much scrubbing as he might if I was wounded

173

and couldn't reach most of my body myself, but he sees the holes the thorns left no sooner had I got my shirt off.

"Fell in a few nail traps, Driw?"

"I fell in the arms of an Ososi girl I met at the Ilkashun lodge."

"Really?" He stands in front of me then, big smile on him. "Was she half a rosebush, half a woman? You're a hot sauce for sure, and if you prefer kissing plants these days. Well, I won't take it personally."

"Her name's Ufra. I can't describe it, Cal, how I feel. I can't stop thinking about her. Her thorns have given me her blood, it runs in me, grows in me and it thrills me."

I guess from the moment he's taking in what I said that he knows what the Ososi bond might mean.

"How much of it is her, Driw, and how much the pull of the plant she's put in you? You've known her for days, weeks?"

"I know I've not spent much time with her, Cal, and it's not that I haven't thought about my feelings being pulled about by her blood. She was a thrill to look upon the moment we met and she's chosen me for her blood having known me in equally short measure. It's not something they give about freely. I was with her on a brew, an Oskoro brew, the blood of the Master of Flowers, their chief. I've never seen anyone so fully and clearly as her and she was beautiful all the way down."

"I get it, Driw, I just need to know she deserves you."

"It's more I don't feel I deserve her."

He's still a moment, takes both my hands in his and squeezes them. He's trying to find words, but love fills years, not words. He lifts my hands instead to his lips, kissing them.

"Fuck, Driwna, that makes me happy. You have changed and it suits you, love. You know, if you can get me a vial of whatever's in her veins maybe I can bag the woman of my dreams too." He steps towards the bath so that he can help me in it. It's cool, the water, but once I'm standing in it he gets the mitts and the pot off the fire and pours the water in around my legs. It's a lovely feeling and I sit down. He adds some alka and tincture of euca leaves.

"I hope you can meet her. But that isn't up to us, is it?"

"No, love. So let us talk of duty. Tomorrow, Driw, you're seeing that shitpot of a castellan, right?"

"In the morning. Wants a report of what happened with the Ilkashun. I need to get a parley agreed by midwinter and Marghoster needs to be at it to answer for why he supported the Hidzucs in their attack on the Ilkashun. Claims he knows nothing of who's buying the slaves and plant that were getting moved on up to the mountains and his crew didn't seem to know much, not unless I wanted to undertake some torture. You've heard about the kidnappings, but all over the Lakes there's some big Ososi hunter scaring the shit out of everyone."

"Scar?"

"Yes. He's supposedly taking children and the old from the Ososi, yet he's not fussy about who his crew kidnaps of the kurches there," I say. "The Ilkashun chief thinks it's Farlsgrad and he's willing to go to war, perhaps believing he'll get some other confederacies, support if they've suffered like his with the kidnappings. Now, tell me, have you seen Crejda? You're not in your cloak and haven't said why."

"I haven't. I stopped by Lindur, saw Morril before taking a messenger here. The Brask merchants came to Morril while we've been away, and a messenger had come from the Gate, from Rogus, a roll that instructed us to do our best to supply the Brasks with whatever farlswood, iron and plant for soldiers we could spare, at barely pennies over cost."

"Rogus?" It makes no sense.

"The seal was genuine. Morril could do nothing else. I came here to see if Crejda had received a similar missive,

175

before riding on up to the Gate to understand the why of it. I thought, as Crejda's barely met me and her crew not at all, I could keep some sort of watch, to tally what she might say to me with what I see of the lots going on the wagons and coming in from the field or other traders. Cost me a fair bit of coin chasing after those that were unloading barges and cogs off the river, and what's bound for us is, mostly, iron and leather, the latter hides of course, but also quivers, feathers, ash and yew wood."

"Arrows then. The sheds have a forge?"

"Here, yes, but we never saw it. You can hear the hammering from the gate and there's more than one at it."

"Really? One smith's a luxury at an outpost like this, and no high cleark's sanctioned two in peacetime outside of the Gate or Epny I'm sure."

"I agree, Driw. And more again, there's armourers, both linen and leather I've seen passing in and out of our gates, two curriers were here yesterday evening talking of how busy they've been with both us and the Marghoster sheds. Crejda can't hide it all, Driw. I'll bet my cock it's going west."

"She wants a report about what's gone on out there tonight, before we meet with Gruslatic. Didn't demand it of course, but it makes sense, while we're pretending to be on the same level with each other, that I go along. Cal, I'm going to ask Bray to go in my stead."

"Why?"

"I can't prove it, but I think she tried to have me killed on the trail out from Hidzucs to the Ilkashun."

"You think Crejda did that? Fucking Sillindar, Driw, you've got a seal can bury her just for your even suspecting such a thing."

"It's not how I want to work this. It'll seal up lips across the whole crew and put them against me. She can deny it was anyone but bandits. But Bray is her man and in asking him to give an account of what went on, to lean on their friendship, I might find out what she's hiding."

"Or she'll think he's yours now and say fuck all. But if he's really her man?"

"That's a chance I'm going to take. I see a change in him, Cal, some fire in his belly, like a lion waking up after a long sleep."

"A fat, old lion."

I have to smile at this. "A fat, old lion. Fine. But I need an ally here and he's my best bet so far. Will you tell Alaqua that she should fetch him up here after I'm dressed?"

"I will. What do you need me to do?"

"We need to know if Rogus really did approve the trades at cost. If not, then we know there's someone corrupt at Posthouse Amondsen and Rogus'll help us. I can't see him being involved in this, but who knows."

"My second's seal should be enough to get me on the messenger horses up the Fifth to the Gate quick enough I can be back here for the parley, if you're aiming for midwinter. It's two weeks, which I should manage if I take the messenger horses."

"I need you here, Cal, no matter what might happen with the parley, at least until you have to leave me again to fulfil your role at Lindur. I'll do what I can to send word out to the Ilkashun and Hidzucs tomorrow."

"Morril's going to have a new second by the time I'm back."

"I'll have to make it up to her."

"Will you go see your mun?"

He reads the guilt I feel about as quickly as I do, knows to let me feel it and not try to soften it.

"I must, but not before the parley. I have to call Gennic

177

here from Lindur as well; his testimony will be important in what's to come."

"See her as soon as you can, love."

"I will. Right, fetch me the orobanche grease. I know a night on that mat in the corner would make me a feast otherwise, and I'd like to go a day or so without some lice."

"I'll get Bray sent up shortly. I'll see you at the parley."

"Another farewell not an hour after you walk in. Sillindar follow you, Cal. Be safe."

He fetches the pot of grease and kisses me. The wounds of the thorns send a tremor through me.

"Bath's getting cold I see," he says with a wink.

"Filth, go on with you."

The ancient, white tower that gives the Spike its name looks ready to withstand a siege, though it's not since before the border troubles that cost the Bridche confederacy our kurch-lands that it's witnessed one. The arrow loops have not been made into windows at any floor of its height, excepting the floor beneath the battlements where the rich, and Cal, pay a fine few pennies to lodge. The battlement that skirts the roof's cone still has a watch keeping an eye on the lands about in every direction. Closer up, the fragments of wall spikes from sieges past remain as splinters in the otherwise huge stone blocks. I imagine the wall surrounding the tower, being well kept and manned; is meant to remind all who pass through that the Spike is ready to prick the ambitions of anyone looking to trouble the south-west borders of Farlsgrad.

The courtyard before the great farlswood doors to the tower itself is mostly in the shadow of the walls, themselves ringed with the stables, workshop and barracks of the small garrison. There are no stalls or anyone not expressly on business with the tower's castellan, clearks or craftsmen. I'm made to wait at the bottom of the steps to the doors, attracting the attention of some of those off duty washing in barrels, or grooming and feeding the horses, sweeping dung and forking straw. There's two in the smith's shop singing as they work. One blows me a kiss so I blow one back. I'd rather see a smile than a scowl, and I'm struggling to keep the latter from my own brow at the thought of having to treat with Gruslatic. I've done my best to prepare.

"Good morning, Fieldsman." Crejda this is, walking up to stand next to me, a small satchel in her hands. She wears the cloak but no leathers. I wish I could feel safe enough not to wear my own, but it doesn't hurt to flaunt my status here and it took much of last evening cleaning them and polishing the metalwork on all my gear.

"Good morning, Reeve. My apologies for not seeing you last night; I have had missives from Lindur and the Gate to attend to, and I'm sure Bray was more than happy to relay to you the details of our journey into the Ilkashun lands and back."

"He did," she says. "Most thorough. There's much trouble in the Lakes at the moment I fear. I don't expect much success with this idea for a parley, do you?"

"I wouldn't waste my time petitioning for one if I didn't. Why would you say that?"

"From Bray's account this Ilkashun chief has problems with his kurch chiefs and he'll be making impossible demands on us to allay their fears."

"Yet against their wishes he agreed to see the Marghoster and Post lots returned, minus whichever slaves chose to leave, for those are their beliefs on the matter of slaves."

"You'd know best."

"What the fuck does that mean?"

"Begging your pardon, Fieldsman, nothing whatsoever. Did you imagine I was speaking ill of you as Sathanti? I was

179

only pointing out that as Sathanti, you'd know better than me what to expect of them."

She's failed if she thinks polishing the facet of her words that the insult relied upon would erase it. I'm tempted to tear into her about her bullshit when a guard appears from inside the tower to gesture us to follow him in.

For all the torches lit and sconced about the walls, I imagine the dark of the passages and lack of furnishings add to Gruslatic's image of himself as a hard and uncompromising man. The screams from somewhere below us are no doubt useful to him in that regard and the cells of the Spike are famous throughout Farlsgrad for their squalor and brutality.

We're led up one stairwell to the first floor. Three gloomy rooms full of clearks we pass before we're shown into Castellan Gruslatic's room. There's a fire going, taking the chill out of the air, and it's well lit with lamps otherwise. Other than a dresser and his mat in the corner of the room, the only furniture in here is five chairs and a table on which sits a jug and some pewter mugs.

He's sitting cleaning his pipe. Next to him sits Lighroz, already puffing away at his own pipe. Odd that a young man smoking is made to seem younger and more foolish than an older man with the same.

"Sit," says Gruslatic. He's wearing a leather jerkin, worn smooth to a shine over the years. He sees me looking at the rather primitive carvings on the chair he's bid me sit on.

"I've always had a liking for carving and too little fucking time to do much about it, eh, Crejda? Always clearks needing their arses wiping, tallies checking, tithes counted and lotted. But I'll get some done today. I made all the chairs in this room."

"They're strong, big enough for giants, these chairs,' I say, finding nothing else good I could say about them. The

180

insinuation regarding Scar passes him by, as I expected, but it pleases me to have said it all the same.

"I won't have a fat merchant embarrassed if he's visiting and a profit's to be made, and all the rich ones are fat. So let's get this done and I can get on. Fieldsman, you have called for a parley at which we'll have Hidzucs and Ilkashun, recently having been killing each other, along with some tree fuckers, your Post lot, and you're asking for Lord Marghoster too."

"That's it, yes. I would send word to them immediately, for any grievances held will not profit from festering."

"Do you imagine you'll be in charge of all this, Marghoster? I'll save us some time. You won't. If Crejda can't manage it, and I'm sure she's too busy, then I can trust Stroff, but anybody else, no."

Cock.

"I'm grateful you've invited me along to tell me that."

"Lighroz here believes a parley might better achieve a profitable resolution. Easiest way to manage it all in my view as well. I ask myself if you even need to be at this parley at all? You must have more urgent things to attend to as a, what is it, fieldsman? It sounds grand, and your leathers look grand, sewn-in plates I'll wager. But I'm castellan here, the parley concerns Farlsgrad and these Sathanti. I speak on behalf of and in the interests of King Hildmir. I am King Hildmir as far as you're concerned, girl. Lighroz here's grateful for the lots that were returned, though crewmen lost and sixty slaves freed will be part of any settlement discussion I'm sure." He gets his pipe lit, holds up his hand while he draws on it to bring the bacca to life. "Ah, is that a satchel, Crejda? You remembered?"

"Of course I remembered, Castellan. Two pounds of bacca, two bottles of Cassican rum."

Gruslatic claps his hands in delight.

"Crejda and Lighroz here know how to manage their sheds, unlike some that trade here. Stroff is always pleased with how efficiently our trade goes. Do fieldsmen not . . ."

"Bribe, Castellan? Of course, when the advantage is clear and it doesn't interfere with the Creed that all in the Post must now follow."

"Creed? Crejda, have you some new set of rules to put in the cesspit with the rest?" This makes him laugh.

"The Farlsgrad Creed no less, Castellan. Honour the purse, Peace through trade, Help the helpless." Crejda this is, speaking the words with the measured, faint note of a child's recital.

There's a moment of him just smiling, looking about us as though we are to get the joke, before he tips his head back laughing, again, and slaps his thighs in delight. Lighroz does his best to stifle his own mirth, while Crejda has to keep her face straight as she sits next to me.

"Help the helpless? Well, I've heard it all now, Marghoster, I really have."

Of course my blood's boiling, but I glance down at my hands to count through my breaths and I find myself amused, grateful that Gruslatic has brought attention to my leathers, reminded me of my status. I represent Yblas. I need to pursue our interest here.

"I've been asked to meet and bring in the Ilkashun and the Ososi parties. They may not trust anybody else given recent events. I will therefore need to be at the parley."

"What have they to fear from us, Marghoster?"

"Most of the Hidzuc chief's strength in battle came from the Lord Marghoster's mercenaries, while some were heard to say they were on Hildmir's purse. I'm sure the tallies and the dead would find alignment in the records of Reeve Lighroz or Hildmir. As such, the Ilkashun might fear that as Farlsgrad has backed the aggression, passing through Hidzuc land to get here leaves them exposed."

The smile leaves his face, of course. He draws on his pipe, clenching it in his teeth and leans forward.

"Crejda, may I trouble you to break the wax on that rum?"

"Of course, Castellan, thank you. Such fine spirit from so far south is beyond the coin I earn."

I'm meant to see them exchange a brief glance.

"Is such rum beyond the coin of a fieldsman, Marghoster?"

"Yes and no, Castellan. Yes because I have not yet received a penny for my service as fieldsman, being new to it, and no because I have been given sufficient coin to execute any and all duties I see fit to by Yblas."

He nods at this, then drops a small knife from his sleeve into his hand, working away at the wax on the bottle Crejda's given him.

"The chief of the Ilkashun is a desperate man. A hard winter beckons his tribe of mud-fishers and he thinks a few lots won't be missed by those rich, well-fed Farlsgrad folk to the east. The slaves might have been useful as food for those Ososi animals they worship, in exchange for their plant and their promises to persuade the snow to stay in the north and the sun to burn a little stronger on us all. No good lord would leave his crews and lots to be so stolen when they could and should expect the vans to pass through according to the treaties and agreements we all work to." He pours us all a generous measure of the rum. I know each cup probably has a silver's worth in it, such is the price the Cassicans charge for it. "This chief talks of people all over his lands being taken for slaves, going missing and never to return?" he says. "That an Ososi, one of their allies, might even be leading a crew in the undertaking of it all? Forgive me, Fieldsman, but do you believe all that?"

"Yes, Castellan. Many summers of good trade and good relations under Chief Yicre's leadership come to this, while troubles along the Sathanti border north suggest something is wrong."

He takes a mouthful of rum, savours it, then leans back in his chair, the only one that's had a padded cushion pinned to it.

"Crejda tells me you are Bridche, in truth, not Marghoster? But you take the name of Marghoster given you in shame and presume to wear it, I imagine, with a view to numbing the insult, to wear the needle of it to a nub."

"I am Bridche."

"You killed Eirakh, the Hidzuc chief."

"I did, or I would have been killed by him."

"Your fa must be proud of you, if the news has carried as far as the Rethic Fens."

"I doubt it has; few wagons need go through the fens."

"Need or dare?" Lighroz this is. I let this one go. It's good rum and the only cup I'll get from Gruslatic.

"If something bothers me, Fieldsman, I'll come out and say it. I do, don't I, Lighroz, come out and say it?"

"You do, Castellan."

"You bother me, Fieldsman. No, that's not right, you concern me, twice over. The one concern is that your fa and you are not such strangers as you'd have us believe, and you're cutting a deal with the Ilkashun to see the Hidzuc land returned to you. Who'd want to scratch a living in the fens? It stinks, it's bad land that Edral Rulger was glad to have some tithe from." He holds a hand up before I can reply.

"But that's outlandish, I've no evidence for that. You are young, though; perhaps it's the chief that's put some thought into your head regarding compensation for your service to him, for ridding him of a rival. I'd pay a fine purse to be rid of my rival and not have the blood on my own hand, but on a citizen of Farlsgrad. I might promise a cut of any land to those that have their kin's bones under foreign kurch-poles, make myself an ally at the same cut."

"There opia in your bacca, Castellan?" I say.

Calm as you like he says, "Don't fucking dare to presume you can play a game under this nose, girl. There's many reasons you're not fit for this parley and I gave you some at the outset. I'll head out to these Ilkashun and Ososi fuckers myself and bring them in. You'll be nowhere near the Spike, because it is the will of the king."

I finish my rum in a swig, and I stand.

"It's important I give you a fair impression of my remit as a fieldsman, Castellan. None but the king himself is above you in the lands you run. So it is with me and the Post, over the wide world in which we trade. If I think it's better for the Post to pull out of the Spike entirely then that is what the Post will fucking do. Ten per cent of all that coin each and every month might find its way to Lindur's reeve and not you. Sorry, the king — I meant the king, of course. I won't ask you who provides the biggest tithes each month to your coffers because we both know the answer. If you wish me to leave the Spike I can do so tonight. The Post will soon follow."

He stands himself, sharply, steps towards me, a far bigger man than I am a woman. He jabs a big sausage of a finger at my collarbone. I'm sure I'll have my knife in him before the one in his sleeve finds me, so I hold my ground.

"You're not above Stroff you arrogant little cunt, nor the king of Farlsgrad," he says.

"Nobody is above the king. As for who has the ear of the High Red, I suppose we'll see."

"Get out, Marghoster. I don't want to catch sight of you, not until I get Stroff here."

185

I search for a comeback, but decide he isn't worth it. He knows I'm going to be at the parley.

It could have gone better, I know, and the way Crejda was mooning about him should have told me that clearer; she's no mug. But fuck his games.

I haven't eaten yet today, so I decide to head for the Post sheds, find Bray.

There's only two weeks until the parley if the Hidzucs, Ilkashun and Ufra are summoned in good time, and depending on how I wish to interpret the Creed I had better let Gruslatic be the one to manage this. I've made an enemy of him but only because I won't serve him or give his cock a good pull. Brutal a man as he is, he's comfortable, if that makes sense; had it his way for too long. But he's small, in the eyes of the world, and the world is going to show him just how small he is.

Our sheds are busy. I'm reminded of all the trade Gruslatic would lose, for he's skimming a nice sum I don't doubt, on top of whatever gifts we're giving him. I see Bray on the gate again, the boy with him looking a fair bit more alert this time. I recall the first time I saw Bray, leaning on his pike, but he's a bit more upright this time. The shakes are there, but perhaps they're diminished. Seems he's had a bath and all, trimmed his beard, cut those tufts of hair growing between the scars on his head, his jerkin's clean and even a bit of wax on it. The boy asks for my seal, Bray smiles as he does so.

"Morning, Bray, how are you?"

"Good, miss. Reeve with Gruslatic?"

"She is. Say, what's this one's name?"

"I'm Eukricz, Fieldsman."

"Eukricz, I need you to find a good baker, fresh bread

and brin, and a farmer'll give you a couple of pounds of butter, five pounds of cheese. Breakfast for the crew here." The Post doesn't normally give meals, only rations to those travelling in its service, and messengers get a hot meal and looking after if they're running something urgent. Messengers are our lifeblood, so we have to take care of them most. Eukricz almost jumps with excitement, can't have had much to eat this morning by his reaction. I give him a bag of coppers for it all and he's off.

"What did Crejda have to say to you last night?" I say.

"She listened to I accountin' our travels, asked about the Ososi. Everyone does when they know you met one; always want to be testing their idea o' them wi' what's real an' even then never seem to believe I anyway. She asked if you was always tight sewn-up or if a laugh could be 'ad wi' you. I said a bit o' both."

"That's true! Did you say we'd been attacked on the Hidzuc border?"

"I did, said bandits nearly got us. She said nothin' to that. Kept on about the battle we was in, what was said with you an' the chief, but I was wounded o' course. Asked about the slaves the Marghosters had, then said I hadn't bin paid a rise in a long time an' she was sorry an' would sort it out this week an' I should be expecting a bit of an easier time if I wanted it, helpin' the drudha out as I's some field lore."

"That's good news, Bray, you deserve a rise. I expect she was worried you might have told me her secrets."

"Fuckin' Sillindar, miss, you be tellin' her that, about what's off books?"

I can't help but laugh. "No, Bray, not until I find a way to learn it so's you're not in the frame for breaking her trust. I won't do that to you. It's enough that I know, for now."

187

He shakes his head, hands on his hips, a right fear on him for a moment.

"I can pay you far more, Bray, if you want to help me. Keep an ear out for the things Alaqua says and pass it all on."

"Aye, miss. I be fine with it an' the coin's welcome o' course."

"Good."

He clears his throat. "And, well, if you needs a man wi' you in the field, you could command it, could you? Of Crejda?"

"I could. That means a lot to me, you saying it. You mean a lot to me, Bray. I'd embrace you but tongues'd wag fierce. I hope with the betony gone you can keep off the drink a bit more, keep getting sharper, stronger."

I take five silver pennies from my purse, drop them in his hand. His eyes widen at this, for it's a lot of coin.

"For your service to me so far. I can get more, Bray, don't refuse it. Fieldsman's seal lets me take what I need as I see fit."

"I be most grateful, miss. It's too much, mind."

"It's a purse for keeping me informed. You manage that as you see fit. Nobody trusts me here. I'm staying at the Doris. I've made an enemy of Gruslatic this morning and done myself no favours with Crejda. I'll keep low until this parley comes for us. Might take a horse out for a few days and find some fresh plant to make my belts up with."

"Always glad o' some goldthread if you can find it. I brew's a tea helps make the taste o' drink foul for days after."

"I'll see, but won't be easy to find much this time of year."

I'm about to leave when he gestures to stop me.

"You upset Gruslatic?"

"He was upsetting me, disrespecting me and all."

"He's ice cold, miss. You might be in trouble, for 'e comes down like a mountain on any that offend him, an' that's how he keeps order."

"I'll be careful, Bray."

"There's many been as canny as they could that's not heard of again. Hold there." He hands me his pike, walks back into one of the sheds. He returns with two small pouches. "Titarum seeds in this grey pouch, chalk dust in this brown one."

"I've heard of these seeds, stink bad enough to put you on the ground. Is the chalk to neuter it?"

"Aye. Long as they're not crushed you can hardly smell a thing. Put 'em at your doorway, an' about the sill, if that room only 'as you in it. Anyone comes in while you're sleepin', they'll be sufferin' bad before they can do you in."

"Thank you, Bray. I'll do it, I promise."

Seeming to be satisfied he gives me a nod. I turn and head back to the tavern. While I know Gruslatic is bad news, it's helped to have Bray say as much with these seeds. As with our camp in the field, I'll need to take precautions in my room at the Doris. I don't get far before I see Eukricz walking back with Crejda, both carrying the breakfast I'd bought for the sheds.

"Crejda, I'd have a word."

"Yes. Eukricz, here, can you manage these? Get Bray to help you. These are from you, Fieldsman?"

"They are, something for the crew." I take one of the brin rolls as Eukricz passes us. "Didn't manage to eat anything before heading up to the tower this morning. Look, Crejda, I know it didn't go well and I know he's not a man to be fucked with . . ."

"Do you? Is this you being sorry before heading off somewhere and leaving me to work out how to stop his militia

189

checking every fucking barrel and sack, box and pouch, slowing us up, putting us bottom of the list with the work we want done from the craftsmen about; stone workers, coopers, farriers, you name it. My job's got harder, my crew'll be up in arms, and he'll be sure it's my name and your name they'll be cussing out. And if you'll pardon me, what kind of fucking threat is you telling him you'll pull the Post out of the Spike?"

"I won't have him or anyone thinking how I'm working in the field, and in Sathanti, is in my own interest and not the Post's, though fuck knows I'd love to give my pa our land back on a plate."

"And that's reason enough to wreck all the years I've put in here, what I've built up? You're young enough you haven't yet learned how to swallow some horseshit from someone we're tenant to. You're not thinking of this crew, and what they and their families'll do then, when he calls your bluff on it and tells us we're out."

"He's never going to do it, is he, Crejda? He's pocketing so much of our tithes he'd be cutting off his own legs."

"That's his business. Ours is to make sure he don't raise them like he's going to now thanks to you. I run a tight ship here and keep him on my side for good reason. I had to fucking grovel back there to bring him back off the ceiling. You'd be best finding somewhere else to follow your creed, because I can't keep you safe here."

"His warning or yours?"

"Mine, Fieldsman. You don't know him."

"I know enough. And it's *our* creed, Crejda, there's no escaping it, there's no choice in whether you follow it."

"I've read what comes with that piece of vellum being sent to the Posthouses the world over, the sanctions, the threat of me being removed from here if I'm found to be corrupting the Creed. Is that what I am? Corrupt? A few bags of bacca or do you think there's more going on?"

"I'd be sorry to find it's true."

"Fuck you, Fieldsman."

"Pardon?"

"I'm reeve here. I fought too hard for this; you should know it having babs and a cinch yourself. Thought you'd have my back. You know how clean my ledgers are."

Her tallies and ledgers being perfect don't make her guilty, though it's as clear a sign of guilt as any. She isn't stupid enough to keep running things off the books while I'm about now she's made an enemy of me. I know she's corrupt, remembering what Bray told me, but seeing the way she bent over for that spaf has wound me up.

"Some advice, Crejda. If he's fucking you about when he's not happy with you, and you're doing nothing wrong, send word to Stroff. Can't see how Stroff would blame you for Gruslatic being a cock. Use Stroff to put pressure on Hildmir and so on Gruslatic. Don't be fucking bullied and pushed around. We're Post. He should be glad of us."

"Stroff?" She snorts with contempt. "No, I've had no complaints about my conduct and I'll appreciate being the first to hear of any you have."

"You will. All I ask is you let me know if you hear of anyone passing ingots, arrows, plant and the like to the Marghoster sheds."

There's a heartbeat before she responds, a momentary flutter across her lips that reveals her. "Of course, Fieldsman."

Chapter 9

Driwna

I was in the field hunting for plant for a few days after meeting with Gruslatic and pissing him off. Might have been a few days after I came back that he got me, and what's he's done to me since has taken any clear recall of how long I've been in his jail. But his mistake was leaving me alive and taking me prisoner. He got greedy.

I hear a murmur, sense movement. I must have been sleeping. There's people around me, I can't tell who at first. I can't see. Then the hairs on my skin stand on end, a prickling all over me. Ufra. Ufra is here, and I smell a man unused to taking baths.

"Not much left o' this one, tree fucker. Nice bit o' flesh on the bones, though. I'd be nailing her regular but we all knowen what colour does to a cinch. You be boilin' her for supper?" I don't recognise his voice.

"Where's the other one that was with her, his name's Bray?" Ufra this is, her voice itself a kiss, softened and deepened by a throat used to drinking, eating and even speaking in ways strange to the rest of us people. It makes me smile to hear it, but I can't call out to her, for I'm gagged.

"Eat him tomorrow, will you? I 'spect all the bruisin's softened him up nice."

"If I eat people at all, it's their tongues, all hot and chewy and wagging about," she says. "You'll get him out of his cell, as you will Driwna out of here. You'd best stop speaking as well; there's things living on my skin you can breathe in, and they change you."

I hear a panicked shuffle and nothing else as the door is opened and he leaves us. She comes to my side, kneels, her hand hot and dry on my face. "Oh Driwna." She pulls the blindfold and gag away, feeling for the damage, my broken nose.

"Get her a robe," she calls.

I hear the squeaking of buckles as she finds what she needs on her belt. I can't see her, can't open my eyes; my face has been tenderised by a mailed fist.

"Where is she?" Cal this is, sounding like he's descending steps, now standing in the doorway.

"She's alive." Ufra strokes a cool, tingling ointment across my eyes. I still wince, feel how swollen they are by her touch. Then my face goes numb, I can't feel anything.

"Her nose," says Cal.

"I will, in a moment," says Ufra. "She's lost some teeth. Ribs broken."

"Bastards. I'll fucking kill that castellan, string him up by his ballsack."

"No, Cal. She's suffered for the parley. It cannot be for nothing."

I can't tell if she's spreading more ointment on. There's a tugging suggests she's moving my lips, my teeth, and a single sharp pain makes me flinch before I feel nothing there either.

The pain reminds me that teeth were taken. I shudder, an act of weeping I can't register in my skin, my eyes. Just the memory of the pain shrinks and cows me. It was going to be a tooth for every one of Gruslatic's crew I'd killed; they'd got as far as three, trying to break me for the recipes in my belts, the Post's fightbrew. Shame thickens as I recall how close I'd been to giving him what he wanted. It would have made him rich beyond measure.

"Rat bites?" Cal this is. I am moved about.

"Only three, perhaps when she was bound, unable to move. Untie her legs, fetch rags, I need to clean her up and cover her."

"Wait till I tell her she's shat herself again."

"You would do that?"

"A joke we once shared. I'm glad you're alive, Marghoster filth," he says to me.

I'm glad he's alive, at least until I can move again. Then I'll kill him.

I hear a crack then, rather than feel it. She's righted my nose I think. She must have put something in my mouth because I feel tired suddenly, weightless. I slip away.

"Chief Yicre, your people are calling her 'Brother Red'."

"Yes, I had called those of the Post that fought alongside us brothers, and she took it in good humour, having proved herself more than a match for all men that day we fought the Hidzucs and the mercenaries from Farlsgrad."

"That alone makes her unfit to lead this parley as you have requested. She won't represent the Lord Marghoster's interest fairly." Gruslatic this is. These are voices in another room. Wind rattles shutters. I'm out of the jail.

"She's shown us no favour, nor prejudice. She's not come at us with a hundred spears, men of Farlsgrad . . ." Yicre this is. Shouting then, argument. A woman's voice cuts through it, smooth like the flat of a razor.

"She is Bridche, but she bring home to me, to lodge once her own, my keep Eirakh. His tongue, his eyes, were not taken and we are grateful to her and to Chief Yicre for this."

"Lady Leusla, she killed him for fuck's sake, your own keep!" Gruslatic's voice is the highest I've heard it.

"A fight to death has this outcome, Castellan. I wish it was her dead but she does him greatest honour."

"Well, Grus, I personally want to meet this woman they're all wet for, then we can see about a parley." I don't know this voice.

"She's sleeping in the next room. Guards were rough with her, against my orders you understand, but when she's killed so many of their own they wouldn't take well to it. Please, friends of Farlsgrad, I ask that you return to your camp and come back to this tower tomorrow. I hope she'll be well enough. She'll be given the best of care."

"I know," says Ufra. "I'm not leaving her. You don't appear to have any control over your guards and you've yet to give a reason for her arrest."

"I'll punish the guards, you can be clear on that. But trust must begin somewhere. Her arrest is a matter for the crown and for me."

"It begins tomorrow, the parley. With Driwna Bridche." Yicre this is. He leaves then.

"I'll take a stroll down to my sheds, Grus, back here in a few hours. Ososi, umm, Ulf? Uffy?" It must be Lord Marghoster, a warm, clear voice, as little of Farlsgrad's flavour in it as education could afford.

"I'm Ufra, heir to the Ososi Master of Flowers."

"Of course, of course. I mean no disrespect. Will she be awake then, this Driwna? I would meet with her."

"She will be ready for the parley," says Ufra.

"Let's leave her then, Grus. Walk with me."

Some muffled voices, men at a further door. I must be at the top of the tower, near or in the room Cal was staying in. The door closes. Ufra kneels back down beside me, kisses me gently, my cheeks, eyes, lips. I can't feel her lips on my eyes, just the pressure of her chin on my nose. I can't open them to see her, a press must be on them. She runs her hands up inside my robe, fingers pressing, her strange thumb running over my ribs, my belly, my skin tingling as it passes. There too, the ribs, something's caked on to me and the pain of drawing a breath means a rib's cracked as well, maybe more.

Her thorns scratch me. She knows they do. My skin thrills to it, almost as though it's missed her as much as I have.

"You're awake."

A dry, hoarse whisper is all I can manage. "I am, Ufra. I wish I could see you."

"Lie still, Driwna of the Post. Let me heal you."

The skin of my lips feels like they're cracking apart as I try to smile. She lets the fibres of her thumb brush over them.

"This thumb, root of the achoa, likes the taste of you, your blood. It moves when you're near."

She brings a flask to my mouth, a few drops of water, then a few more, patiently waiting between these trickles.

"What happened, Driwna?"

"He should have killed me when he had the chance."

The first attempt to get at me was, I recall now five nights after I'd spoken to him, Crejda and Lighroz in this tower. I'd been sucking vadse sticks in the days as I went hunting for plant beyond the Spike's plant runs, in the copses and heather, and I'd return to the Doris, sleep through sunset, the better

196

to be alert at nights. It was floorboards creaking that woke me from a doze. There was a rustling of a bag; they must have oiled the door's hinges, it opened more quietly than it otherwise did. Then they stepped in the titarum seeds, crumbling under their soft leather slippers like nuts. Bray had told me to put some euca oil about my nose, and I was glad of it. Fucking Sillindar, it couldn't have been worse if you'd piled forty rotten corpses about the room. They coughed and choked. I was up from my mat, knife ready. One stepped forward, hadn't checked for caltrops, cried out as they pierced his foot. The poison would soon deaden his leg. Two more with him, one swept the 'trops away. For all her speed on a brew she'd not reckoned on my being ready, for she wore no mask and it didn't look like they had a brew of any quality. I threw a sporebag into her chest and it filled the air about the both of them. They were trained enough it slowed them only a moment. The other leaped the distance to my mat, couldn't have known I'd pried up the floorboards and filled the hole with field 'trops, as we'd use for horses. He too got pierced, his balance gone as he fell through the mat. I stabbed him quick in the neck as he fell towards me. The girl was coughing and thrashing about, unable to open her eyes. The other one had hobbled out of the doorway. The girl was dangerous enough, soldiers being trained to fight blind, the brew more than compensating, so I pulled her dead friend onto the caltrops before her, grabbed my sword I'd left on the sill, then climbed out and dropped to the ground a storey below. I opened the pouch that contained my dayer, a vile curd I scooped into my mouth. I was at the side of the Doris and I heard the other one's faltering steps as he headed out of the main door. He heard me, of course, coming at him; his brew was going to make him hard to kill, even though he had only a knife. I couldn't land a blow on him, even with his leg slowing him and weakening his stance. Then I felt the shiver, almost buckled with the violence of the dayer, like plunging into an icy sea, savagely awoken. I could make the difference after that between the blades count. The barkeep to the Doris was watching as we fought, watching as I cut the man's head off, my experience and training winning out over the speed his cooker's brew gave him. I turned to the barman before the body had fallen.

"Know him? Or the two up in my room?"

He shook his head. He was full of shit. "I know Gruslatic runs the Spike and anybody crosses him is fucked. It's worse for you if you cross me."

As I walked towards him he held his hands up, panicked. "I see them about, these men. They do work for him. I had to let them in or he'll take her off me, the Doris."

I stood up close to him, breathed in deeply, keeping on with the patterns. He looked down at my sword and then at my feet, cowed.

"There's one left alive up in my room. I'll cut her head off out here, so the blood won't need cleaning up. I'll still want the room. Will that be good with you?"

"He knows I have a boy. Y – You don't know the man. He's worse than a wolf."

He was right on that score. I don't blame him. I left the three headless bodies in the street outside the Doris, stripped bare. I took what I could for my belts and put the rest in a sack with their heads, threw it in the river before dawn brought the day crews whistling and shouting at each other on their way into the sheds and jetties. There's many was gathered about as I returned to the tavern, to look at the bodies before the militia came to cart them off. I freshened the caltrops in my room, chalked the floorboards that had the crushed titarum on them and gave Alaqua help with the blood from the one assassin's neck. Bray came to see me that day, for the tavern was going to be watched. The failure of these mercenaries put Gruslatic in a difficult position. I might have gone back to Autumn's Gate, petitioned Hildmir himself to have him removed for the attempt on my life, but the parley was more important, for without it there was a war the Sathanti couldn't win. I feared also that Stroff might have worked against me in a court full of powerful allies. A fieldsman must solve their own problems, Yblas had said.

Bray knew Gruslatic wouldn't let this go. He wanted me to leave, to get out of Farlsgrad. Three bodies that had paid the colour was a "fuck you" to Gruslatic's that the Spike's denizens would blab about in all corners.

Alaqua it was told me that they'd be coming back, that the barkeep had been ordered to leave for the night when it was time to close and others that had taken rooms were leaving as well. I slept off the dayer and ate some brin and some fish.

I couldn't take a proper fightbrew, as I didn't know when they'd come. Couldn't be paying the colour when they chose to make their move. I shouldn't have worried on that count, for I heard the shutters get smashed in all about the ground floor an hour after sunset. Oil was thrown in, torches after them. I took a brew then, not a full measure, but it would be better than a dayer. Hard to describe how much tougher it is without someone to prep you, to hold you down while it happens. Hard to ignore the smell of smoke, the sound of flames, a dry rumble beneath me. I pressed my hands to my mouth to keep the brew down, stoning the fear to stop my gagging. I was in the room with the bathtub, its window opened onto a different side of the tavern. I glanced out through the open shutters. A mistake. I saw movement on the roof of the sheds opposite and ducked, an arrow

199

whipping through over my head to stick in the wall behind me. I put an arrow against my bow, stood and readied myself. Two figures, one the archer, another behind him, hand over his mouth, knifing him in the side. Bray. He took up the bow himself. He shot arrows left and right of him. I jumped to the ground, strong enough now it couldn't hurt me. I notched another arrow, stayed in the smoke that was pouring out of the smashed shutters as it filled the air. I killed two more. Looked up to see Bray hit with an arrow. He fell off the roof, enough in it I knew he'd done it with purpose. He landed across the lane from me, arrow in him broke and he couldn't help but cry out as it did, stunned by the fall.

There's never time to weigh up the right course to take. I could have run, could have made out the right course was to find the Hidzucs and Ufra, find another way to ensure the parley happened, that they wouldn't be ambushed. Bray would have wanted it. Running to him to fix the wound, neuter the poison, that was a decision that would get me killed. One sword, no matter how fast, wasn't going to beat a row of pikes. I still went to Bray. I hadn't asked him to help me, or watch out for me that night, but he did. I wanted to thank him, that's all. It's that that moved my feet, made my mind up.

Gruslatic was there, behind his militia and their pikes. They'd waited; perhaps he hoped for a different outcome this time. A bell started ringing, calling all about to gather water from the wells and put out the fire, though the Doris's stone walls would limit the damage. I kept at Bray's wound. Only moments had gone by, barely time enough to realise I'd chosen to die, that this instinct not to leave Bray there, not to leave without somehow making it right, was a bad instinct; unprofessional, stupid, fatal.

"Put a bag over that scraggy cunt, and the fat one. Bring them." Gruslatic this was, thinking about the profit, the odds of getting the Post's fightbrew and making himself a fortune.

Some time has passed since I spoke to Ufra. I must have slept. Wind's hammering at the shutters, they're rattling against the catches. I smell cooked meat.

"Can you open your mouth a bit, Driwna?"

Some pain, an ache in my jaw from where they'd got the teeth out. Gruslatic had held my head, fingers in my nose to force my jaw open, tongs ripping a tooth free, and I was choking on the blood, sure it'd drown me.

"Driwna?" She eases a sliver of warm, greasy meat into my mouth, small enough I can swallow it.

I can't thank her before the next piece of meat is at my lips. I need my strength. I'm proud enough of myself for having held out on the secret of our cyca, the Post's brew. It's all I've got, because if I'd given that up I'd be asking Ufra to kill me.

"Be strong," she says. "You've gone still. You look inside yourself and I expect you find yourself wanting because that's what I find behind my own eyes, each day I think of our people taken and their songs that I could not save."

"How can I manage this parley? I can't even sit up."

"One hour at a time, my love. You will need help to get downstairs but we will get you there. You matter too much to us."

I'm grateful, but the thought of matching wits with Marghoster, even to get peace? I don't feel I have it in me. I eat more than I'm comfortable eating.

She puts down the dish, kneels at my side. There's silence that I interpret as her being ready to tell me something.

"I feared the worst when they told me you had been

brought to this tower, for I would choose you, Driwna, to share my milk and bond our blood, though it would mean you become Ososi." There's a nervous catch to her breathing, fearing I do not share her desire.

"I choose you, Ufra." It's said quickly, recklessly, given what it will mean for the woman I am now and the woman I will become. It is my body that has spoken, reason that has been made to listen.

Ufra takes my hand in hers, starts humming, rolling a sound about her mouth. It's a sound that draws fear, becalms the wind. The sound gets deeper, heavier, like she's struggling to contain it. I can't tell, for I can't see. She starts her next breath before the sound's ended, as though there's something in her chest still vibrating. Her hands get hotter about mine. The sound, the breathing, it could be mine I'm feeling, but then she'd not be breathing at all, for the sound is continuous. My own lungs buzz with it as it fills me. The heat from her hands grows, fills my arms, rolling in waves with the sound as it rises and falls. I'm dizzy, I feel off balance as the twisting vowel, its ebb and flow, strips away my fears, memories, plans, everything that is of times gone and the time to come. I feel those edges burned, bridges taken up, an island in a seething ocean of bubbling orange and blood-red sand running as sheets across my skin. Driwna is far from here, trying not to make herself heard, mute in the hope of never leaving the Song, the pressure of the sand, as its softness finds edges, whorls of blue, filling me. I'm breathing in without end, far beyond this small grey chest. There's a tower of air inside me, stirred to its own note, fusing with Ufra's, a tangle at first, off-key, a buffeting wind that finds the current and feeds it, shivering the sands in which we lie, rattling each grain till I'm raw. I feel myself writhing with it, a truth in blood not words, and still the breath, our breath, our air binding us to this timeless point until I can no longer bear the scouring pain that cleanses me and readies me to become an Ososi.

I open my eyes. The tears and the milky mix that was under the press Ufra had made blink away. My eyelids are still puffy, but the swelling's almost gone. Ufra is in my arms, her thigh between mine. She has undressed us. Her thorns are in me. We are bound, deliciously. I cannot describe how I feel. It is as though I've been fed, no, nourished to my bones.

I have changed.

I know that dawn is many hours away. A man snores outside the door, our guard. I look at Ufra sleeping through this quiet hour and I understand. She's chosen me as I had chosen her the moment I saw her. Or the Song has chosen us for each other. There's no real difference, is there? I have been infatuated before, who hasn't? Yet unlike infatuation, I don't strive to give myself up, to leave nothing of me that can be separated from her. She's answered a question I couldn't form, a question I may have sought to answer with my devotion to the Post. What am I for?

These words have not the wit of a poet or else they might render better the Song of the Earth as I now find it. I worry my blood has weakened her sense of it, in the same extent as her blood has strengthened my own. But she has chosen me.

"I have."

"Why? Why me, Ufra?" I'm not surprised she could hear my thought. Had I heard her voice?

Her eyes are open. I should not be able to see them so clearly in such darkness.

She smiles. "The Song was so strong in you, when we

first met. You shaped it about you, as an island shapes the currents. And I find you beautiful." She winks then, knows the echo of our experience as if it is inked on my skin for her to read. "The etza-Ososi, he will approve of you."

"Your pa?"

"Yes, Ushnor is his name; he is what you would call my pa, blood and seed, though he has shared his blood with all our Ososi kin. I want you to come west, after the parley? You are Ososi-wen now, Ufra-wen. My own."

"Yes." I try and find words to add to it, but I realise there's no need. "I will come west, Ufra, but I cannot go after the parley. My mun, she's not well, she's sick, so Cal tells me. I mean to see her, for it seems I will never get another chance."

"It is east?"

"Could you come with me?"

"Our people are hunted, Ufra-wen. I am here too long and there are no allies here I can promise the etza-Ososi, none who will stand with us and the Sathanti against Scar and his crew. They find us wherever we hide. There must be a reckoning."

"The Oskoro chief, Master of Flowers? He will help?"

"Yes. His song, his mastery, with ours . . . we may yet breed and splice and seed towards the essence, towards divining the source of the power the magists wield so readily. And we will discover new recipes, empower our blood, give it more eyrtza."

"Eyrtza?"

"More . . . the closest meaning is majesty and mastery and focus."

"We say, when we drink a fightbrew, that we stone it, a way of giving it a channel to improve its clarity and strength, to stop it overwhelming."

"That is something of it, Driwna. Know that a change quickens in you. Will fill you. It began on that field and now, as we are joined, you have in your blood and muscle and bones plant beginning to grow, taking root, seeds of flowers for which you have no name. I hope you can welcome them, for they cannot harm you, yet there are ways in which they might hurt you. You stone them, as you say, train them as vines are trained, but you must, must find their song in you. If you can bring it into yours, you will have more eyrtza than any in Farlsgrad."

"Will I grow such plant inside me as you? Will I have this vine?"

"It won't reach this size for many years, but you'll feel it. You and the vine become each other, if you work for it. It's a kind of listening; again, no one word you have describes it. Perhaps your fightbrews will nurture it more quickly. I am excited to find this out, Driwna." She kisses me and I would fuck her if it wasn't an agony to move; the need is there, that thrilling heaviness of lust between my legs, her scent making me drunk. I let her lips wander, savour the sense of their sweetness where once I only sensed their softness; savour the hot, wet sting of thorns as, in the town about us, the sniffers blow their whistles in the dawn mists and raise their dogs who wake, in turn, our snoring guard.

Chapter 10

Driwna

The long table Castellan Gruslatic uses for feasts and celebrations is a bit too intimate, too narrow for a parley like this, leaving us close enough to each other we can judge the breath of our opposite. Such meets are done in fields around firepits when the Sathanti parley. The closest the sky gets is through a few arrow loops along the curved wall of the tower. It feels like night while outside midday approaches. It is Gruslatic's just, the room in which he hears complaints and grievances and makes judgement.

Gruslatic has put himself at one end of the table and me the other. I'm grateful for it, as I was to see him look me over as I walked in with only the aid of a staff. Ufra had cleaned me up, washed me and put me in the robe of a cleark that Cal had given her, my red cloak over it. Gruslatic would have expected a woman far more broken than I appear.

On my right as I look down the table to that cunt are Ufra, Chief Yicre, Lodre Canendrigh and Cal. Yicre and Lodre will bring a doomed war to Farlsgrad for the aggression of the Hidzucs and Farlsgrad mercenaries if they don't get their lifeprice for the slain and their kidnapped kin. Behind them are their Ososi guards, bright and twitchy on their vadse. Marghoster and Gruslatic's guards along the wall to my left look uneasy at the presence of Ososi. For all that fightbrews are forbidden at this parley, there is nothing they can say to the plant that runs through or replaces the guards' skin. One of them breathes with the creak of bark.

Bray must still be far below us in the jail and the attempts on my life meant I could not fetch Gennic from Lindur to speak on behalf of the Post van also taken by Yicre. Ufra said Bray had been beaten up badly and was despairing. Another motivation to make life as hard for Gruslatic as I can. To my left, with Lord Yeismic Marghoster, sits Lighroz his cleark, Crejda and Eirakh Hidzuc's widow, Leusla Hidzuc, along with two of her kurch chiefs and a notary. They seek their own price for the caravans taken by Yicre. There is an empty chair between Yeismic and Crejda. Marghoster looks well. There's some grey in his beard now, a dab at his temples as well. A plain velvet jacket and a cotton shirt have obviously been carefully chosen for a parley with nomads, while his beard and hair have been plainly braided. For a lord he's got some sun in his skin and kept his shape up with his interest in breeding horses, which is the latest fling of his fancy these last few years.

"Are we expecting someone else, Castellan?" I ask, lispy with the bruising in my mouth and face.

"We are, but we should begin." And I'm about to speak when Gruslatic continues. "There's much anger about this table, wrongs done that require a kurchgeld or, as we'd say in Farlsgrad, the lifeprice. I speak for King Hildmir in this serious matter. The Sathanti kurchmen wish for this red, Driwna Marghoster, to be here to ensure a just hearing. We will see."

The door into the room is behind me, facing Gruslatic. It opens and he immediately stands, as does Lighroz, Crejda and the notary. Ufra's eyes widen and I sense her trying to control her body, her manner. Cal is less subtle and looks shocked. I turn to see Administrator Stroff enter with a young girl. I won't stand, for it would be awkward and painful.

"Pap, Pap!" she shouts, running from Stroff to Marghoster.

"Liucha, my rose," he says. She jumps up onto his knees and puts her hands on the edge of the table. He kisses the top of her head as she looks us all over.

"Look at her, Pa, look at them." She points at the Ososi present, at Ufra, and then scrunches her nose. "Thorns, Pa. Are you hurt, lady?"

I've seen Liucha once before. Six summers she is now. It was last summer Cal and I ran a van up to the Marghoster estate. His only child, she was born with a twisted back and had never been able to walk. I recall too her head would find its natural rest turned a way into her left shoulder. Here there is no such posture. She ran and now sits straight as any of us.

"Sit down, sit down. Thank you. I'm sorry to have been delayed," says Stroff as he takes his seat between Yeismic and Crejda. "You must try not to blame Liucha, but some things are more important than war and peace to a young girl." His smile encourages our amusement and those on my left smile and laugh, those on my right not so much. Cal and Ufra, the other Ososi, can't take their eyes off him.

"Rulger, good to see you again," says Stroff. "Pass on my best wishes to Gennic and Morril at Lindur."

"—I will, Administrator," he stutters.

"Gruslatic, it is dismaying to see a murderer at this table. You say she is here at the behest of our friends in the Sathanti?" Yeismic Marghoster this is.

208

"Lord Marghoster, the crown will pursue sentence on the fieldsman and her ally Bray in the jail below for their refusing an attempted arrest, but my hope is that the good faith we're showing our friends will be recognised in the settlement of the lifeprice and any other negotiations."

"Is there a law in this land says you cannot defend yourself from soldiers entering your lodgings and meaning to kill you?" I say.

"Soldiers? We found no belts, no heads either, my Lord," says Gruslatic. "A savage and brutal killing this was, bodies left on the street for all the good people of the Spike to see."

"All those who saw the bodies spoke of the titarum they could smell, seeds that I'd laid inside my door. I don't believe they entered my room naked and headless, Castellan, for the dead follow few orders. But that is how they ended up."

"Could someone fetch Driwna a mug of wine, some aloe in it too; she is having trouble speaking." Gruslatic this is. "Driwna Marghoster, I cannot imagine why anybody would try to kill someone so well trained and, to that point, so highly lauded for the good work she's done for the Post. I sought your arrest for questioning. I regret to say my captain was fearful of you mistaking his intent. He saw no other way than to smoke you out of the tavern where our militia could escort you here. You and your Post friend Bray decided to kill as many as you could. I'm all that's keeping you alive."

I look over at Stroff rather than him.

"All that's kept me alive, Administrator, was my unwillingness to yield the Castellan the secret of our fightbrew."

Gruslatic slams his fists into the table, making us all start. Liucha shrieks and begins crying.

"Let me take my young girl back to her maids, perhaps then we might execute the main purpose of our parley, yes?" Marghoster this is.

I shake my head, cross with myself for how this is going, but the pain I'm in is his doing. We wait as Marghoster leads his daughter out.

"Administrator," I say, "I must apologise for my words so upsetting the Castellan. I must also ask the Castellan to ensure the parley keeps our contributions to the matter at hand."

The look on Gruslatic's face should keep me warm for a year. Ufra's head is bowed, awaiting a sense of respect. One of the Ososi guards is trying to control his breathing and a tear runs from his cheek. He and the other Ososi of Ufra's party are shuffling as though the flagstones are hot. Then a ray of sunlight breaks through the arrow loop behind Lighroz, the first of the day, for there was heavy weather overnight. It stills the Ososi, but their nerves are making the guards opposite them nervous also. Gruslatic continues to stare at me but otherwise says nothing as Marghoster enters the room again.

"Now we've got all that done, our good Castellan should lead us forwards." Stroff this is.

"Right, this began with some vans going missing," says Gruslatic, "held against their will by Chief Yicre of the Ilkashun Confederacy. Two Marghoster vans out of the Spike and a Post van out of Lindur, representation here through Cal Rulger."

"It began a while before that," says Yicre. "Mercenary crews, according to kurch-kin of mine, have been taking our people. This last year I can count one hundred and twenty missing, where we might lose to the land no more than twenty. Other confederacies, the Odrack, the Roskills, have lost similar numbers, whole settlements gone, bloodless and silent." He looks then at Ufra.

"We have been hunted for two years. We will not be hunted any more," she says. While the Ososi look less nervous, they now keep their eyes lowered until they feel respected.

210

"If Sathanti tribes are not doing this to each other, if vans of slaves from Farlsgrad go into the mountains in greater numbers than any in my lifetime, we are sure that this is where our own kurch-kin are taken," says Yicre. "And if Farlsgrad has some agreement, or alliance, with the mountain confederacies across the Spine of the World, then we demand answers. I did not expect that this Marghoster would instead send Eirakh with a hundred soldiers to kill all the kurch of my sib, the Canendrigh, and to kill me as well, for it is no accident of timing that I was there."

One of Leusla's chiefs stands sharply, forty summers at least but lean as a wolf. "We are no puppets of Marghoster. These Ososi are all that saved your feeble kurch. You have no heir, Ilkashun. Your land calls for strength and we answered."

Lodre stands to face him, guards behind them step in. "Chief Marak, we each have our allies. Yours killed our children while we fought, ours killed your chief and broke your mercenary army and your own kin grown fat on the teat of Farlsgrad, and weak on its kannab. Tell me, whose coin filled their purses?"

I watch helplessly as Marak, a veteran soldier, grabs Lodre's neck and smashes his face into the table. His other hand whips a knife from his belt meaning to bury it in his back. An Ososi leaps forward, fast as an arrow, catching his wrist and wrenching his arm savagely, bone snapping and the knife clattering on the table. Marghoster panics and falls backwards off his chair, scrabbling to get away, while his guard and the others on the left wall draw their swords.

"Stop!" Ufra is standing, her shout loud as a horn, heavy as a barrel of sand. We're silenced as much from the shock of such a deep yell coming from her as from the way it rattles our bones. Yicre lifts back his brother's head, puts a kerchief to his nose and mouth to stop the blood. Another of the

Ososi steps forward to help him, his hands on Lodre's shoulders as he writhes in an effort to stand and retaliate.

"Chief Leusla," says Gruslatic, "if you can't control your animals, leash them outside."

Her head is bowed in shame. Korba, one of her kin-kurch chiefs, has risen quickly to put his arm around Marak and pull him away from the table. He's hissing into his ear, words in their lingo. Stroff has risen to assist Marghoster, who stands and then takes his seat in a silent fury. Korba gestures to their guard to escort Marak outside.

"Forgive us for this, Castellan," says Korba. "Many that be loved be dead that we known since they be in cots."

"It's to be expected."

I bite my lip. I have to concede how well crafted an insult this simple comment is.

Yicre whispers in Lodre's ear as the Ososi guard applies a salve to his nose and steps back to the wall again. Lodre is fighting back tears, his face flushed with the pain and, no doubt, humiliation. The words Yicre speaks will save this parley if he can settle Lodre.

"Chief Yicre." Marghoster this is, looking to push him in the moment he's preoccupied. "You accuse me of supplying Chief Hidzuc with mercenaries in order to invade your lands. I didn't provide soldiers to Eirakh for him to take them to war. Eirakh was going into Ilkashun lands to recover the vans if he could. My vans. My property that had been kept by you despite not one man or woman disrespecting or flouting your customs. Why would they? It isn't good for my coffers or their purses. Eirakh was not sanctioned to kill nokes and children." By noke he means "no colour", anyone who isn't a soldier.

"You agree with this, Leusla Hidzuc?" I ask, to give Yicre some time to finish settling Lodre.

"I not in his counsel." She looks to Korba, older by twenty winters at least; scarred, dour, fidgeting as Bray would do in a battle where wits and not plant are the decisive weapon. Hard to read what lies there. She won't have his respect and didn't have Marak's, given his actions. There'll be a summons once they're back from this parley, the lodge will host it and the Hidzucs may be supplanted by either Marak or Korba. Stroff speaks, as though he'd heard my thoughts.

"Chief Korba," he says. "You are a veteran soldier, a man of your wisdom must speak at a time like this, I'm sure Leusla would allow it."

She nods with as much dignity as she can manage. Korba clears his throat. I sense his embarrassment for he isn't well spoken.

"They Ososi, they be what's at the back of this strife. One be Scar, a mountain on legs he be, fast as a wasp he be and all, quiet as a bird on the wing. This Yicre be in league with them. Eirakh has to defend hisself from the Ilkashun who be raiding us."

Leusla's looking at me. She's sensed, as I have, what Stroff's trying to do, raising the importance of one of her kin-kurch chiefs to undermine her status and sow discord among the Hidzucs.

"Daith-nu Yicre cannot see trouble Ososi bring because he loves them. Driwna has mark of Ososi, Ufra. How we know what Ufra wants here? Daith-nu Yicre, he think on why no ears at the Councils when Council see him and Ososi." He's got sharper in tone while saying it.

"Yet you wished Driwna here?" says Gruslatic.

"Before she lie with Ososi. We pay debt for return of Eirakh to Hidzuc lodge."

"Korba is wrong to blame Ososi, for we have all suffered at the hands of Scar." Yicre this is.

213

"Then why Council shut door?" continues Leusla. "Why make hostage of vans, except look strong for kurch."

Yicre laughs alone, and it echoes about us briefly.

"Scar was long banished from the Ososi, Daith-ru Leusla." Ufra this is, not yet raising her eyes since her shout, not yet bestowing that grace upon the other side of the table. "Sometimes a seeding will go badly and the blood rots the will, fractures the Song. We have no desire for the lands of Hidzuc, nor the lands of Ilkashun. We want only peace in our own land, freedom from those who hunt us like deer."

"Scar was in Lindur. Cal will confirm it," I say, looking to push the talk away from the differences between Hidzuc and Ilkashun. "Scar was at the Brask sheds overseeing a lot that went onto Marghoster wagons headed for the Sathanti."

"Horseshit! Lies!" shouts Marghoster. "You'll find no Ososi mercenary on our ledgers. I would recall a giant Ososi in my sheds were he in my pay. I fear for you, Stroff, if this is the future of the Post."

I ignore that. "All of the Sathanti speak in fear of Scar, not only your kurch-kin, Daith-ru Leusla," I say. "For if Daith-nu Yicre was lying about this, why then waylay the vans yet do them no harm? And Daith-nu Yicre does not control the voices of those other confederacies, nor yet the voices of those in the mountains along the Tongue we know to have cut the bridges down in the border passes."

"Enough," says Stroff, a command I can feel in the stone of the tower; an ache, a heartbeat. Gruslatic is smiling as he looks at me.

"The first crime is Yicre's," continues Stroff. "All else is speculation on the part of Yicre and none of it established as fact here. Yicre, at the least, must compensate Lord Marghoster for the slaves that he freed, for he had no right to free them. His customs, as he well knows, do not apply to the vans passing through his lands. Such understandings are a given wherever peoples trade with each other. If Yicre does this, we can and must begin again. The Post will fund two hundred soldiers to patrol the borders of Ilkashun lands. I will petition for Fieldsman Driwna herself to oversee this, to look into the threat posed to our allies from these marauding bandits preying on the good people of the Ososi and Sathanti. We will also provide guira, salt and alka lots at cost, and half the cost of bacca lots through to midwinter of next year. I hope these terms will encourage the Daith-nu to think of his people and allow vans through his lands again."

By the time he's finished I'm trying to stifle how hard I'm finding it to breathe. All the time he was speaking I had the fear I was drowning, yet without the panic of my body. My blood has chilled; I was steady only if I held to his words and did not think of how I would respond. Ufra has pulled a woollen shawl about herself, the look on her face one of enduring great pain, and it is the same for the other Ososi. Cal looks over at me, wide-eyed, sensing the same discomfort he had was in me.

There is a moment's silence, an absolute silence. I want someone to call out again that it is Marghoster's vans of slaves that are going into the mountains, but none do. Yicre clears his throat.

"As we are making our claims here in respect of the kurch-geld, I have a field full of my dead, from an unprovoked attack aimed at killing my Canendrigh kurch outright. Tradition demands land for such crimes, being three acres of tillable land or livestock in the quantities laid out in the Sathanti Accord for each chief or heir killed, one acre for each else. This must be considered before we can consider the administrator's request."

"Lord Marghoster, what is it you expect from this parley?"

I ask, recovering from the strange cold and heaviness I felt while Stroff spoke. I realise now I have the thread of the way through this. Marghoster gives the appearance of composing his thoughts, but I think he's too clever for that. He's known his predicament long before he walked in here, which is why Lighroz is not here alone on his behalf.

"I am sorry that Eirakh Hidzuc, so long an ally of ours, is not here to account for his actions, but by any measure the invasion of Ilkashun land was wrong and certainly was not sanctioned by me. This aggression, Administrator, cost me my slaves, for without it we might have had parley on Canendrigh land and recovered them all. Now, we have a Hidzuc confederacy at our border without a leader and, I would imagine, in trouble at the Sathanti Council when next it meets. You have no allies there now, Leusla, Chief Korba. But you have allies in Farlsgrad, the greatest ally in the north of the known world. If your lands came under my steward-ship . . ."

Inevitably, Korba stands and in his own lingo is telling him what he can go and fuck. Leusla seems lost; she looks over at me, unsure how to continue. I nod quickly at Korba, a signal for her to get him under control. Then I see it. I don't know if somehow it is this Ososi blood I have in me now, but I feel a swell in her, the other Ososi do as well. She's showing her hand.

"Please sit." She lays a hand gently on the forearm of Korba. He shakes it off, is about to speak again.

"Sit, Korba." It stops him, and he sees enough in her eyes he sits down. She takes a breath to compose herself, then looks directly at Marghoster.

"If you steward, my people pull up our kurchpole, take Farlsgrad colours, must see herd-walks and plant runs spoiled by those looking to make settle on our land and more tithe for you, and enough tithe we pay now for bringing our wagons through your clearks. My kurchgeld, it is simple. You stay out. You give proper price now, thirty a head for deer, three point blocks of kannab for four silver. This is not much, Lindur pays seven from Rulger land. Eirakh give you passage through our kurches. But when you bring slaves through my land and Daith-nu says no, Crejda comes, this Lighroz comes, oily words, crying stories. Yet you have fat Crejda, our kurches not fat, wait for vans we had paid for last Jenna, when Eirakh come for lots of barley, ash, horse-shoes, three harnesses for drafts we put to work, and alka. But you took our coin, then kept back the lots until we fetch you deer as I have said.

"You want run slaves through our lands, Daith-nu Marghoster, then pay iron, arrows and chainmail. Or you go Lindur and stay off Hidzuc land."

Crejda's shifting in her seat but Stroff doesn't even blink. Gruslatic is glowering and Marghoster's looking to Stroff and Gruslatic, widening his eyes as though insinuating this needs to be stopped. Leusla lifts her hand from the table, quelling subtly the rising restlessness.

"Daith-nu Marghoster, I look at Driwna Bridche and see daughter of the last family Marghoster steward of. They lost seat at Council, given your name as insult. No longer are Bridche Sathanti. Castellan, you speak good for King Hildmir. We want only peace with Farlsgrad, even though I have lost keep. I tell you here about way we have been used. I wish my keep had not hide from me deals he made these merchants. Fair prices again I ask."

Korba eases himself back into his chair, respect in his eyes, pulls his pipe from out of what I'd call the water loop on his fieldbelt's shoulder and starts rooting about for his bacca and bones, as though he's heard what he needed to from the woman who would be his chief. It's bad news for all the Spike's merchants if she goes about stopping vans at her borders and no longer agrees trade with us.

I see then a few of them are looking at me, for all that are here seeking their kurchgeld want justice.

"What do you believe we should do, Fieldsman? It's you has been chosen for this, not I." Gruslatic this is, thinking I'm pinioned, absolving himself of a decision beyond his wit. He sits back in his chair, steeples his fingers like a scholar. I look to Ufra and Cal, who are both looking back at me. Here is either peace or war.

"Try and do this without swearing, Driw," says Cal. Ufra laughs. It gives me a lift, because I'm fretting about not letting them down. It was Leusla's words that put the final bit of the puzzle in place. I imagine it's why people think Sillindar must be behind moments in your life, for good fortune happens so rarely in these hard lands. Part of me wants to ask Gruslatic to recall his demand to lead this parley and take on drawing a conclusion from all that's been said. He has not the wit and would prove it before us all. But too much is at stake and I must keep cold my need to see him suffer.

"The High Red recently gave me this title of fieldsman and with it gave all the Post a creed that I am to enforce with the other fieldsmen created. The Creed states, 'Peace through trade.' This is true. Good trade discourages war, makes allies of all. The kurchgeld among Sathanti demands the land or lifeprice for the slain Daith-nu Ilkashun has suffered when no provocation or invasion was made on the Hidzuc. Nobody can dispute that. There would be a parcel of land agreed between them that Daith-ru Leusla cannot deny and that would satisfy Daith-nu Yicre.

"That kurchgeld cannot be executed if Daith-ru Leusla loses her status at the Sathanti Council, for her confederacy and that of the Ilkashun will suffer if it is not legitimised in the Council's eyes. The Council is made up, in part, of the Hidzucs' neighbouring confederacies. This keeps peace at their borders. Without this sanction, the Daith-ru's kurches, in hardship, might turn hostile to our vans. Attacks on our vans means Farlsgrad's trade suffers. Farlsgrad, the Spike, Lord Marghoster, the Post, all of us need a stable Hidzuc confederacy that has a voice at their Council and an ear to it as well. Reeves and clearks must make profitable judgements on the crewing of vans, the rates to pay, the rates to charge. We can only do it with a fair reckoning of what they owe. Daith-ru Leusla remains an important ally and Marghoster undertaking stewardship of her realm might as well render the Sathanti lands beyond her borders a mystery, for then there are no longer the eyes of kindred there. We should back Daith-ru Leusla's desire for peace and continued trade and should back also a fair price. I cannot speak for Marghoster, but I will petition the administrator and the High Red that we maintain a fair price for Hidzuc lots and follow the Creed in all our dealings with them. The administrator's offer is one I support and respect."

"It had a condition, Fieldsman," says Stroff. I'm buffeted suddenly by that strange tightness in my mind; I fight to continue my thread.

"Yes. Lord Marghoster wants compensation for the slaves freed by Chief Yicre. I would support the awarding of that. Much as I and the Chief hate slavery, we can't expect Lord Marghoster to consider the return of the wagons, horses, lots and only a quarter or less of the slaves payment enough. You both will agree a price and Lord Marghoster will remember how much was returned, how his crew were treated well until they started killing nokes, when considering what that price is."

I have a cup of wine before me. I'm about to reach for it when Ufra takes it up, trailing her achoa root thumb over the lip of it first. It's subtly done and I'm grateful, for I had not thought, stupidly, my life might be in danger here.

I look about the table. Marghoster is whispering to Lighroz, Gruslatic is staring at me venomously, Cal is smiling to himself and nursing his cup, head bowed. Stroff nods at me, and I can't tell if it's in appreciation of the judgement or if he's got me on some scales in his mind and is measuring my cost. Leusla and her chiefs also are conferring, while Yicre and Ufra are whispering. My heart pounds, waiting for the arguing and bartering to begin. Then Yicre clears his throat, a glance at Ufra, who wills him on. They've an agreement of their own, it seems, and it gives me hope, for they will look to support my judgement and in so doing make it harder for the others here.

"I accept the judgement on the kurchgeld and I look forward to agreeing a price with Lord Marghoster."

"I represent the etza-Ososi," says Ufra, following quickly. "We will not hinder Umansk vans, be they Sathanti or Farlsgrad passing through our own lands, though we never have unless they meant us harm. I find much to admire in Daith-ru Leusla – she has strong eyrtza – and I look forward to riding with her on our return to the Sathanti."

Leusla nods at me, smiling. Ufra has shown favour to her in front of her strongest chief. Much as Korba spoke against the Ososi, I suspect it was borne of envy. He won't be ignorant of their benefits as an ally. Leusla then speaks.

"I agree to kurchgeld of land for Ilkashun dead. I hope we heal border, Chief Canendrigh. I agree also passage of Post vans through our lands at a market price, but do Castellan Gruslatic and Cleark Lighroz change price?"

Gruslatic is about to speak to that when Stroff raises a

finger, silencing him. I tense as he readies to speak, but I can't put my finger on the fear.

"I commend the Fieldsman on her deft handling of our dispute; there is much to admire and much agreement. I would not spoil that. The rate on lots, blocks of plant, livestock, all these shall be reviewed with Crejda and contracts written up with immediate effect." Crejda's jaw drops a moment, but she thinks better of speaking. I wonder at his game.

"Gruslatic, I imagine that with us paying a higher price now for Hidzuc lots, you'll need to amend your own position to remain competitive. We value our allies and we follow the Creed. Eyes on the Sathanti are at a premium in these uncertain times there and news from the mountains would be most welcome at the Gate, for we're troubled by the closing of borders along the Tongue as well as by these kidnappings." Gruslatic nods at this, meek as a lamb I think.

"Lord Marghoster," says Stroff, "will you see this done?"

"Certainly, Administrator."

I don't understand how such men, used to getting their own way, are like children before a stern pa. I expected a fight, with me most of all. The ease with which this parley has been settled leaves me, strangely, with a sour smell, of something rotten being hidden.

"And to all our friends from the Sathanti Peaks, might we put our commitments to vellum in a short while, that you might yet have some light to make the journey home? I have some matters to discuss in private with the Castellan and Fieldsman first."

As smoothly as that, a practised authority I hadn't thought him capable of, the right side of the table all rise and clap out their thanks. Leusla puts her hand on my arm as she passes me, Ufra the same. Cal kisses my forehead through a smile. The chiefs, both Canendrigh and Korba, nod their appreciation. Then they're gone and the guards close the doors.

Stroff is looking at me. I begin to feel faintly dizzy, my throat tightening. I try to clear it and I'm about to question his relentless gaze, an attempt to break the strange, solid power of it, when he smiles. "Efficiently done, Fieldsman," he says. He sips his wine, barely a fingernail's worth. "Gruslatic," he continues, "during that tiresome meeting I had some time to think over the sentencing and, indeed, guilt of Driwna and that fat one whose name escapes me. You said that our fieldsman might yet be tried for murder and so be killed in due course. I petition you to consider the difficulty that would pose in a fair trial."

"She killed my men, Administrator. I am judge in the Spike; there's no time or room here for a court as there is in Autumn's Gate."

"I know. You run the Spike with strength and surety. But leaving aside why there was a crew in her room, what's important to all of us is that we may continue trading. Those chiefs might actually honour the new contracts if they see she's alive. Dead, well, that poses a problem, doesn't it? Notwithstanding the High Red himself finding out his new toy was killed by a Hildmir castellan."

Gruslatic's eyes widen, and I sense, I don't know how, that he's holding himself back, that there's more to what's just been said than the words themselves. I'm glad I took a moment to register the arrogance of Stroff's tone or I'd have missed it. It fuels my control, as Stroff continues talking.

"I'm told you dragged her and the fat one—"

I interrupt him. "His name's Bray. At the very least it's easier to say."

"Don't make this harder, Fieldsman. Gruslatic, you dragged

them both here and I'm sure many saw how badly beaten they were. I think we can forgo killing her. Why don't we see her and Bray out of the Spike overnight? While she's alive the wagons run west." The last is spoken more slowly. I feel again some ache in the stones and timber, a pressure in my ears.

Gruslatic stands. "I appreciate your wisdom on this, Administrator, as I do in all things."

"Thank you, Castellan. Driwna, you'll need to go back to the jail while I arrange things."

"Right. Cal will help, he's not known here." This is not what I'd intended to say. It was − it's hard to describe − it's what was the easiest thing to say.

"I see. Very well."

The pressure is building in my head; I feel I need air, to escape this room. I ease myself out of the chair and take the staff I used to walk in. As I do, Stroff offers his hand to help me balance. I grasp it and catch my breath so sharply I vomit. I have enough wit to turn my head aside and not spoil his fine, bright red robe. My blood screams in my veins. His hand, it doesn't feel like a hand feels to hold − the bones aren't quite right. He lets go of me. I fall to the floor, cry out in pain. The door opens before the guard inside can react. Cal it is.

"Driwna?"

"Ah, Cal, she's hurt, unsteady; she tried to stand but needs some help," says Stroff. "Perhaps it's the beating she took."

"Come on, Driw."

"You'll take her to the jail," says Gruslatic.

"What?"

"It's in hand, Rulger; we'll talk later at the sheds," says Stroff.

223

Cal lifts me, wipes my mouth with a rag from his pocket. I want to be sick again, but I slow my breathing down, swallow what's still in my mouth. I hear a song in my head, one my mother hummed often in our kitchen, and I can't recall the name of it. Then the memory returns of a bark-fly, landing on my skin as a girl, and me squashing it, the worst thing you could do.

I get my arm around Cal's shoulder and as he helps me walk I stop us a moment, half turn to get Stroff's attention.

"Administrator, I couldn't help but be delighted to see Lord Marghoster's daughter. She was unable to walk, to run or move like she did today when last I saw her. Do you know what drudhanry, what plant, could make such a difference to her?"

"I'm no drudha, Fieldsman. I know the price of everything and the taste of nothing, according to the High Red. Perhaps Lord Marghoster will tell you, though you won't be the first to ask I'm sure. Sillindar lives, according to Yeismic, and who are we to argue with such evidence?"

"Indeed. Thank you, Administrator."

We have two guards follow us all the way. Ufra joins us. She tells me that Leusla, Yicre and Canendrigh were talking together despite what happened and that she thought Leusla had eyes for Canendrigh, he being flattered, rightly in my view. Cal says he will spread word of "Brother Red" and how she prevented a war. He tells me how proud he is of me, how he loves me, and right there, for all my pain, I am held by two I love more than life itself. Slowly they manage me down to the cell. Cal demands he draft my report to Yblas, but I tell him they hadn't started on my fingers, only my teeth, so I would do it. I tell them both of the plan to get me and Bray out and Ufra promises to tend to Bray. The pair of them fuss over me and it's welcome,

224

but I'm so tired. At the edges of my thoughts slithers an unrest, a shadow that feels like some deep part of me knows something's very wrong and I can't get at it. I see my ma in the fens as I fall to sleep, Scar begins singing with Cal's voice, and all I can do is hold my baby Oskoro as she tells me the future.

Chapter 11

The Magist

There are times when I'm almost sorry for those brilliant people who I find myself opposed to. The very qualities I admire in my allies — determination, integrity, humility, loyalty — all combine to render them implacably opposed to my goals.

In this girl Driwna's case, there is no engineering the events that could alter how she sees her mission in life. To get her to go against Yblas? The boy Rulger? And now the Ososi girl Scar is tracking? I might as well attempt to turn the tides. She has the smell of Ososi, the only reason I can think of for why she'd have reacted so strongly to my proximity at the Spike two weeks ago. With her little victory at the parley, peace at the border and no corruption to find at the Spike she should hopefully stay clear of the Sathanti mountains. Wherever the Ososi hide it is not there, and Scar may have already found them. If she persists in pursuing the cause of the kidnappings I will find her family and apply the usual pressure.

I must return to Autumn's Gate as soon as I'm done here in the Sathanti. With Yicre now dead his confederate chiefs will meet to agree the succession. Lodre Canendrigh will be chosen. With his own wife dead and his sister now the widow of Yicre, he's the frontrunner in respect of continuity, but he's also going to be in the same position as Yicre, a fragile hold on the leadership with no heir and thus amenable to the terms I can offer him.

It was no great hardship to kill Yicre. The form of Yicre's guard, a man called Tresle, was easy enough to refo, especially as the armour meant I wouldn't have to spend time more finely orchestrating a copy of much of his body. Our multitudes entered him nonetheless, emptied him in the understanding of his shape, and as we found and assumed his brain, an impression of his manner and certainties was gathered. I'm nothing if not thorough. I'm pleased also that I have retained enough of my old refo capabilities to assume the form of someone other than Litko and Stroff. Of course it's frustrating, this skulking about. One doesn't always have the time to manoeuvre the will of allies with the precision required. Things would have been a lot easier if the attack on Yicre at the Canendrigh lodge had been successful. And it should have been. Marghoster and Hidzuc had a reasonable plan. Driwna Bridche and her Ososi friends were unforeseen. They have forced me to intervene directly.

I buried deeply what was left of the guard Tresle's body. It took me only moments. Then I returned to Yicre's camp. Three days at his side was enough to see that Leusla Hidzuc did lust after Lodre Canendrigh, and he was not immune to her beauty. If Marghoster's and Crejda's crews can behave themselves through these lands, the coin Leusla makes will allow her to be munificent with her chiefs, and thus amenable to a union with Canendrigh and the Ilkashun. The peace this brings facilitates our work in the mountains. Driwna's judgement at the parley at least allowed me this opportunity. All I needed to do now was kill Yicre. One touch would be enough.

The first day I could watch from outside his tent the comings *and goings of the crew that had travelled to the parley. They felt safe, so the mood was good, and I'd ensured with Crejda's help some gifts of plant, wine and sugar, which they all call white honey here. Yicre talked of seeing his keep again at their lodge, of a concoction given him by Ufra that might help her to conceive.*

The second day brought the sun and a clear view to the huge Sathanti range they call the Spine. I can't deny the beauty of this part of the world. So much of my time has been spent in the Old Kingdoms and before that I had utilised the burgeoning Orange Empire as it grew out of Harudan, attracting other magists, both friends and enemies. It was the last time I saw Lorom Haluim. He escaped two of us, we almost had him. Ever since he's proved elusive and ruthless in the unpicking of the many threads of that empire I've spent so much time and effort in weaving. It is more sustaining than food to think of the ways I shall make that man suffer. It is a war that none here can understand. Centuries in search of the one they call Sillindar here, Haluim his follower, as I once was. This low work, this manipulation of empires, is the price of my obedience to a new master, a honeypot of misery and death to bring Haluim to us and perhaps then Sillindar when he learns of Haluim's plight.

Yicre tried to talk to me during his last day alive. I knew little of the guard's family and life, so couldn't afford to raise a concern in him by answering any questions wrongly. I did my best to counter his questions with my own. I would kill him at night, when escaping would be easier. He spoke of the fallow fields and the planting to be done as spring approached, spoke of how glad he was to be out of the "shithole" that was the Spike and its castellan. He's not wrong. Gruslatic is useful, but he's not clever. Meanness and savagery thrives. It always does. That much was clear with his treatment of Driwna, although to see her suffering and having difficulty moving about the tower, especially knowing I could have healed her, was worth a sugar in my tea, as they say in Marola.

Yicre was alone in his tent all evening, which was perfect. Lodre Canendrigh had left the camp to return to his own lodge that morning, so couldn't be blamed for the death of his chief.

I would be replaced two hours after midnight, judging by the sentry candle. The killing was simple. Inside the tent, an hour before the end of my shift, I kneeled next to Yicre as he slept. I took his hand in mine and stilled him. After a few curt words with my replacement an hour later I told him I was heading into the trees to relieve myself.

Now, with empty plains before me, I can run as fast as I please, for it is a disturbing sight to any but animals. I head to our camps high in the Peaks, a tour to ensure all is in order before returning to the Gate and readying our allies for the downfall of King Hildmir.

Chapter 12

Driwna

We stopped at Lindur-Bray, Cal and me. It was a slow journey. The cold was savage and it snowed on the milder days, which we don't often get this far south in Farlsgrad. Ufra left me to go back west, and it was obvious then to Cal and Bray what we meant to each other, but they seemed happy, when they weren't wondering when I'd get my first thorns. I miss her and would have gone with her if my mun hadn't been so ill as Cal has said.

Cal had told me how strange it was to see Stroff at the Spike only a day after he had arrived himself, and that by messenger. He did not look as worn out, stiff or tired as Cal, who's thirty summers his junior. Certainly, it takes a life of regular horsemanship such as us vanners have to be strong enough, "field ready" as Cal would say, to manage such an exhausting journey.

We talked much of Crejda's involvement in moving lots through the Sathanti after telling us she hadn't, and that had killed any residual respect Bray might have had for her. Cal had spoken to Rogus, and Rogus had not been aware of his seal and sign being used to secure supplies with the Brasks and others. He promised Cal to keep it quiet for my sake, or to tell Amaris at least if he saw her.

At Lindur, Gennic, Morril and the rest of the crew cheered us. Gennic had told them of "Brother Red" and he got on with caring for us while everyone made a fuss of me being a fieldsman. Morril gave Cal up as her second, him being needed to look into any more miracles such as had been done to Marghoster's daughter. He'd start in Ullavir with the merchants there and then head up to Autumn's Gate. He would find out what he could of those merchants with ties to the Post or Marghoster. Bray, healed well enough from his beating at the hand of Gruslatic, I asked to head up the Wheel to the Stalenfild, the mountains that snaked north from the Sathanti into Farlsgrad. He was to start in Cathrich Valley first and then go north to Stalder's Vale. All these requests for iron and coal might have their source in the contracts held by both the Cathrich and Stalder reeves and their guilds. I asked him too to keep an eye on purses being put up for soldiers, and what the detail of them was.

We took better horses and I got an old fieldbelt and some leathers that our currier and armourer made for me, mine having been stolen by Gruslatic, though it was probably for the best.

Morril told me she'd had word from the Gate to buy up ash and get leather cured and cut – iron too, if she could get any from Roan – and pass them on to the Brasks at cost. There was plant wanted as well, all for recipes that would go on fieldbelts. She questioned the orders, being concerned for the craftsmen and the farmers that she normally bought from and now was having to divert the Post's coin from. Their livelihood depended on the supply we sought. The good prices she'd cultivated for years with them she'd now see shattered when it came to drawing up contracts for next winter's furs, plant and peat that these hams sold us. It's the sort of thing that used to matter to Stroff and why Garn and Morril had their promotions.

I said my farewells to them all, and to Cal and Bray. They were concerned for me, being alone in the field after what happened to me and Bray. I was pleased to see Bray get fitted properly for leathers, a good belt and some instruction on it, as his was of an old layout that had its problems, not least the plant he was used to that we'd now improved. He was given a new sword as well, the first he'd owned in years. He'd know how to use it well enough against all but a veteran soldier. "You look like a new man," I told him. And he embraced me, much to my surprise. "Thank you, miss," he whispered to me, then he was on his horse and away, pipe in his teeth and his back straight. He was bearing the pain of our beatings better than I was, but at least the plant I'd had and salt water had stopped the swelling in my mouth.

The run over to the fens was hard going in the Jenna cold. I must have tracked a similar route to those our kurches used in being sent here. The surviving kurches of the Bridche confederacy, exiled from our lands by Marghoster, had been wandering all over the borders of the Roan Province, Rulger and Marghoster lands for close to twelve winters. We'd become enough of a nuisance we'd had papers from Yeismic Marghoster and Barolt Rulger that the local reeves had to respect in giving us some of the commons around the fens, mostly in the bogs of course. If you can call being a nuisance trying to avoid being lynched or burned. We were guilty only of being starved.

That was my childhood, as I've spoken of before. Pa was trying to make a good start of things. He put a new kurch-pole down there and got all of us together who had survived the twelve years since we lost our homeland. These lands had no kurch or clan who cared enough to claim them, so we'd begin a new pole and make them for our borders and we would be the fathers and mothers of the Bridche going forward. We began calling them the Bridche Fens, and there was even a song sung of that day and of my pa, "Aguelet a Dreis", for Dreis was his name and Aguelet was a word that means avenger and protector rolled up. It couldn't be argued that he'd suffered with, fought for and defended the lives of all those present. I think my pride in him back then makes my despair and sadness at him now all the keener for how I see him fallen. The memories that stay are happy and sad and never in between. My pa would sing "Buttons of Gold" and Mun would join the chorus, a foraging song calling for the yellowtips to show themselves. Mun had a lute and was always called upon to play it, for the fineness of her fingers as she worked leather was as well applied to the strings.

She was teaching my brun to play the night before he was taken and killed. These memories are clearest of all. I'd laughed every time he pushed his tongue out in concentration while trying to get his fingers right for the notes on the strings. He was angry at me, he always was when I mocked him for it, but it was forgotten by the morning as we took our wagon on which Pa had put pickled eggs from old Oaky and the baskets from our cousin Ebra. Most of our coin would come from the eels of course and these we'd either pickle or smoke; sometimes we'd have a few still alive in water. We had a lot of peat blocks too, but usually couldn't sell peat even at half the cost of those who lived these lands and sold their own.

Leif, my brun, was in a good mood, as was Pa, and they had me along hoping I might help make those at the market see we're families like they are. We'd have to go in the dark as it was three hours to the market, but almost as soon as we joined the other wagons making their way to Arriman Moor the Rulger militia would hold us up and be looking into everything we carried. In exile and wandering, Pa would find it hard to resist getting back at those who came looking for us, to burn our wagons, kill our horses. When they managed to get some of our sniffers, or when others of us, children and all, were found killed and hanging from trees, Pa would join their kurch-kin in digging the holes for them. He'd be gone then for a day or two, with some of our kurch-kin. We all knew what it meant and Mun would have me packing up and helping her make the wagon because we'd have to leave. He'd have been raiding and getting his revenge. Sometimes I'd hear him boasting, telling all in earshot that he'd killed and hanged those who'd killed ours. I have to confess I was glad too for him doing it. I didn't know any better. I just saw that those I remember playing with or harvesting with, those boys and girls I'd sit with on the wagons and run about with, were gone, or their pas were gone and they were crying in turn and wouldn't speak to me, or they'd say they wish it was my pa who was dead.

That day at the market, however – the day we lost Leif – the militia were worse than usual, and they were always bad. It was a hot day and soon enough it was nasty to be out in it. I was soaked in sweat and miserable and not making it any easier for Pa or Leif. Some at the market had been in their cups, more local to these commons than we were, and they all knew full well we were the "Marghosters". It was bad enough that only wanderers would look at our wares, despite us having lowered our prices to below those others selling much the same as us. The local people would walk straight past our wagon despite Pa and Leif's hollering. Any that came near would get shouted at and they'd turn away to other wagons and stalls. A few hours past the mid-day the drinkers had been singing songs about us savages and a few had come over and were asking Pa to tell them all the prices for everything we had, over and over. Then he ignored them, then one of them said was I for sale, for he wanted a tight mouth about his cock. Leif shoved him off and while Pa tried to calm him the man took a swing at Leif, but Leif ducked out of the way and got lucky with a punch that put the older man on the ground. Militia were in quicker than a ferret in a burrow and they clubbed him while pointing a spear at Pa. Then Leif got a kicking and was dragged away. I was screaming and crying and tried to go after him, and Pa got me about my shoulders and just stood there, the point of the spear at his nose. A few then threw their cups at him, splashing us both with their ale. Militia couldn't have been more than twenty summers, and Pa just asked that we go along and see justice was done right. We were told the reeve would be at the commons the following day and we should come back and talk about getting Leif out of the pens then, and we'd best be prepared to give up coin and whatever else we had, as this was a crime, to strike a militia. So we learned those men who started it all were militia, off-duty. Pa's head fell, and the boy told us to fuck off with our eels and our baskets and other shit they had enough of themselves.

Mun was worried sick when we got back. I hadn't stopped crying and Pa just had a drink that night. I heard him up in the barrel the following morning washing himself, and he put on woollens Mun had washed the day before, making the most of the sun that had burned me pink. It's hard to remember ever being a noke now I have this grey skin blotchy with bark and stains from rubs and old wounds. Pa left with Craihle, chief of one of our kin-kurches and a man who had his letters and a fine way with words.

Pa and Craihle came back later that day and had given over a silver coin and most of what we had on the wagon the day before to pay for what Leif had done to the militia, but Leif had to stay there with them till the following day. I don't know where they took Leif or where they kept him. I heard Pa telling Mun that the reeve had no sympathy for his side of the telling. He'd given Pa a scrap of a roll that he was to bring back and they'd have Leif back at the commons the following day and out of his chains.

They killed him. Pa and Craihle went to the commons at dawn the day following. Me and Mun couldn't keep to our chores that day. I remember Craihle walking the horses back as the sun was setting and Pa was flat out on the wagon, drunk from the uisge that they had taken to share with Leif, uisge that Pa had kept and brought with us from the Sathanti. Leif's body was on the wagon under an oilskin. Pa got up unsteadily and he put his arms around Mun, and he had a good cry into her shoulder, a high, helpless sobbing like it wasn't just Leif that he was grieving but all the years piled up on us all, and he was breaking. Mun just held him and stayed still. I recall she had muddy hands – she'd been in the runs weeding, sweat staining her woollens wet – and now those muddy hands were all over his good clean clothes, this land staining him, leaving its mark at every turn. Then I heard her say, so nobody else could hear, "We'll get our revenge." At the time this made me glad, fierce enough and hot enough I too sprung tears. It wasn't the first time I'd wanted to take up a sword and dreamed I had a fightbrew in me and was killing everyone before me.

Craihle was telling the others gathering about what had happened. Some shovels were brought and both Mun and Pa, though he could hardly stand, they helped dig a grave for Leif, and some of the muns that were there, as they did with all those who had died of our blood over the years, sang "At Sillindar's Side". It was a Sathanti song, a belief that in death we weave what we achieved in life to improve the Song of the Earth. As a girl of thirteen winters I could take no comfort from it. But there have been times since when I believe I hear voices, truths, in the air about me as I stone a fightbrew. There are opia mixes that my pa and the other chiefs would take, some women too if the signs were that they could hear the Song. They tell us the stories of our forefathers and tell us the stories of other animals, other kinds of people as well, which I now know must have been the Ososi.

Pa was clever, and nothing seemed to happen for a long time after. I put flowers on the earth over my brun Leif, and Eliwn, our younger brun, he'd put them on too – we'd do it every week. Pa was away a lot then, back in the nights, and through the curtain I could hear him and Mun whispering each night. Others would come in with him and they'd all be drinking. We began eating better then, some meat for the pot or spit, more bread, and then some hands lived with us, helped with the walling off and draining of fenlands for crops. He never said where he got the coin, but we knew. We stopped going to the commons markets.

We went wrong.

Now I'm back at the fens, our fens again, and if I'm honest, I'm more nervous than last time, fretful for Mun and her health.

It's Eliwn that comes upon me as I'm washing out some plugweed I'd found a good patch of, on the border of the fens. It happens to be near the dell Cal had told me about and I was going to have a look at what slaves there might be while I was riding through. I'm wearing my Post cloak, and I'm not hiding or keeping low as he finds me, for these are my homelands, the only ones I know, and I felt I'd be safe enough I could stop the spotting and sneaking about.

Eliwn is with one of his age; both have bows.

"Where's your van, Post?" he says, not able to see my face.

"There's no van here, my brun. Just me." I turn to look at him and seeing me brings a smile to his face.

"Driwna?" he says. I stand and shake water off the plug-weed I'd had in the stream I was kneeling over.

He drops his bow and rushes over to me, so much bigger a man now than when I last saw him six winters ago, my pa's nose and cheeks, Mun's chin.

"Oh Eli, you've grown! Look at you!" His hair's as black as ale, but he's already losing it at the crown and temples. It happened to Pa when he was young, but Eliwn's is still long where Pa shaved his. He smiles and squeezes me.

"I hardly knew you, Driw. You've paid colour and fierce it seems. There's nothing the like here excepting those mercs we have come through." His smile's gone then. "Mun said you'd come. We saw Cal a while back. He would have told you."

"He did. Who's this with you?"

"Apo, this is my sister, Driwna. Doing well in the Post I hear." Apo nods and shoulders his bow, leads their horses to us.

"You said she'd paid colour Eli; she has at that." He's fairer than Eli, taller by a head. He's got a bit of cooker's colour on him, faint blotches and dried-out skin uncared for. A dayer's the best he's managed by the looks.

"Been a soldier and a vanner, haven't you, sister. And Cal said you were some sort of marschal?"

"A fieldsman they call it. I work for the High Red himself."

"Like fuck you do," he says, chuckling. "Worth some coin then I'll wager. Pa'll want to know how much more you can send us."

"You come out from the dell where Pa's got those slaves?"

His face changes at that, just briefly. "Cal told you of that as well, not the why of it. I'll leave that to Pa."

"How is he?"

"Same but worse."

"He's a hero, your pa," says Apo.

"One way of looking at it," I say. I wasn't going to argue with him about the killing Pa done of innocent people just to hurt those who hurt us. One of the reasons I had to leave all those years ago.

Eliwn gives Apo a look and he understands to keep quiet from now on.

"We look after the slaves well, Driw, no good them being starved or on the droop. Getting more coin than plant would make us. No need to go begging for coppers at the commons now."

"Who's buying the slaves?"

He shakes his head and I know that's all I'll get for an answer. "You want to ride home with me?"

"Of course I would. Pa did say I wasn't ever to set foot in the lodge again, so I'm looking forward to seeing his face when I do."

"Don't make it harder on Mun, Driw. Don't argue with him."

"I'll find a spot where him and I can talk, Eli."

The ride to the lodge, to my home, is proof enough that Bridche fortunes have changed. Pastures we'd use for the animals are now all wheat or plant runs, a good few leagues' worth of trees have been cut down all about us and there's dams up elsewhere. There was a time we'd not have been

239

allowed to follow up on plans like this, much as our kurches wanted to make a go of things. I pass our kurchpoles and see on them Pa along with the other chiefs of our kin-kurches. All are carved into them at the base, a new chapter in the Bridche kurch-fod. He's a king here now, or as good as. And there's something about seeing all this change in the land, these new houses and sheds and the sniffers out, that feels like a world away from the fens I left at eighteen summers. I could almost close my eyes and imagine that this wasn't all fed by slaves and whatever other trafficking and banditry he's doing between Ullavir, Ethmor Hill and the Spike.

There's cords, well made, stretching over the bogs thick with cat-tails, sedge, orchids, foxgloves and frosted marsh-muhly. Being winter there's no flies to speak of and it's welcome, though I miss how bright and beautiful the bogs and fens come in the summer. I've long been used to the smell.

The cords we lead our horses along are watched. On the solid ground and hillocks that are laced through the bogland are willows and spruce, thickets from which I can see people watching us. Pa is wise to keep the bogs and fens about the lodge intact, for no militia could take these lands if he had enough kurch-kin to defend them.

We pass through kurchpoles of our kin-kurches, then Bridche's own. The land seems still but for the whistling of the sniffers echoing over the flats. Ahead I see the gathering of huts and the lodge. It's grown, two storeys now and a wooden stand's been built behind it with someone looking out over the bogs all about us. The land it's all on – Bridche Island it's now called – was raised like an upturned plate about the lodge, enough for twenty huts and runs for plant, pigs and chickens. There's a couple of duts wouldn't have been born last I was here that come up to us as Eliwn and

240

I lead the horses onto the gentle rise to the lodge. They are asking a thousand questions about my colour and my knife, sword and belts.

The only building of stone here is the forge, the peat and pottery kilns part of it. I'm delighted to see Cirne at the anvil through a gap in the curtains that's down for forging, and she's barking orders at a boy the same way she was once a girl being barked at by her pa. She looks over at us and smiles as she recognises me.

"Cirne!" I shout. As girls we used to practise kissing, out in the thickets, hoping to impress the first boys we liked enough to let them kiss us. I was a bit keener for her kisses than theirs that spring. I won't forget how well the bog coppers and canary flies kissed our skin that first new year our kurch-kin settled and began the drainage and 'jacking for the wood we'd need.

"Driwna? It's you?" She puts her pliers down on the bench, tells the boy to keep the fire lively.

"He yours?" I ask. "He can't be, too old, or did you catch a good man young?"

"Ah no, not mine; that one's Lily's, Lily Adibric. She's with a hand had been working the fields out at Ledde's Dyke. One harvest's dancing with him and this one appears the following summer. Doubt you'd recall. He's a good man, they brought this one up well. He listens, unlike most men, eh Eli?"

"I think you're right, blacksmith," he says. She gives him a wink.

"You must have a man hidden up somewhere," I say. "Look at you now, that scarf can hardly keep that thicket of hair up." She's tall and lean, the work does that of course, but the soot can't hide her blue eyes or lovely round cheeks.

I embrace her; she's damp from the work, smells of peat smoke.

"You making mail in there?"

"Wire, yes. Got the turve spades done last week. Gives me a chance to catch up with some armour. Putting some links together."

I won't ask why, for she'll tell me as much as Eli has. Much as chain's always an advantage on a battlefield where everyone's risen on brews, off the field there's no such thing as a fight, generally speaking. If someone's on a brew and the other isn't expecting it, mail won't be a help.

"You're back for your mun?"

"I am."

"I'm glad. You look fierce, Driwna. That boy Cal came through to speak to your pa and told us you'd killed the Hidzuc chief."

"I did. What did Pa say?"

"I think he was glad." It's nice of her to say it, but it sounds instead like he made no sort of pronouncement on the news to anyone. "Not the girl I once went bog-crabbing with, are you Driw? You still scared of crabs?"

"Probably, love. We should have some cups before I leave. I've missed you."

"Aye. Welcome home. And next time, bring that Cal with you. He was nice to look on and he sang lovely while he was about his horse."

There's a few about us have the look of hired hands, and I count seven soldiers in leathers that have paid colour. Two must be mercenaries for how they look, a heaviness to them, years of brews can't be hidden, for they thicken the muscles, change the bones. These men were like bulls with cloaks and beards.

"It's my sister," says Eli as we approach. One nods at him.

"Still have to take the sword, any knives, miss."

"Go fuck yourself."

242

His sword's out pretty quick. Eli puts up a hand.

"Ganet, it's fine."

I shake my head and walk up to the mercenary. "I'm blood, you're coin. I'm sure Pa will appreciate your keenness all the same." I hold out my arm for him, which he isn't expecting. Then we clasp. Usually, clasping arms is all two need to understand the temper and quality of the other, that and the calm, the clarity in the eyes, whether there's betony there or peace. Pa's keeping the best close to him. This Ganet looks down at my hand, sees the marks the thorns made, the redness that's spreading around the hole, into the veins and toughening the flesh.

"Post has some thrannie drudhas. This be a mix I can get a coat of?"

I smile, thinking of her. Sillindar, I miss her. I'm gone for a moment. He takes my silence well enough.

"Your ma's in the back," he says. "Near the runs."

"I don't want her breathing in the lasch; you should have left her upstairs," says Eli. By lasch he was meaning the spores and fumes from the mushroom logs she'd work so well.

"She'll be buried in those runs, brun," I say. "You can't keep her from them."

"Don't talk like that, Driw. You haven't seen her."

The lodge has a big firepit inside, something I only saw in the Citadels, but it's colder there. I think my pa enjoys having the big hall for having more people to listen to him, more chance to show his charity and more room for the thanks he would believe he's due.

There's two sweeping that don't look like kin. My heart sinks to see that we have slaves now. They don't have their hair as we do; they keep their eyes to the floor, sweeping like they're making the work last.

There's a fine job been done with oak posts and boards to build this hall. It's been built against the front of our old lodge, which has been knocked out to allow a double door through to the original part of it. There Eli leads me through our old hearthroom that is now a storeroom. There's a beautiful, heavy smell of bacca, eight or so kegs of it. There's cybins here too, mushrooms forbidden to all but the drudhas, that somehow keep the smell of mown grass on them, even drying on the rails as they are. Too many here for the kurch, this is a harvest for an army to use, enough for a hundred lots at least. I see now it's the lasch from these that Eli's worried about. It's full enough of lots that we have to squeeze through a corridor made out of the chests and kegs. I can't even see the hearth itself, where Mun would once have had her chair, made from a big piece of a rare black seka wood from far up in the Spine, a gift from the chief of one of our kurches now lost to us. She worked the leather and padding herself of course, and I would trace with my young fingers the plant she'd carved over the legs, arms and the back; Sathanti plant, from poppies, arnica, cicely and wheat around the legs, a wolf and horses among them, rising up to elms, alders, and above all the mighty chestnut, the root of so many of our old recipes.

Off to the left of the hearthroom was Mun and Pa's room. The door's open to it, and there's the snapping and wheezing of the fire; it smells like cincha wood along with the peat. One of the shutters is open and a cot's been made for her, my mun, and in only a moment I'm weeping to see her and rush to her for she is so small in the cot, like a child in a man's bed, thin as reeds, the neck of her wool shirt baggy about her stringy throat. I see that big, beautiful chair is next to her bed, like a companion to her almost.

"Oh, Dinna!" she says, a lispy sound to her voice, like it's

244

not coming from her chest but the corners of her teeth. Her eyes light up well enough and her arms, skin as smooth and dry as a bottle cork, stretch out to me. She always called me Dinna, for that's what I first said when I learned my own name.

I drop to my knees at the cot and put my arms about her. It breaks my heart to see her in bed while it's daylight. We once joked about how she must have had caltrops for an arse, for she could never sit still unless the sun had set and we had eaten. Six winters of us missing each other are released in our tears. "My little girl," she says. "My dut, my blood." Over and over. We both laugh at the same time as we settle down, feeling stupid for all our crying when we're happy to see each other. She finds my hand with hers and holds it as tight as she can. Hard to see her colouring in this light but it's not good. She runs her fingers across the stubble on my head, cradles my face in her other hand.

"Eli says they made you up, Dinna, in the Post. Says you sent twenty silver pennies home to your kurch since midwinter."

"She did, Mun," he says, behind me.

"Every month one of ours brings in the purse you send. Your pa won't let Post come past the kurchpoles. Where is he, Eli? He'll want to see her." I look back at him; we both know how it was I left.

"He's not expecting her, Mun."

She's canny enough she must recall then our argument. "Well, I'm grateful for her coin and her letters even if he don't think he needs them any more." The saying of all this seems to get her out of breath; she blows softly for a few moments before she can carry on.

"Besides, she come home. Pa must have told her I've been forced into my bed when there's the runs need attention."

"There's people for the runs, mun," says Eli. I flash him a look and shake my head, because he has to know how fucking angry I am that he's talking of slaves. "And you must remember it was her friend Cal who come by. Pa was shouting at him, but he come in to see you before he left. The one who can sing like a thrush." She's searching her memories for it, eyes looking about as though it's out in front of her.

"The tall boy, he's your friend?"

"Yes, Mun," I say. "Years ago now, a long time past, we came by, before that hall was built next door."

"Oh the hall." She rolls her eyes. "I told him we didn't need such. Who wants a firepit inside unless you're a north-born?"

I look back at Eli again and he shrugs.

"Is your pa not here to see you, Dinna?"

"No, Mun, I'll go fetch him."

"He doesn't shave my hair like he used to; look how long it's getting?" She meant by that her hair had to be kept as it was when they were made keeps and her hair was cut to join his in our oak crown. He hadn't worn it the last time I had come home and must not have bothered to shave her head as the ritual that accompanies those others regarding the Bridche crown.

"Can I get you anything, Mun?" I ask.

"Oh, no, Dinna. Tooey — what's his name, Eli — Touail is it?"

"Toula, Mun," he says.

"Toula had sat me up today so I could see outside." She gestures to the window, her arm only moving a few inches.

"Sit me up, love," she says.

Eli steps in and gently eases her up. She brings her feet around and onto the floor, finds her own balance on the edge of the cot. She's got footwraps on, clean enough, and I'm glad she's well looked after.

"Let me get him, Mun," I say.

"You do that, I want Eli to help me get a pot on. We've got some caffin dried and powdered and it does a good job of getting me on my way. We'll have a bit of uisge in this one as well, won't we, Dinna?"

"Aye." I stand up again, lean over to kiss her head. "I'll fetch him, Eli. Where is he?"

"Might be he's over the east fens, Crasken's Row. There's a lot more sheds there since you last come back."

"See you tonight, Eli; you'll have some cups with me?"
He smiles. "I will."

Eli's right about the sheds. The Rulger reeves would have him hanged if they could see what my pa's pushing through these fens.

The bogs give way to the fens in the east, as it's closer to the Rofany river. There'll be a swell come the spring and it'll fill the fens and there's good sniffing and hunting to be had there. Between fen and bog there's the Andract Way, and I think my pa runs this part of it, from what Cal told me, a road on a finger of land that's raised above the level of the river, inclining upwards as it finds the rolling plains south-east, and much more arable.

There's heavy forest that fringes the road for miles either side and it's no wonder Pa's found it easy to pick off the vans that come through.

I lead my horse out of the bogland and up through the cold and shadowy trees by paths I used to wander with Cirne and some of the others our age. I smell the smoke of a campfire and hear men talking before I see them, the air still and frosty. I call out so they don't try anything and a few urgent shouts are followed by three that come to meet me. I don't recognise them.

"I'm looking for my pa, Dreis Bridche. I'm Driwna."

"Are you? We'll need a bit more than that, soldier," says one, a woman with a broken nose, tired eyes and a pipe in her teeth. She might have been a serious merc once, but not now.

"Course you will. Tell him that I hope he's not bought slaves with that twenty silver I sent him from Autumn's Gate and tell him it's Cal told me that Mun had the wasting."

She nods and leaves the other two with me. Soon there's whistling, a field command I think, and the two gesture me to follow. None look like they got much fight or quality about them, but not even Pa can pay well enough for more than one crew of the quality Ganet seems to have at the lodge.

In the clearing there's a fire with some pots over it and three sheds, raised a bit from the ground, so they must have plant in them. Across the clearing from the sheds are stables for horses and a shed for hay and other provisions. Pa's at the fire with his crew; most have stopped for a bowl of whatever's in the pot. I can smell eels stewing, some parsley and cockles. He drove my mun crazy with taking up good runs for his parsley.

He's put on weight and got greyer in his beard, unplaited, which is unlike him. He won't wear the crown of the Bridche as Sathanti do, so his bit of hair's down as well, dirtier grey. He has a heavy leather coat on, fur's been stitched to the collar about his neck and it alone marks him out as chief here, for all others are in ponches or woollens. He's always had heavy eyebrows and a fat nose I've inherited a bit of; makes him look angry at the best of times, so I can't tell what he's thinking. Then again, I couldn't care much for any problem he has with me. Too many years have gone. I tie my horse at a post and put some hay down for him, give him a fuss.

"Well, here's a sight. My daughter comes home after six winters. That Rulger boy tell you about your mun, did he?"

"I wouldn't be back otherwise, Papy. You made that clear enough."

Nobody'd say anything without his giving an opening for it, so the others stayed quiet, watching me or getting on with their stew.

"Hungry, child?"

"I always liked your stew, Papy. Smell of eel and parsley brings good memories." He gestures for one of his crew to take up a bowl and ladle some stew in. The heat of it is a wonder for my cold hands. I tip the bowl and the broth itself is as good as it ever was, for he never over-salted and would tear at Leif for doing it when he'd be making it with Mun all those years ago.

"Let's walk a bit, Driwna."

After packing his pipe and getting it started with a stick from the fire he gestures me through onto the trail the far side of the clearing from where I came in. I finish the bowl and follow him.

It's early afternoon, but the sun's light is only grey in here and there's a ground mist. The trail we're on would suit a wagon, winding so as not to reveal itself until near the river itself.

He slows a little once he's out of sight of his crew. His eyes have a look in them, something I'd not seen before. Weariness. It's not just there's more lines about his face, but even with a bit of colour that he had from thieving and poaching years ago, he looks much older than he should; his cheeks have slipped, as Cal would say.

"She'll be glad you're here, Driw."

"Feels like it's come on quick, but the wasting always does."

"It has." There's nothing more then that either of us can say to it.

"Us Marghosters are doing well on Rulger land. Keeps his militia away, the tithe we pays Edral Rulger."

"That's good."

"As Marghosters, as tribes that swear fealty to King Hildmir, we've broken with some of our Sathanti customs, and had to."

"I know. You don't say 'kurch' now?"

He spits and has a good draw on his pipe. There's a touch of kannab in there, only ever a touch so he stays lucid.

"The Rulger boy was asking about the slaves, and he from the High Red, as you are. No business of yours, his or his lordship Yblas. But I hear you killed young Eirakh Hidzuc, on the field as well, before a force of Ilkashun. Good for you, you've made a good few of our elders happy."

"But we know I didn't kill him for you, or the kurch."

"No, you did it for the Post."

"No, Papy, I didn't do it for the Post either. I was in the Canendrigh kurch and the Hidzucs came at the Ilkashun camp, looking to kill them all to a child while the Daith-nu was there."

He shrugs. There's another silence and he smokes a few puffs.

"It's going well then," I say. "So much has changed since I was last home. It's all a lot bigger."

"It is. You know some of it and your friend has told you the rest."

"You're getting noticed, Papy. You're taking too much. I'm surprised those in the settlements about don't complain to Rulger, let alone the merchants you're taking lots of. Rulger won't have it if you hit his coffers, and he's an ally of Hildmir."

"Rulger doesn't pay his militia in these parts. We do."

"You don't think all the land you've reclaimed isn't making

the fens a more profitable prospect for Hildmir and Rulger to root our kurch out of. At the same knock they'll win back those grumbling about the lack of law here?"

"We don't touch the fuckers used to spit on us in the commons; we've got those that took Leif and the rest we don't need." He looks at me then, for, though it was a few winters after Leif was killed, it was what he did about that made me leave our kurch, that and looking for me to make keep with some Rulger militiaman he wanted influence with.

"I remember. But it wasn't only those that took Leif that you took in turn."

"I see you're still sore about it."

"We've had this talk six winters ago, Papy. You could have had all this without those hangings and burnings, and still Leif isn't here. Revenge don't raise the dead back, don't turn back the days either."

"All we had and all we have is fear, girl. We wouldn't have all this if they didn't know what we could do to them."

Farmers, nokes, people who could turn earth and cook and grow, none had known suffering an ounce of what we suffered in exile. They didn't stand a chance when Pa put fear of us in them, while our own nokes in the surviving kurches that might have been afraid of having to do what gangers do didn't need much persuading of Pa's cause, not when the spoils were food, coin and most of all respect where none had been given for so much of our lives.

"And when did you start moving slaves, Papy?"

"When I was shown what coin lay in it."

"So we're no longer Sathanti? No longer Bridche? Is this why you saw fit to leave the old kurchpoles out of sight and put the new ones up? You call us Marghosters now, before me. Who the fuck are we, Papy? What are we now?"

251

He whips his pipe out of his mouth, his eyes wild.

"You don't have the right to ask questions of me and how it's done here, girl! A kurch-fod gets written when there's enough alive and eating, farming and herding to have heirs at all. When there's some land under you that's the same land was there the last week and week before. Land you can bury some folk in, land that's not a killing field you leave your own tribe to die on because you've got a girl and a boy in your arms, because your children have to live, to live and lead the tribe when you're gone. But I only got one left of those, haven't I, girl? One left I saved who'll make those about this land learn we are not Bridche but Marghoster, for the other's sworn herself to coin and profit, to filling coffers so's the Post can buy out those it chooses and then undercut those that's left in markets they've built their lives around. Don't start me on the Post and the shit they've fed you."

"Isn't like the Post hasn't fed you either."

"That's you, not the Post. They moved you on for that and still you were screaming for their nipple till they made you a red when you could have come home."

"Slaves though, Papy. They're people, not ploughs and horses or picks and spades. They got blood and they got family somewhere, in some far place. They're in fucking exile like we were."

"No, Driwna! They're fed, sheltered, healed with plant, they earn a bit of coin even, those working for us. Who gave us that in those long years? These Farlsgrad cunts all over the south gave us burnings and hangings and stole our herd, took your fucking brun for a swing of his fist because he had just a bit too much pride in him."

The pair of us are at it again.

"You running slaves west into the Sathanti? How will Eli

ever make them see us as Bridche if you behave like a Marghoster? Have you got trade with Yeismic Marghoster?"

"I'm running slaves from Ullavir to the Spike. Couldn't give a fuck what happens to them after."

"You seen mercs come through? More than usual?"

"Why are you asking me this, Driwna? What's going on? Because it don't just sound like your boy Cal telling me Yblas is pissed about some lots going missing."

"No, Papy. Tribes all over the Tongue have cut bridges in the passes. People are getting kidnapped in their hundreds from all the tribes there, the Ososi too."

"You think I'm part of whatever's going on?"

"No, but . . . but if there was enough gold in it, seems like you wouldn't be bothered about that any more, and I have to be sure you aren't involved because something bad's happening out there and I have to go look at it."

"You're leaving us again, leaving your mun here while she's so ill?"

"I'm not going for a little bit. Papy, I can't just give up my duty any more than you can give up your operations to be at her cot."

"You cheeky little sow. You've been here an hour and you're finding fault in me for being at the sheds?"

"You seem to be finding fault in me for the same. Papy, why are we doing this? Why are we having a fucking go at each other when she's home so poorly?"

He sighs and looks skyward. A breeze rolls through the trees, the sound of the sea. I feel it in my fingers, my legs, my blood and plant responding to this sound. I let myself float with it, like I've become clear and it's moving through me and moving me with it. My pa's voice brings me back to myself.

"Your friend at Lindur, Reeve Morril, she sent a messenger

here to ask what it is we have and want; says that she would find us better rates than others would offer. That your doing?"

"No. But she knows how it's been for these kurches. The Post can be like that, Papy. My purse with them now is to promote the Creed set down by Yblas. Help the helpless. Honour the purse. Peace through trade. Those things we must hold true to in all our work."

"We're not so helpless now, daughter."

"Until you make a mistake. Until you, or those who take a purse from you, kill the wrong person, stop the wrong van. Then they'll burn all of us out of these fens."

"I'll bear in mind your advice."

"You almost sound like you mean it. Don't you have a captain you can leave to run things while you tend to Mun?"

"Tend to Mun? Me? I'm not carrying her about and asking how much honey she wants in her oats."

"She's got a while to live then."

"Get out of these fucking fens, girl. I'm not going to wear your opinion of me and your mun and how it goes with us. Might be women and men are seen the same in the lakes you swim about in, but here we have traditions. I see her enough of an evening and in the night I'm first to call the drudha if she's in pain and needs betony."

I open my mouth, then close it again, and I take a moment to hold my fists at my side, close my eyes. If I hit him, if even I ask him how long she's been on the betony, well, I'll be on my horse today. If I remind him that the traditions he keeps seem to be those that suit him, I'll not have any chance to see her again. I believe him with regard to the slavery. I don't know if I should, but he's never shown himself to extend his interests beyond protecting the kurches who are with him on the fens. He's supplying the trade through to the Sathanti Peaks all the same.

"Can we go back, Papy? I'll be gone soon enough, as it is what you wish. I want to see Mun. When I return to Lindur I'll make sure Gennic will come or will send someone with whatever they think might help her. It'll be paid for."

"Good. Let's go back then. Might be your brun's got her upright. She has to keep her body in its habits of movement if she's not to waste."

And again I keep my thoughts to myself. I'll speak to my brun about what he should be doing to help Mun in her final days. We walk back in silence, him smoking and me feeling like these runs, these trees with our drawings and names carved on them as we ran about as duts years before, they're not mine any more, they're other people's memories, cold to me. There's a lurch in my belly just remembering that feeling of not having a home, of nowhere being familiar. It was Pa himself told me once that a homeland feels like a body and that we're its blood, it lives with us and because of us. We keep each other, we love each other. It's why we bury our dead, believing that our fathers and mothers and theirs and theirs all fill the soil and water, root and rock with their love for us. Is it Ufra's blood? The seed of her plant in me that has frayed this bond? Or is it what Papy's said? Is it that the story of our kurch has changed as he said it must, or that our dead must find their own peace with the fathers of those who lived here before? Our soil is thin.

We are in the clearing with his sheds. He tells me he'll be along, that he must see to a wagon that's moving out this afternoon. I have an urge to get in my cups fierce. Where's his love for my mun now? Why is he not on his knees before her after all that she's done for us? Did she not hold him as she held us to take our nightmares away with her kelahlu, the nightsongs of our ancestors? Nightmares of our cousins gutted and swinging from trees, horses butchered and left for the flies, sometimes alive and screaming in the dark. She whispered the kelahlu to keep us from crying out and being found, covered in blood, hungry to near madness. She was the kurchpole for us all. What every day of our exile broke, she would fix every night. There's not words enough for what I remember of her, now I'm old enough to understand the iron of a mother's love. Too common and too profound for poets, this love.

At the lodge my brun has gone. Mun's been sat up in a chair near the shutters, open to the plant runs beyond. She's got a blanket over her, hands clutching the arms of the chair as though she might be torn from it. Looks like she's had the caffin, a cup on a small stand next to her. Her eyes are closed but her jaw twitches and trembles. She's managing pain. Then her eyes flick open. She's heard me.

"I asked him for some sweet butter. I can walk about a bit once it's on my tongue." She smiles a drooper's weak and shameless smile.

Eliwn comes back then. He pauses a moment, knowing that I'm about to see him give her some betony. He digs a spoon into a pouch. It's waxy, this betony, mixed with guira I expect, or perhaps even some white honey. The spoon shaves a large flake from the top of the block and he puts it into her mouth. She takes the spoon off him and sucks on it greedily. My eyes fill with tears to see it. Eliwn looks at the floor. He goes to take the spoon back and she shifts away from him.

"Come on, Mun!" he says, too harshly.

It takes a few more moments and she sags slightly, the fervour of her movement slowing, the anxiety burning off her. She lets the spoon dip in her mouth and he snatches it away.

"I understand, Eli. Don't be like that with her."

"Where's Pa?"

"Said he'd follow, had some wagon he obviously couldn't fucking trust a captain with."

"Can't you see it, Driw?" he whispers. "It's because he's as upset as we are. He stuffs his heart away in his pipe and his cups or in going about asking how others are and looking out for them, because he can fix all that."

"He never could let his feelings go much, your pa. A daith-nu can't." Mun this is, talking while her eyes are closed, her hands hanging off the arms of the chair now. "Think how it would look, him crying in front of the other chiefs or his soldiers, him running after me for me to sit down so he can prepare our pot, skin our rabbit or buck." She holds out her hand that's nearest to me and I take it. Her fingers run over mine.

"Strong now, Dinna. Strong as I was, you are. Enjoy that strength while you have it." She sniffs then, leans forward a touch, some effort, and brings my hand to her nose.

"There's a smell about you, not just the colour." She opens her eyes, the pale blue of a winter morning. She holds my hand close to her. "It's strong, this smell, like a red lily."

"I thought you'd taken to dabbing a bit of oil about you as I've heard is the custom among those with coin enough to fuss about such things," says Eliwn.

"Whores, you're thinking, Eli," I say.

Mun frowns. "Oh Dinna, no, this is something . . . like it's someone else you smell of. I know your smell, girl; I wore it as I wore you as a bub and dut."

"Didn't mean that, Driw, you know I didn't," says Eli.

"Are you in love?" she asks.

"I think so, Mun."

"Aaah, away with you, 'I think so'. It's beating at me like waves on rocks; you're hot with it, girl."

Eli's smiling.

"Who is he?" she asks.

"An Ososi." I can't expect her to understand and I'm sorry for it. If she hadn't been taken with this wasting I'd have loved to bring Ufra home to meet her.

"Ososi?"

She makes a circle with her finger over her head.

"No Mun, no flower in the braegnloc." She breathes deeply again, sees me properly for that brief moment of lucidity, the freedom from pain the betony's given her.

"If you're happy, if he makes you happy, then I'm happy. Sillindar knows there's not happiness can't be snatched from you in a flash."

"We know it and all." Eli this is. "Are you staying tonight, Driw?" he says.

"I am. I think I might have to go tomorrow."

"You don't have to go, Dinna."

"Me and Papy, Mun, we argued again, about the slaves. I, I can't stand it. I upset him with my talk of them."

"He'll not mind you staying longer. And look about you, girl. Look at what he's brought us to, your pa."

"I know. Things are growing. A lot for Eli to learn and manage."

"He's clever, your brun. Pa's showing him what's to do."

I look at Eliwn. Obvious why Pa's so concerned. Eli's no ganger, no soldier either. He never went with Pa and Leif on the runs, or poaching. Leif was on dayers in the years I recall up until he was killed, listening and spitting back up all Pa's thoughts he'd fed him. I expect Pa's filled Eli with his thoughts as he would have me if I'd stayed home longer, but my brun hasn't got that same chill in his manner; I don't see him looking a father in the eye before beating him in front of his children for not clearing a debt. He's too much like Mun and I wonder how often he's been told that by Pa along the way.

"Can I lie down again, Eli?" says Mun. She's struggling being upright.

"Pa wants you to have a bit of a walk about first, take a few steps."

"Maybe I can manage that."

"Really?" I say.

"A few steps will make him happy," she says. She's drowsy with the betony, like she's not bedded into her body. We both take an arm, me and Eli, and I can feel her wobbling at her hips as she tries to lock her legs straight, set herself. Despite the betony she struggles to move a foot forward; we have to lean her over it. This is fucking stupid, but to make her happy, which is what I want, is to put her through this so she's making him happy. She improves briefly, as though her body's remembering what to do on its own, one leg taking the weight, muscles responding, her other leg moving through, her arms wanting to be free of ours to do what they must. She can't though. We brace her to cope with twenty or so small steps and she's blowing by then, gritting her teeth with pain and concentration.

"No more," she says finally, a smile escaping with the gasp of that being spoken. I nod to Eli and he lets me sweep her up so I'm carrying her. She weighs less than a vanner's pack. I carry her to the cot and put her on it. She seems to crumble as she hits the boards.

"Did she take some steps?" Pa this is. He's moving about outside the room for a moment, moving some chests.

"A few," says Eli. Pa comes in then, pipe still in his mouth, but the bacca must have gone out.

"Good." He comes to the cot, kneels next to her. Her smile springs up on her face as she sees him.

259

"There you are. I had my walk, love. Dinna and Eli helped me."

"Good. Can't let it win, can we? We're stronger than that. Now, Eliwn, give me a hand to move this table. Driwna'll want to eat with Mun before she leaves tomorrow."

"She's not leaving tomorrow, Dreis," says Mun.

"Eliwn, fetch us all some wine, we have those bottles up from Cassica somewhere next door. Driwna, you'll go to the kitchen and bring in whatever you find there, but I'll have some of the bread and butter that's there. The girl baked it this morning and she's learned well off Mun. It's almost as good, isn't it Mun?"

Her eyes are closed. "Say, Mun!" Pa barks. She opens them with a start.

"What's the matter?" she asks.

"We're eating in a moment. Go on, Driwna."

I follow Eliwn out of the room. I could scream as Pa starts on at her about the troubles he's having at the sheds. I want to saddle my horse and go now, but my feet keep moving to the kitchen and the shelves and benches where the jars and linen-wrapped meats are. This kitchen has been extended, the old wall knocked through and rebuilt with extra room for tables to prepare feasts. I find a tray and put a spread of food on it. The bread has a good brown crust to it, a hint of being burned on the edges where the dough was scored, and I love the ashy taste this gives it, that and the salted butter.

I put the food out on the table. Pa's sitting in Mun's chair as she lies in her cot. They're holding hands and she's lying on her side, able to watch me.

"Good to have our girl back and waiting on you, isn't it Mun?"

I'm trying to understand why he's being like this, baiting me.

"I wish I'd never left, Papy."

Fuck him. I go back to get a plate to put Mun's food on.

"If you have a clean knife, cut Mun's up small. It'll help her as she has trouble swallowing big bits of food."

Eliwn returns with some cups and the bottles in his arms.

"Make us a fire, Pa," says Mun.

"Eliwn'll do it, won't you, boy?"

"Course, Pa."

"I expect the Post has you busy, Dinna?"

"Yes, Mun, always."

"Where must you go that's more important than here, Driwna?" says Pa.

I blink away the baby girl, the welling up of tears as I put her back in the alka, back in the dark.

"The Post would have me go to Sathanti, to our old lands and beyond them, to find the Ososi and render them help." The Post couldn't give a shit about the Ososi unless it was cycas of theirs, secrets of their fightbrews, but he doesn't need to know that. I smile then, realising that because I'm a fieldsman and I care about Ufra and her kurch, the Post really does now give a shit.

"Seems the Sathanti are more important than you are to her, Mun," he says.

"For fuck's sake, Papy. Our mun's happy with you, happy here, and life has become comfortable and even safe at last. I have my life with the Post like you have yours. Might be I'd have stayed a bit if you hadn't told me not an hour or so ago to get out of these lands, but here you are making out to her I'm being a cunt by not staying."

"Dinna!"

"Stop arguing, the both of you, it's making me sick." Eliwn this is. "We'll have a drink, for us and for Leif, try for an hour to forget how we got here."

261

"Sit me up then, I'll have a cup of that wine," says Mun. Pa helps her, and he's bubbling, keeping a lid on it. He gets hot in a rage but I go cold. Eliwn puts his hand on my shoulder as he passes me a cup. I have a sip and watch Pa settle her upright on the edge of her cot, put her lips to his cup, for her hands are trembling.

"Eli's right," she says. "Where we've been are memories we had and where we go are dreams of what's to come. You've all made me proud, there's fire in your bellies and I'm glad of it." She gives herself a few breaths. "Each day on those wagons we was helpless, each day the world was taking cuts of us, taking our marrow out a spoon at a time. Nothing we could do but endure it. Now our girl's changing the world. Our pa's led us to a good life out here, better than we had back in the Sathanti, and I don't care if you think different. Remember our people who didn't get this far. I might be dying, might even seem like there's not but a nugget of reason left in me, but I thank Sillindar for every day I got left. One more day with all of your love's worth a score of years without." The wasting's gone for a moment. She shines, empties her cup and licks her lips. "Dreis, I'll have another and we'll drink to being Marghosters; stubborn, stubborn bastards we are."

Chapter 13

Driwna

Might be the plant that's forming in me, but for all I drank of the wine that evening, and it was a lot, I never felt as bad as that after being in my cups before. Cirne stopped in and we had a good sing and dance. We got drunk enough even Pa calmed down and Mun did what she could, waving her arms about from the bed and mouthing the words to verses about things I never thought I'd hear my mun say herself. Me and my brun did a jig and it was lovely to see him laughing and acting up. I know it's not easy for him having to get involved in the life of my pa, a brutal and ruthless one.

I could hardly bear to let Mun go when it came to leaving the following day. In the quiet of the morning, when the reaction to the wine had me doubled over and crying out for some betony or kannab, it was just me and her awake. The drudhan, the apprentice drudha, came by with Mun's betony and I had a bit with her, just a nail's worth to get me straight. It gave us enough time to talk over some things. In her head she was her old self, sharp and funny, more than a match for the men she'd grown up with I think. She bid me leave, not wanting me to see her weaken, and she told me she was proud, proud of what I did to the Hidzucs and proud of how I was helping the Sathanti from being fucked over by Farlsgrad again.

It took me some time to get back to Lindur. I was grieving for Mun, but I was sick as well with the twitching I could feel in my arms, in my body. I had to ride half a day and rest half a day, for I had a fever and my skin burned and stung all over. It was worse than paying the colour and, even now, riding out to the Hidzuc lodge, I'm puffing on a kannab pipe to calm the roiling of my nerves and muscles, the pain in my head. As foolish as it is to say, I'm fretful of how sensitive I am; to light, to dark, to the rub of my woollens on my skin, the smell and feel of the air. Either I'm going mad or I have some sense of the weather now, a surety that rain will or won't come, like the air has its own deep currents as the sea does, that the stillness of the blue sky is a deception.

At Lindur there was no word from Cal or Bray, but it had not been so long since we'd parted and they had further to ride than I. Morril looked after me until I was well enough to move on, and she put up with all my stories of Mun as I was coming to terms with that. She'd lost her own mun and pa, understood the emptiness, the regrets that could fill a lake. I was delighted at seeing my old shadow and runner Livvie as well. She was waiting when I rode up, running out to greet me. She's got red ribbons in her hair now, not the blue ones she'd always worn. I swept her up in my arms, but after the beating I had and all the travelling, it wasn't as vigorous as I'd have liked.

"You're hurt," she said.

"I've been hurt, Livvie. I'm much better now."

"I did what you asked, Driwna; I kept about the Brask sheds and watched and then told Morril everything I saw. But then the Brasks came to our shed and talked to her instead."

"Thank you, Livvie, you've been a great help for us. I'm sure Morril keeps you busy now, doesn't she?"

"She does." She fussed with the one of the ribbons that was tied about one of her tails of hair.

"You've got red ribbons now."

"Conti said his favourite colour is red." She smiled then.

"Is he still apprentice to the farrier?"

"He is."

"Well, if he can keep to a trade and he's good to you, perhaps you might let him take you for a walk, or show you what work he does in the shop."

"He's asked me that already." She was thrilled by this and it warmed me to see. She kept with me for the time I was in Lindur and I was glad of it.

A few at the sheds there were calling me Brother Red, were recalling to everyone how I brought them back alive or would have brought back the cloaks. Without a view on the politics and madness of the work of Yblas or the administrators, they were insisting I'd do a better job. Morril put them right, told them it's the Post in the field that need their stories telling to the administrators, reeves and high clearks and I was made a fieldsman for that. I asked for any crew she could spare for my ride west back into the Sathanti after Ufra and the others. I meant to ensure that Leusla was undertaking her commitment to the kurchgeld and go on to discover more about the vans going to the mountains. I wouldn't do it without an ally.

Morril whistled for a gathering at the front of the main shed. She asked for anyone that wanted to ride with me to the Sathanti Peaks. There's about five that put their hands up. She thanked them and told one to come forward. He got jeered of course. She barked at the others to be about their work.

The one Morril had chosen I struggled to recollect, until she told me he was one of the mercenaries she'd sent out after Gennic's van who had decided to take up the red afterwards.

"I'm Curic, Fieldsman. It's an honour to ride with you."

Morril had chosen well for me. He was Bray's age at least, but tall and lean. He had eyebrows as thick as my thumb, and grey bedding in with the brown on his head. He was rounder in the cheeks than Farlsgrad or Sathanti, the soft crescents of skin under his grey eyes giving him a deceptive air of tiredness and age. He had to be from Roan Province or Alagar, his face was shaved after their custom, and I sensed a calm and a warmth in the way he looked at us. I saw also good waxed and stitched pouches and cups in his belts, not a frayed seam about his leathers, the chain he wore also oiled.

"Where have you taken purses?" I asked.

"I've took purses in Roan Province, but mainly Khasgal's Landing, at the Hartista border. I'd bet myself with a bow and I can manage a spear well enough. Got a bit too fond of living as I got older, so come north to find some vanning."

"Sounds like it, you coming with me into the Sathanti."

"You come for us and brought us back, Fieldsman; you're friends with the Ososi, as all are in Khasgal's Landing. All the reds spoke well of you on that Lindur van I went after for Morril here. Won't lie that I'm canny for a chance of some Ososi plant for the fuckin' colour while helpin' out against slavers, who I always hated. I expect also your purse'll be good as you've got a seal from the High Red."

"It will. You think it's slavers taking the Sathanti and Ososi then?"

"Can't be anyone else. They're not taking fighters, not burning the land or their kurches as they call them."

I wished I could have had Bray and Cal with me and all, then. Would be a good crew to go after Scar, for he was going to show his face at some point, I was sure of it. I could only hope Ufra could give us plant worthy of matching him.

"We'll make out a purse for eight pennies a day, cloak's tally is three silver for family or one silver penny if you're back and breathing. Post sees you for all other expenses."

Curic agreed and we clasped arms on it.

We rode from Lindur over the border to Hidzuc lands. In those days and nights of riding and making camp I had to explain what was happening to me, why it was I could not quench my thirst, or had the strangest urges to eat mud, worms, mushrooms. He was good enough to take most of the sentrying, despite his own troubles as a veteran of fightbrews, to let me get what rest I could. Not even kannab could settle me, though it was worse without it. He had a lingonberry jam preserve and was happy to see me devour it in one go, which settled me for a few hours after. "You're eating for two," he said, laughing, for such lusts for food were common in women with child.

He was right in a way. In the nights he'd try and soothe me, telling me I was mumbling in a language he'd never heard and not shy either about telling me I was strong smelling, though not of sweat or dirt so much, a smell more like burned blood. My sense of smell was improving, enough I stopped needing the snuff to pick out plant and droppings. I was feeling the cold a bit more as well, I found myself taking off my leathers and tying up my sleeves when the sun came out. He said little about it beyond asking me not

267

to turn into a tree before the purse was settled. The real pleasure of it was that with the sun on my skin I could smell Ufra, the plant in me reacting to the light, which explained why even in battle she could stand to have no sleeves over her arms.

Feeling also surged within me, feeling of all kinds. I had to apologise more than once from not being able to control laughter or tears at his easy jokes and stories at camp or while the horses grazed. At times it frightened me, but he took it all in his stride as a veteran would.

Once more we're at Crackell's Run and paying our respects to the kurchpole, arriving then at the Hidzuc lodge. There are many about the lodge armed, some with belts, full colour. Agitation colours the air. All about are busy but unable to stop looking over at the soldiers.

"Can't see many mercs in there, Fieldsman. Mostly Hidzuc-looking." Curic this is.

"I agree," I say. "I wonder if there's been a new daith-nu confirmed."

"You killed the old one," he says.

I hadn't thought about that. "Let's dismount anyway. Leave your spear on your horse — let's show we're not trouble."

One of their daith-wa, their drudhas, comes over to us then.

"Post? Are you scouting for a van that's coming? I doubt we'll need much from you if you are, unless there's some alka jelly."

"Has another van been through then?"

"Yes, a big one: Brask. More slaves, but a lot more wagons besides. They made us gifts, from Marghoster."

"That's . . . good to hear. No, no van, we are riding west. Messengers. Has Leusla or someone else been made Daith-nu?"

"Leusla is Daith-nu." I'm thrilled to hear that and have to compose myself.

"I am glad. Would you tell her our horses need caring for, but that Driwna Bridche is here? I was at the parley over in the Spike in Jenna."

"I will. Follow me with your horses."

He takes us to the bloodstone where Curic follows my lead with the oaths. I've had the chance on our ride out to tell him of what happened at the Spike. I've told him Crejda's running lots on Brask wagons that are off the ledgers and told him also that Marghoster was behind the attack on the Ilkashun. He's surprised at Crejda for he'd heard only good things about her running of the Spike's Posthouse. I told him also of the Oskoro girl, the reason this all began. I tried to get him to understand it was all as much for her as it was for the Post, happy for him to think me mad on that score. He says nothing to this but for a hand on my shoulder, a promise to help me find her again, for we both believe her fate is one with that of the slaves and the Sathanti that've been kidnapped.

Leusla is wearing the headpiece of the Hidzucs, her coal-black hair woven through it. The strength she found at the parley seems to have flourished, given her a presence, a calm authority that to me makes her all the more beautiful. Korba and two other chiefs are with her at the lodge. She's speaking to the soldiers gathered there. Stablehands have many horses ready at the edge of camp for them. We wait, the daith-wa having taken our horses to the now emptied stables.

"Something's not right." Curic this is, gesturing at the gathering and readying of soldiers.

"We wait until she finishes addressing them," I say.

She follows Korba and one of the daith-wa as they inspect

the soldiers' belts; each soldier receives their fightbrew bags from her. Each then turns as they're dismissed to pass us and say their oaths and seek help from the bloodstone before moving to the edge of the huts where the horses wait. With the last of them turned, the rest of the camp watch on. There are men and women lining their route that put their mouth-pieces in, akin to those the horse whisperers use. The pieces change their voices to a deep buzzing; long rolling notes that blend and clash, calling the dead to join the Song of the Earth and give them a fair wind and the strength they've grown since being committed to the soil.

Leusla sees us then. She wears a pale brown leather dress with finely stitched patterns, animals and plants, paw to tail and root to leaf, in chains about the hem, waist and neck. It's practical, those patterns enough to confer status along with the crown of wood. Eirakh's knife is in its sheath on a slender leather belt, not a finger wide. She can't fight with it, but it too is decorated and the sheath itself is a strange bright green leather that I couldn't tell the dye for.

We wait for the soldiers to mount and leave. The lines of people fragment to their duties and many about are tasked with taking care of those visiting from other kurches, for many more fires are made about the huts than is usual, more pigs are spitted. Leusla then calls us to her at the firepit. "Brother Red!" she says, coming over to us. A few are surprised by her embracing me, not least me, for it is done usually only with great friends or honoured guests, and the latter I hadn't assumed for us. I introduce her to Curic, she introduces me in turn to the chiefs and the daith-wa I hadn't met at the Spike. Word of the parley must have carried, for I clasp arms with them all and they each speak to me, but in their own lingo, to which I can only nod and smile in response.

"They are thanking you for honour you've done us, with my keep and kurchgeld. We had not justice without you. I could not have crown without you."

"I'm honoured by you, Daith-nu. You are the right choice for your people. Yet I see soldiers being prepared for war."

"You not heard. Daith-nu Yicre is dead. He had camp at Lake Fildric, days from lodge."

"Fuck." I can't say any more for it's shocked me, and upsets me as I think again of how good a man he was, how important to this peace we've made here.

"How?" asks Curic.

She shrugs.

"Some might not be happy with the kurchgeld," he says.

"I don't believe it's Lodre would have done this. Not his sister's keep."

"He'd be likely the Daith-nu because of it, when their confederacy chiefs decide on it," says Curic, "and as good a choice as any of them, from what you told us, Fieldsman."

It fits. And it fits too easy is my concern. Of course some would want blood and more; vengeance boils all reason dry. Canendrigh lost kurch-kin, children among them. Lodre might think Yicre gained too little from the Hidzucs or Marghoster for his dead. He was quiet at the parley, but he had to be as Leusla's chiefs had to be. I could read nothing in his face about how the parley concluded. He has peace on his border. Could he want more dead?

"Do you think Chief Canendrigh might attack, take more than the kurchgeld?" I ask.

Leusla bids us sit at the firepit with Chief Korba, who must have advocated for her at the gathering that decided the Daith-nu after how well she spoke for their confederacy at the Spike.

Tea is summoned and Leusla packs her pipe. "We agree

271

kurchgeld here, at this fire. Yicre, Canendrigh, Korba, me. I offer good land, he know it, Lodre pleased."

"Still could be him. He gets extra land with the kurchgeld and the crown," says Curic.

"It is not him," says Leusla, and there's a flicker in her eyes makes me believe her, some mote of feeling in thinking of him. "But we must defend ourselves, show we strong at our borders."

"You are right to. I must go west to speak to Lodre and I will find out who killed Daith-nu Yicre and why, if I can."

"I help you. One of my own to show our loyalty to kurchgeld and parley. Ensma!"

One of Leusla's own guards steps forward. There's a stillness about her that I can feel, a silence in the Song that speaks of a harmony rather than an absence. She's small, barely shoulder-height to me, the build of a miner or a deckhand, yet with hardly any bark on her. She's kept some hair, the colour of wheat, but it's cut high and square on her forehead. Her nose curls up like an eyelash and she has a deceptively sleepy look in her face, little expression there.

"She a stoner," says Leusla, taking an ember from the firepit to relight her pipe. "She a cold wind blowing." By stoner she means that Ensma is able to get a fightbrew under control quickly, a rare gift.

She looks us over, this girl.

"She stones brew well?" I ask.

"The best. Like storm. She will follow your order as I command it. Help you bring peace."

Ensma bows to Leusla as the order is given.

"You are a welcome boon, Ensma. I am glad you are with us. Daith-nu, I am honoured and humbled." I make the greeting gesture to Ensma. "Daith-nu, I would leave today, waste no time. We would appreciate water, feed for our horses."

"It is done." She puts her hands on Ensma's shoulders, leans forward to speak in her ear. Barely a sentence. Ensma hears it with no expression I could discern, but as Leusla leans away, I can see a tear tremble at the edge of her eye, blinked away quickly.

Leusla bids us farewell in their way, fingertips to her lips, and two hours later we're riding out to their border. I feel a bit more hopeful than I have in a while. It doesn't last. It never does.

I become less troubled by the plant in me as the days pass since leaving the Hidzuc lodge. I find I can read my horse better, how she feels. It seems ridiculous, but her hunger and thirst, weariness, are clearer to me, the signs of such fatigue evident before the others can recognise it. The sense of being watched has sharpened, something I had only felt before this strongly when I'd taken a fightbrew. Fewer animals pass us by unharmed, and we eat better in our camps. I see better also the forms that Curic and Ensma run. For all their differences in style it's clear how well they run them and it helps that a bit of pride spurs them to work thoroughly through them. Curic leads by example with the care he takes regarding his fieldbelt and the mixing of rubs for me. Ensma has no aches or wounds that need treating. I might have thought this showed a lack of experience in battle, but her song tells me not to trust such thoughts. I still wish that Cal could be here; his singing lifts the mood at any camp and we've been on edge not only with my diminishing illness but also because we're as far west into the Sathanti than we've ever been; the trails are hard to find, foraging and hunting harder still.

We round the neck of Lake Fildric to the north of it. Clear skies are the coldest, however. The lake is iced over at the shores, reeds frosted, the earth hard as stone and few travellers about but some hands needing any scraps we could spare. We pass bodies of those starved to death, savaged by wolves, cats and boar. Always more such dead south of the Spine than north, for they work the land less there, need less a surfeit of hands at harvest that then are sent away to survive as they can. It makes me wonder if the loathing of slaves is at least partly to ensure only the kurch would be fed in the winter months.

There's little sign of the battle against Eirakh at Canendrigh's lodge. They that greet us as we pass his kurchpoles remember me from that day and we are welcomed. Ensma bears no sign she is Hidzuc, which I'm grateful for, but we put a red cloak around her to be sure. I know well enough that even the way a knot is tied is a sign of someone not being of a kurch.

A herder directs us to the camp where Yicre died, though at first he feared for his life as we approached him. He tells us that some of his kurch have been taken, that strangers have been seen in the hills that border the lake, foothills to the Spine's vast range of peaks stretching away west and east out of sight.

At the camp where Yicre has been bound and wrapped for his journey back to the Ilkashun lodge, we meet his keep, Carli, with her brother Lodre and others from their kurch-kin. That six of their soldiers ride out to us on dayers, calling to us to drop spears and bows from a distance, seeing us as a likely threat, makes me worry for Ufra. I feel twitchy, faint almost, and only because I somehow know Ufra isn't at the camp.

We do as they ask of us and we are escorted into the camp. Yicre's body is in his tent under guard. Our escort led us to a tent with the Canendrigh colours hanging next to the opening. We meet Carli and Lodre here, themselves surrounded by further guards. I make an introduction to Curic and Ensma and we are invited to sit with them on the mats that cover the ground of the tent.

"You are Driwna Bridche," says Carli. She's soft, fleshy, but her eyes are red like they've been branded, her black hair hasn't been brushed, her dress is stained with wine, food, whatever they ate the previous night I'd wager.

"I am, Daith-ru. I would know how we have come to lose a good man, a man I fought alongside and a man who would have secured a peaceful future in these parts."

"He spoke well of you, Driwna; you have secured a good and fair kurchgeld." She speaks Farlsgrad lingo well. "I would have said he had died naturally. Such a thing in a man so strong is strange but not unheard of. Yet his guard, Tresle, has disappeared."

"I assume he was most trusted," I say.

"He's guarded the Daith-nu for as long as we've been joined. We must go back and tell his own keep and children he has gone. Might you have had word of him as you came through Hidzuc lands?"

"No. But it would be difficult to note or track a single man if there was no suspicion attached. That the Hidzucs have manned their borders in fear of being blamed for this action makes it even more doubtful he fled that way. There could be nobody else, then? No poison in his food?"

"It's always tasted, even when I cook for him, and I welcomed that, for many hands pass over the – how do you say it? – materials for our food."

"When did Tresle leave?"

"As soon as he was replaced as guard; nobody saw him the following morning, nobody saw him leave."

"And Tresle at no point left the Daith-nu's service? No

opportunity he might have had to be forced to betray his chief?"

"He might have spent time with the Marghoster vans at my lodge before the attack," says Lodre. "That they attacked us on hearing the horns of Eirakh Hidzuc may tell us they were informed of it. They may have made him promises."

"Doesn't smell right, that," says Curic.

"Why not?" says Lodre.

"They would have expected victory with the ambush, for only the Oskoro and Ososi turned the fight, as you recall it, Fieldsman. So they would not have thought there was a need to turn someone assassin, especially someone so loyal in such a short time."

I'm not convinced by that either, for Tresle knew the Oskoro to be at the camp. Such a powerful drudha as the Master of Flowers would not have been discounted had the Marghoster vans tried to turn Tresle to their cause.

"It's a possibility, Curic. On the one hand, the risk that his loyalty would expose their offer or threat might mean they knew he had a weakness. On the other, to have planned this would mean knowing him, and gathering such knowledge feels like we're reaching too far for our story. The only one out here he might have joined that has done you all harm is Scar, but how he has come to his cause I cannot say."

"Yes, Driwna, this may well be true," says Carli. "We have lost more of our kurch-kin. We are preyed upon as badly as ever before. He may have joined Scar."

"You've seen him? Scar?"

"No, but who else would it be?"

"It would be a pleasure to meet this Scar," says Ensma, though she says it without any feeling.

"We may yet, Ensma. The Ososi, Ufra, were they here when it happened?"

"No," says Carli, "they carried on out west to their camps near Lake Bouskill itself."

"We are looking for anyone who knows of the vans that go into the Spine, where the slaves have been taken. What Sathanti clans are there?"

"The Flintre are north of us, thirty leagues to the kurchpoles. Then beyond them are the Cargamun. They've not been seen on the plains for a long time and were rare enough before that. They cause the Flintre trouble, for there's better fodder and hunting the further down you come from the mountains, into the Flintre land."

"I assume you've not met the daith-nu of either?"

"No. Our elders say the Cargamun are 'naitta uku', what the Farls would call 'plate lickers', half animals. Will you look for our missing, Driwna?"

"More of your people have been kidnapped?"

"Three sniffers two weeks ago, four days ago a woman out foraging the commons of one of our other kurches, the Acoerie. They've lost five now. My keep, our Daith-nu, he held those vans because we are powerless to do otherwise but sting the bear to the east. The bear bit back soon enough, but nothing has changed and two daith-nu are dead that had no quarrel with each other or Farlsgrad. But this is Farlsgrad, Driwna. It stinks of Hildmir and of conquest."

"It's hard to disagree," I say.

"Not hard, impossible, Driwna. The Sathanti would convene a Council now, we would declare war, but the confederacies in the mountains, where such Councils are convened, they have pulled up their bridges. The Flintre Daith-nu would not meet with Yicre. Yesterday a van passed us a league to the north, slavers, thirty spears at least, supplies with it. They said nothing to us and we were not equipped to hold or subdue them. You must help us, Brother Red, for we

Sathanti cannot, for whatever reason, forge an alliance against this enemy. Seek the Flintre Daith-nu, tell them we must ally, stop these vans until they reveal their motive and their route's end."

She speaks well, a fine keep for Yicre, her words spoken a little louder than necessary that those nearby would hear her say them, be reassured of her.

"We'll track the van. It must be heading into the mountains at some point. If it takes us beyond Flintre kurchpoles we'll have our answers. Lodre, you are neighbours with the Hidzuc. They fear blame for what has happened, but we know it was not them."

He frowns, wishing, I think, for an easy foe to shape his anger against.

"You would have me go to their lodge and seek alliance?"

"If Farlsgrad, or whoever it is behind this, seek division among the Sathanti, you resist them through alliance. Do not set guards against your own borders, but guard together against the threat. Daith-ru, when can you summon your chiefs to the lodge to agree the next daith-nu? Your chiefs need commanding to go south and west to their own borders and secure alliance with the confederacies there."

She glances at her brother. "When Lodre returns from the Hidzuc lodge the chiefs will be here."

"Who is daith-nu there now?" asks Lodre.

"Leusla."

"Not Korba?"

"She spoke well at the parley, if you recall. Her people love her. She wants peace, the kurchgeld is made."

"It is," says Lodre. "Sister, I will leave at dawn, but I will take my hours at the vigil until then." It is a sign for us all to stand. He clasps arms with us all.

"Brother Red, I'm glad you're here," he says. "But why

are you here? Are you here as Bridche or Post? Do either have so much to gain from us that you risk your life?"

I think of the baby Oskoro girl in my arms that morning with Cal at the camp of the bandits we'd killed. I remember her face being so peaceful as to be merely asleep. I realise, suddenly, it was her mother that killed her. Could only have been, to spare her unbearable torture.

"It's love that brings me here."

Chapter 14

Driwna

It isn't hard to pick up and track the van, given the wheel ruts and ashes of campfires and the cesspits dug about them. The trails east to west are well worn, generations of Sathanti finding the truest paths across the foothills of Kristuc's Folly, between the lakes, Ilkashun, Adendrigh and the mountains of the Spine. The sickness the plant in me caused has mostly passed. I am now so much thirstier than I was, and ravenous as well for whatever meat we can hunt and kill. There's a strong blue colour to my veins and it's bleeding out to the skin around them, changing it, so it feels more like shaved tree bark, smooth, tougher, dry and less sensitive, as though the skin is numbed. I haven't dreamed for weeks now, and I have had to be woken forcefully for my sentry duties.

My crew have bonded well. Ensma took her time, an instinctive wariness around us, being strangers, but I think Curic's experience in the field has won her over. She's given us the impression there weren't many that took their forms and spear mastery as well as her. What might be taken as bravado in a younger soldier was only her earnestness, and

I am grateful for that. We have sparred and even with sword she is strong, though she prefers an axe, for such are well known to all Sathanti. To my surprise, for someone so serious in all else, she has all manner of rude verses and tales from her time travelling with Leusla and Eirakh about their kurches and in their negotiations with merchants. She made Curic blush more than once and I feel he might quite like her, though his sense of duty in the field has overcome any lust. I spoke of it when I replaced him as sentry one night and was surprised to hear him conclude she could do better than he, not least because of the difference in years, he said. I know by this he means that he's paid the colour far longer, that she would be caring for him as she might a frail elder before she's got more than a handful of grey hairs of her own. As is to be expected he has needed more help than Ensma in his mixes and rubs, for he has counted nearly fifty fightbrews done to her thirteen, not counting the training that goes with taking on the colour. I have only had twenty-nine measures and what we don't tell nokes, or joke much of, are the shits they give us, the vomiting, the pain in every drop of blood like we've been peeled to our bones, the visions that echo long after, when we see ghosts and hear voices, dreams of violent death that will wake us up crying. These are the stories we tell each other, how we give our sympathy and kinhood to those that pay the colour. Curic's woken screaming more than once on the days we've been out, and it's taken kannab to help with that so he doesn't give away our camp in the night.

We're at the end of a long and miserable day of rain when the van we're chasing after is attacked. We caught it up and have tracked it yesterday and today, so we're close enough to hear the whistles calling the line of wagons to a halt to begin setting up for camp. We're behind them by only a mile but in the treeline, knowing it's almost impossible to see us in here.

"I'll fetch water from the brook we crossed an hour back," says Ensma.

"Good. We'll not get a fire going on this; we'll have some bilt and get in our skins. I'll take first, Ensma second. Curic, can you do the horses?"

I shiver then, feel a stab of dizziness that almost unbalances me. Something's building, crackling like logs in a fire. "Ensma, wait. Curic, come with me." He'd not even begun removing the bridle and saddle from his horse.

"What is it, Fieldsman?" says Ensma.

"It's Ufra. The Ososi, they're close; something's happening, an attack on the camp maybe. Stay with the horses."

"Yes, Fieldsman," says Ensma. "How do you . . .?" she begins to ask before realising it must be the plant in me.

We take our bows and spars and run along the slope.

"Brews?" asks Curic.

"No, not yet. I hope we'll only need dayers."

"Bilberry? It'll help if there's no fires."

I stop, for he's right. We get it out of our belts. He puts a hand on my face, eases my head back to face the sky, fingers on my forehead, and with his thumb pulls the bottom of my eye down. He taps out a few drops of the juice from a small leather-bound vial. It's cold, momentarily, then warms and it's like needles drumming at my eyeball. We repeat it for each other and walk on, more cautiously, breathing hard in our attempt not to cuss out loud at the pain of the mix filling our heads.

The bilberry mix lifts the gloom of the night as it stretches over the heavy clouds we've been snivelling under for the day so far. A horn blows from the camp, shouting begins.

282

Curic looks at me, surprised that I called some trouble before he could sense it. We alter our run to move down the slope to the edge of the treeline. The cries and shouting, the horses braying, all intensifies. The van's found a good open area of scrub beneath the trees along which we've been tracking them in which to camp. They had barely got the wagons turning when the attack came. With my blood running high the change in me from the plant is more pronounced and I sign to Curic where the attackers are coming from. They're moving at a frightening speed, riding the boar as Cal would have said, on brews. Bags are being thrown in, slingers rising to hurl them from stony slopes the far side of the trail from us, bushes, fissures in the narrow shelves of stone hiding them from sight. The van's dogs are released from their leashes and run for the attackers. The vanners have not had the chance for their own brews to be stoned, not nearly quick enough as the whistles across the fields alert those attacking to the approaching dogs. Pepper bags are thrown out and despite the rain limiting their spread, the handful of dogs not sent into a frenzy by the peppers take no more than two I can see before being killed.

"We go in, Fieldsman?"

"Yes, these attackers are Ilkashun and Ososi. No dayers, they will quickly finish this and I won't want to be mistaken for a vanner right now."

We walk towards the wagons as the soldiers of the van form a line against those attacking. They have shields up against the arrows, many still staggering from the brew they've just been given. They won't rise in time, there's too many Ososi. Half of the soldiers are killed with spear or arrow before the others, some still rising on their brew, drop their own weapons in surrender. They must have seen it was Ososi; they knew they were no match. The Ilkashun and Ososi

283

shooting and slinging run to join their soldiers as they line up against the vanners whose hands are raised. Some drop to their knees, fingers in their throats, vomiting out the fightbrew, sparing themselves more suffering later.

My breath catches in my throat as I see Ufra step forward from the Ososi lines. I hold my hand up to halt Curic, not wanting us to disrupt this moment or risk anything happening to Ufra by the distraction.

I see then, filling the gap in the line she's left, the Oskoro chief I met back at the Ilkashun camp when it was attacked, the Master of Flowers. He turns his head calmly towards us as we hide. Neither of us could have taken another step if we'd tried. He shakes out his arms, as he did the day I first met him. This time I shiver with it. I have a notion of acceptance, edges of things my body wants to tell me he's saying, but I am a dut yet in my becoming an Ososi. His eyes are like points of fire, an artefact of the bilberry mix I'm sure. Even from this distance the Flower of Fates stands strong and bright in his braegnloc. It is he that has brought these vanners to their knees, for he is the only one of his kind, a story they will tell all their lives. As with the Ososi, he is a legend, a terrible monster that will have haunted these vanners' darkened tents and houses as fables for children, warnings not to run too far from camp, to shout at strangers. As soldiers the fables become tales, awe-struck accounts of sightings, escapes. But all here know the Flower of Fates, all eyes are on it, even the stone below us holds its breath.

Silence. Not even the wounded dogs or soldiers moan. There's the shush of rain on grass, pattering on the wagons' oilskins, the leathers and greaves of armour.

"We will not kill or torture you, if you surrender arms." Ufra this is, that beautiful deep voice carrying across the wagons and fields.

284

"Agreed." The Guard that's spoken, it must be. He says something in their field lingo. The soldiers throw down their weapons at Ufra's feet. A few spit at the ground near her too, but, as I'd hoped, this isn't the kind of insult would upset her enough to get them killed. She speaks then in Ososi lingo, gestures, some signing of her own, and they move in among the wagons while the Master and the Ilkashun stand ready. The slaves start stamping in their wagons, rattling chains. The Master then says something to Ufra. She looks over in our direction. There's a moment where I fear, desperately, she is not pleased to see me, that she has forgotten me or no longer cares for me. But she smiles then, delight.

"Fetch Ensma and the horses," I say to Curic before running out from the treeline towards her. When I reach her she throws her arms about me and I lean back to pick her up, squeezing her and kissing her neck, pressing my face into her chest as she holds me to her. We're still for a few moments, then I feel her sag slightly, her breath catching and turning to weeping. I lower her gently, keeping her in my arms.

"What's wrong, Ufra?"

"It's all gone, Driwna." She speaks into my ear, her eyelashes moving against my cheek as she blinks the tears away. I bring a hand up to cradle her neck. "Scar," she says.

"Where's your pa?"

"Taken. Some taken with him. We escaped, the rest are dead. All that's left of our people are those tribes of our cousins in Khasgal's Landing. All that remains of this Ososi tribe is about us here."

"I . . ." But I don't know what to say to that. There are so few.

There's going to be war now. There's nowhere left to run for these peaceful people, so they will give more air to the flames of the dark stories told of them.

"We go into the mountains, Driwna. Will you come?"

"Yes, we have to try and stop this." She leans back so we can look at each other, wipes tears from her eyes with the knuckle of her thumb.

"There are none left to open my head, and no seed of the alkaest, the Flower of Fates, to plant in me. Without my father I am etza-Ososi, chief of Ososi, but cannot be the blood of my people, cannot truly be a Master of Flowers. I have no eyrtza before my people if I do not have a flower."

"The Oskoro Master? Can he not plant it in you?"

"We have talked of it. Their way is different but a tribe must have its blood. He has seeds enough from his own flower, but the time it would take for me to regain my strength is too much, there would be no Ososi left. I must find my father, our etza-Ososi. It is our best hope. We might find and kill Scar."

I look up to see some of the Ososi have gathered about us, the Oskoro chief among them. I had heard none approach.

One of them speaks in Ososi lingo.

Ufra turns so we face them. She takes my nearest hand in hers, holds it up. The only words I recognise are my name and "Umansk", their word for outsider. She moves our hands against her breast, her heart.

"You are Ufra-wen," says the Master.

The other Ososi there are at least surprised, some are shocked.

"I have told them you are in my blood, all through me, that I have found my wen, my keep."

The Master comes up to us, puts his huge hand over ours, tightens his grip. He's barely twitched, but I almost cry out with the force of it.

"Ufra's seed is here. Their song . . ." His words decompose to his own lingo. I imagine then he is describing it, though he is making sounds, a rhythm of sorts, and he's pleased. If it is a lingo, if I could learn it, I would speak it all my days.

The Ososi about us look at Ufra, needing her own acknowledgement of our union. She glances at me and I feel the heat of her, a rush of blood, of excitement.

"Driwna Bridche is Ufra-wen. Driwna Bridche is Ososi-wen, second of the outsider. She has my seed and it grows strong in her. She has a strong eyrtza."

I look at each of them, nine of her people about us, and it hurts me to realise now I have seen no children among them, or should I say, I have felt none, for while they would not have brought them to field for the ambush, the pleasure they take in her delight, in this declaration of a union, is fragile, a moment's joy in a wide field of suffering. There's hurt at the edges of their eyes, weariness, hollowness too. They each in turn come to embrace us. They speak Ososi words of welcome to me, though I only learn what they are later. At the Spike she had surprised me, left me at a loss for words when she asked if I would be her keep. I fear for this happiness; I have done since she stayed with me the night before the parley. We may not see the spring. It's something I saw well enough when I brought back the cloaks for the lifeprice of our vanners, or when we got back all alive from a purse and their keeps and their duts would be waiting with bitten fingernails as the van rolls in, watching us for wounds or for laughter, our story written in our faces. They would bob their heads, tilt them, looking for a familiar shape in his or her hood, for a red doing the same, trying to find their love, their family, bringing a purse to keep them fed another month, another winter. Now I know their hearts, their fears; now I know what it costs, what it takes to let such love in.

"Two come from the trees, I feel them." The Master this is.

"They are with me, Master. Curic, the man, is of the Post. Ensma is of the Hidzuc, commanded to protect me and their interests by Leusla."

"You are with us."

"We are."

The cuts that were made, to give the Ilkashun and Ososi his blood for this ambush, have stopped bleeding. Around his cuts, under his skin, things move.

"Let us free the slaves," he says.

The Master did what he could for the slaves that had been brought on the van from Farlsgrad. Most couldn't be free of their addictions. He knew that the droop mixes they were on were not all they needed curing of. Like many of the crew that took this van, they were silent before him, or frightened, crying. Each of them – the raped, the beaten, the old with their cowering, silent humility – he took in hand, whispering, rolling the long notes of healing that Ufra gave to me at the Spike, his hand on their heads, the other moving without the aid of his eyes, about the field-belt he wore, or the satchels he carried, finding the plant that would help them. We were entranced. They were healed as far as he could manage and all were led away or left with provisions and seals that would see them safely off Ilkashun lands.

Now we sit about a fire, Ufra, the Master, Curic and Ensma. Their clasping arms with Ufra and the Master had the effect it would on anyone. Both found they could say nothing before him. Ensma spoke his name in the Hidzuc lingo, and as with Curic, he had been only a legend until now. The other Ososi, Oskoro and Ilkashun have fires of their own and are going through the wagons for supplies and weapons. Those who crewed the van have been marched away to the Ilkashun lodge. They'll not be able to get word back to Farlsgrad of this, not until we're in the mountains.

"If your father is anywhere, Ufra," I say, "he is in the mountains, where all these vans are bound. We must man this van as its crew, head north and find the pass for ourselves."

"One of the Farlsgrad gave us the way," says the Master.

"Is this a Marghoster van?" asks Curic.

"No markings on the wagons, no manifest," I say, "for I had the chance to look them over earlier while you saw off the slaves. But they are Marghoster. His smith marks his work with a stamp, a 'Y' and a crescent moon above it. It's on the spearheads, horseshoes and knives. There's Post lots in there too, I'm sorry to say. No obvious markings, but it's Gennic's mark on the wrappings of plant; he binds skunk cabbage in spearmint-soaked linen. Nobody else I know does that."

"Seems like this Marghoster is putting an army of slaves together, you think?" Curic this is. "Has Farlsgrad put an army in the Spine, taken what Kristuc Hildmir couldn't all those years ago?"

"This far beyond the border? I can't see it. There's been no rumours of any great army forming in Farlsgrad."

"Enough have been taken from the Ososi and Sathanti," says Ufra. "But no more. If I cannot be made a Master, we will become the terror they make of us in their songs before we die out."

I reach for her hand. She brims with tears.

"You will not be the last etza-Ososi," says the Master. "We will find and kill Scar. Then we can grow again. We will find a new home. These wilds are vast and stretch far beyond Farlsgrad's reach." He makes other sounds, puts his branch-like arm on Ufra's shoulder. A sap fills some of the channels in his arm's bark, a smell then, sharp and sour as a yellowfruit's juice. I'm slow enough of wit I wonder what the sap is for, for it reminds me of summer. Which is what he intended. Ufra smiles with it, puts her hand over his huge, hard fingers, each running to a fine point, like four pickaxe heads and a shovel for a thumb.

There is no need to ask Ufra what she saw when she arrived at her tribe's lodge, or whatever passes for their hearth, after Scar had been. I just put my arm around her and hold her close as we make our plans.

As a disguise, the chains that bound the prisoners are merely gummed closed around the ankles of Ufra's Ososi, who will act as our own prisoners. There are twenty and they huddle together with weapons and belts under the straw beneath them. Sporebags and fingerflasks of the Master's blood are hidden in their vests and skirts. The Master of Flowers wears the long loose robes of a cleark, for his body would be too misshapen not to arouse comment in anything more practical. The hood is large enough and loose enough his face won't be immediately visible, though we had to scout a good way forward of the van to ensure he had time enough to fold it carefully over the Flower in his braegnloc if we were to meet anyone out here. He brings eight with him, but these are more experienced soldiers than Ufra's kin, all he has left of his people that hailed from the Almet forest in faraway Hillfast. Had he met the founder of the Post, Teyr Amondsen? I hadn't thought to ask, for the Ososi live much longer than the rest of us and so must the Oskoro. The three who looked most like us were armoured and would ride with us as crew, the rest were also chained. The Ilkashun were split equally, ten riding, ten in chains. They told us they were from a border kurch, did not wait for Lodre or Carli to allow this action. This is an act of vengeance for Yicre.

We were grateful for the provisions we were able to plunder. There's food and water enough, arrows and much plant that all of us could mix in our different ways. The Master of Flowers was happy to share his recipes, and Curic, for want of a roll and ink, marked a piece of wood with his knife, scratching out his cyca for the recipes shared. "I won't have to work for the Post again," he said, waving it in the air, and I gave him a clip round the top for it.

It's the Flintre confederacy that must take the wagons north out of Ilkashun kurchlands and six of them meet us seven or so leagues beyond their border poles. Practically nokes, none of them have any more than the colouring of a cooker's brew about them. They expected they'd be able to accompany us, and they ask for the bacca and white honey promised them, along with blocks of betony and other plant such as guira, which is hard to come by in the heights. We give them what they ask but bid them leave us, for their own safety. They try to sound aggrieved over the lack of sport they're usually allowed with the slaves and I'm proud of Ensma's improvised tale of the death of one of our crew whose cock had rotted after putting it in one of the Ososi. We ask for news of the vans that have come before us, tell them we'd heard Scar had got a good number of these Ososi fuckers, including their chief. Only one of this patrol had seen that van, tells us the chief was there, Ufra's father, big flower in his head and looking sorry for himself, skin all burned and cut all over. Ufra turned her horse and rode forwards of us on hearing this.

With gifts of plant and white honey given, we walk the wagons up through stands of pines, the farms shrinking with the lack of good soil to rice fields, the air getting colder with each day passing and the snow thickening; hard-going mud giving way to frozen ruts that break the wheels of one of the wagons, pitching the Ososi over the side of it. We cram them onto the two other wagons and do our best to hide their belts and spears. It's hard on Ufra, for we cannot dress them in the furs the van has ready for this part of its journey and she can do nothing but watch them suffer with it. Scattered about are hamlets, tucked into the banks of the great rivers and falls that spawn in the heights above us. Their duts surround the van and their men push their women inside their huts as they point at our wagons. They present us with poles of smoked mascha fish, stinking bear hides, yak-bone carvings. We gladly buy a bag of two hundred black walnuts and the bark of the same tree, a treasure almost unheard of in Farlsgrad. Even the Ososi are lifted to see it and there's much chattering in their tongue with the Oskoro Master regarding the various uses to which it can be put. Five more slow and demanding days on steep trails see us at the Cargamun border poles. We're not quite at the snowline and we're grateful for the trail flattening out to a high valley, a wasteland of stone and boulders spotted with rhododendrons and birch trees. The mountains have been sharpened to axe heads, as though Sillindar's carved them. Giant rock bowls have been made of the land here and there's the welcome sight of a fast river whose rapids and falls we'd passed on the way up. I call the van to halt to let us and the horses drink and rest.

What must be the Cargamun lodge is ahead of us, surrounded by sixty or so huts about the river, pens of yaks, chickens and tuikas. The huts are all mud-stone and wood, two roofs to each of them, wide overhangs. Ufra tells me it is because of the rains here. There's a little soil they can work for lentils and it takes me a moment to notice that all of those planting them are in chains. A guard that's watching over them whistles back to the lodge on seeing our van having arrived in the valley.

"You should put your hood over," I say to the Master.

"I will not hide the flower here. They will believe I am Scar's brother and I do his work."

I'm surprised to see they have horses up here. They're led quickly out of stables that must sit behind the lodge, itself larger than the Ilkashun's. Fifteen riders trot out to us.

"The trail's cleared here, see? These boulders have been dragged away, many ruts ahead of us and snaking off over there, through that narrow valley. The vans move on up there." Ufra this is, pointing over to the right of the lodge. I take the chance to wash in the icy water and it thrills my skin. This isn't only the shock of cold water, but something else. I have no words for it; a sense of the water's life is what I want to say.

These are all soldiers, the riders approaching. At their head must be the chief, yet he wears a steel helm and a chain shirt, the helm chased with great artistry, a decorative helm such as would be worn at a coronation. He has similarly detailed boots and his horse too is extravagantly barded, with a fine shaffron and petral unmarked by battle. Some of the other horses have leather barding, mail crinets. In this land it would be less surprising to see a bear with wings.

The chief of the Cargamun dismounts clumsily. As I approach him I see his yellowy eyes, a drooper. He stinks, both his body and his breath, confirming it. We clasp arms; there's a faded strength there, good muscle gone bad. In his mouth is a bone pipe, chased silver rings on its stem and carved fit for a king. I'd laugh if we were in any other place.

"I am Marghoster, of the Post." I want to see if there's any surprise in him at hearing that. He has not reacted to my red cloak.

He points to himself. "Chief Ifmot. You been due many

293

days," he says, his Farlsgrad limited. "We take betony." He's about to say more when he looks past me to the Master.

"What?"

"He is brother to Scar."

I'd say he was coming down off some betony, a twitchiness about him, but thankfully his reason, any suspicion he might have had, are doused by his come-down and the mention of Scar.

"We take betony. What blocks you have?"

"We can spare eight points."

"Eight? No, no. We get twenty. Twenty?" He uses his fingers to show me. He turns then to the men behind me, and they're all men. He cups his hands about his chest and chuckles, flicks his tongue out and they all smile, looking at my babs.

"I like strong. I like fight on my mat," he says, looking me over as he would a prized yak.

"Eight." The betony blocks are ready; Curic holds up the blocks, two four-pointers, before putting them back in their linen.

He nods, as though he's forgotten his original demand. He walks over to the wagons where the Ilkashun and Ososi posing as slaves are. As he does one of the Ilkashun starts crying out a name, "Lughre! Lughre!" She reaches out with her arms over the side of the wagon, looking into the field. There, a child, also in chains, turns and looks back. She immediately tries to run to us — "Ma! Mata!" she shouts — but the chains trip her and she falls. Still she scrabbles, howling with longing.

Fuck. I turn to Ensma behind me, speak in field lingo, "Shut her up, now! She'll fuck us all."

There's a flicker of surprise in her eyes until she remembers the stakes, then she takes out a knife and starts shouting at the woman to sit back in the wagon unless she wants to lose her tongue. The woman's mouth drops in horror; understandably she's lost all reason now she's seen what must be one of her kidnapped children. Her eyes widen then, fixed as they are on the field behind me, and I turn to see one of the tribesmen grab the girl by her throat and shove her to the earth, pulling a club from his belt. He cracks her twice on her back and the girl is silenced, shaking with fear and grief.

Ensma talks rapidly in another lingo, must be one they know something of, the Ilkashun and Hidzuc. The woman looks at me and then at the Master, but we cannot react. She stares at the Cargamun chief and spits in his direction. He pulls out his sword and reaches for her.

"Enough!" I shout. He turns, in a rage; his men dismount and take their swords out, all of them fine and shining blades, the work of Farlsgrad smiths I don't doubt, gifts to appease this kurch while the vans roll through.

"Chief, not one can be hurt," I tell him. "They are my orders!"

He's trapped between two courses then. I can't have him look any closer at the wagon, see the weapons and belts in the straw.

"More betony, yes?"

I gesture to Curic. He understands immediately, holds up another two four-pointers.

The chief's eyes flash with hunger, and it appeases his men too, gazing at the betony like moths drawn to a candle.

I take my chance to catch the Ilkashun mother's eye. She reads my plea for her to calm down and I touch my belt so she knows I'm fearful of Ifmot seeing the weapons in the wagons. The sorrow in her eyes is hard to bear as she looks for her girl again.

"Fine horse," I say to Ifmot. "Fine blade as well."

He swells at these compliments and bids me follow him so I may inspect the barding more closely.

"We can set camp, Chief Ifmot?" Ufra this is.

"Yes. There, where others stop before." The grass has gone and the soil is torn about by the vans that previously stopped here after the days on the hills up from the Flintre kurchpoles.

His crew settle back down. They puff themselves up a bit as they face us soldiers; none have much colour or posture about them. They don't carry full belts, just some muster belts as would be used at ceremonies. More than one has struggled to get the belt near his belly, and they curve under instead. Curic whistles those crewing the vans to move the wagons away from the lentil fields into the common. I don't see lookouts about us. They do not guard their kurch and it is as if they have no need.

I sign, behind my back, for Ufra and Ensma to join me as I follow the chief, Ensma taking up the betony blocks Curic had held up earlier.

"Who has made you such fine gifts as these?" I ask, gesturing to their armour. "This is beautiful work."

"The man in red," he says, pointing to my cloak. "He promise more whore, more young."

"Who?"

"He is older then he is younger and he smell same."

"*Ekri-mustau*," says one of his men, and he mimes something like lumps being pulled from his head."

"He dream catcher. Ekri-mustau, Dream Catcher," says Ifmot.

"What do you mean?"

"You sleep before him. You touch, you see dreams. He takes. He happy. I'm happy belly now." He slaps his paunch and smiles.

I look at Ufra and Ensma. We're all struggling to understand his meaning.

"You follow for smoke," he says. "Bring Scar," meaning
the Master.

"I will secure wagons. I'll follow you then."

Ifmot takes the bag of betony blocks from Ensma, holds
it up to his crew, all of whom are delighted with their new
supply. I wait until they're far enough back they won't hear
us.

"You did well, Driwna," says Ufra. "They are droopers."

Ensma looks about her with disgust. The string for the
lentils has been laid in long rows to the right of the river,
where most of the sun will be at this time of year. There are
many from the plains here and they are being beaten back
to their work after stopping to watch as the girl was beaten
and her mother threatened by Ifmot.

"What is her name, the mother of that girl?"

"You must ask her, Driwna," says Ufra.

I see no way to free the girl as it stands. I must persuade
her mother that we go on, that we will come back for her
daughter.

"Did you follow what that Ifmot was saying?" says Ensma.

"No. Hope I can get more sense from him about where
we have to take these vans and what sort of place it is we're
taking them to."

But something is bothering me about what he said. About
the dreams.

"He wasn't surprised to learn you were Post, Driwna,"
says Ufra.

"Yes. It's become clear the Post is involved; he spoke of
someone in red. Crejda's ledgers being too clean and her and
Morril being told to move lots through the Brasks and
Marghosters proves it anyway."

297

"Stroff?" asks Curic. "Out here?"

"This red he spoke of must have some command to be treating with him. Stroff wouldn't, couldn't come up here. A marschal perhaps?"

"I have to stay with the wagons," says Ufra. "They will not believe there is another Ososi like the etza-Oskoro."

"I think your people will be glad of that anyway. I hope we can leave here in the morning with directions north."

I kiss her. Such is not forbidden on a van, but neither is it encouraged when discipline and clear minds are required. Ensma clears her throat, making us both smile as we kiss.

She and Curic then join me in walking along the riverbank to the lodge ahead.

I can see how angry Ensma is, a Sathanti looking across lentil fields at other Sathanti in chains, their slavers calling themselves the same.

"How can they do it to their own people? This is Farslgrad coin." She spits, takes a breath to manage herself. She might be cursing her own kurch for their relations with Farlsgrad as much as the slavery here.

The men wielding the clubs over the slaves are all armed and armoured for battle. I've never seen so many swords in a kurch, so many mail shirts. It saddens me as we approach the first of the huts that I am reminded of my own kurch, my pa's house. There are barrels here, crates full of rope, sacks of what must be rice piled in newly built sheds. A child, a boy ten winters at most, is in ankle chains and is cleaning clothes at the edge of the river. There's three stood about him, kicking him, trying to get him off balance, Cargamun duts, themselves a similar age. The boy looks at us approach; he's in tears, but still tries to do his work, beating at the robes and shirts he has laid out on the huge rocks the like of which are strewn all about this valley. The

298

children follow his gaze. One has a pipe, I can smell betony. The other two move with a predictable slowness and care.

"We wash, we wash red, two silver!" They gesture at our Post cloaks. The boy in chains is pulled back by his hair. "He good wash." They start barking with laughter, fuelling each other's humour until they're almost insensible. They forget about the boy for a moment and he turns back to the pile of woollens in baskets about him, another armful into the river to have their dirt trodden out of them.

The Cargamun are all those who are not working. Women, elders, cripples, all those who might be expected to keep the kurch, its tuika runs, chickens, yaks, plant, all are sitting about, some singing, most smoking. It is the afternoon and they are in their cups, flutes playing jigs, bacca and kannab filling their pipes. To me, it is some strange reflection of what could be seen in any king's palace, between nobles and their servants. Some of the men and the older boys stand over the Ilkashun slaves as they do everything from make butter to weaving and cooking. There's none come near us as we walk up through the huts on the main trail to the lodge. It is being extended: there is a work party a hundred yards off at the face of one of the cliffs rising high over the camp; carts for the stone, more slaves, men and women of prime age I expect, working with picks and hammers. In appearance the lodge is a grander version of the huts about it, three roofs with great eaves that are supported by six stone columns, creating a large verandah on all sides, enough for firepits and, it seems, the provisions they've earned as tithe for their acquiescence to vans like ours moving through. Stone steps lead up to the main level of it, straddling a gulley cut all about it to manage flood-water from the river. The kurchpole stands before the steps. We pay our respects to this storied twelve-foot length of a vast trunk of some fir tree I don't recognise, easily three feet wide. At its base, leopards and wolves dance with yaks and Cargamun hunters, speaking of worship centuries past, the offering of babies even. My ma told me of similar stories carved on our own kurchpole but hacked away by my greatpa for fear it would harm our relations with Farlsgrad. The carvings at the top of their story, five or so feet up, are more finely worked, and it's here that Ifmot has himself standing on the backs of men on their hands and knees, his erect cock carved to be the size of his leg, and from his hands appear to flow water, or milk, a river in which stand Cargamun soldiers with their spears and drums.

I am used to such poles and the lodges they announce being places of veneration, of respect. But from the Cargamun lodge I hear only laughter, shouting and more singing from inside. I hear the grunting of sex from open shutters along one side of the lodge. There are only three guards outside, as ridiculously dressed as Ifmot and the other Cargamun.

"We would see Chief Ifmot," I say.

One of the guards walks across the verandah to the doors, giving them a knock with the end of his spear. One door opens a crack and, shortly, more widely to let us past.

"In," says the guard, as though this has been more effort for him than we deserve.

The fug of betony, roasting tuika and ale is heavy inside. It must be Ufra's plant; my growing senses — my sight, hearing, smell — snag on something, as though squashed. The Song of the Earth cannot always be called pretty.

There is a hall, a firepit in it tended to by a boy and a girl, both naked, grimy with ash. Doors along the sides of the hall would, in other kurches, lead to rooms saved for esteemed visitors. Most doors are closed, but the door to the room I heard grunting from is open, and it sickens me, what's being done in there. I reach for Ensma's arm, squeeze it, for she's seen it as well and we have to keep calm.

"Chief Ifmot!" I call, trying to bring my crew's attention to the end of the hall, away from the gasping and short cries of pain, to where Ifmot sits, predictably, on a small dais in a grand chair that has the cut of Farlsgrad craftsmen. Ifmot fancies he's a king here. Between us and him sit ten or eleven of his crew, in two groups, at long tables either side of the pit. There are sconces along the walls and on the tables candles are lit, for despite the roofs being far above us, their tiered design lets only a dribble of light in.

One of his men opens a door to our left, halfway along the hall. The slaves here are whores. He has nothing on but an unbuckled leather tunic. Behind him a woman sits with her knees up to her chest, her face against her thighs, breathing heavily, shuddering. The man stares at us, and absently rubs his gums with his thumb, which must have had a sliver of betony on it.

"He fuck for hours, Ekrad, bang bang bang," says Ifmot, his words spoken through teeth clenched about that stupid fucking pipe. He laughs and we're encouraged to smile, to share his humour. Next to him, on the steps of the dais, sit a Cargamun woman and one of the men we saw earlier. She sits on a higher step, and between her legs sits a boy. She's got her arms about him and a pipe in her hand, which she pushes into his mouth and on which he draws in kannab, its sweetness thickening further the awful stale heat of the hall. On the other side of the dais must be Ifmot's champion, or what passes for it; big and heavy, shirtless, a ratty unkept beard, the build of a rockbreaker, though he's likely done little of that since the vans came.

"Tuika!" Ifmot claps his hands and the two children at the fire run to us, point to seats on the end of the table nearest to the left of the dais. They cannot look us in the eyes and I see Ensma's own fill up, for they are beaten, that is clear, scabs and bruises where there shouldn't be, dried lines of blood from their heads that the ash sticks to. They find two tin plates and some rags to get at the tuika spits.

I bow in thanks to the chief and we sit at the table. His crew are paying us little mind; they've got the linen bag of blocks open and are shaving off slivers to shred into their pipes.

"We will not stay long here and do not need to fuck. We go north with the slaves but don't know the way. My first time." My meaning is completed with gestures.

"You go to big camp," says Ifmot. "Biggest camp. Two day, up, up. Maf take you."

One of the men, must be Maf, on the table opposite the firepit from us, speaks in their lingo.

"What does he say?" I ask, for it is more than a simple "yes" to the command. I'm glad at least we'll have a guide and glad that we'll get to kill at least one of these fuckers out of sight.

"He will tell me of the army," says Ifmot. "We smash the Flintre. We grow stronger."

I share a look with Curic and Ensma sitting across from me.

"It is your army, in the mountains?" I ask. I immediately curse myself, for I ought to know what the vans are for.

"You don't know about the camp?"

"I know the camp. I ask if it's your army to command, to fight Flintre. It is not Marghoster's army?" In for a copper, in for a gold.

"No, no." He speaks nervously. "Marghoster promise land for us. Allies. Brothers."

"Kings of the Spine!" shouts one of his crew from the same

group as Maf. The others in the room shout it back. They say it awkwardly, like words they've heard but not understood.

The children bring over our plates, cuts of tuika on them. One returns moments later with two hard loaves. She's hobbling, makes a show of placing the bread on the table, trembling as she does so.

"Thank you," says Curic, who cannot look up at her for more than a moment. The anger's rising in all of us, I can feel it. "We cannot fuck this up," I hiss in Post lingo, for only Curic will know it. "We must make it to the camp, find those responsible."

Ifmot leaves his chair. There's a scream from a room behind us, which pleases him. He sits next to me, gestures for the boy who served us to come over. He does so quickly, stands next to Ifmot. He squeezes the boy's buttocks. "Krsa. Go!

"We drink to Marghoster. Drink to army." He begins packing his pipe, his fingers and reflexes slow with the drink and betony. It's as though he forgets we are there, picking at the hot, greasy cuts of tuika while he shaves betony off one of the four-point blocks we'd given him and packs it into the bacca in the bowl. His attention returns to us after lighting his pipe with a candle from the table. He puts his hand on my thigh, then looks up and watches the thick smoke he's exhaled rise lazily up. He squeezes.

"Strong, eh! Strong woman." This was meant for the hall, and there's some banging of cups as they watch us with a little more interest. I look over at Ensma, worried she'll react, the disgust at these fellow Sathanti barely contained. Curic puts his arm around her, a gentle hand on her shoulder, signal enough that she should restrain herself.

Slowly, Ifmot moves his hand up my leg, watching my face as he does it. I look back at him; he's hot with lust. Perhaps he knows that there's nothing we can do to retaliate.

I put my hand on his, curl my fingers around it and lift his hand onto the table.

"Not today, Chief Ifmot. I will bring the van back." I lean gently into him. "Then I will smoke your pipe, King of the Spine."

This he takes the intended meaning of, his eyes widening with approval and pleasure. I put my hand on his, squeeze it gently. It works.

We endure the cup of krsa, a honeyed ale that we are duty bound to drink. He settles for putting his arm around my shoulder as he tells us of his plans for the kurches about his, but especially the Flintre, who will be wiped from the land and their kurchpoles burned. He tells us nothing will withstand this army. We encourage him along before refusing the offer of one of the rooms in his hall, telling him we need to keep watch on the slaves, for it is dusk. We return to the wagons in silence, Curic with his arm around Ensma who has suffered with what she saw there. We all suffered with it, but she has not seen the world, not seen what those who call themselves civilised are capable of, how seductive their wealth and vices are to such poor Sathanti as these.

The Master has made those pretending to be our slaves comfortable, for we are far enough from the Cargamun huts and in sufficient darkness that they could not raise a concern.

"Do you have the way?" he asks. Ufra is with him; she can sense we're upset.

"We do. One of Ifmot's crew will lead us. Two days north to a camp, they must be training an army, using the slaves for it."

"For what purpose? This is a Farlsgrad army being trained in the Sathanti mountains?"

"Ifmot spoke of being an ally, that the Flintre would be

overrun, and he made master over them. This must be Hildmir, seeking conquest, and he's gone about it cleverly, stirring up trouble with the kurches in the mountains and the plains, stopping a Council being formed. He's learned."

"All his life King Hildmir's shown no sign of desiring conquest. He's dragging his people to war with the Sathanti. It'll be bloody," says Curic.

"I agree," I say. "I can't fathom it, but if he has the mountains, if the kurches up here are like this one, already in his service, then he might well sweep all resistance aside. The mountains resisted his forefathers, in part because Marghoster did not join them and so cost us Bridche our homeland."

"You are Post. You are Brother Red," says Ensma.

"The Post cannot get involved in this, the Post does not want it; it goes against our creed."

"There's plenty of profit in war, Fieldsman," says Curic.

"For a while. But unlike some in the Post, I don't see what we do as being about how many bags we can fill with coin for a few seasons. Fuck it, Curic, I don't want this. I am Sathanti, for all I bear the name Marghoster about Farlsgrad. I want to stop this and I know Yblas would want that too."

"What do we do about Ifmot?" Ensma this is, packing a pipe with some kannab. "He shames all us Sathanti."

"Nothing yet."

"This is wrong, Driwna. We should lay waste to this fucking place, throw every one of them off of those cliffs."

"I would. But if one of them escapes to raise the alarm ahead, we're too few to stop a barracks of soldiers if that's what's up there. We need surprise, we need to know what we're up against or we're all dead. Scar is up there and he's fearsome enough. There are slaves here and ten times more there I'll warrant. We must keep to the greater good, break them at their heart."

"We leave allies of theirs behind us if we don't kill them, Fieldsman," says Curic.

"They are droopers," says Ufra. "They are nothing. We will come back and kill them all."

"Let's get some rest, we've a long day ahead and I want to get out of this shithole as dawn comes. Curic, come with me."

We walk a little way from the wagons, out of earshot.

"Everything all right, Fieldsman?"

"Yes and no. Yes, because I think this is the right thing to do for these people, and no, because we're Post, and this no longer seems to have much to do with the Creed or the Post's profit. You agreed to come with me to investigate what's behind these vans, guard me and support me in that, but follow us tomorrow and you're signing up for trouble — a proper fight I fear, unless Sillindar favours us greatly. This isn't a crossroads purse."

"I know, Fieldsman, but I'm with you. You and these Ososi, and that Oskoro. It's all I can do not to get on my knees and thank you for the gift of meeting them. I never thought I'd live to see such a wonder as the Master, and your Ufra. My greatpa would sing me songs of them, yet in his they were not monsters, they were shepherds of the world, healers." He remembers the words with a smile, holds up a hand to conduct the tune that's in his head. "'*As I was dying, on a forgotten path lying, a flowergirl came to me. Your bones I'll bind, if you'll help me find, this forest's Heartknot Tree.*'" The memory brings tears to his eyes and to mine on seeing them, for I'd not heard this song in many years and I have said before how prone us soldiers are to the feelings and memories of home and family.

"You're right, Fieldsman, Yblas is right, with this creed I've signed up to. This is what the Post must be for, if the

Creed is to mean anything. I would give my life to see these Ososi live and prosper again, for they've shown me kindness and taught me recipes for which they've asked nothing in return." I hug him. I'm glad he's here when Cal cannot be, and I fear I'll not see Cal again.

We walk back to the wagons and I look across at the Cargamun lodge. A kind of grief overcomes me, that such love and suffering can be close enough one could throw a blanket over both, whether it's in this cold valley or the halls of kings.

Chapter 15

Driwna

The Cargamun, Maf, leads us north, past the waterfall that brings their river to them. As we walk the wagons up through the narrow pass, the Master puts his hands to the face of the rocks around us. He looks back at me, Ufra, the other Ososi and Oskoro, begins hugging himself, as though he's grieving. The rock has been worked through here, but worked finely; the sides of the track are almost smooth. Who would or could take such care over the widening of a trail such as this? The stone beneath our feet, in the middle of the path, is a different colour to that at the sides, a dusky blue unlike the pale grey of the main path, polished by the years of boots and hooves.

I feel something too, a queasiness throughout me. Something isn't right on this path and the whole crew are silent as we shepherd the wagons along. These hours are a chance to be with Ufra. She fears for her pa, fears too for her people when she has not yet got the Flower. I'm as helpless with her fears as she is with mine for my mun. She's wiser than me, coaxing out our stories, mine and Curic's.

She asks question after question, lets us talk, the words a kind of river that she can stand in, making others feel better as well as herself.

At dawn on the second day, Ufra and I bring Maf some of the brin and lentil broth we'd been given by the Cargamun. We ask about the path ahead and he tells us of the old iron mines and quarry that the camp is set in. Once, the Cargamun moved iron from this quarry, south to the Flintre and along the Tongue. Bitterly, he tells us of their losing trade to cheaper iron, the betrayals of the confederacies about them, how it robbed them of their lives. The belly cramps start hurting him an hour later, the poison is deliberately slower than it need be and I fill his mouth with cotton and bind it to stop him screaming in his final hour.

The firs and spruce thicken and cover the bluffs about us, finding an uncanny purchase in the steep rock faces. There's a stillness to these trees as we pass through, just crows scritching across the canopy, a lone thrush calling out. The Master halts the wagons before we pass out onto a glade of shale and rhododendron bushes, pink and red buds beginning to flower, lifting our mood in the mist surrounding us.

"We'll scout ahead," he says.

"Is it near?" I ask.

"I hear the camp, it is beyond the ridge at the far side of these *raxmor*." This must be his lingo for the rhododendrons. "I need some Ososi, we climb more quickly, we will circle the quarry." I look to our left and see a sharp drop, a cliff face that curls away from us. If the gates to the camp are straight ahead they'll be able to bypass it and come to the lip of the quarry without being seen.

The rest of us that's not chained to the wagons watch as they move like spiders across the rocks, signing to each other the handholds they find. I watch Ufra, who's gone with them, thrilled by her strength, the fearlessness with which she makes her choices on the face of the cliff. The Master is every bit the wonder that so moves Curic, leaping to the handholds he sees till he finds the cliff's edge some two hundred feet along from where we stand. Once he's listened for anyone in the trees beyond, he uses rope to pull the others up that are still making their way across. They vanish into the trees.

It's understandable that we're all restless as we wait. There's plenty of kannab on the van and it's carefully portioned out. Curic and I pack our pipes and settle into its sweet and pungent smoke. We wait in silence and once I've knocked out my pipe I go through everybody's packs, Ilkashun included, demanding they run through the pouches, vials, bags, pockets and scabbards, inspecting everything. Two there are who could not instantly put their finger on the plugweed they carried, one who needed to gum the lip of a sporebag that was getting dry. Many are nervous, and as I inspect their fieldbelts I ask them if they have family in the camp beyond, or if they know someone taken, or who it is they have at home, girding their will to the killing, to the necessary ruthlessness that will help them stone the Oskoro blood, thankfully far easier and more potent than the mulch we use in the Post, "the Amo".

An hour or so later, against faint cries and an occasional note from a horn that rise from the quarry, the Master and Ufra scale the rocks back towards our position. As they arrive and stand before us, they look at each other and the Master tilts his head back, a surprise to us, for it seems he's holding back tears.

"Driwna." Ufra this is. She also struggles with how to begin. "Arrows. The others, the Oskoro and Ososi we've left on the other side of the quarry, they'll need arrows. The

310

quarry is in a kind of crescent, and over the ridge there is a high wall with the gates. There are no guards on the far side where we've left our kin, for the land there is either impassable or else cliffs. They'll not expect attacks from that side. There are caves in the quarry, iron bars over their mouths, pens about the foot of the quarry where the bloomeries would have been. Near the gates are the tents and huts of the drudhas, captains, merchants. It's big, Driwna. Hundreds of slaves are there, soldiers." Her breath catches as she recounts what she's seen.

"I am no soldier, Driwna Bridche," says the Master, filling the moment that Ufra's needed to compose herself. "But if the wagons would be led down to the foot of the quarry and you begin a fight there, with the bowmanship of my Oskoro and an attack on the gate to follow, we confuse and disorientate any attempt at a defence. We may stand a chance."

"It is good reasoning," says Curic.

"How do we know our prisoners will need to be led with the wagons down to the foot of the quarry and not held up near the gate where many of the guards would be?"

"The rock has been hewn wide enough for wagons, as would have been necessary for the iron they once mined," says Ufra. "It may be that the guards can be persuaded to let you lead them down because of the dangerous nature of the Ososi we have in the wagons. The drudhas are down there. I saw tents against the bloomeries that survived; they're being used for whatever they're doing to the slaves. They'll want my Ososi there."

For a moment I wanted to ask why she implied she would not be with me at the head of the wagon, but she's too obviously an Ososi for that to work.

"There were sounds from the caves there, howls of pain. I do not know what lies in them that has to be caged so,"

311

says the Master. "You should do what you can to observe, and sign as such if you can do it without being observed."

"I will. I think we should go now, for they might not take us down to the drudhas if the drudhas are back near the gate at night for whatever food and entertainment is made in such a place for those who work it."

"I'll gather up arrows," says Ensma.

"Driwna," says Ufra, "tell them to stay calm. What we saw in there, it's not easy to see."

"I will, love." I hold her for a few moments, breathe her in, kiss her. "Stay alive, Driwna-wen."

"Our song thrives, the Oskoro say. We will live."

"We will. Sillindar follow you."

I go to the wagons and speak with the soldiers there. We'll begin the killing on my signal, the Oskoro archers will wait for it, and one will shoot a fire arrow into the sky to signal the Master, Ufra, her three Ososi not in the wagons and four of the Ilkashun to attack the gate. The rest will be with me.

We leave the Oskoro chief to distribute the arrows to his crew, one of whom goes back to the cliff face to take quivers to the other Ososi and Oskoro hidden above and behind the quarry. Then we start moving the wagons through the glade and up the slope. The noise grows as we approach; screaming, shouting. As we crest the ridge a horn blows from the wall. Ahead of us are giant gates, a portcullis is down. The wall is made of the stone of the quarry, smooth and strong as a castle wall, another strange and unnerving sight in such a barren place. My breath quickens. If the baby Oskoro girl has been brought into the mountains, then it's here I'll find her, it's here she waits to be held again.

About the gate are tents, twenty or so, and there's no cover between here and there. I fear for Ufra's crew making this ground up and getting over that wall. I have to hope our distraction is enough to draw the lookouts down inside. One of the tents outside the gates is a pavilion, though the others are all smaller, and all are weather-worn. There are some fires about and we pass some shit pits. This is a long-established camp.

I look over to our left where the wall ends at the edge of the cliff; I see one of our Oskoro move through the trees, but there are no guards at that end of the battlement.

"Why the fuck is such a wall needed here?" asks Curic. It's a question we can't answer. It makes no sense.

Then the smell joins the noise. Disease, shit, rotting meat. It's a stench as heavy as the deck of a whaler at work on one of those giant beasts. The horn rouses those in the tents. Two soldiers appear from the pavilion, no fieldbelts, putting on woollen shirts. A curt whistle brings out a mountain of a woman who leans on a thick staff, hand on hip. She whistles, shrill and clear as a bird, and her whores step out from the tent and line up. It's sad to watch them summon the strength to raise their chins and look us straight on. Some glance nervously at their master, who is rapping the staff on the ground. The soldiers walk forward with her. The other tents spawn men, women and children in a frantic rush to fill empty tables with their dried plant, cooker's potions, kegs they weren't expecting to need until the evening, along with all manner of worn-out robes and leggings and boots, most likely from those enslaved.

"Rough goin'?" says one soldier.

"First time up here," I say. "Pass is tricky; the Cargamun were a great help to us." This in case he was a Cargamun himself.

"We being no trouble for the masters here. Lick their lips at all these Ososi cunts, won't they, Crish?"

"Will do, brun."

313

"Welcome, Guard, I'm Yaen." The whoremaster this is. "You come back out here later, have your pick of these. I broke and trained them myself." The woman steps forward. "Hard journey up to this shithole needs some rewards, doesn't it?"

"It does, lady," I say. I look behind her, see one of the girls with her arm around a boy, maybe her brun, giving him reassurance as he looks nervously at us all.

"See you tonight, then. I have more than enough for your crew, long as you don't mind the sight of each other at it." Her laugh is wet with phlegm. "Smell's not so bad out here and all; better for business and better comfort for you soldiers. When you get inside you'll see."

The others approach us then, scritching about their wares and speaking like poets to the merits of whatever they're selling.

"We just want to get this lot in the camp; it's been a long road," I say to the soldier.

"You have betony on there I hope," he says.

"We do."

"Marghoster's not that stupid," says the other one.

"Follow me," says the first. "Yaen, I'll be back tonight for another go at that Ososi boy." _

"I'll have him ready for you, Dron."

I dismount, Curic following, us being the only ones not riding the wagons. We'd put our red cloaks in bags before approaching the camp, wanting nothing to distract those guarding this place into taking an interest.

Two of the guards at the top of the gate wind the portcullis. A bar is lifted from its lip across the gates and two from inside push them out. As they open, the smell of burning flesh hits us, the wind blowing smoke towards us as it hits the lip of the quarry. As the Master of Flowers said, we pass

314

through the gates and look at a deep crescent, rising across from us, a bowl of sorts, flattened at our edge of it. A wide stone path winds down to a shelf on which some of the remains of the bloomeries are used for other fires. My heart pounds, yet here is a sight to break it.

"Where's the chief, the captain?" I shout, taking deep breaths to control myself.

"He's down to your right there, big hut. Scar's standing outside; can't miss him."

There he is. He's watching us. As big as the Master, no hood here as he wore back in Lindur, though he stands in leathers, a sleeveless vest like Ufra, but his is chain, mighty arms bare and thick with vines and bark. His head is covered in scars and stitches, a mostly blackened patchwork, misshapen, as Ufra has told me it would be from his trying to repair his braegnloc with the skulls of those Ososi that forbade him becoming a Master in his own right. He leans back to hammer the door with his fist.

The path slopes down past where he's standing. There's a smithy and stores next to the captain's hut. Further down the slope I see the bars over the cave mouths along it. Below I hear crying out, someone singing. The smell of burning flesh is hard to breathe. I move closer to the edge of the path as I gesture the wagons forward. Below are a pile of bodies burning, eight or ten, and two slaves, it looks like, manacled to each other, are doing their best to drag another pile of bodies to the fire. Many corpses have been opened up in the careful manner of drudhas. Some have no skin. Limbs and heads are stuffed into a fire in a big open barrel that might once have caught water. There are many of these barrels. It does us no good for me to dwell on the horror here. The path winds down the crescent of the rock face to the pit below.

315

From the captain's hut comes a man who would look big against anyone but Scar; his head's shaved and his mighty beard, thicker even than Gennic's, is grey and patchy about his chin and lip with the orange that comes of smoking. He's wearing full mail, a fieldbelt and all, though it's not buckled for a fight. He carries a whip in his hand. He reads me as the vanguard.

"Welcome." I can't place his accent. We clasp arms. He's got a nose like a plum, as if it's been burned, his beard's spotted with food, hair matted in places from a lack of washing and brushing. His is a sharp, sour smell. He looks tired, though his colour tells me he's used to proper fight-brews.

"How many?" He flicks his head up to the wagons behind me.

"Seventeen Ososi, ten Ilkashun."

"Seventeen Ososi?"

"The Ilkashun chief had been hiding them."

"Which one?" He's suspicious.

"Yicre. We didn't find out from him. Not seen him for a long time."

"Doubt you'll see him again. Tarstrik will be happy you've got this many. Have you seen their thorns drip with poison? Dangerous fuckers."

"I'm looking forward to an ale. Can I leave the supplies here or do I need to take them down there?"

He walks past me, clasps arms with Curic, looking along the train of wagons.

"Dron," he says to the man leading us, "before you go back, get a few off their bunks to move those three wagons to the stores. The shift's changing anyway in an hour; they can get an early start on it."

"Yes, Captain."

"Lindur." I look back to the hut and Scar is now standing only a few feet from me. "I saw you in Lindur," he says. "Post."

"She's Post?" asks the captain.

"She was at Brask's shed," says Scar. "Post."

"You wear no red here. What's your name?"

"Driwna. I am a fieldsman of the Post, a marschal of sorts. Morril, the reeve at Lindur, has supplied some of these stores, as was requested by High Cleark Rogus from the Gate."

I do my best to hold Scar's gaze. He sniffs the air. Just then I realise that if I were alone he'd be able to tell I was becoming an Ososi, that their plant was growing inside me. The soldiers in the wagons acting as our prisoners must be masking it.

Scar turns, looks up at the trees overlooking the quarry. I follow his gaze but see nothing.

"How do you get used to this stink?" I ask, looking to distract him.

"We don't burn them every day." Scar's voice has the same soft, sandy quality I recall from Lindur, a voice not used to speaking, or speaking over others perhaps. "We must get those Ososi in cages. They're dangerous."

There's an implication in there, subtle, that it must have been hard or even impossible to subdue this many Ososi. Scar looks at them and they don't hold his stare. They know well enough that to challenge him, defy him, might bring him close to the wagons, to what we have concealed there.

"We've had them on some droop. They'll have another mouthful as we bring them off the wagons, while they get chained back up with your guards below."

"Lead them on," says the captain. "Any of the guards below will help you with them."

I need no more encouragement to get away from Scar while

317

we ready ourselves with the Oskoro blood. We tie up our horses on a post next to the captain's hut and I lead those pulling the wagons on down the slope.

"Don't look back at him," I whisper to my crew, "he's Ososi. I'm learning that they can get a sense of things we can't. We take the Master's blood on my mark."

Each step I'm waiting for something to go wrong. The slope winds down into the shadow of the quarry. The burning bodies light up part of it. Other fires are lit in the broken bloomeries and outside the tents below where the drudhas must be working. We pass by two caves, their mouths barred, dark within. At one there's nothing, a mumbling from within, echoing. At another two men and a woman watch us. One's braegnloc is open, flies swarm at it, crawling about his face and over the amony planted in it. He's panting, sweating, and I'd think it was tears leaking from his eyes if I hadn't seen his head. The woman is in a filthy robe, barefoot. Her one arm is mostly bark, creaking as she flexes her elbow. I smell dead skin, but I'm unsure if it's from her or all of them. She watches us with some interest, maybe hunger, for the front of her robe and her chin are covered in blood. There's little of what animates a person in her eyes.

It is horrifyingly clear to me now why the Ososi are so important to what they're doing here. This whole camp is set up to find a way to grow what the Ososi have, to create soldiers and brews their equal and so greater than any soldier I have ever come across. This is the army King Hildmir must be building. With enough time their drudhas will create an unstoppable force, tortured and twisted enough to think only of killing, to want for nothing else, no coin, no fear.

I sign back to the wagons, and the Ilkashun acting as their guards open the flasks and give the slaves our fightbrew before finishing the flasks off themselves. The path carries on and at the bottom stands a guard. She's before a line of slaves, eight of them, none are chained, all staring at her as though they have no will in the matter. I see better now the parts of the quarry hidden from the gate above. Curic passes me the Oskoro blood. I drink and pass it to Ensma. The force of it builds in me; I'm more ready for it this time. The Song grows in strength, kindling but not burning me.

We move the wagons out of the line into the space at the pit of the quarry. Here there are cages crammed with people, barely room to stand in each. There are some lying dead, others standing on them. Those facing us watch us. Some are in cages on their own and chained up. They have lost their minds, but they are bigger, fresh with colour, grinding their teeth. Some watch us with eyes so dead they could be blind, others with a dark and fierce wit. One has a man and woman chained to him; they are naked, bitten all over, and the flies are thick on them; the woman is weeping, trying to wipe the insects from her. There are two more dead in this pen, skin torn open over most of their bloated bodies. They've been eaten.

"Welcome," says one of the guards, the only one close to us. She lowers her staff and as she does so the eight slaves before her kneel: trained pets. I look back at the wagons and my crew all stare back at me, revulsion and rage simmering. I nod and raise my arm. The guard has time only to widen her eyes as I leap forward with my spear and run her through. Those of my crew pretending to be slaves take up the hidden weapons and fly off the wagons as the slaves in the pens start screaming. They had practised the fitting of each other's fieldbelts on our way to the Cargamun camp. The fire of the Master's blood streams throughout me from my belly once more, a great heat, a giddy and thrilling lightness. We need confusion. I reach down for the guard's belt, cut the loop of keys free. We have jumped from the wagon in all directions; some run for the drudha tents, a couple of whom have rushed out on hearing the noise. The drudhas are slick with blood, and I look back up the path. Scar and the captain see the chaos below them and the captain runs back to a bell hanging outside his hut, begins ringing it.

"Curic, Scar is coming. Ready your sporebags." I signal for the Oskoro that have been hiding at the top of the quarry across from the gate and huts to begin shooting.

There are only six keys. I open one of the cages filled with slaves and they fall and stagger out, some pushing at others, the whole cage shaking with the fire of their hope. There are few guards here and they had been in the drudha tents. Our Ososi and Ilkashun are at them, spearing them on the fine cool high that this blood gives us. I hear our bows from above us then, the strings, and as soldiers pour from their huts, swigging their own brews, many are hit, the rest trying to get their bearings on where the danger lies. Scar runs down the slope at us, the captain and a group of others following. Curic throws sporebags up the path, and three of our Ilkashun shoot at each. Scar stops at each of the cave-mouths we passed, opens the barred gates. Soldiers have followed behind him, throwing through the open gates swords, spears, axes. A roar comes from within the caves as they answer the call. Those that watched as we passed them moments ago calmly pick up these weapons. Scar bellows at them to follow, though his other soldiers are hesitant. Men and women pour out of the caves; they're fast, picking up weapons and either leaping from the path down into the pit or else following Scar as he runs at us.

"Form up on me! Archers cover!" I shout. I unlock two more cages, shout at them to take up weapons, fight for their lives and freedom, before running to join Curic, masked up, eyes juiced, set with his spear before the onrushing Scar, his experience stilling all thought, bringing joy to the Song itself.

I look up quickly as I ready my spear. The fire arrow's gone up now and I pray for the Oskoro and Ufra to get here fast. These are men and women such as I've never seen, the proof that these drudhas are improving their arts of splicing plant and flesh. These feral slaves, no armour or belts, they move like wolves, leap like antelope over the wagons right at us, as fast as we are, hitting our line of spears hard. And the first of them have no hesitation, throwing their spears at us and running freely onto ours, holding them and pulling them down so those behind them can leap over. Scar, however, is armoured; his chain shirt turns a glancing blow from a spear, slowing him a moment. I pull my spear back as one of them leaps at me; I get him in his gut, watch him get up, in no apparent pain despite his wound. There aren't enough of us. Scar is at Ensma on my left, and she matches him. He's surprised, I think, by how fast we are. Arrows fly at us from behind them, the height of the slope an advantage. The spores have not affected them as we had hoped. Our line's broken then on my right. An Ososi is hit in the throat and one of these strange soldiers is through, stabbing the Ilkashun next to me with his spear. He takes an arrow from one of our archers above, but snaps the shaft and keeps stabbing, heedless of it. I am risen now and I can see a thrill in his face, no concentration of a man stoning their brew. He is a match for me. I catch him in his gut, a stab with my own spear, less effective this close, thrust again to his face, but he's read it and rolled the bind. I feel the weight of it; I know my fate and drop as his spear passes my shoulder. He is huge, muscles swollen grotesquely, the brew or something else. I thrust again, try to unbalance him. He knocks my spear

321

aside, has read me again, but an arrow punches through his head as he stabs me; a few inches of his spear dig into me, cracking a rib. Desperate, I kick him over. The line's broken. Behind us the slaves are cowering, backing against the far wall of the pit or running for their cages.

"Kill them and live!" bellows Scar, a command that's felt as much as heard. There's some that cry out then that are so afraid of him, so broken, that I hear them charge us. Ilkashun and Ososi are caught up, some killed, others turning to fight them off.

"Spores! Schiltrom formation!" I shout, for these slaves do not have whatever is in the soldiers before us to withstand the spores and we need the schiltrom's shape to make some advantage from our lesser number.

More of their soldiers drop from the path further up the slope from us, and still they pour from the caves, fifty or sixty at least. They run up the slope to the stores to retrieve weapons. I have to hope that Ufra's crew is at the gate and can stop them, but this crew, with me, I have to lead. Curic is cut, slices to his legs, Ensma's lost her mask; she's wailing and screaming at the monsters before us, finding an equal foe for the first time in her life, no longer sure she'll make it. We all know that keeping our circle, even as we move back, is our only hope against these soldiers. Only three more join us, their spears over ours, raised. Still they choose to leap at us, some climbing the face of the quarry, looking to drop onto us, oblivious and uncaring of their own injuries. The bell rings again up in the huts. Ufra's crew are over the gates and splitting the captain's crew. Arrows still come in, finding those that are shooting at us on the slope, many now weaving among the wagons for cover as we're forced back to the open pens. There are men, women and children all around us choking to death from our spores. I hear a cry behind me; one of my crew grunts as he's killed. I glance back. A man's buried an axe in his shoulder, has flanked us, another that's had work done in his body. His chest is massive; I can't imagine what's inside him. He wrenches the axe free; his strength has forced it deep into the Ilkashun's breast. My knife's out, dripping with its own venom. I step to him, reading the fractions of his instinct, his left arm rising forward to counterbalance his right as the axe rises. He has no armour; a cut is all I need. As I slice his arm I feel a hand clutching at my leg, then a spear hits my shoulder from behind me. I kick down on the hand, but an arm hooks around my ankle. My footing's gone and I fall back, land on the legs of one of our fallen. It's a woman that's holding me, an injured slave coughing and retching, frenzied. She writhes, bites at the leather of my jerkin. I let go of my spear, grip one of her arms and snap it clean. She goes limp with shock. I get to my knees. The soldier's arm is cramping where I slashed it, fingers rigid, the speed of his blood, the might of his heart, making the poison work all the more quickly. I leave him, take up his axe. Ensma's now covering Curic, who's been hit in his hip. Scar's not fought the likes of us, but each small mistake, despite all our stern defence and telling counters, means we cannot hold back this press for very long. Scar has cut many of us down, keeps trying to get at Ensma. We give ground to him all the time, his speed and power. They're falling on us from the quarry face now, they're flanking us from the far side of the path, dropping into the pit and running through the slaves, most of whom are huddled together, back in their cages, hands over their mouths, desperately trying not to breathe the spores in.

I realise then how their brew could come so close to ours, why it is we are being overrun despite the Master's blood.

Ufra's pa. This is Ososi blood that's in them. His blood, I fear. I draw my own sword, the axe in my other hand. I'm not trained to fight with both, but I have to protect our flank, the one archer we have left with us. The others are dead or out of arrows and taking up their own spears to fight among the wagons and cages. There'll be little the Oskoro archers at the top of the quarry can do to help us down here in among the fires and the dead.

A shout; two are running across the pit, charging me at our flank.

Stone it, Driwna. I have to trust in Ensma and Curic to watch my side.

They read the danger I pose, read my song. They hesitate, then come at me together. I get one, a good stab into his ribs. I fall towards him, take most of the weight of an axe blow away and it cracks against my thigh, the chain and leather holding. They have not trained as I have. I wait, find the tells, their balance. The first dies quickly; the second has a club, a few nails in it, a simple, brutal thing, and in the moment I find an opening and cut into his leg, I misjudge him, he leans into it, the opposite of instinct, dumb to the pain of it. He brings the club down onto my arm as I raise it in defence, one of the nails punching into it. I bury my sword in him and he falls, the club still stuck in me. I tease the nail out of my arm and plug the wound, not registering the reason I might even have a moment to do so.

"Driwna, Scar!" Curic this is. He's down on one knee, only a few feet away. One of our Ososi is working on him, they're covered from sight on the slope by the wheel of one of our wagons. Curic points past the wagons; Ensma and three others are left fighting only a handful of soldiers that came from the direction of the cages, the rest of them now following Scar up the slope and away from us. I can hardly register it, relief at first, then fear for Ufra on its heels. Coming at them from the sheds and stores is the Master, Ufra beside him, glistening with blood, her Ososi with them. The few that meet them are dealt with savagely for the Master is a man apart from them, the Song made flesh and thought. His spear finds them with arrogant ease; no bind, no parry can withstand him. I think for a moment Scar means to run at him headlong, but he turns into one of the caves at the side of the slope, his soldiers following. It's fear; Scar fears him, has left the line, and it's broken the will of those soldiers remaining as it's bolstered our own. I run up the slope past Ensma as she kills the last of Scar's men, and I reach the gate as the Master and their crew finish those defending it, the cave into which Scar has just fled.

"We go in," says the Master. "It ends here." He holds out his hand, curls it around my head and brings me to him. The claws of the branch that makes his one hand hold me still. I know better than to move. He tenses, his eyes shiver in his head and a pale, oily water seeps from them. It stinks, like bog water. Ufra takes it on her fingers, holds my eyelids open, brushes the oil over my eyeballs. I cry out briefly, then staunch it, trembling with the effort of holding myself still, my jaws clenched.

"She will need bandaging later, Ufra." He speaks in their lingo, then. My blood feels his command to follow and we walk into the cave mouth after Scar.

Twenty feet inside there is utter blackness. I'm breathing hard with the burning in my eyes. As tears pour from them, the pain spreads to my temples, it sinks into my head, my ears throb with it and I drop to my knees spluttering in my attempts to stay silent, to not scream the quarry down. My skull, my veins, feel hard and stretched as wire through a draw plate. Then I see the cave in a new way, something

325

that isn't like sight at all. Our breathing paints the sound, it rolls against the stone and so I see the stone. Ahead I can sense a larger cave, hear the *thap* of feet, the crack of leather and hiss of chainmail, which can only be Scar himself.

The Master walks forward, not heeding the darkness with his heavy, loping stride. I follow by the sound he makes, for it carves a path to keep to. I don't soften my own steps, so I can create a path for Ufra and those that follow us. He stops, suddenly, stabs out with his spear; the breath and moan of one of the soldiers hiding by us is thick with heat. The smell of another is near. I attune to it, as the chief must already be doing, must do innately. A woman leaps forward at him; her sword is knocked aside by the shaft of his spear. His fist hammers into her chest, breaking her ribcage in two punches, stopping her heart. I barely saw it for how fast he moved.

"Listen!" he says, and while I might have cursed that he spoke, forgetting for a moment that we aren't intending to give our position away, he is using the sound, its echo, to paint the larger space about us. "Will you stay, Scar, or will you run again?"

I can perceive only silence, but he reacts to something.

"I hear you, coward. You are hunted by all the Oskoro now. They surround me, fill me; they guide me as I drink the secrets of this land, the truth of you and your shame. All around us you have your soldiers, thinking this an ambush? Their scent, the blood they've drunk, their sweat, their beating hearts are a chorus as loud as thunder." He holds his hands high, plays the conductor. The faint shimmers of air he makes by moving his arms draws them clearly, the eddies bring shape to the soldiers surrounding us, thirty-one, some kneeling left and right of us, among old mine carts and piles of rotted tunnel supports, others higher along the cave walls above them, or hanging from ropes high up.

We are nine.

His hands stop and I hear the chainmail moving, fading at the far end of this giant cave. "Oh. Scar has left you all," says the Master. The ropes tremble. Now the air moves as they breathe, as they realise they are seen. He speaks an Oskoro word, there's movement behind me and then I hear the arrows being drawn from quivers, the brush of feathers against each other. The creak of the bowstrings. Scar's soldiers must move or die. The cave comes to life, the first arrows hit.

It is decided as much by boots and fists as it is by the sword; gouging eyes, tearing open noses, crushing throats and battering skulls. It is knuckles and teeth, knees, stones, strangling, no duelling in this darkness. We stumble, for all the refinement of our senses, hollows in the ground, rubble and rubbish about us. I am hit with rocks, my cheeks are torn by them, by the gravel of the ground as I wrestle; I snap all the fingers I get near, but these soldiers are so full of their own brew, so changed by whatever these drudhas have made of them, that they punch me with broken hands, broken wrists, quiet and unyielding in their attempts to find the advantage. What soldiers with hearts and a desire to live would stand against them? Our movement and breath, our heat and curses, work to help me see the cave as my eyes would see if we were in daylight. I would be dead if I were only on the Post's own fightbrew. But whatever they are using, it is not the measure of the Master's own tears.

I realise then, among its other virtues, that the smell of the oil that blinded me and filled my head is a marker, a way to tell friend from foe. With the Master we gain the advantage, corner them as they look for a way out, kill them as they throw themselves at us to die. In a moment's respite

I draw in ragged breaths, for my chest and belly are battered and sore. I feel blood on my neck, trace it to only half an ear, a deep gash in my head that the brew has congealed. A stone skitters, away from the melee; Ufra it is who runs past me, to a soldier must be escaping. I follow her by the echo of her movement as she sprints after them. She is speaking in her lingo, teeth gritted. Her quarry moves quickly, making for the passage along which Scar escaped. He's clever, drops caltrops behind him, big ones used for horses. They ring out as they hit the stone, cause her to misstep, turn over on her ankle and fall. She cries out as her falling leg is impaled. I drop to her, turn her and pull the 'trop out. I suck at her leg, draw some mouthfuls of blood bubbling with the poison, smear a bellwort mix on the hole.

"Hold still, love, he's gone."

Her left hand finds mine; she places it there clumsily. I touch knuckles bloody and swollen from the savagery of her punches.

"Driwna, he's gone. I know he was here." For a moment I thought she meant Scar or the soldier she'd just been chasing, but her voice cracks as she says it. She means her pa, for they must have drained her pa as the Master has us drink his own blood.

"We'll find him."

"I cannot lie here. Gum a strip to the hole, my wen, stand me up. We must go back to our crew outside."

I love her for her loathing of self-pity. She cannot but do, act. I would be glad to catch my breath, to make a tally of the damage done to me, but I am not poisoned, the rest of me will mend.

I pull her up and she hobbles with me, back along the passageway to the cave, now silent but for the Master, weeping. I feel the heat of the bodies about him, bodies

328

everywhere. There are three Ososi left alive and they are working on their wounds. I reach down to touch him, as does Ufra. His wide shoulder hardly moves, he is not much out of breath.

"You have saved us, Master of Flowers. We survive yet," she says.

"So few, Ufra. Forgive me for this despair. I will not deny it. Despair is a thread we must weave if we are to have all colour and hear all of the music."

"Driwna! Ufra!"

Shouts from the cave mouth. Ensma. It is a delight to hear her alive, to think we have overcome those running this camp.

The Master stands. "Let us heal and free the slaves. Driwna, you are blind for a while, necessary for what we needed to do. It will wear off."

He leads us out. My eyes are open but I see little beyond smudges of movement, as much what I can still sense with my ears as with sight. Smell is strong as well, and it tells a story of the death and suffering in this camp.

"She gave the order." A voice, approaching us, one of ours, one of the Ososi that was with us on the wagons.

"She had to. Scar was rallying the slaves against us." Curic's voice.

"Etza-Ososi, she killed them, this Driwna. Others suffer."

"Ebanre, sister-Ososi, explain, we cannot see," says Ufra.

"Spores, bloodcap belets. These Driwna's crew put about her soldiers as they were attacked." The Master this is. He whistles, calls out in his lingo, answered by what must be the Oskoro archers now in the camp with us.

"Driwna?"

"I gave the order, Ufra. It is as Curic says. I opened the pens thinking the confusion would trouble Scar and their soldiers, thinking too that the slaves might want revenge on those that caused them such suffering . . ."

"They were safer in the pens, were they not? Until we killed all or were killed ourselves?" Ufra this is.

"I . . . We were outnumbered, confronting fifty or more as strong and savage as you have seen. I thought . . ." But it is obvious to her. I used the slaves. I hoped, somehow, they would fight alongside us, and yet against soldiers so spliced with and consumed by the brews and mixes of these drudhas, how could that have made sense?

"You'd have them shield you," she says. "How many have we killed Ebanre, with our spores?"

"Thirty-six dead, children among them, Ososi and Ilkashun together. Half of them were killed by Scar's soldiers. The rest still alive need the Master of Flowers to flush the spores. They want you, etza-Ososi. Come with me."

I feel an arm, it must be Ebanre's, releasing my hold on Ufra, separating us. She smells of blood, of the offal of bodies she has chopped and torn at. She leads Ufra down the slope and it breaks my heart.

"Brother Red." Ensma puts her arms around me.

"Help me, Ensma, lead me to the cages, to heal them."

"Driwna, no." Curic this is. "The Oskoro chief is down there; he will do better than we can."

"If you are guilty, Driwna, so are we, for we have killed those slaves that had become animals, killed those who only death could give peace to." Ensma this is. She leans in and kisses my cheek. I can think only of Ufra, of how stupid the decisions I made were.

"I smell the dead, we must get them to the earth," I say. "I cannot see, but we must load the wagons, bury them."

"Yes, Fieldsman," says Curic. "But let us see to your wounds before we go. The fight is won. Against great odds we have ended suffering here that would have gone on for years and worsened at that."

"Maybe." I tolerate his pastes and dressings, though with the Oskoro blood I don't feel much of the pain that I will when it fades.

"Report," I say, as I am treated.

"The Ososi that didn't follow you into the cave went at the soldiers remaining in the quarry. Some of the Ososi had bows, cut down ten or more, but whatever has been done to these soldiers, whatever brew they had, they took all our arrows and fought on. Their training was their only limit and had we only Ilkashun or Post fightbrew it would not have been enough. One of the Ososi with Ufra told me they had rushed the gate with no trouble thanks to our diversion. They left no soldiers alive at the huts and pavilions around the gates; the Master tore them apart."

"The drudhas?"

"One lives, the others we killed. Their workshops and benches are those of butchers."

I look back into the cave. It is not silent like stone, it tastes differently.

Whatever brew they had.

Ufra's pa.

I realise suddenly, agonisingly, they could not have killed him, could not have lost such a prize, for while he lived he would bleed a fightbrew better than any.

"Load the wagons for the dead." I head back into the cave.

"Where are you going?"

"That's an order, red."

"Yes, Fieldsman," says Curic.

Without the shadows and haze of the daylight left outside I find it easier to settle into the other senses the chief's mix has grown. I pass through the cavern in which we fought, sense now the dampness of the place, feel running water nearby in the stone. A faint smell of wax tells me that they would have lived here, the soldiers that Scar released at us, lived here in candlelight. I step about and over their bodies, a wisp of air guiding me to the passage at the far side of the cave. I shuffle through the caltrops, kicking them to the walls. The sound of running water gets louder, rolling about the walls of the cave.

"Ufra?" A husk of a voice, dried and thin. I sniff for him, Ufra's pa. The passage opens out to another small cavern.

"Here, girl, hurry." I feel my way to him, over sleeping mats, closer to what must be a river, running, chuckling down through stone, a drop to some further darkness.

"Etza-Ososi, Master of Flowers, I am Driwna."

"I smell Ufra, she is here?"

"I am Ufra-wen. She tends to your wounded in the quarry outside."

He is on a stone table; in my blindness my fingers brush his thigh, enough to know then that he has cuts all over him.

"I will fetch them; the Oskoro Master is here."

"No, Ufra-wen. I am done. My last moments will not be alone and I'm grateful for that. I can admit my shame and beg forgiveness, for I gave myself to Scar in the hope he would leave the rest of our people." I find his hand. It is bound with a heavy iron shackle to the stone of the table. He can barely curl his fingers. They are wet. The smell of his blood is everywhere, his sweat, the fluids leaking from the bark I can hear on his chest, creaking with his breathing.

"They took too much from me, to fight you. They took my seeds, every one of them. One said he'd found a use for them, a better place. I wondered at his meaning, but he took them from my own flower, from here." He guides my hand

332

towards his head, his hand weak, trembling. I touch the leaves of the Flower of Fates, soaked in his blood.

"It's so hot," I say.

"It uses me to survive. I'm failing and it draws all of me to sustain itself. As it must. Look for the seeds in his soldiers. Take this alkaest from my skull, empty its cradle and find somewhere in the world it might once more take to earth."

I move our hands away, bring his to my own belly.

"She has given you the milk of her thorns. My own thorns tingle." I can hear his smile. "She loves you, Driwna."

"She should be here, etza-Ososi, but she fixes the mistakes I have made in our assault of the quarry."

"She told me what you've done for our people, for the Sathanti, when she came home from the parley. You are a good woman. The etza-Oskoro will be able to give her the seed for the Flower that I cannot. You both shall lead us from this war that comes. You must find a way to the Hanwo'q jungle far to the south, for it is there you'll find Lorom Haluim. He has the strength to save our people."

"The magist?"

"Yes, he is a friend to us all."

I am struck dumb by this revelation, that he knows where a magist might live, that he must have met one. I want to ask a thousand questions but he coughs, his chest and breathing heavy with muke. He is quiet for a moment, his breathing softening. I try to think of something that will stir him, bring him back.

"What was she like as a girl?"

He breathes, more deeply, a sigh the colour of which I cannot read. "The brightest sun, the darkest storm. She loved me and ignored me, did not learn the written word yet gave her growing garden the highest eyrtza. But her course is the Song's, they are joined more closely than I had perceived.

For a long time I didn't know if the Flower I bore would bring out her best or her worst and there are too few of us to survive the worst. I failed us, and now my seeds are gone." I squeeze his hand, feel his mood lift, then a sudden flush, a fierce strength in his grip, and I hold my breath. "Love makes the song and the singer. I'll see you again, Ufra-wen."

He's gone in a moment, his last words fading on his final breath.

For a short time in the silence that follows I want to walk on through the passageway that Scar escaped along. It's tempting to think there's a trail out there that leads high up in the world, a place of peace. But nobody belongs in such a place, not for long. We must run with our tribes; eat, fuck and fight as the seasons wring us out and then take us.

I've always faced my mistakes.

I search about, bump into a drudha bench, find a key to his shackles among the knives and jars. He's not a small man, her pa, but the Oskoro brew still runs in me; the edge is off it now, but it gives me great strength still, enough to pick him up and carry him in my arms, feeling my way back through the cave and out into the side of the quarry. Much of it is cold with shadow as the afternoon wanes. My lack of sight registers only that everything has darkened. The merchants and whores from the pavilions and tents outside the camp have crept through the gates further up the slope, but I hear Ilkashun survivors shout at them to stay away from the stores. Other huts are being looted.

"Ufra!" I call.

One of the Ososi hears me, calls to her.

"She is healing. She will come," they say. I kneel down with him on my lap until she's ready. She knows I have her pa and knows he's dead; she is right to try to save a life, the life of one of her own. She is the etza-Ososi now.

Gradually I begin to make out shapes. I cannot help this process, for I hold Ufra's pa. Tears clean a great deal, inside and out, and it is easy to find them now as I kneel in this awful place. I can just about see Ensma has put all the shackles from the wagons in a pile at the bottom of the quarry and she's tending to the horses as they drink at a trough there. I see now the drudha that's still alive, bound and being tended to by the Master. It makes me glad, for the easiest thing in the world would be to slice off his eyelids, ears and nose, feed them to him, watch him go blind. The Master knows we need answers; he can always turn to torture.

Curic is standing with one of the Ilkashun, throwing bodies up to the wagons, where two others pile them up.

"Curic, get those looting shits from the tents outside the quarry to help dig," I call.

"My thinking too, Fieldsman. Is that Ufra's pa?"

"It is; they drained him."

He stands and stretches out his back, looks about him. "I'm getting in my cups heavy tonight."

The blood in me, her plant, tells me Ufra's walking up the path from the foot of the quarry. I'm trembling, I can't bear her wrath. She wipes her hands on her jerkin. I can't see her properly, but she's looking at us, standing still a moment. I can't read her thoughts though my blood, my heart, beats for her. Then she kneels before me. She caresses his face, tracing on and around the thorns there.

"He said we should try to plant his Flower," I say. She looks up sharply.

"He was alive? He spoke to you?"

"Yes. I wish it had been to you, more than anything."

She looks back down at him. "I'll take him to the glade; it will be good to leave the Flower here. None will come by for years after we're done."

335

I help him over into her arms, squeeze her shoulder, but I don't presume I could kiss her or hold her. She strides up the slope to the gates. The Song fades as it did on the plains against the Hidzuc, like the world steps away from me and I'm trapped behind my eyes once more.

"I'll help you dig, Curic. I need to sleep like a stone tonight and the Master's blood still has me on edge."

I walk down to the quarry floor, help Ensma bring the horses still alive back to the wagons.

"You've done your people proud today," I say. "There'll be no more kidnappings of the Hidzuc."

"Should you not be with the Oskoro chief? We've got enough shovels and picks for the burial pit."

"Those we've freed should be with their kin. I don't expect we'll move them out until tomorrow, until they've eaten good food, slept on a mat or straw at least. Look, he washes each of them."

Many are on their knees, Ososi and Ilkashun alike, for the Master of Flowers to do what he can to heal them and make them right, singing to them in his strange way. There is reverence in their eyes. I would not intrude on the song he draws from the world to give to them.

As he sings, as his voice fills the air and changes it, I remember once more a promise I made.

I go into each of the drudha tents. My work is made harder by my not being able to see properly. Here the flies are thickest, my fingers trace buckets, and the smell helps paint the rest of the grisly detail, of the insides of people, their hearts, rolls of skin, ropes of the belly. There are heavy wooden healing benches, more like huge butcher's blocks now than the benches in a warcamp. Blades and cleavers, bloodied rags and clothes, pots of plants, jars of preserves, tinctures and ointments. This is research with no concern for suffering. The need for slaves is clear; these are recipes trialled for the purpose of conquest, time a foremost concern. I seek the baby I once held, the girl I put back in the darkness. Her purpose can only have been to give these drudhas a guide to planting the seeds of the Flower of Fates into braegnlocs. They could not keep her in the keg, for they'd have opened her up. The thought makes me sick, makes my head pound. I take a chisel to the crates and baskets that are woven shut or nailed. Through the sickening stench I catch the sharp, savage smell of alka, a vat that might once have been used for making wine, yak's skin thrown over it and tied around hooks. As I reach it the smell intensifies; I have to hold a rag to my nose, my eyes watering as I untie the knots. There's almost nothing to reflect the fading light outside, but the lantern across this tent from me casts a light that catches the curves of a hand, a torso.

If she's in here I can't leave her; if she's anywhere in this camp, even in the ashes of the burned bodies outside, she will be buried. I'm glad of the tears this alka causes. I lift a head out first, an old woman, the back of her skull cut away, parts of her braegn removed. A child's body then, four or five winters, the belly cut open and a dead weed I don't recognise spilling out from it, a slick, greasy black. A larger body next, a soldier I think, for the skin, despite the damage, looks to have had colour. I find a butcher's hook, for he's too slippery to heave out of the tub without one. He falls with the slick slap of the alka splashing off him. There are hardened parts of bodies, not clean cut, trails of veins and muscle hanging from them, to allow, I expect, plant to be grafted to the stumps that remained. Then, my arm now most of the way into the fluid, so close I have to vomit into it, my fingers wrap around a limb, a leg. I know it's her. I

337

look down, but the alka is black. For a moment I don't want to see what's become of her.

"There you are," I tell her, gasping. "I said I'd come. I said I'd find you." I pull her up and out of the vat. Much of the Flower of Fate's roots have been exposed, but in every other regard she is the same. She is as cold. The leaves and heart of the Flower have been cut off. I lie her on the nearest bench while I find a big enough sheet of linen, though dried and bloody, to wrap her in.

"Come outside, girl; let's catch what's left of the sun. There's someone here who wants to see you very much." Someone I know now must have been her father.

The dead are buried. She is last.

The Master asks me to help him dig a hole for her. He doesn't need the help, but he knows she brought us both here. He speaks to her in their lingo as he lays her down and covers her over, his great hands rolling the earth over her gently, dropping a few seeds in from what looks like a pink thistle on the trunk of his one arm. Then he sings and weeps for her, my hand in his. I hear my name in that song and it must be gratitude that he can put her in the ground himself. The rest of the dead we help dig a pit for in silence. Finding her has put me at a strange kind of ease, almost a pleasure that despite the sadness I felt to have lost her, I could help find her and bring her to her Master of Flowers.

Many of the merchants have packed away and left, fearing retribution, fearing as well the Ososi, who they've not seen in such numbers before. Every whore took up a shovel or pick and helped with the holes for the dead, who have been stripped of their clothes for the Sathanti and Ososi that are still alive. Their whoremaster could say little to this, for she would not earn a penny from us and she knew it. Instead she watched as they shared cups of ale and wine, rubbed betony on their gums and sang along with whatever ditties and ballads could be recalled. The Ilkashun have singers who are trained to remember and sing their stories, their war songs and their kurch songs. Ensma sang laments in her Hidzuc lingo. One of the slaves who survived the torture sang to the skies, his voice made huge by his training and the brews taken to grow his chest.

There is only one prisoner left, the drudha, and he's kept in the whores' pavilion, out of sight of those freed, bound and guarded. The ones that have fled will tell the Cargamun and their chief, Ifmot, we will be coming. If they have any sense, the Cargamun will also flee for their lives.

I spend the hours of the evening looking out for Ufra, but she does not return until the watches are called and set out and I'm in my furs, succumbed to the bruises, wounds and the deep tiredness of pushing my body too far.

Voices, coughing, chopping wood echoing in a heavy mist wake me. Ufra's arm is across my belly as she lies behind me. I keep still, hoping to let her sleep a little longer.

"You're awake, my wen."

"I am, Ufra. I . . . I'm ashamed. I cannot look a single Ilkashun or Ososi in the eye."

The hand on my belly that holds me against her finds my own hand. I can feel the soil on her fingers, the greasiness of the dirt; her hands are swollen from the fighting still.

"They hurt, Driwna, the choices we make. Some there are who felt you thought their lives cheaply bought. More there are who saw how you and your crew fought those that tortured them, far outnumbered but steadfast. Some did indeed run for you, unwilling to deny the command of Scar. It is easy to understand that compulsion." She shudders. "Some, when it came to it, were too broken, like emptied shells or else

339

they were savage and nothing the Master could do would settle them. These were also killed, given a mix by my hand. I deserved the blessing my people gave me for freeing them no more than you deserved my hatred, wen."

"You only killed those who couldn't be healed."

"Blame. It's easy, a well that never runs dry. I was angry and I'm sorry. Now, my wen, you need to get up, eat, drink. We lead these Ososi and Ilkashun back home, but we kill those Cargamun first, free the slaves they keep if we can."

"We should have kept those merchants here," I say.

"We did not have the people to do it. Some fled while we fought, when they saw us coming over the gates. They feared for their own lives."

I turn over to face her, trace my fingers over the cuts and bruising on her face. "I should be in more pain than this."

"It is our blood that feeds you." She slides her hand under my wool vest, around my side and up my back. The plant that she has for a thumb settles on my skin. She presses her thorns in, tenses her arm. There is the familiar tingle across my skin, the warmth spreading.

"I'll lie here while you fetch me some of the oats I can smell being boiled," she says.

"Will you now?"

"I have a mix you should take now the plant's growing; a few mouthfuls you won't enjoy, so mix it in with the oats."

Reluctantly I free her thorns and stand. The Master is with the Ilkashun and Ososi that have all still kept together despite no longer being in pens. I pull on my leathers and walk over to them.

"Can I help?"

"Bring bowls of the oats. We found hazelnut butter, cured tuika and yak."

"I will do that, Master. The Ososi Master, Ufra's father,

340

he told me that I should inspect the bodies of the soldiers we faced. He believes they have had his seeds put in them."

"Then I'll come with you. Some may yet be salvaged." This lifts his spirit, stirs him to stand up himself.

They're heartbreaking to look upon, the fifty or so slaves that remain. Some of our crew are among them, for a handful have friends or family here that they haven't seen since they were kidnapped and they are helping dress them, wash them. I see some have lost arms, their sight, or have bloodied wraps around their heads where their skulls had been cut. Hands, fingers, legs, so many have had linen wraps and poultices to heal the wounds the drudhas had given them as they experimented with grafting plants into them.

"Have you spoken to the drudha?" I ask the Master. He directs me to walk with him, to the fire where they're making the food.

"I have. This is one of many camps. There is an army forming; all this is Marghoster's doing."

"Not just Marghoster," I say. "There are orders from the Post to provide these vans provisions at cost. You'll find Post marks on the provisions somewhere, the rope, arrows, salt perhaps. I'm sorry to say it, but the Post is involved. I have to get back to Yblas or Amaris and tell them."

"Amaris?"

"She is his mentor, as she was mine. If Yblas is not at Autumn's Gate, she will be, and she will help us."

"Must you go back?" he says. I'm thrown by this; for a moment I have no idea what he means.

"Master, these camps, this army, are surely being bred to conquer the Sathanti? The Post have involved themselves in conquest, are already responsible for the deaths of hundreds, and it will soon be thousands. These soldiers fight without feeling, no light of mercy or conscience."

"Is your duty not to Ufra and the Ososi? We are fighting for our survival; we cannot win if there are even a thousand of such soldiers as we fought yesterday. Thirteen of us in all, here in this camp, are the last of the Oskoro. We will not survive without becoming Ososi. I am keeper of our songs, our history, our recipes and our blood. I am the last of us and must give the seed to Ufra and whoever she chooses, man and woman, that the lines may continue. I must persuade her to come south, to preserve the few of us that are left. I fear she will not."

Ufra has chosen me, so the Master is right that she must choose others to have our children. I find I do not mind if she herself is to try and bear a child. I know little of their ways and I cannot assume they are as ours.

Those that are well enough help to feed those we rescued and I get Ufra her breakfast, though by the time I've finished talking to the Master she is up and checking on her crew.

The Master, Ufra and I go back into the camp. I watch as they turn some of the bodies over onto their bellies, taking knives to the backs of their necks, between their shoulders. Four bodies they carry to a spot near the drudha tents. They lift one onto a table that they've dragged from one of the tents. The soldier's back is bare and between his shoulders they've cut away the skin. In the bloody and glistening meat, a seed for a Flower of Fates has split, its bright orange fractured by the black tendril of roots, finer than spider's silk. The flesh and muscle around it are stained.

"Scar has taught them what we have kept secret. These stains are evidence of a mix we use to feed the alkaest seeds, help them to bed into the body," says the Master.

"Four of them have these seeds and in time they'd harvest them from these soldiers as they did from my etza-Ososi." Ufra this is.

342

"It's clever. They might have discovered a way to put these seeds into bodies without the training and conditioning of years that we follow with our young. These might be, in time, soldiers that are always risen like you Umansk are with your fightbrews."

"They would go mad," I say.

"Do you not already go mad after years of drinking your brews?"

"We do. Can these seeds be salvaged, for the Ososi?"

"They can, I think; the ones that haven't taken deeply."

"Can you plant one in some part of my body?" says Ufra. "If these drudhas can achieve this, can you not also, Master? I can help grow the seeds for our children, even if I cannot undergo what it would take to plant alkaest in my braegnloc."

He puts his hands on her shoulders. "I can do this, but I cannot be sure how it will change you. I can only hope to be with you and guide you as it does. There is great danger in it. I am surprised Scar had such knowledge to succeed even this well."

"He was to be a Master of Flowers, as you are, as my father was," says Ufra. "He will have learned much from our drudhas before the judgement against him. If I'm to go for the other camps and burn these Farlsgrad murderers out of our lands, I may well need alkaest's potency. There are too few of us to fight Umansk such as these without your advantages, Master."

"And you, Driwna?" asks the Master.

Now it comes to it; now I'm to decide whether to stay and fight or return to Farlsgrad.

"I know what is expected of me. You have spoken of it. I am Ufra-wen. Your tribe's vines grow in me, they are changing me and I am becoming, in a small way, Ososi. Ufra, I don't know if my path is back into the mountains north to find and burn the other camps, or east to confront the cause of them. I see what has been done to you all, how few of you remain. I see what all the peoples of this world lose if we lose you and your capacity to heal and do good, for the Post's own fightbrew and many of your recipes have fed it as it's grown and thrived and done good work."

"Yet what has become of it, Driwna," says the Master. "You need only look about you. I despair of you Umansk. How can so many be so deaf to the Song?"

"I know. And I see more reason than ever to stand against it. Yblas, the High Red, he wants what Teyr Amondsen wanted, what many of us do. A strong Post — and adherence to the oaths we took. We have to fight our corruption as she did."

"You speak of Teyr Amondsen. I know then that you understand what the Post can be. How do you know of her?"

"Yblas has shown me her writings, the good work she did with you."

"I was a child, but I knew her; I knew too her family who helped us thrive. You speak true enough, but the Post now is far larger a beast than the one she nourished. It eats now for the sake of it. It pleases me to know Yblas follows our old friend, but he cannot watch all the thousands you have in all the lands and waters you cover. Neither can you."

"Are you with us, Driwna?" Ufra this is. "Are you with me?"

Chapter 16

The Magist

Once before I've seen Scar shaken as he is now. Twenty years old and alone, wandering the southern shores of Lake Bouskill, cast out from the Ososi on the cusp of becoming an elder, perhaps even the chief. The dreams of the Ososi are rich; sweet and hot as boiled treacle, and who can bear more than a cup of that and not vomit? I found him as I sought them and his loyalty has been tireless and magnificent. I understand such rejection.

We're in the slums of Autumn's Gate, where we usually meet. His size and the difficulty people have of maintaining a close proximity to me are enough to ensure no tongues go wagging as we make our way to the room I keep there, a lodging over a cooper's shop.

I opened my room's shutters to the lane outside once, years before. It was dark then as well. I saw two figures make short work of a drunk. She was stabbed rapidly in the chest, five or six times, while the second of the two cut off pouches from a belt under the woman's robe. Dogs had got to the body before any militia. Some growling and the occasional cracking of bones

345

accompanied my reading. The smell was unpleasant. There is no benefit from opening the shutters.

The dust and shavings of farlswood and oak that permeate this house are a comforting smell to me. I've furnished the room with chairs and tables the cooper has made for me, and I give little more than an ease to his joints in exchange for it all. There are too few like him, men who ask only for what they need, men who seek to retain sovereignty over their flesh that they may continue to pursue their calling, succeed on their own terms, as I have.

Scar is tired as much as he is shaken. When I arrive I find him sleeping, a rare enough thing. He is wounded, rarer again. On entering the cooper's shop it's quiet but for the cod sizzling in a pan in his room at the back.

"He's up, Master Litko," says the cooper. "Quiet all day. Not eating. Left a dish o' water with him." He shrugs, sees, I imagine, nothing more than an upright animal.

"I'm grateful, Lewdog."

He nods to a candle for me to light my way to my room.

Scar wakes once I put the candle on the table and set about bringing the coals in the hearth to light. Now and again I take pleasure from teasing the kindling to life with flint and a crumb of patience. When I turn back, Scar, who was lying on his side facing the fire, has opened his eyes and is watching me. His right hand is balled to a fist in front of his mouth. It trembles. His eyes lose focus as he finds memories.

"I've brought some slices of beef. A flask of clean water." I light two other sconces in the corners of the room.

"You've no fieldbelt?" I ask.

He gives me the subtlest twitch by way of acknowledgement. I don't press him; he'll be ready shortly.

"Look, Lewdog's cleaned my pan; I can give this beef a searing when the fire's up. Would you like that?" His silence is his agreement.

I move the stand over the coals and sit the pan on it. It's good beef, topside, fringed with fat that he'll suck on afterwards, grinding lumps of it between his teeth, savouring it.

"Camp one is gone. To the Master of Flowers, the Fieldsman, Ufra of the Ososi."

I look over at him. He cringes like a dog, averts his eyes.

"How?"

"Ambushed the Brask Eleven van, south of the Flintre kurch. Killed or exiled the Cargamun, fooled the gatehouse they were our van. Three points of attack."

"I see."

I don't fucking see. I can't help what follows: a momentary slip of the mind and the walls shake, floorboards spring free of their nails, curling towards me from the edges of the room, rolling him over to his front, his fear bringing him to his feet, crouched, trembling more violently than before. The boards crack and groan as they seek me. I bring my multitudes back into focus. The floorboards fall back, bent and exhausted.

We breathe. I close my eyes. I remember that I move in centuries, they are my currency, the appropriate unit of time. I should be grateful to our enemies for bringing me so close to these small hours that I can feel anger, desperation. These are aspects of me that are long unexercised.

"You did well, child." I kneel before him as he kneels, an absurd mirror. As I put my arms around him, the dust on my fingers ready to take shape, to make him strong, I tell him I will deal with the Fieldsman. I tell him that we are strong enough to begin. I just need to light the fuse.

Chapter 17

Driwna

There's movement behind the shutters of the Doris. Candles are being lit, the barkeep's coughing and gets up a spit heavy enough I hear it hit the floor from outside the main door. This is the edge of dawn, cold, but nothing like the mountains. I knock on the door softly. The sound carries in the still air nevertheless, alongside the distant shouts of the fishers out on the river and about their jetties.

"Be coming, hold there." A man much older than the last barkeep unbars the door and the locks.

"Where's Pusikh? The loaves?" He stands with his hands at his lower back, supporting it. He's bald on top but has a good long beard. His skin hangs from his face, his throat, a much bigger man once.

"I believe Pusikh is yet to arrive. I'm not here for ale or service, but a room, and word of any that are staying here."

"There's a few coin needed to open my lips for that. Come in, miss, I'll find some caffin I can put in the water I got on the fire. You look like you had a bad stint in the field."

I'm initially surprised at his sympathy until, by the candle-light, I see he must have paid colour himself many years past.

"I'm grateful."

"You got a horse somewhere?"

"In your stable."

"Heh, fine, fine." He stands back to let me in. I smell linseed and alka in the darkness. He lights some lanterns about the main bar. The flagstone floor is dry, not the sticky mess of food, ale and mud I trod through the last time I was here. I drop my saddle and bags down, grateful for a seat and the warmth.

"Alaqua being paid overtime is she?"

He's opened a stone jar and he's putting some powdered caffin in two big tin cups. "Oh, you're meaning the floor? Yes, it's had a stiff brush and alka grits? It took a good few days to get all that shit up off it. Alaqua's one that keeps it right, good worker she is, but there's a few more I've got in to help her. Life serving as a soldier gets a need for order in your bones, doesn't it? Can't stand a place to smell and feel like shit; it's not right."

"I'm with you. You the castellan's man?"

"He's a cunt."

"Then I'm Driwna and I'm glad to meet you. I'm wanted here, by him particularly, which is why it's this hour I've chosen to come by. I'm hoping a man of the Post, Cal Rulger, is staying or has left me some note."

"Name's Gilf, I'm down from Stobrel, Cathrich country. Now, Driwna? Driwna?" He's trying the word out on his tongue, remembering. "Driwna Marghoster. Yes, Cal Rulger, he asked me to let him know you'd be by. They're calling you Brother Red, then, despite you're a woman."

"Some have called me that; a Sathanti chief it was called

349

me it first in jest, because I saved his life despite I'm a woman."

He smiles at that. "Can't count the women I fought with who saved my life, braver and stronger than me. You're Post and good to hear you're high up and all, like a marschal or their highnesses at the Gate."

"I am, but I'm not welcome there either. Post has me rooting out the rotten apples in its barrel, so to speak."

"As you say, you seem to be making all the right enemies as far as I can see. There's reds here who said you saved their lives out over the border, ones up from Lindur can't speak high enough of you. All I need to know, that. Happy to keep you here quiet; there's a space upstairs for you. Been putting powders down and they've got most of the lice and rats, but I'll have Alaqua sweep it out."

"How is she? Her baby?"

"Well, I think. Another you've done a kindness for. Speaks well of you and Bray she does." He takes a cloth to hold the pot of water, pours into both our cups.

"Early start?" I say.

"Body seems to know when dawn's about. I don't take to cups like most, pipe either, so I rare has trouble finding myself in the morning."

"You sound well, in your chest, for a man that's paid colour."

"I'll take that." He blows and sips on the caffin brew. "Now, your Cal, he'll be first door on the right at the top of the stairs, in there with a couple of fishermen from up river. I'll have Alaqua knock him in a few hours; she's due at sun-up proper."

"I'm grateful, Gilf, for this shelter, your silence. I'm bone tired and getting over the border, into the Spike, it's been tricky."

"You bring anyone with you?"

"No. It's just me."

How much can one woman expect to do? I saw Ilkashun slaves reunited with their Ilkashun kurches, the same with Ososi and Hidzucs, seeing once more family they thought dead, and these were days of joy and weeping, songs and feasts. "Brother Red! Master of Flowers! Etza-Ososi!" were the shouts. For the rest of this short life I'll be glad if I manage only that on my tally; the look on a mother's face, a son's face, to see each other again, despite their mutilations and the torture. Their suffering is over for a while and perhaps the usual bruises life itself gives will feel like kisses for years to come as the memory of the camp returns, as it surely will, in the dark hours.

We found a way to keep ourselves busy on the van to the Ilkashun lands, Ufra and I, but the furs we shared each night were heavy with my decision to leave for Farlsgrad. Once did we speak of my leaving the Ososi, over a campfire at the Ilkashun lodge, the night before we parted. There was none else there to hear it, and, knowing this, I was more forthright, asking her what the point was of bringing all these families back together if Farlsgrad was going to come through with an army of near unstoppable, inhuman soldiers to finally lay the ghosts of its past failures to rest. I couldn't, I can't, leave them to their own fate.

"How much can one woman expect to do, Driwna?"

I held her close. Told her I loved her. Told her I'd find her again once I had learned what Cal and Bray had found, once I'd told Yblas and Amaris how the Post has been used by Stroff, given them my evidence as I had sworn to do, forced a confrontation with Hildmir and Marghoster.

Six wagons returned to Leusla Hidzuc, eighteen kurch-kin

among the lots recovered from the quarry, but half unable to work again, unable to help themselves. With them I left the drudha, safe enough there until I got the lie of the land in the Spike. The surviving Hidzucs would be burdens on their kurches in turn, so we left provisions with Leusla, some compensation to appease those who would speak against us bringing back those as good as dead. She at least did not see it so. Neither did those of her chiefs that she could convene in the short time I was willing to stay, for I felt keenly each passing day that brought Scar closer to Marghoster, for that is where he must have fled to. All the Hidzucs were proud of Ensma for the honour she brought to them and Leusla ordered a carving to be made on their kurchpoles, of Ensma fighting Scar alongside me. Their wood-cutter was generous with me, to say the least. The Master's Flower of Fates he carved so its leaves spread out to form the ground and a canopy. He must have spoken to one of the survivors when making the carvings of the soldiers we fought, for while they are frightening to look on, their faces show great pain. For all that such carvings tell stories kindest to their own kurch, this at least speaks the truth.

Curic would not listen to my asking him to head back to Lindur. Knowing of the danger I'd be in, the importance of word getting to Yblas, he disobeyed my orders and said it was in the name of our creed. He got a cuff for saying it and I am glad that he remains near to the Doris, watching its doors under the guise of being a drooper.

It is a thrill to see the look on Cal's face when he brings down the plate and cup taken to him for his breakfast and sees me sitting on one of the benches in the main room. He kisses me, tells me I look terrible, kisses me again and bids Gilf fetch us a flask of wine and some food for me. I've eaten

352

less, I know, since Ufra's plant has taken hold. Cal finds touching my skin exciting for it has changed and there's an ache that I can only attribute to the growth of my own vines beginning. Alaqua comes in no sooner than we have had our first cup of wine, helping their baker's boy in with the loaves for the day, and we take one with a plate of butter. I give the boy some coppers to take a loaf to the poor old drooper across the lane.

"It's you, Driwna!" she barks, putting the loaves down on the bar and coming over to make a fuss of me. "Your handsome young man and all, isn't it?"

"You look well. Gilf seems to care about you a bit more than your last barkeep, from what he's saying."

"He does, miss. I gets a few more hours with my boy; you should see him now, like a bear he is, drinks me dry, an' your coin means a few less men I have to flatter out of theirs. Say, now, you look like you need a bath. Me and Cal can do you one again like we did last you were here, couldn't we, lovely?"

"She needs that and some sleep, I know," says Cal.

"I'll start the fire up there. Gilf, you can watch down here for a bit?"

"Yes, Castellan." He winks and leaves us alone as he takes the bread through to their kitchen.

I tell Cal everything that's happened since last we spoke. It's hard to recount without my crying a bit. He comes and sits next to me on the bench and holds me for a while as I let it out.

"I missed you," I say, when I finally got the tale done.

"I missed you, love. I hope you're not expecting good news from me, either. If I'm honest, I'm scared. You asked me to find out if there's been other miracles worked like there must have been with the Marghoster girl. There's been

353

healings all right. 'Blessings from Sillindar', they're being called. I went to Ullavir first and spent a few weeks in my cups and in droop joints. Along with the notices to come to the Sathanti border for anyone that's paying colour, I found the slavers doing the most trade recently were taking it all west. It's all going out to the mountains, along with any and every mercenary. Cayorse & Bruler you know of, a guild with big interests around the ports. Cayorse's son is in charge of their interests now since the old man died. His little brun's always trouble; got himself into a fight and took a bad, bad beating from four or five deckhands he was mouthing off at. By the time they were done with him he couldn't walk any more, slurring and not making sense when he spoke; would have been kinder to have killed him I heard. Was a month or so later that the little fucker's right as light, walking proud, not a mark on him, though a good bit less cocksure. I thought it might have all been tale-telling, as you must think, but there's a good few that saw his brun feeding him and having him carried about. He took care of him, fair's fair to that, but the lad's changed mightily overnight.

"I hear then from a droophouse on the docks a story about a trader from over Hillfast that has plant runs on the Sixty; shiel, cicely and flag. Had a withered arm all his life, until about six months ago, but now it's good as the other; he'd also lost most of his hair as a young man and now it's growing back. There's more, Driw, a farlswood merchant up north at the Gate, two more besides." We're through the wine and now there's some of the early crew coming in for some brin and tea before heading onto the river and the sheds. Alaqua's got the bath ready so we go upstairs and bath together despite its size, for he's good at getting the knots out of my back and neck, not to mention the dirt and all. I'm so tired he gets annoyed at my fumbling about my fieldbelt straps and the leathers I'm in, and I give up and stand there, let him undress me like I'm some princess being waited on. The water's still hot as I get in and I close my eyes with the bliss of it as he undresses and gets in behind me.

"This water's thickened up quick, Marghoster filth," he says. I'm sitting between his legs and I lean back against him, reaching up to cuff his face. "Fucking tub's sticking in my back and all."

"Do all Rulgers whine like this?"

"Been a long time since we had a bath," he says.

"It has. What you said, down in the room, has me thinking. All these miracles, well, they're miracles in the sense that they're not things you can buy at any price. The Cayorse family's got Old Kingdom's money, these are no flatbacks. Marghoster wouldn't have enough gold or silver to buy the plant and slaves as he has, aside from Stroff obviously working something very clever under the nose of Yblas with Crejda and whoever else. So he's getting what he needs to build this army up from somehow being able to do what no drudha, not even the Master of Flowers, could himself do."

"Driw, who could do it? I've seen the Cayorse boy if not the Hillfast trader and the talk is that the trader claims to have met Sillindar. I know how stupid it sounds, Driw, but is it a magist?"

"Sillindar? Haluim? Oh Cal, I can't see it."

"The tales of the magists recount healings such as these."

"They've all gone, Cal. They were rare long ago and none have been seen for centuries, have they?" I thought of the last words of Ufra's pa, of Lorom Haluim, but if he's in the Hanwo'q jungle then he's many months travel from here.

"They don't walk along streets with their arms out and wave away sickness and hunger either, not unless you believe the legends. But here we are."

355

"Who heard of them healing slavers? Sillindar, Haluim, Mephe, all of them are supposed to have done virtuous things, and it's harder to believe they're alive and doing this now so Farlsgrad can conquer Sathanti lands. I don't believe the legends for the same reasons I've never seen a horse with wings, or a tusk growing out of its head. Legends are cowshit."

"Don't hold back, Driw," he says. I pinch his knee.

"I don't know what else to say, Cal. They're a way of explaining it, but what do we do if we sit here believing a magist has allied with Marghoster and plans to help in a conquest of those people? Who could fight a magist? We're fucked if it's true."

"It doesn't make sense, I know." He pushes me forward, grabs the rag floating in the water in front of me and squeezes it over my back, working in circles.

"Have you seen Bray?" I ask.

"No, he had further to travel, didn't he? But I still would have thought he'd be back by now given most of his travels were on the Wheel."

"I want to wait for him, Cal. We need as much evidence of what's going on as we can get, because of what it all means."

"You said earlier you had a drudha that had worked that camp in the mountains, one that you took prisoner up there. He's with the Hidzucs?"

"Yes, we'll have Ensma, one of their warriors, to bring him back to us. She's up to it if I send over Curic to help do nightwatches on the journey. The drudha'll come with us to Yblas and Amaris and tell them himself. I couldn't risk bringing him here until I got the lie of the land."

"We'll have enemies at the Gate. Yblas isn't there either, only Amaris and Rogus who can we trust. Are we not going to deal with Crejda, now you know enough to be certain she's part of it all?"

"Word getting to Stroff I've thrown Crejda out will make it worse. I need Amaris's guidance."

"Scar will have got to Marghoster and he'll be telling them all anyway, won't he?"

"Yes. Fuck. Oh, Cal. I need to think on it."

My chest and arms feel thicker, the growing vines are spreading. I'm trying not to use kannab to ease the pain of the plant pushing about and infiltrating the core of me. I'd be concerned about it if I hadn't also felt how much more keenly my body responds to Ufra's presence, and feels with more precision the world about me. My colour's lightening, according to Cal, and I can feel the grits he's using to wash me more keenly than ever, though it's no longer as simple as whether I'm more or less sensitive to it. It's a change in how it feels; each grit is sharp and hot, but leaves a cooling trail behind it. I sense my skin is thriving on the treatment and Cal patiently gives me more of a rubdown than I could normally bear.

"I must get word to Yblas, send a messenger I can trust to bring him back to the Gate. I have to recommend Amaris takes control of Farlsgrad and that Stroff and Crejda go in chains, at least until the administrators can convene. All this before Farlsgrad goes to war. Which means an edict to stop us supplying this war, authority I don't have over any instruction Stroff's given the Posthouses and sheds about Farlsgrad. It needs Stroff's seal, so my road points to Autumn's Gate and Amaris."

"I'll help however I can, love. Now, you can do my back before this water gets cold."

I do Cal's grits and his lice rub and I find fresh woollens from my saddlebags.

I'm cleaning and waxing our boots and leathers while he's down in the main tavern getting us food when I hear raised voices. There's nothing to concern me looking out of the shutters, but with footsteps on the stairs I draw my knife and get a sporebag ready. It's Cal, then someone I don't recognise, an older man, a face scarred with poisons that's pocked his beard and left him with nothing but scars and bark over his head. The rest of him's in the leathers of a Post marschal. He's not fresh off the road and has no belt or weapons. He's been waiting.

"Fieldsman Marghoster?" he says. "Marschal Latimer." We clasp arms. A marschal's role is to keep reds honest, but they work for administrators. This one's Stroff's.

"He saw you arrive this morning, Driw," says Cal.

"Good. We should go back down to the tavern then, as I'm no longer in hiding. A lot more comfortable down there for some food too."

"Thank you, Fieldsman. I have a roll for you, from the Rethic Fens."

It's the heartiest food I've had in some time. My belly's full and I eat it despite what I think is Ufra's plant making it somehow harder to enjoy the smell and taste of cooked meat. Curic has come in now he's seen Post enter the tavern. Latimer's had to give me the roll before Cal and Curic. All the while we ate I was thinking of Mun.

"I don't understand why a marschal's giving me a message that's written by my pa," I say to Latimer.

"I wasn't at your kurch in the fens. It came to me as I was visiting the sheds we have at Marghoster's estate. I knew you'd be here if you were in Farlsgrad at all, given your work west."

Of course I don't fucking trust him.

"What's it say? Is it about your mun?" Cal this is.

"My pa's saying I should go home. It's not telling me why. Seal he's paid for is a messenger's, so he wanted it here quick and he's a tight bastard at the best of times." And I don't understand why Latimer's been hanging about here and watching.

"When did you get into the Spike?" I ask him.

"Day before yesterday. Needed to rest the horse before moving on. I was heading to our sheds early when I saw you coming from the stables out back."

I glance at Cal and Curic. None are betraying more than a hint of doubt about that. I have to go. I don't doubt this roll's come from the fens, and I don't doubt it means that my mun's gone.

"Marschal, thank you for bringing this to me in person. I appreciate it."

"I'm sorry if it's bad news, Fieldsman."

"I would have you go to Amaris, to the Gate. I'll draft a roll for you to take, but it's urgent. Farlgsrad is going to war and the Post is supplying the army. This isn't our war. Can you leave today?"

"I will, Fieldsman. I'll gather a few supplies and leave in an hour or so, if you'll have the roll ready."

"Thank you." He stands with me, clasps arms and leaves.

"Lying cunt." Cal this is.

"It stinks, Fieldsman," says Curic.

"I know. I'm still going. If my mun's gone, if she's died, I will pay my respects. I owe her more than I could ever repay."

"Forgive me, Fieldsman, but with what we've seen," says Curic, who I can see appreciates this isn't an easy thing to say, "I know you must speak of your ma to your ancestors, commend her to them as is custom for Sathanti, but could

359

it wait and still matter? It's still paying your respects and if we can do something to make Hildmir think again, to make Stroff and everyone pay for what we saw out there in the mountains, we should do it."

Cal straightens, drains his cup.

"It's good sense that you speak, Curic," I say, "but I have to go. I might feel little for such traditions, but they meant a lot to her and gave her strength to care for us growing up."

"I don't trust it at all," says Cal, interrupting. "What if it's about getting rid of you? If Scar's gone to Marghoster, he could be anywhere along that run, if he's not coming here after you. They'll know that's what you have to do in respecting your ma."

"I understand, both of you, I do. I've not the words to put over to you why I must go." And I don't; it's a pull in my gut when I think of her, her smiling, her arms about me when the nightmares came. I recall how she would always find scraps of hide and leather and would cut and stitch them to make an owl or a wolf or the amony flower. These would be the gifts she'd give us on our birthdays in the shelters we'd rig when hiding out in woods. I doubt she'd think I'd remember all those times she put the scraps of rabbit and pigeon on our plates and not hers. But I remember. And I won't have my pa saying anything against my love for her, I won't give him an inch in that.

"I'll go with you," says Cal.

"If I'm needed, Fieldsman, I'll go," says Curic.

"I be wantin' one fuckin' hour, miss, an' a few cups o' beer before I get up on that bloody horse again." A familiar face has just walked in and seen us.

"Bray!" I jump up off the bench and run over to him, put my arms about him. He stinks of the field; sweat, sour breath

360

that'll want some ash, but thinner again than in all the weeks since I last saw him. He puts his arms about me.

"You've had a bath, miss; this won't help any." He takes my arms and eases me back to look at me. "I'm fierce glad you're alive." His eyes shine and he gives one a wipe, looks over to our table. He nods to Cal.

"Get me an ale an' a plate of eggs an' pitties an' I'll catch you up."

Chapter 18

Driwna

There's been no trouble on the run from the Spike to the Bridche kurchpoles in the Rethic Fens. We've stayed off the main trails where we had a good reckoning of other routes. Bray was the main help with this, keeping us away from the River Iblar. I sent Marschal Latimer back to Autumn's Gate with a roll in which there was nothing more than some observations of vans in the Sathanti south plains that I thought required further investigation. I don't think he was clever enough to feign surprise at my claim we were funding a war, and while he is Stroff's man, as Yblas said all those months ago, Stroff will worry that I might have spread this news about the crews or others. The moment Latimer or Stroff open the roll they'll sniff out that it's bullshit. They won't know that I've sent Curic to the Hidzucs to fetch Ensma and the drudha and take them up the Wheel to Autumn's Gate, with my seal to ease his passage. I'm hoping that by the time the seal's use itself is reported to Stroff, Curic will already be there and will find Amaris directly, so she can hear all of what befell us and what trouble is coming.

Bray is with Cal and me. What he told us as we left the Spike four nights ago confirmed our fears. At Cathrich Valley he spent time with the clans there that mostly mined the hills, and while the Post has its own tin mine, we've been buying up the coal, tin and iron from the other clans and moving them on at cost, on the instruction of Rogus, according to rolls Bray had seen. He found some work and so found his way in with the crews to the taverns and ale tents about the various mining camps and settlements, and there were many more mercenaries than the merchants and militia would usually see, all passing through to Gethme's Tongue, the western border as Cal had said. Going north to Stalder's Vale he saw yet more wood and iron being moved on vans and was offered a number of purses to join their crews, all heading into the mountains at the border. What I didn't understand was how, in either Cathrich or Stalder territory, or even at Nailer's Road, he never saw any of King Hildmir's merchants involved, though they grumbled a good bit about the trade that was going on. The workboards at the fort of Nailer's Road showed what all the interest was for from the mercenaries flooding west from the coast. The boards directed mercenaries to a camp nearby. There were no Farlsgrad militia there, but he found drudhas and purses worth three silver a day: a fortune. They made him promises of recipes and plant unrivalled in the north and he tasted a brew that, from his description, sounded like some of Ufra's pa's blood had been drawn off and thinned, an effective snare for any doubting the usual claims that are made by cookers and the like. He saw twenty sign up in the short time he was there before he turned about and rode back to the Spike. If they're paying that much for every mercenary, then this is a purse far beyond Marghoster, tallies that would stretch even Juan coffers, and yet no tax rises have been recorded, nor tithes to the castellans and lords about the lands, by my reckoning. I can't puzzle it out.

As we pass through the fields at the borders of the fens they draw comment from Bray. There is a peace here, an order to things that can easily be thought of as natural, not because of my pa's gangers. It's heading towards the evening when we get to the guards at the fens themselves, at the start of the maze of paths that lead to my family's lodge.

"Driwna Bridche?" says one of them. He has the look of a mercenary, young to look at but none of the cock about him; he's seen too many dead, it's like a scent on us that's been in the field for years. The other with him is Bridche-born, not much colour, a spear and a decent-looking belt.

"I am Driwna."

"Just you then. No crew, no matter how much you want them, is coming any further."

"I trust them with my life."

"I'm pleased, but I lose this purse if you all get to the lodge and it's likely there's others back there will see you don't. You understand this, Driwna."

He's right. I look at the other two. "Can you camp here? I'll come out at dawn with some fresh food for you and the horses."

"Aye, miss. Be glad to, you're home now."

"There's a stock of good bacca here. I'll have a few pouches of that for us as well."

"Give my respects to your pa and Eliwn, Driw," says Cal.

"I will, love."

The mercenary takes up and puts on his helm from the ground near his post and leads me into the fens, over the paths as the shadows grow.

"I hate wearing helms too," I tell him.

"Can't hear a thing wearing one, pointless for this work, really, but I'll be scolded if I've not got it on when I get to the lodge." He's sure of the way and takes a lantern at one point from one of the huts that's standing on a knee of ground out of the bog. The moths love it, and as we come close to the lodge there's a handful fluttering about it, but he's calm with them settling on his helm and cheek-guards.

Cirne's not about as I pass her smithy and it's Eliwn that comes out from the lodge on a whistle from this merc.

"Driwna?" He holds his own lantern before us and with his free arm puts it around me, squeezing me to him. He looks excited, a thrill about his smile. "I'm so glad you're here; come."

I follow behind him, but I feel nervous, queasy, like I want to sick up the bit of bilt and bisks I had at the midday.

"Mun! It's Driwna, she's come!"

As he opens the doors to the lodge, she appears, my mun, and I catch my breath for I had spent these last days thinking about her and trying to manage my grief, trying not to picture her in the wraps, her lips sewn to protect the seeds we put in the mouths of our dead.

"Ah, Dinna!" There's lanterns about the door so it's easy to see that she's standing firm, her back straight. She holds her hands out and I feel a cold sweat, my belly lurches like I'm at sea. She's well, her hair's shaved again and she's looking strong; her voice is clear and loud as a bell, as it always had been.

"Are you tired, Dinna?" She walks up to me, kisses my cheek. I hold her still; she's warm, the muscles of her arms firm, the smell of horseshit, her garden on her.

"You're well, Mun. The wasting? It's gone?"

She puts her hands to my cheeks, her thumbs smoothing

over them to my nose, and there's a sense of strength restrained. For a moment she looks me straight in the eyes. She's searching for something, thinking, trouble flickering at the edges of her. I think she might then have said something, something that really needed saying, something vastly important, for I held my breath.

I hear movement behind her, at the door. She looks to the floor.

A man walks out from the door behind her. My skin itches intensely. It takes me a moment to recognise him, the red leathers, the smartly kept beard. Though he steps softly and with grace, the air has the taste of flint, as though it's ready to spark a fire.

It is Litko, Stroff's man from Posthouse Amondsen, who was there with us when Cal and I had audience with Yblas and Amaris.

"As remarkable as you are, Driwna — and you are — your mother, Salan, is quite another thing. Testament to the iron in the bones of the Sathanti, this kurch, your father as well."

My mun kisses my cheek then. A flash of sadness whips by her eyes, but she turns and walks past Litko, head bowed, into the lodge. The mercenary has gone back to his post, leaving us alone.

"What the fuck are you doing here, Litko? Though I should know, shouldn't I, for Stroff has to have some connection to all these lots that my pa's putting over west, along with the poor fucking slaves he shouldn't disgrace himself with. More to the fucking point, how is my mun walking about? I had a roll from your Marschal Latimer suggesting I come back quickly, as I'd expect such a missive would if it's to tell me she's died of the wasting."

"I'm here, Driwna, because your brilliance, your stubbornness, have become a nuisance. I'm here to help you understand why you should consider spending some time with your mother, who is indeed cured of the wasting that had taken her so close to death. I'm glad I came when I did."

"What? Are you saying you've taken away the wasting from my mun? You are not a drudha Litko, but even the greatest of drudhas cannot cure the uncurable?"

"It would be good if we could go inside. Your father's in there. We've been expecting you and it's getting a little cold out here, is it not?"

I can't help a tear escaping. I'm still trying to reckon with seeing my mun standing before me, and she wasn't just stronger, it was that she was somehow younger and that she hadn't come to terms with the wasting not having taken her. I feel a flutter of delight in my chest, but it's in the clutch of a dread I can't shape. The Song feels distant, far beneath the ground, Ufra's plant gives me a sense of the air and it's empty, if that makes sense; it has no flavour, no scent.

Litko's leathers and leggings are clean, his beard is still trimmed, a faint scent of lavender to him. He steps back to allow me past him. Inside, my pa has the firepit lit, a small fire, enough for the time of year. There's eels smoking on hooks over it, maple chippings giving off the rich sweet smell I recall from being a girl when we first settled here. It moves me, the smell, as such forgotten things do when you find them again unexpectedly.

"It's good to have you home again, my girl." Pa this is, sitting with Mun on a bench at the head of the firepit. Eliwn's ushering out the slave they've had tending to the eels and raking some chestnuts in the fire's bed. Eliwn then tends to it all and, barring Litko, there's nobody else in here. I sit on a bench side on to Pa's, and Litko sits opposite me.

Pa drains his cup and he's not taken his eyes off me. There's something there: a triumph, a joy.

"Mun, fetch us some more wine," he says.

"A small measure for me, but Dreis, you should perhaps not drink too much too quickly; it rots your liver," says Litko.

"My what?"

"Your insides, your stomach."

"Right, right. Yes."

Pa never took a command from anyone on his own land. Mun gets up and hops over the bench to a long table along the side of the room where there's a few large flasks of wine. She pours us a measure.

"With your wine we should toast the return of your daughter, your family back together again with the brightest of futures ahead."

"What's going on, Litko?" I can't take my eyes off Mun, the way she's moving about, like I still need evidence to accrue before I can accept she's alive and well.

"Salan here is cured of the wasting. I cured her. I have also confirmed to your father that Rulger is no longer lord of these fens; he is. There will be no more tithes, such as they were, for a man who's shown such unswerving commitment to our cause."

"By our cause you mean joining the fucking Farlsgrad Post to King Hildmir and Marghoster in attacking the people of the Sathanti? I've seen it, Litko, seen the camps in the mountains, the work that drudhas are doing on slaves, on the Sathanti themselves. To what end is such research if not conquest and bloodshed? Does the king think to begin some new Orange Empire? It's beneath the Post and it's against our creed, but he'll need more than a few thousand soldiers spliced with plant to counter the wrath of our allies and the Old Kingdoms if an empire is his aim."

He pauses a moment, before smiling. "A new Orange Empire? Yes, yes I can see why you'd think that."

"And how did you cure the wasting?"

"I'm not a drudha, as you say. So what would that make me?" I'd expect a smirk from him, the way he says it, but he's looking at me as though he's expecting an answer. I'm annoying him.

"I have no fucking idea, Litko. I feel as though you're keen to tell me, so why don't you get rid of your stiffy and speak plainly."

He raises his arm towards me, hand cupped. Something's in it, I can't quite see what. Then he brings his other hand over it with a clap, a faint puff of dust from between his palms as he rubs them together. The lodge is stilled by it. I can't move my legs, and the others here feel it; Pa puts his head in his hands, Mun brings her knees up to her chest and hugs them, looking sorrowfully at Litko. He is a dust-storm, like the violent swirling funnels that pull everything into them and tear it all apart. He slides off the bench to his knees, the fire between us so I can see him shimmering through the heat of it. My head feels like it's being pushed in from my ears, I'm shuddering, we all are except him. The walls and doors rattle, a growing storm. He slaps his hands onto the flagstones and it feels like blades plunge through me, up through my legs, skewering me. I arch my back with it, I can't help but scream, and I grab at myself, looking for wounds and seeing none.

"These eels are done, I think." Ice spreads from his hands, thickening over the stone, as if he's guiding a freshwater spring towards the firepit, thick as a snake, wide as a rug, slowly at first, mesmerising in its spread, then, in a blink, with a mighty crack like stone shearing, the fire is gone, the peat vanished and the iron rack alone is standing in a block of ice some eight inches thick. The lodge, all of us, are released in that moment, as if we've been pulled free from drowning. Pa stands up, drops his cup, Mun drops hers as

369

well. Eliwn screeches like a gull and falls back on his arse away from the fire he'd just been tending.

Litko's a fucking magist.

A magist. I can't speak, I'm gasping like a fish out of water, fighting to return to that which I normally breathe and live in. Wisps of cold begin to rise from the block of ice. Litko, still on his knees, sits back onto his heels to admire his work. He waits for us all, for he's done such things before. I can't take my eyes from the ice, as though searching to relive its instant summoning, the flames vanishing so quickly I close my eyelids and still see their residue. Here is the cause of the miracles Cal has seen.

"While you stare at the ice before us, Driwna, I'll save you asking why it is I've not killed you. It would be the easy thing to do. I could turn every inch of this kurch into a fire; it would take little effort. But I have a huge respect for this family's trials and how well you've come through them. Your father's told me much of your exile from the Sathanti lands the Hidzucs now call their own. This family never laid down, never did anything but fight for its life, tooth and nail, as it were. When opportunities have come your way, you've taken them with both hands, for the fear of exile haunts you still, the fickleness of a lord's whim, the brutality of a mob. You need no reminding of the latter. Your father brings order here, he is just and fair with his kurch for they have stood by him, and you.

"I confess I hadn't known you were related to him and this family until recently, for our allies have needed to move much in the way of provisions and slaves through Ullavir to Marghoster land, the Spike, and beyond. Your father's done much to assist us, sometimes at the expense of those who might oppose us." Litko stands up, wipes the dust from his knees before sitting back on the bench.

"Well, I can hardly kill his daughter now, after all this good work in aid of our cause, after agreeing such enrichment for his loyalty. He would rightly think I could not be trusted."

"He should be thinking you're evil. I wouldn't shit in your mouth if you were starving, you bastard. Shall I tell him what you and Marghoster have been doing to the people of the Sathanti?"

"Save your breath, girl." Pa this is. "We've spoken a good deal about his plans and we should be grateful such a man as he is here. Not in my darkest days did I hope that us Bridche would have the blessing of a magist, that he would bring your mun back to you from the arms of the dead to see our prosperity, our kurchpoles raised proud on soil that will be ours for ever. You are in shock, girl, and it is only that which stops me from forcing you onto your face before him."

Eliwn has a wild look in his eyes; he's still trying to compose himself. I look at my mun and her head is bowed and there's tears in her eyes.

I take a good slug of the wine in my cup. The air's chilled quickly with the ice, it's dry and all, such as you'd only find in high mountains.

He's a magist. There's no fighting or poisoning him, no surprising him. No beating him. The silence as I come to terms with the froth of contrary thoughts, the unrelenting presence and truth of it, infuriates my pa.

"I'm sorry for her, Litko. She was always seeking the contrary, thinking of herself over her kin. She was a good girl once, our pride."

I look at him as he speaks, babbles before a man that is like a god, like Sillindar and Haluim. Is this him? My heart tells me not, even while I could not assay that which would tell me otherwise. What did I expect of a magist? An older man in field leathers isn't it, one who can make a table of ice in an instant and then sit there like a rich man's guard a moment later. There was no aura or unnatural look about him while he took, as the legends go, the material of the Song itself and unpicked it, his hands in the flow working it to his will and not, as we all strive to do, simply finding a way to join it with the least disturbance. If a guard walked in now they would see everything as it was, apart from this block of ice and air that strips all spit from your mouth.

"You finally getting your revenge on the Hidzucs then, Papy? On the Sathanti?"

"Oh, girl, you know nothing of it." He takes out his pipe and jumpcrick bones, preparing for a smoke. He was going to say more but Litko clears his throat.

"It isn't the Sathanti I'm interested in, though Lord Marghoster feels quite differently."

"What could interest a magist in all this torture and bloodshed?"

"You couldn't possibly imagine. I do not mean to demean you in saying that. You simply couldn't imagine what goals I pursue. The army you have seen is going to march and is going to achieve our objective. Lorom Haluim is my enemy. He won't ignore this army, and in coming for it he'll find me and he'll find my allies. Only the suffering I can cause will deliver him. Your success in destroying one of our camps changes nothing except how swiftly our triumph comes. How could it?"

"I had heard stories of magists preferring some kingdom or confederacy over another so that its king could feel good about invading another land," I say, "and I've heard stories about magists just helping people. Heard nothing about magists overseeing prison camps and people being kidnapped and tortured. How could you sink so low when you can do so much good with your power? You make me sick. And you, Papy, what are you doing supporting it all?"

"We live, Driwna, we get to live and we get our pride back in a world that never give a shit about us and give us no justice all your life."

I stand. "I would like to leave this lodge. Am I going to be able to?"

Litko stands. "No, Driwna, you cannot. Not until we are done."

It was as I expected. Bray and Cal are camped on the edge of this kurch. I'm worried for them, for Litko will have no problem killing them.

"If you want me to do nothing you'll have to let me speak with my crew. You wouldn't want them raising questions or to be concerned about me."

"You're right. I think they should keep you company here. I think it would make your decision to stay a lot easier, knowing I have been merciful with them."

Cock.

I sigh, to convey how unhappy I feel that I am forced to acknowledge his decision. As with other powerful men, he has a need to have others bend to his will, only with Litko it's worse because he answers to no one. As I expect, he seems satisfied with my response.

"I'll fetch the others myself," he says. "It'll give me a chance to help them understand the need to have you all here and not cause us further trouble."

What's unsaid is obvious in his manner, obvious with a moment's consideration of how powerful and old he is. He will kill us all if necessary, he'll kill my mun, for why else cure her except to use her as leverage? But he can't stay here in the fens if he's to oversee his army and its purpose. I just need to use this time to plan.

He leaves us alone then, my family and I.

"No need to stay up with us, Mun," says Pa. "Why not

rest and get an early start on those runs in the morning? Spring is almost here, the beets, spinnec and radish will want planting and you'll want to oversee our hands with the bogbean and rice."

"Yes. Yes, there's lots to do," she says. She stands, seems distracted. She comes over to me and kisses me and Eliwn. "I'm so proud of you both." She walks past Pa through the doors into the old lodge and her room there. There's no kiss for him.

"I might leave and all, seeing as you two will be arguing in moments." Eliwn this is. He leans over me and kisses my head before crossing over the edge of the firepit, looking down at the ice there before walking out of the main doors to the lodge. Neither him nor Mun looked happy considering they've got the support of a magist.

"How many lifetimes have passed in the world without the magists, and here is one in our lodge, bringing your mun back from dying. You need to understand, you and your friends, that you're not leaving this kurch. There'll be no way out. Litko's been clear about it; he can bring back the wasting as easy as take it and your choice, our choice, is have your mun fit and well after these years of suffering, or not. Do you want her to die, Driwna?"

"No, Papy. How could I want that?"

"As I expected. She deserves a longer life, your mun, deserves to enjoy the peace and coin we now have after all our days in exile. You don't need me to tell you what it's cost us, and cost her. Your brun's died because of it and Litko, in his wisdom, has not taken her only daughter. He's spared your life today. You'll be grateful for it."

"Aye." I can't say anything to that. I'm trapped. How could I know what I was up against? The miracles make sense now, everything Cal and I have seen with Marghoster's daughter

374

and those others that must all now owe Litko their lives and allegiance as my papy does. They'll do his bidding for they cannot resist him, cannot fight him.

"You might think of this as a chance to rest. You'll return to your duties with the Post at some point soon and we can all move on with our lives. You might visit your mun a bit more however; she has missed you."

He's enjoying this, watching me nod, watching me give up.

"I'll have an eel, if they managed to cook before that spimrag froze the fire," I say.

"They're close enough." He gets off his bench and takes some eels off their hooks, throws me one so I can start on it with a knife.

"More wine?"

"Yes, Papy, I'll have a few more wines before I try and sleep tonight."

"Good."

"I might take a hammer to that ice as well. I'd like a fire again."

"You aren't breaking that much ice without a barrel of salt. Let Litko sort it out."

He's right, it's a lot of hard work with a big hammer. Litko can show off a bit and I can get a bit more in my cups.

Eli won't return, he'll be away for the night I expect. After an hour or so of nursing my thoughts over a pipe, Litko arrives with my crew. They've been stripped down of their belts and weapons. Through the open door I can hear the horses are being led off and tended to.

"Welcome to the Bridche lodge. You are guests and you shall be treated well," says my pa.

"Everything right, miss?"

"Yes, Bray, as far as it can be."

"I need some ale, wine, something," says Cal. I stand up and go over to them, embrace each one, tell them I'm sorry. They are shaken.

"I can see we'll need a fire again," says Litko. "Cold in here, no?" We all watch him clap his hands together again, a fine powder spraying out once more, and then he holds out his hands and the ice cracks, chips fly off it, steaming to nothing. The air dries again, the beams of wood above us creak like timber on a ship. The peat and wood catch fire, glowing orange in the blink of an eye, as though they'd been lit for hours. My crew sit silently with me as my pa fetches us all some cups and flasks of wine, which he leaves with us. Litko sits down across from us, as he did earlier. My crew's silence, the way they watch him furtively, tells me he's proven to them he's a magist before this fire.

"Happy to help about your kurch, chief, come dawn," says Bray. With a glance at me and Cal, I see that Bray means to play along, to avoid conflict.

"That'll be welcome. We've not been introduced, Driwna. Only Cal here I know."

"Sorry, Pa, yes, this is Bray, he's good Post, saved my life in the field."

"Then I'm grateful to you, Bray, and I drink to your health." He drains his cup. Litko nurses his. I sense that he might not care for eating or drinking at all except to fit in with those about him.

"Saved I an' all, she has, from I's self, from drink an' the like." It moves me that he'd say this.

"Fascinating," says Litko with sufficient venom. Bray's set enough in himself that he smiles at Litko, knowing what he meant by it, but holding his gaze all the same. "You know, it's good you're offering to help about this kurch. It'll keep you from worrying about the change that we're bringing about. I imagine that by the summer you'll be able to return to your work and the Post."

"I'm grateful, Litko, that you've seen fit to leave us here," I say.

Cal's struggling with this, though he knows what's going on, has learned what's at stake.

"Imagine you'll need to head off soon to oversee this massacre, won't you?" he says.

"Yes, Cal, I think tomorrow. This has been a necessary diversion, but still a diversion."

"A pity, that," says Cal. I almost spit out my wine. I'm proud of him, proud of them both, for the guts they're showing in the face of someone like Litko. That it's got my pa uneasy makes it all the sweeter. It's lifting my spirit to have them with me.

"Are we able to sleep in here tonight, Pa? We've got our furs and skins with the saddles."

"Yes. Litko, will you not take my room in the back there?"

"Ahh, no, thank you, Dreis, I don't sleep a great deal. I'll head outside I think, wander the woods."

"Right."

Nothing more is said. The peat blocks wheeze and the wood cracks and spits for a while. We're all thinking, plotting, but in asking to sleep in this hall it means it's my pa and Litko that stand and bid us a good night. Litko asks Pa to walk with him a while, take a pipe. We're quiet for a good bit after they've gone out into the night.

"We're fucked," says Cal.

"I be expecting a bit more from one calls himself a magist. Proved it right enough, an' a shock it was to see, but he's killin' those can't hold a sword to him. Might as well be ants runnin' round to him, way he looks at us. What sort o' man is that?"

"I don't know what to say to you both. You know well what price me and all of us pay if we try to leave here and these lands that my kurch know far better than us. We got no belts, no weapons. But if we left and Litko found out, he'd kill my mun, wouldn't waste a breath thinking about it."

"He'll be calling that army together then, if there's more camps like the one you tore down. Looks like you've pushed him into beginning whatever it is he's been planning." Cal this is.

"He said it's an invasion of the Sathanti Peaks Marghoster wants, from the mountains where they have this army already, with more coming down the Tongue from Nailer's Road and across the North Sathanti plains. Bray, you said that no Hildmir merchants or the castellans you met seemed part of what's going on?"

"Never saw a Hildmir involved, miss. Castellan at Nailer's had no idea what it was with the mercs an' such comin' through and goin' to camps west."

"Was he keeping his own counsel in the face of a stranger such as you asking?" says Cal.

"Might be that, Cal."

"Could Hildmir not be involved? Could it just be Marghoster, with the help of the Cathrich and Stalder, the other noble families? They all hate Hildmir, the Ullavirs have been out of the court for a while and all. Only Rulgers have a clear allegiance with Hildmir," I say. "It was Rulgers that my pa's been preying on most; bet half of all the lots he's got stored out back are off Rulger vans. Remember what Yblas said to us, Cal?"

"I do. No sense in stealing lots from someone else that's working for Litko, is there?"

"Unless the Rulgers in't backin' Hildmir on this," says Bray.

"Possible," I say, "but if anyone's had their hands burned by invading the Sathanti Peaks it's the Marghosters that might be reticent to send soldiers anywhere in Hildmir's name."

"Not with a fucking magist they won't be," says Cal. "They'll be burning hottest for revenge and to reclaim some honour. Which magist do you think he is, given I've heard of no Litko in tales and song and I know all the songs sailors have sung the Sar over?"

"He'd be himself, wouldn't he?" says Bray. Cal laughs at this, fills our cups with one of the flasks that we've got at our feet.

"I heard stories that magists do walk this world; they've supposedly been seen in Mount Hope, Harudan," says Cal, "and a few go by many names. I met Marolans when I was working a tavern years back and they believe Lorom Haluim and Sillindar are one and the same, which any in Farlsgrad or Sathanti would dispute."

"Well, you might be getting up early to help Driw's pa tomorrow, Bray, but I mean to have a few more cups and leave the dawn to itself," I say. "I'm going to drink to the woman I love though she's far to the west and facing war."

We toast her and I toast them, a cup of wine for each, despite the price Ufra's plant will make me pay. As Cal starts his singing, delighting us all with sorrowful ballads in his peerless voice, I wonder why Sillindar has abandoned us all when one of his kind is here causing us such misery.

Through gaps in the shutters and around the main doors of the hall, a bright day. I can hear the yap of dogs, the echoing calls and chatter of duts, the men and women at the churns, Cirne's hammer going at the anvil in her shop. Too much wine. My lips and gums are dry as rocks. A door closes out back, in the old part of the lodge. I hear my pa's voice, some laughing that fades as he moves away with whoever is there.

I dreamed of Ufra. Our vines, our plant were as one, joining us skin through skin. I would feel her twitches, open my eyes and see myself through hers; I'd blink and my sight would switch. I felt lost, happily lost as my toes dug deeply into the soil to hold us still, to settle us so we could reach out and bring earth and sky together.

"Dinna."

I sit up. Mun's standing over me, an old leather apron on, gloves, in one of which she's holding some blue flag flowers, earth still clinging to their prized roots.

"Cal still sleeps, Dinna. Your pa's gone, Litko's left the kurch. I hoped we could talk."

"Of course, Mun. I'd love to."

"You can help me wash and press these."

"Do you have any beech for my head, Mun?"

"At the shed I do."

She holds her hand out to pull me up. I'm moved by it, holding her hand and feeling her lean back and pull strongly, helping me right myself. My head pounds in complaint. I'm grateful for having a bit less wine than I did last time I was here, for it's clear the vines growing in me don't seem to enjoy it like I used to.

Mun takes the shawl off her own shoulders and puts it around mine. I keep hold of her hand as I wait for my balance to catch up with my senses. I look about us. Bray's gone, Cal is sleeping near the firepit.

The sky is a flawless blue, hard and shining as the head of a hammer in my eyes. We walk around the side of the lodge and up the steps that lead to my mun's plant runs, as well kept as a king's now, stakes and threads solid, trellises clean. Like a smith's shop, her shed is open on one side, tables set out, her jars, alka and tools presented as though for inspection. It can be no surprise that she judges someone's character by their runs, the care of their tools. She has a small hearth in the shed and over its fire I see a kettle hanging.

"I'll chop up some beech and put a poultice on your head, you'll feel better soon enough, love," she says. "We'll have some caffin and all." Out from the shed she brings me a weather-beaten old stool to sit on. There's little shade here as the trees about put a shadow only at the edges of her run and that's as she would like it, putting there the plant that prefers a bit of shade in the day.

"You sit and let this good air fill your chest, Dinna."

It's a delight to watch her moving about. She puts the poultice of beech together and I press it over my head. Then she puts a cup of brewed caffin in my hand. I watch her at the roots of the blue flag while my brew cools. She taught me so much about plant before I went to the Post's academy at Epny, over in Citadel Hillfast, that even their drudhas remarked on it. She put me ahead of so many I trained alongside when learning to become a red.

"I had your friend Bray help me a bit this morning," she says.

"He out with Pa somewhere?"

"No, he saw some of our hands going out sniffing and wanted to go along, see what plant we have here in the fens. He's had sadness; takes years to get it out of the eyes, don't it?"

"He seems to be doing fine now; lost some weight and been working well for me, Mun."

"He loves you, Dinna. Not like that of course, I mean the way he speaks about you."

"I gave him a chance is all. I needed an ally at the Spike

as they're all under Crejda's spell and I was given not to trust her, rightly as it turns out. You're right, he seemed sad, like a shell without a crab, standing guard there when I first turned up. I felt it was right to give him something worthwhile doing and he moaned about it but soon enough he proved himself more than I could hope."

She nods at that, blows and sips on her caffin. "He spoke of you, what you've been doing out in the Sathanti, what he's been doing and all."

That makes me smile, for I suspect he's done it to give Mun a good view of what's feeding all of this prosperity we have.

She carries on washing out the roots in a bowl for a few moments, then stops.

"I keep saying it, but I'm so proud of you."

She carries on. Stops again. "Wish you'd told me more of it, though I know the last time you was here I was . . . unwell . . ." She's staring within herself, eyes empty.

"It really is a miracle that Litko's done on you. It's more than I could hope, more than anyone who ever begs Sillindar could hope to have come true."

"It is, love. I know what this Litko is about, but as he put his hands on me, as I breathed in the dust, I could feel, I don't know, feel something return, like I was coming back to this body, waking it up. I had the strangest dreams and all when he had his hands on me; I felt quite out of myself and in another place."

"Think you were in the Song, Mun?"

"No. Not quite. It didn't come closer as I know it does to you who takes those fightbrews and now, it seems, have taken Ososi blood, along with an Ososi woman into your furs. Ufra, Bray calls her. Don't know why you made out it was a man last time you was here."

"Oh, Mun. I thought it'd kill you."

"What do you think of me, Dinna? Think I've not tickled a minnie in my time?"

"Oh, Sillindar. Mun!"

She cackles, then roars laughing, leaning over to put a hand on my shoulder.

"Don't tell your pa."

"I should. Just to see his face."

"You love her, that much is plain. Bray says she's shared her milk, that the thorns are coming and the vine's growing in you now. Your colouring looks a bit different, I'll say that." She goes back into the shed and gets a rag to wipe her hands along with another stool, which she puts down next to me, sitting alongside me with her cup of caffin.

"Why isn't she here, Dinna? If you're in love you should be together."

"She's the etza-Ososi and had to lead her people back home, those few they could rescue from slavers, to hide them from the war that is coming. I wanted to help her by coming back to expose this war to the Red, Yblas, so that we might stop the Post being part of it, part of warmongering and slaving."

She looks at her feet. She's not easy with the slaves and I'm glad. She knows as well that she's the reason I can't leave.

"How's Eli doing? Has he found a girl yet?" I ask.

"Aaah, not yet. I'd had hopes for Cirne, she's a worker, looks like she could push a big family out for me."

"Mun!"

"At my age that's what you're wanting, isn't it? Some duts about that you can worry over and'll fill this big lodge with some noise in the days? He's a good boy, doing what his pa needs him to do."

"Has he got the iron for it, Mun? Pa has some serious people about him, to put it lightly. We know he's a ganger, Mun, and that Eli isn't."

"All the more reason I think your Pa's happy to have the support of Litko and Marghoster. No more tithes means our freedom here, and in Rulger lands and all. He won't need to, well, do so much of what he's been doing." She can't bring herself to talk of it, thinking it necessary and yet feeling guilt over the stealing and poaching, the banditry.

"Don't mind if I have a pipe, do you, love?" she asks.

"No, Mun."

She's got big pockets in the leather apron and she fishes out a small clay and a pouch, her crickbones to light it. I breathe in the fens' air and finish my brew.

"I had made my peace with my life," she says, scratching out the pipe's bowl with a nail. "I stopped resenting the years we was exiled. Stopped resenting what your Pa's become, for he's hurt people who was not the cause of our suffering. I have forgiven him for making himself a stranger to me, to protect me from all that, for playing out this idea that we're still the same man and woman as we was in the Sathanti, making a good living.

"And this wasting, Dinna, you don't notice it getting into you. You feel tired and slower each day, worse in winter, hard to stir in the dark, hard to think, remember things. 'Rest up,' your pa would say, 'I'll get another to do this and that.' And over these years I've let him do it more and more, these thousand small surrenders, until it become obvious to us, to me, the pain was growing; my robes, shirts, leggings getting too big for me. Years to think about my dying." I reach out and hold her hand. "Years, too, to think about my duts, out in the world or under it. I'm glad we got here at all, to see this lodge go up and the huts and the dams, the fields we've grown and you all growing with them. I've had years to think about me, the woman I might have been if not for the Marghosters, all those leathers I could have worked, whole saddles for kings that would have been the envy of all. These old fingers did not tremble then and, see, they do not tremble now."

She packs and lights her pipe.

"But now I'm well, now I'm strong again, how do you think I feel?"

"Happy, Mun, I hope. Sitting here with you in the sun makes me happy, and I came here expecting to see you in the ground and gone from me until the day I'm brought back here in powders and a sack and they put me alongside you." I can barely speak straight while holding the thought of her in the ground and not here, now, as much herself as she's ever been.

"But I'm angry, Dinna. This man putting his hands on me, and only agreeing to it if it meant your pa would back him though he could have healed me without. Like my life is theirs, Dinna, like I solve a problem for your pa and this Litko, like I fucking asked for it when I never did. Now they've tied you to me and all; I'm the rack on which they're pinning you, holding you back from standing up to him, all the killing he's done, of us nokes and children. I see they're using me against you, my love, my brave, brave girl. 'We're so grateful, Master Litko,' says your pa, 'She's so grateful.' 'We owe you her life, our freedom.' How free are we, you and me?"

"I couldn't stand up to him anyway, could I, Mun? Sick as it makes me, he's given you back to me and is only doing what I couldn't have stopped him doing, because he's a magist, Sillindar help us."

"There's another fucking magist don't do us good, love.

385

Fuck Sillindar." She has a draw on her pipe, offers it to me, and I have a draw myself. There's kannab in it, and she winks as I look at her.

"Tell me, Dinna, if Litko hadn't brought me back like this, if you found out otherwise that he was a magist and was free to do what you wanted, what would you do?"

"We can't talk like that, Mun? It's not where we are."

"Still, Dinna, what would you do?"

"I'd be with Ufra, because I now know I could not, nor could anyone fight him. I'd be at her side, helping those people we got out of the mountains, helping those tribes survive however we could. Her Ososi are mine now, aren't they?"

"They're more your kurch than we are here, Dinna."

"Mun, that's not true."

"What's left of the Bridche now, love? What price have we paid for this?" Her arm sweeps out to indicate all of what's about us.

"We paid the price we had to pay, more than we might have wanted to, Mun, but it was that or die out in the plains or forests, as our kurch-kin did." This is an anger I had no idea was in her, for I'd not heard her speak except in defence of Pa and the kurch all my life. I tell her so.

"I said I had time to think, Dinna, but in all the years you was growing up, all what we hid from and then, here, all what we had to protect, it was about you and Eliwn and poor Leif. You was all I cared about. I couldn't have spoken against Pa when you was too young to know the whys of it. Now, with all what's changed here since we settled, I wasn't strong. But now I am. These are hours I don't deserve, stolen hours, girl, hours to burn up and burn bright. Don't you see, I'm already dead."

She's looking at me all warm and calm as a cow, a smile

on her face, and here, in this place where Litko's been and the Song is frayed and bitter, sour almost, she's like a heart that's beating shining, thick honey into the earth and air, filling me, that smile, feeding me. Here's the woman my pa fell for and I wonder how he could believe his luck when she had her head shaved for his crown, for she could lead an army, she could have led this kurch. But such is a woman's lot. Litko has no idea what he's woken and my pa's forgotten.

"Seems like the life of this and my own life are to be set against the lives of your Ososi and all those Litko'll kill."

"Yes, Mun."

"I'd rather have died."

"What's that, Salan?" We turn to see Pa has walked from the trees behind Mun's shed.

"I said I'd rather die than see all those people in the Sathanti, Driwna's love, the Ososi, all of them dying in my place."

"Is that right?" He stands before us, looking out upon our view across Mun's runs to the trees beyond. "She's not leaving. We know the price."

"It's not right, love," says Mun.

"It is."

"Because he'll kill us if she goes, if we let her leave."

He turns to face us both on our stools. He's sweating, must have been at work somewhere in the woods.

"He will. Small price to pay to have you back, Mun," he says. "We've got everything now."

There's peace in him, I'll give him that. He seems younger, and his hair's now tied back out of the way, his beard in plaits once more.

"Driwna's not happy, Pa," says Mun. "This Litko goes off to hunt and kill the woman she loves. She's got Ososi blood in her."

"What?" He didn't know. "An Ososi woman, then, that's who you're making your keep?"

"I am, Papy."

"Sorry to hear it."

I take a breath.

"Why are you sorry she's in love?" says Mun.

"Couldn't find a man good enough for you?"

"No, Papy."

"Can't say I'm surprised. Well, I'm sorry if your Ososi woman is having to face Litko. If she had any sense she'd stay in the Sathanti, far from Farlsgrad."

"Why?" I ask. "That's where this army's going, isn't it? To take the Sathanti? She'll be defending her tribe and herself."

His words sink in.

"You just said she'd be wise to stay in the Sathanti, to stay away from Farlsgrad. What's going on, Papy? Sounds like you're saying the army's not going into the Sathanti."

"Course it is. Where else would it go?" He's simmering, lips thinning as he suppresses his frustration at saying what he just did.

I see it then, I finally understand. "There's been no Hildmir vans or merchants involved in this Litko's work. This is all Marghoster, the other nobles. No Rulger vans have been involved and it seems it's the Rulger vans that have got hit by you and your crew and nobody else's, Papy."

"Course we hit Rulger vans, we're on – well, we were on, Rulger land, though thanks to Litko this is all ours now."

"Thanks to Litko? Does he speak for the king? Would it not be Hildmir that compels Rulger to give this kurch land?"

"What do you mean, Dinna?"

"Mun, this army isn't going to the Sathanti at all, it's going for the king. If Hildmir's not involved in this army and it's not going for the Sathanti people, then they're going for the king himself. It's a coup. Marghoster wants the throne and Litko's giving it to him." A rebellion and the Post part of it. Does Yblas know? Have Amaris and him tricked me? Lied to me? I feel sick in my stomach as the questions tumble out.

"So your Ufra is safe? This Litko won't go to the Sathanti Peaks?" Mun this is.

"She won't know that; she'll be marshalling her people to go burn the camps that have these soldiers in them, risking her kin's life when the soldiers there aren't meant for them."

"Too late for you to reach them anyway, Driwna. At least we can be sure your mun will be alive here, and your own kurch will prosper."

"Is that how you'd think if it was me out there and you here, Dreis? Really?" says Mun. "You disgust me." She stands before him. "I might not have wanted to die, nobody does, but if this is the price of it, I'm not paying it. I'm not putting myself or you before our girl."

"You'll put her before Eliwn, your only son, heir to this tribe?"

"If he wanted to go, if his love, your keep-daughter, was in the Sathanti about to risk her life, would you deny him?"

"It's not a question I need answer, Mun. Litko's seen to that."

"Has he now? You been leading all your life and you'll put what Litko wants before us all. You know you'd find a way to let Eliwn go; you'd find a way to go yourself if I was out there."

"He's a magist, Salan. There's no going against him. I put the tribes first — us Marghosters that remain — those that helped get us here. It's the price of being chief."

"I'll leave then," says Mun.

"What?"

"You heard me. I won't stay and be the reason our Driwna's about to lose who she loves. I wouldn't stay if you was in danger, whatever Litko says."

"Sit down, Mun. What are you saying, you'll leave? This is the kannab that's softened you."

Mun knocks out her pipe on the stool she was just sitting on and puts it in her apron.

"Dinna, saddle my horse."

"Mun? What are you doing? You can't leave here," I say.

"No, Dinna, it's you who can't leave. I can go and warn your Ufra myself. Litko said nothing about that."

"Salan, sit, what's the matter with you?" Pa goes to put his hands on her arms, an attempt to comfort her, to soften the rage that's building in her. She pushes his hands off.

"Are you going to stop me, Dreis?"

He's stunned. I'm surprised by it, but my heart soars to see her fierce like this.

"You can't leave, Salan, to do what Driwna would do, for the same death would be brought on you and all of us as if it were her that did it."

"Horseshit. You'll think of something if he comes back this way, but I know the quiet ways about these fens and I'll leave now. You can tell the kurch I'm going to the markets."

"You won't go anywhere, old girl."

Her slap is sudden, hard, moves his head sideways. "Call your fucking guards, Dreis, if you dare it."

He grimaces in a moment's hot fury, his hand rising, clenching. I jump to my feet, stand alongside her.

"You fucking touch her, Papy, I'll lay you out cold."

He grabs a handful of the shawl around my shoulders, trying to push me back and away from Mun. But I'm strong, much stronger than he has ever been for he's a noke. He can't move me. I put my hand around his wrist and squeeze. The pain makes him cry out. The shock of this challenge, of it being his daughter, redoubles his fury and he throws a punch. It's too slow. I block it and send the heel of my hand into his nose; his head jerks back with a meaty snap. He's stupefied, dazed by it. My own anger overran the self-control I'd intended and he falls to his knees before us both, his wrist in my other hand, head swaying now, blood pouring from his nose.

My mun's on her knees before him, patting my side to let his hand down, reaching into her apron for a cloth to hold to his face. Yet I think we can both still hear and feel her slap. I've never seen her stand up to him before, confront him. Here are the years of her duty to him, toughening and burnishing her authority. He's blinking, trying to right the sight in his eyes. I wipe his blood from my hand onto my undershirt, for I'd come outside only in that and the shawl.

"You are no longer my blood, girl." His words are clogged up in his ragged, bloody breaths. He pushes Mun's hand away, holds the cloth himself and slowly rises to stand before us again.

"Salan, we must talk it through," he says. "Driwna, you'll leave us be for now."

"Fuck you."

Mun puts her hand on my arm then, to shush me.

"What's the good of talking it through, Dreis? You either let her go, with her friends, or I'll go. You can make us another brew if you need that time to choose, but by the time I've drunk my cup I'll have your choice and we'll think of how to make it work."

He looks about us then, suddenly worried someone may have seen him being put to the ground by his daughter. I see his lips tighten with anger, with planning.

Mun hands him her cup. He gets up and gingerly walks to the kettle over the hearth, his head back slightly, the cloth good and bloodied over his nose. She looks down at her hands, wringing them with her nerves, the difficulty of confronting him.

I sit back down on the old stool ready to cry. Mun takes a deep breath and goes over to him. There's angry whispering and then he's gasping with pain as she finds some salve. She hollers then at someone that's moving about at the side of the lodge. It's one of their hands and she barks orders at him. The hand returns soon with a chair and a small bag, must have more plant in it for Pa.

He cries out then, suddenly. She must have righted his nose. I don't look over, for I know he doesn't want me to, would consider it cruel. Oddly, I feel the same. So I look up at the vast blue, let the purity of it fill my eyes as I blink away my tears. I feel almost sick, as my mun surely does, at the violence we've done to our blood, my pa. More than that, more than simply being stronger than him, I was shocked by how much strength he had lost, his eyrtza fading with age.

"Sit down with us, love, when you're done," she says to him. There's a silence. She's waiting for him to make the caffin she asked for, something she'd have done for him and not ever asked of him before.

He returns and sits on the spare chair that's been brought out, hands Mun her caffin. She's packing her pipe with a good bit of kannab for him, and I'm expecting him to refuse it, but she lights it, passes it to him and he takes a few draws on it, looking out as I am on the sky over the treeline, buzzing and bird calls filling the air of the fens. Mun's quiet, waiting on his words.

"It's not been easy for you, Salan, these last few years.

But they've not been easy for me, either. I thought I'd lose you when the wasting came on and took hold. I been watching you dying slowly and I've been helpless about it. You tell me that I should let Driwna go to see this Ososi woman she loves yet when Litko tells me he can save your life I shouldn't agree to it?"

"Did you ask me? Did you tell me the cost of it when he put his hands on me? I was healed for a price and you have paid it gladly and without barter."

"Oh Salan, what barter's to be had with the likes of him? And Driwna's woman might be alive after all of this and we all win because of it; she does, the Marghosters do and fuck the rest of them."

"The slaves and all, Papy?" I say. "The ones tortured to madness and death, all that sits well with you? It must be seeing as how we have them now."

"We've done this over and over, girl. I'm not doing it again."

"Our girl's opposed to what Litko's doing," says Mun. "So we are supporting her or supporting them against her. I'm for our blood, love, not against it."

"But isn't she against our blood if she acts so as to bring ruin upon us?"

"She's trying to do some good for people. There's hundreds owe her their lives, and by accounts I've heard she's stopped a war between Sathanti families and protected them from Marghoster who would have killed our old border kurches of the Ilkashun. Aren't you proud of her, Pa? Isn't she as much as we could want of a daughter of ours? She brings honour to our name all over the southern Sathanti, even if it's not the name we have taken for this lodge and this new life. She brings our name back there, back from nothing. I'll carve her story into our new kurchpoles myself."

"Before Litko smashes them to splinters?"

"What then would you have on them? A bit of poaching? Banditry? A kurchpole of farmers and herders is all fine in times of peace and much of our old poles spoke of such before the Marghoster bastards came to us and turned us off our land. But there was heroes there too, your own pa, his greatpa who led the Council and whose crown you now don't wear."

"Leave it, woman, leave it! You're speaking in a way that shames me and I won't have it. Marghoster denied me a place to show the Council my worth. Fuck knows I'm paying for that and our whole confederacy aside."

"It in't shaming you, Dreis, you fool, for what you done with us, bringing us over here and keeping us alive, that's what's carved there, isn't it? Survival of us Marghosters is what you done for us and I'm proud of you. We did win, love. But nothing goes on forever, nothing goes as we would have it. And we have a girl here who brings us more glory, who puts us right in the eyes of the world again." She leans forward and holds out her hand to him. He looks across at her, then takes her hand in his, a great love in his eyes.

"I have seen death, Dreis. There's no Leif there, not my own mun or pa, or yours, just a quiet we take nothing into and where we forget all that has gone. And when I knew this, when I felt it, I saw I had nothing more important to give than all of my love, for what then happens without me in the days that come is not for me to shape, not for us. It's our girl and Eliwn that have to shape it all, with what it is we leave them. I can't leave her betrayed, kept a prisoner far from who it is she loves, who she's shared blood with and fought alongside."

His jaw's clenching. And it means he's listening, properly, and being him means trying to find some way to be the man that chooses the path, the guide and carer all his life. He's forgotten what it is to have an equal, I realise, and Mun's more than his equal in wit as he's rediscovering.

"What do you say, Driwna?" he asks, phlegm in his voice, staring down at his lap, cloth over his nose.

"Mun knows I wouldn't go if it meant her life. Seems like it means more to her than her life that I do."

He's quiet for a time.

"I shouldn't be surprised, should I, that Litko's given your mun her fire back too. I can't lock you up, but you go and you kill us all." He stands.

"I'll say my farewell here, girl. I've got work to do saving what lives I can before he finds you and then comes back to kill all of us."

I stand as well, face him. I can't read what thoughts pass across his eyes as looks me up and down. He nods slowly to himself, as though something's settled. Might be pity, might even be pride there, I'd like to think, but he says nothing more and walks slowly away.

Mun stands to put her arms around me as I start crying, for I know in my heart it is the last time I'll see my pa and I wish it could have been different.

She holds me while I weep, while I fall silent. I'm treasuring her embrace that's strong once more. This is our own farewell, too. I'm taller than she is, we seem to sense it together, how much bigger I am than her.

"Hard to think you come out of this belly," she says, leaning back to look at me, to put her hands on my arms and squeeze them. "Whatever Litko might take from us he has at least given me this hour. And this farewell he can't take. You give people hope and you bring peace. No mother could want or ask more. '*Lai luk ebecz a funtre, lai gurut ehr halsce.*'"

"'You sow our summer, you children of gold."

"Not forgotten your Bridche lingo, Dinna."

"No, Mun. Never."

Cirne and Eliwn stand with her as I leave the lodge for one last time. Eliwn's got hold of Mun and she sings a song for soldiers, proud and clear across the fens. Cal's head is turned to hear more of it, but soon enough the calls of thrush and sparrows take it from me, heralds of spring.

Chapter 19

Driwna

I thank Sillindar for the rain and thunder that's driven everyone to their hearths. Cal stands shivering in his oilskins at Alaqua's door, third in one of the many rows of wooden two-room huts on the edge of the Spike, built by castellans past and surrounded by the heavy, muddy fields full of traveller's tents and the pens and sheds of the markets for livestock and slaves. The pens are silent, the tents not so much. I'm crouched at the side of a well.

"Who's there at this hour, Dullan? We can't have men in here tonight, you promised." An older voice, though sharp as a knife, meaning to be heard by us.

"Ma, you'll wake him. I'll see them off before we have a bite."

She opens the door, its hinges creaking for the lack of oil. There's a good fire and the glow of candles reflecting in the puddles in the muddy ruts of the track on which Cal's standing.

"I remember you. The songbird. You know I'm not—"

He doesn't let her finish; he whispers and she looks over

397

his shoulder, makes me out behind the well across the track. She opens the door wider and stands back to let us in.

"Who's this bloody lot, Dullan? Bloody soldiers and all. Make 'em pay silver and I'll go in the other room with the boy."

"Where's Bray?" she asks.

"At the sheds, love," I say. "This your mun, then?"

"It is," says Alaqua. "She calls me Dullan though I have changed my name. She won't take to it."

"Bloody Alaqua she's calling herself now. To think I give her the name of my own ma, for her to spit on it with a highborn fancy like Alaqua."

"Boots off, Cal, we'll not muddy this house for it's well kept and a pleasure to see." Of course this puts a smile on her mun's face, a nod of approval for my manners and the compliment, as it was meant to. They have little here but chairs, tables and a few shelves for food and their clothes. A stone chimney and hearth makes a partition of the rooms with the fire under it heating them both. Ashes are swept, as you'd hope in a wooden hut, and with the coin she's got from us there's provisions filling those shelves, logs stacked and a small chest with woollens and linens stacked up on it.

"I'm Driwna," I say to her mun.

"Cuslin, me. Welcome to our home. There's pegs for those oilskins behind you." She's Alaqua in twenty years, old age putting a good bit of weight on her, long grey hair and jowls, a big round belly and hips to frame it. But her forearms are thick, fingers swollen and scarred, a story of a life's hard work. She can't stand straight, bent out of shape with picking in the fields and all the other labours that come with being poor, but she's over to a table to cut us some bread and open some jars: jam, butter, beer.

"Alaqua's been good to us, over at the Doris. We're sorry

to have to come here, but I'm not wanted in these parts and might be arrested."

"I see. Dullan tells me you tip her well and I see you're respectful, that's good enough for me."

"How's your boy?" Cal asks Alaqua.

"Oh he's good, sir," she says. "The coin you've give us, it's put some meat on him and given us the logs that's seen us through the winter. But the purse you give us, you can't, Ma said it, you can't give us it all, that silver."

"Least we could do, love, for the help you're giving us," I say. "I just want us to dry off before we prep for our visit to the castellan and bring his bullshit to an end. Will we wake your boy fetching the chainmail, plant and belts from the other room?"

"If this thunder won't wake him, neither will you, miss."

We had come northwest, from the Rethic Fens to the Spike, for news of Ufra and the revenge that was being planned in the Sathanti. I hoped to persuade them not to begin a war on Farlsgrad. They couldn't win it, even before I knew a magist was pulling the strings. To me it was likely Ufra and the Master of Flowers would not go after the camps in the mountains, for it would have been slow, hard work to find any of the camps without the lie of the land and any willing natives to share it. Made sense to me they'd attack the Spike, being so close to the border, if only to hamper any forces following them up along Gethme's Tongue as they went in search of vengeance on Hildmir, his own lands being far to the north of Farlsgrad. They could not have raised the northern Sathanti kurches, let alone those so badly used in the high peaks themselves, so I feared for them if their plans were of an ambition greater than their number and quality. I feared also that in trying to take the Spike with its being prepared, there'd be a lot of unnecessary bloodshed on both sides. My hope was that I could divert her force away from it. That hope would prove forlorn.

Bray was convinced there'd be support for me in our sheds, so went with our horses to the Doris to stable them before walking out there. Yesterday this was. Bray had told us where Alaqua lived and we'd have come here this morning but for two Hidzuc who stopped me as I sought some eels from a catcher in a shovelful of huts at the southern edge of the Spike, a mile or so east. They were careful not to call me by my name, instead calling me "Ufra-wen", which was enough evidence of their being true as any I could have asked for. They had been watching the Spike with four others, pretending to be trading lots out of Hidzuc. But they had been gathering news and assessing the Spike's strength ahead of an attack by Ufra, the Master and over a thousand Sathanti. They were young, these two, hot for revenge on Farlsgrad and what it had done to their kurch-kin. I was surprised Ufra and the Master could muster as many so quickly, but if this was only a thousand they would be trained, Oskoro mixes in their belts and blood. Formidable. They were indeed coming for the Spike, would arrive in two days. But I learned also that many of Gruslatic's garrison had taken vans up through Gethme's Tongue, a summons that called fully three thousand of Marghoster's own tithed and sworn from all his clans to march north with him along the Fifth, to Cathrich and no doubt beyond to Autumn's Gate. This proved the truth of my pa's loose tongue: that this was a coup against Hildmir, a civil war.

I knew no birds could fly with warnings of the Sathanti army that approached, as that might divert the forces going north back here, so I told these two to leave for their own lands, to tell Ufra, Leusla and the Master that all would be well when they arrived at the Spike. I could not risk revealing to them what I knew of Litko and the real plans they had until I saw Ufra myself. I confess I wanted the pleasure of ending Gruslatic's reign as castellan and Crejda's as reeve of the Spike, but for all that I would be overstepping my authority as a red in imprisoning Gruslatic, the other ways this could play out were far worse for everyone. I could only hope that the people of the Spike would understand when it came to it.

The seven reds that Bray brought back to Alaqua's are enough to wake her dut, that and her mun squawking about the mud and crowd in their hut. "You're Brother Red," says one red as we clasp arms, and Bray's rolling his eyes at the way they are about me. Another's thanking me for helping his cousin get home from the Sathanti and another says he's grateful to Yblas for making up a role that saw "one of us" have the same influence as an administrator, and for a creed that speaks to them that work the vans and oil the axles of the Post's fortune. It gladdens me to hear this.

I'm expecting we only need dayers for this work, getting into the tower and to Gruslatic. They want assurances that Crejda will not retaliate, and I have to tell them the extent to which she and Gruslatic are aligned in slavery and cheating the ledgers, how they've been used in support of Marghoster's attempt to take the throne. It becomes clear that some of their ardour for this work is because of Gruslatic, the chance to end his tenure as castellan, having been aggrieved in various ways by his militia over the years.

Bidding farewell to Alaqua we leave for the tower. The outer wall isn't manned, as we had expected. We take three different routes, breaking up to look less suspicious to any that might be watching. Only the gates, open unless under attack, have guards at them, standing under a hide shelter fixed to the stone before the archway. Cal and I are to clear the way through the open gate.

I put my arm around Cal and we take a flask each and he begins singing, the pair of us staggering as though we'd been in our cups. About the arch are empty stalls and some two-storey workshops, dark and shuttered. We have only the guards to worry about.

I can see they're reluctant to step out into the rain, sheets of it sweeping past us.

"You got business inside?" shouts the one of them.

"Staying at the tower, in't we old girl," says Cal. "I have the top room." We move towards them, fifteen feet, ten feet. The one that's spoken gives a sigh and steps forward out of their shelter, the rain pattering on his helm. He lowers his spear a foot or so, a gesture for us to halt. We take a few more steps.

"He's got a big one, hasn't he, old girl?" says Cal.

"Bigger than yours, love," I say.

"There's old Bukelin in the top room," says the guard, "comes by from Roan, always stays here. You sure it's the top room you have, son?"

While I can't believe he hasn't noticed how filled out our cloaks are with fieldbelts and swords, I can't take the chance he will and then give a shout to the other guards in the barracks beyond. I leap forward, throwing a flask at the guard who's with him. I kick this one's spear away before he can bring it to bear on me and I make short work of him, a punch to his head, the metal studs on my gloves smashing in his cheek. Cal's moved in at the other one, who's barely risen off his stool to reach for his own spear. Cal gets his throat, stops him from screaming, and two good blows to the side of his head put him out. I do the same to this one to stop him moaning. I hope I haven't killed him in doing so, but the dayer's burned out any more thinking about it. The shelter being on the outside of the wall, nobody inside would have seen us. Through the archway the outer bailey's full of houses for the richer men and women of the Spike, as well as more sheds and workshops, giving us some cover from which to look up to the inner bailey wall. The cullis is down, as we expected. There'll be two up on the wall, no doubt at their hearths in the turrets either end of it. I leave two on the outer wall to act as the guards should any others come their way, while the five left along with Cal and Bray I bring together at the side of one of the sheds that belongs to Gruslatic.

"Cal and me will get to the wall, throw grapples up and you'll follow, three on each rope, leaving Bray here to start going through the sheds looking for what we can take that'll help Ufra and the Sathanti when they come."

"That don't seem right, this working for the Sathanti," says one of the reds. "Thought we was doing this for the red, the cloak, not some Sathanti looking to invade."

"Right now, they are the only allies we have, for none but Gruslatic himself knows the deceit he's guilty of. If we are to see that he does not retake this tower, we need allies. You're Skoler, aren't you?"

"Yes, Fieldsman."

"You might have said all this sooner, but I won't have you doubting what I do. I can't say the right and wrong of this is easy, what it is we're doing and who we're doing it with. You see it as many in the Spike might. The Sathanti come here for revenge on Marghoster, not your families and those who make a living here. Marghoster's a traitor to the crown, as is Gruslatic, Crejda, the Brasks, any that's affiliated. They will be punished and some order must be made here once they're in the cells below the tower. Then I go to the High Red and tell him how Stroff and Crejda have betrayed us. Will you follow me, Skoler?"

"Yes, Fieldsman."

"Good man. Now, once we're up on the wall, just follow us. Cal and I will take care of the guards that's there. Then we'll go straight for the tower, you'll head to the barracks and you'll powder them so's they can't fight you. Lead them out into the courtyard and that'll calm them down while I deal with Gruslatic. Let's go."

Cal and I step out from the shed we're behind, walk up to the inner bailey's wall. The guards are inside at the turrets, shutters leaking slivers of torchlight from within them. Lightning fills the clouds above us. I count and on three there's the grinding, shattering blast of thunder. Cal moves along the wall, so we're near the turrets. These Ososi dayers we're on give us a calm and easy strength. Lightning again, rippling and lighting up the sheets of rain. We swing and throw the hooks and they hit the stone as the thunder fills the air. Hand on hand, we scale the walls, making use of the holes and remains of spikes from sieges gone by. I pull myself over onto the parapet and crouch, the rope creaks as the next red begins climbing. I step to the door to the turret. Two voices, laughter inside. I turn to Cal, thinking that both guards must be in the room beyond, but he's opened the door to the other turret and has gone inside. There's no noise. I take a deep breath, open the door. A good fire in the hearth, both guards armoured, armed, their backs to me only a few steps away. I leap forward, knife out, arm around the face of one, pull back his head and slit his throat. The other one, barely twenty summers, is so shocked he tries to stand too quickly, falls back off his stool. I fall on him, break his nose, straddle his chest.

"Live or die?" I hiss in his ear. He's choking, gasping with the pain of his nose, my weight on his chest. His hand slaps the stone floor, a training drill remembered, conceding, surrendering. Knife at his throat I take a pinch of mandrake powder, cover his mouth and put the pinch into his nose. He snorts it, wide-eyed with the fear I've killed him, but he's soon limp and asleep.

Cal comes in with two other reds, smiles, then leads us on down the steps to the base of the wall and into the courtyard. The remaining reds are creeping along from the bottom of the far turret to the barracks. I gesture our two to join them, and me and Cal go up to the main doors of the tower itself.

"You want to put him in a cell, Driw, but we have to kill him," he says.

"We can't, Cal. Now move." I rap the door. There's a moment while the guard inside shuffles up to the door; he must have been half asleep.

"Who be there?"

"Someone at the cullis wants Grus, something urgent he said, give me a roll for him." Cal this is.

"This hour?"

"Why it's urgent I reckon, I don't fuckin' know."

"You that new lad they put on last night?"

I look back at the rest of our crew crouched waiting about the door into the barracks, looking for my signal.

"That's me."

"Next time, lad, tell 'em to fuck off till morning."

The bolt goes, Cal puts his boot into the door, smacking the guard full on. I shoulder-barge it and run for the stairs, first floor, Gruslatic's quarters. I hear a chair scrape on stone somewhere else below me. Cal knows to use powders for any that might be in the tower, most likely the servants in the kitchen and stores there.

Gruslatic's door's not guarded. I draw my sword and walk in, just as the shouting's beginning outside, just as he wakes. A torch burns next to me on the wall by the door. He has an axe by the side of his cot. He's taken it up, standing now and squinting at me, but I'm still hooded.

"What is this? Who wakes me?" He's thick with sleep, slow.

"It's a good friend, Gruslatic. You gave me a cell of my own last time I was here."

I pull back my hood, move forward.

He squares up, takes his axe in both hands.

"I'm on a brew, Castellan. Throw down the axe, over in that corner will do. I'm undecided on killing you; don't take my choice away."

"You're that fieldsman, that bitch of Yblas's, Driwna."

"I am. Sit back down while my crew settles yours."

"Fuck you."

"I'm wearing a fieldbelt, Castellan. I have many ways to hurt you in its pouches and pockets."

He rubs his eyes, getting used to the light.

"What a mistake this is. What horseshit plan has a fieldsman looking to master the Spike? Are you still with the Post? Do you think an army won't march up your fat arse and tear you to pieces when someone gets away to alert the Marghosters and Cathrich forts? Because someone will; my allies are not all within these walls."

"I won't pretend it's a great plan, Castellan, but it's one that means almost nobody under your command or governed by you dies. The alternatives would soak this town in the blood of nokes. Your nokes."

"What the fuck are you talking about?" He shouts for help, desperate to take some initiative. From outside there's a lot more shouting now; the soldiers from his barracks are being led into the rain I expect.

406

"There's an army marching on the Spike. Looking for some form of recompense for the torture and slavery they suffered at the hands of you, Marghoster, Crejda, the Brasks, and most of all, Litko."

He stiffens at this, gives himself away. "Yes, Litko," I say. "I know who he is, I know what you've been working towards these last few years. It's over for you, as castellan."

He laughs. "Mind if I have a cup of wine, while I consider how stupid you are?"

"Of course I mind, you fat cunt; this isn't a tavern. Go near a flask I'll take your hand off."

He raises his hands in mock surrender before sitting back on his cot.

"The axe?"

He casts it to the floor just a few steps away from me. I sweep it behind me with my boot.

"Well now, our king will be dead in a few weeks at best. If I'm not dead, I'll be made castellan again, castellan of a larger territory than this. The Sathanti will suffer if they don't retreat the moment they reach our border."

"We both know Marghoster will have far more on his mind than going after the south Sathanti confederacies."

"So you accept Hildmir's fucked. There's a thing I'll be happy to see. And what about you, once you've gone from here? Traitor to the new king, traitor to the Post."

"Stroff isn't the Post."

"As you say."

There's more shouting outside; something's happened. I hear someone approach the door.

"Cal?" I say.

"Aye, love. Fuck knows what's happening out there, but there's a few of the militia dead and the rest arguing. This fucker still alive?" He stands in the doorway.

407

"I am." Gruslatic this is. "Seems like you're needed out there, Driwna Marghoster, my militia proving themselves a handful for your crew, even without a brew. Never thought you'd run a crew well, too soft, making out you're on their side. No general won a war with that outlook."

"Mask up, Cal, I'll have some powders ready. We bind his hands and ankles, he can shuffle his way outside to join his beloved militia. You can try and have a go at Cal when he comes near you, Castellan, but these powders will make a mess of you."

He shrugs, stands and turns to face the wall, puts his hands behind his back ready for them to be tied. He offers no resistance to Cal as he begins his work, a few grunts when the rope is tightened to his skin. Cal turns him back and steps away from him.

"You or me?" he says.

"I'll do it, love." I take my knife out of its sheath, wipe the blade with a cleaning rag to get the poison off it.

"All that to then kill me, old girl?"

"No, Castellan, you're being stripped." I take the knife to his shirt, cut it away, then the leggings he was sleeping in. There's a moment when he twists his hips as I start cutting at his waist, trying to piss on me, and I dig the knife an inch into his side, stilling him.

"I would love you to try that again."

"Sorry, Marghoster, I didn't quite understand you; you're a bit lispy now without those teeth I took."

I say nothing to that, just cut away his leggings until he's naked.

"Let's go, Gruslatic, cool you down a bit."

Twelve naked militia in all, not including the one I put to sleep who now lies sleeping besides his brothers in arms.

The ones alive are mewling or panting with pain from the powders that will have got in their eyes and noses. Three of these militia are dead, the others are kneeling, heads on the ground, arms out in front of them. Skoler's with them, kneeling, and he stripped and all. He's bound and as he sees me he spits blood on the stones before my feet as I throw Gruslatic forward to the end of their line, next to him.

"That fucking Skoler nearly did for us," says one of my reds. He gestures towards the barracks and lying against the stone of it is one of our crew, a young woman.

"Get her cloak, red, she'll get her tally."

"She won't, none of you will for what you're doing. Sathanti fuckers!" Skoler this is.

Gruslatic laughs. "This one knows the meaning of loyalty. Well met, Skoler. I'll see you well in the new regime that awaits us."

I kneel before Skoler. "You have sworn to the cloak, to the Post, yet have killed one of your own, one who would not have harmed you. You disobeyed an order from your Fieldsman."

"Suck me."

"Kill him," says one of our reds, spitting at him. "If we was in the field that's what we'd do. We'd kill him."

He's right. It goes against how I feel, for in that regard Gruslatic also is right. I haven't got enough ice in my veins for this to be easy. I jab my knife in its sheath a few times to get a good coat of poison on it again and kneel before him. I want there to be another way, something more merciful, but I can't without risking all that we're doing here.

"You knew what would come of this Skoler and I'm sorry for it."

He begins to mouth the word "no" as he sees the blade in my hand, and lightning makes his face shine briefly with the rain running over his head and hair. His eyes are huge as he begins to lean back, a gasp as I slam the blade into his chest. It crunches through his ribs. He starts rocking with the shock of it, his head looking down at my hand, the hilt up against his skin. The knife slides out easily, blood sputtering from the wound, fast and thick then, running away down his belly. He falls forward silently.

"You should thank me, Marghoster. You took my comments to heart I see. I told her, brothers and sisters, I told her she wasn't tough enough for this sort of work, not—" A single punch, a hook so fast to him without a brew he's stopped still; the rough metal on the knuckles of my glove tears skin from his cheek and he falls forward stunned, moaning.

"There is a soft heart in here somewhere, Castellan, for it lets you live. You're all living, I should say, bar our traitor. None are dead that couldn't be helped. I expect none of you would give me any quarter were you on a brew and armed, despite your lives being spared. You are loyal to the crown of Hildmir, though Gruslatic here has betrayed the crown, has supported an attempt to take control of Farlsgrad by the Lord Marghoster, who marches north to Autumn's Gate with an army for just this purpose."

"Speak carefully," hisses Gruslatic.

"We're for our castellan," says one of them, older man, his voice thick with muke from where he'd breathed in the powders. "He's seen us right all these years. Hildmir's given us nothing."

The others there, emboldened by this, say the castellan's name, aligning it into a short chant. He looks up at me. "That's how you do it, Sathanti fucker. Will you kill us all now? Leave widows and widowers and duts with no food?"

I look about me at my crew. Gruslatic knows I can't kill him and the militia, or at least it will diminish me, demean the red and what I've stood for till now. He knows as well that I can't win, that if I talk of a magist I will only confuse and do me no good even if they believed it, for Litko is on Gruslatic's side. I've taken control of the Spike but cannot keep it or change it for the better. Once we're gone north, who then sees order and trade are maintained here? Who, in the whole of the Spike, could win over a fort that Gruslatic has diligently cultivated with his bribes over the years?

I look up into the pouring rain. I face the truth of it again, as I had to in the Fens. There's no way out of this for me where I get to live. I've known it since Litko showed his power. My will has been fraying with each dawn since the Fens, each meal, at every shadow in the brush, all pulling on my heart to give up. But alongside me stand, nevertheless, Cal, Bray, reds who haven't given up on what we're trying to do. What I'm trying to do.

"Help me get this lot in a cell," I say.

"There's more than one free down there," says Gruslatic.

"It's nice to know, Castellan, but one will be enough."

"Won't be room to shit."

I break his nose this time, a fast, straight punch that puts him on his back.

"Have you got any more pointless shit to tell me, Castellan?" He groans.

"I can't hear you, love. Was there something more you had to tell me?"

He's quiet.

"Wonderful. Cal, let's get these soldiers down into the cells. Can you carry him that I put to sleep earlier?"

"Yes, Fieldsman." He smirks, pleased with seeing me punch Gruslatic flat.

There's cursing and spit aimed at us and the reds with me are happy to follow my lead and beat it out of them. I can see it's helping my reds to burn some of the dayer off on beating these militia. They're a sorry-looking lot now they're naked, cold and soaked. Cal leads us through the main doors of the tower and past the cook and servants, who watch us take them down to the dungeon. I see one of the servants is bound, a big man; perhaps he thought Cal was there to kill them all and so made a nuisance of himself. He's calm enough now.

The cell that I had been tortured in is empty, so we open it up and push them all in. As I'm doing it there's two that's prisoner in the next cell along tell me there's plenty of room for Gruslatic with them. I nod to Cal, who takes him and shuffles him along to the other door.

"Think about what you're doing," he says to me as he passes me, his words hard to make out with the blood in his nose and the swelling in his mouth.

"You'll have room to shit in this cell at least, Castellan."

"We'll take care of him, woman," says one of the prisoners in there. I see them both standing there, waiting. Whatever they did to end up in the tower, they look like a strong couple, though both have been worked on by Gruslatic or his guards, as he worked on me. They are bruised and cut, a heavy intensity as they see Gruslatic and a chance to get some revenge on him. Cal shoves him forward and they set on him quick. The iron door has a grille in it that means we can hear the sound of their fists and feet as they get to pay him back. There's shouting in the next cell, curses and threats, the militia coughing up the muke from the powders to shout harder at us.

"Best leave them a bucket of water in each cell," I say. "That way they'll last a bit longer. Might even live if anyone in the Spike can use a grapple like we did."

I don't care what anyone says, revenge is a good feeling;

it feeds like a leg of lamb or a plate of fried potatoes, it settles me. I run my tongue over the holes where my teeth were, the reminder sufficient to ease my mind as I walk back up the steps to the ground floor of the tower. The servants are still there.

"Well, I thank you for doing as Cal, my friend here, has bid you," I say to them. "Did you like your castellan? Did he treat you well?"

"Course he fuckin' didn't. Bastard always on at us for shit," says one of the younger ones. "An' always grabbin' me too, wavin' his bloody thing at me when I brings him his oats."

"Well him and his soldiers are locked up. You might push a bit of food through the bars in the doors in the coming days, but that's up to you. For now, if you'd like to fry us all something nice to eat you can have as much of it as you like."

"Thank you, miss. What's all this for? We thought you was here to kill us all."

"No, miss. A couple we had to, but Gruslatic is a traitor to the crown, so is Marghoster. We lock them up and we hope that one of Hildmir's high reeves will come down and do the king's justice."

"Got too greedy, did he, miss?"

"Is there a man that doesn't?"

I kneel before the man that Cal's bound up. "I'd like to cut your bonds, if you'll be happy to carry on and help serve up the food. Can you do it?"

He nods.

"You got a family?"

"I haven't. Would only come in for dawn otherwise."

"Well, if there's anyone in the town you love or care for, you should take some provisions from the shed at first light,

413

take them down to them. Same for all of you. We're doing some sharing out instead of it all being used on the rich that come to do their deals with your castellan."

There's a ripple of excitement through them. The routine has been broken and, while they might fall into line again with the next man to hold a whip to them, they give me the impression they'll take advantage as best they can until then. I cut the man's bonds, give him my arm so he can pull himself up.

"Who are you, miss?" says another of the men that's there.

"I am a fieldsman of the Post. I root out corruption in it. Here in the Spike its reeve Crejda and your castellan Gruslatic also have been corrupted by the Post's administrator, Stroff, and your lord Marghoster. He goes north now to overthrow King Hildmir and take the throne."

"Castellan told us that Marghoster's soldiers were marchin' north to fight the Sathanti."

"It's horseshit. They have already attacked and kidnapped Sathanti and Ososi these last six month or more. Marghoster's drudhas have used them, tortured them for their secrets, to make new fightbrews. I have seen it. One such drudha was sent captive to Autumn's Gate weeks ago, and will prove the truth of it."

"Why should any of us believe you? Post gets richer without a conscience," continues the giant that I'd freed of his bonds. "And grateful as we are for you sparing our lives and of those in the cells, you might well be clearing out any resistance here for a Sathanti army to come through. I've seen you here before: Gruslatic beat you, there was Ososi with you, though you don't much look it. They was callin' you Brother Red. You the one brought all those vans home?"

"She is," says Cal. "Saved a lot of lives, some you might even know."

"Might be I do. Hard for us to know what to believe when Gruslatic has you down as an enemy, and you chasing after Marghoster as a traitor yet saving the lives of his vanners. I'm sure you all know what you're doin'."

"She's showed us mercy, Furig, and has given us the run of the larder, so let's cook a feast as she's asked and get ourselves some sacks to fill." They head to the larder and kitchen to prepare us some food.

"When are we taking Crejda and her clearks prisoner?" asks Cal.

"We'll be there when they show up at the sheds. I need to get a fire going in the just, first, dry off. Can someone go get Bray and all, tell him I'm expecting an inventory of the lots." One of the reds with us gives a "Yes, Fieldsman," and he's gone out into the rain.

"Have a plan for tomorrow?" Candler this is, another of the reds that's come with me from the Spike's sheds.

"I don't, beyond getting Crejda and her crew put down in a cell. If you can commend a cleark to me that might keep the sheds going without making a fuss that'll help."

"Guthurin will; Crejda's never got on much with her nor she Crejda."

"Perfect. I expect without militia watching things some might turn up here wondering about it during the day, so I'll have you, Cal, dress up as a guard and making out Gruslatic has important work on. I'll go out then to meet Ufra's army, see what I can do to make sure they don't start killing."

"Your wen won't do that, would she?"

"Can't see she would; Ososi don't kill unless they have to. But if the Ilkashun are with her, we can't be sure. We need to get us provisions for a full field spread, be ready to go as soon as we can."

"Let me get my head down for a few hours then, Driw,

415

after I've had a bite to eat and got warmed up, assuming this dayer won't still be filling my blood for many more hours. Going to be a long day as it is."

"I know."

"We buryin' Skoler, Fieldsman?" asks Candler.

"What do they do with the dead here? We got guards and all that's been killed."

"Family takes them normally, militia'll call on those who knew the dead."

"You'll play militia tomorrow then. Dust the bodies, sack them up and find out from one of those servants where their kin might be. You got a busy day too, tomorrow."

"Yes, Fieldsman."

"You did well today, Candler, all of you that's joined me. You'll be commended to Yblas when I get to him."

"Dangerous road you're travelling, if you're wanted all over. Hope you do get to see Yblas, but if you don't I'm glad we done this. You seem to have us reds first in your thoughts, Fieldsman. Means a lot to us, even those that Bray couldn't talk into it."

"I appreciate that, Candler. Now find yourself some militia leathers. I'd help with the bodies but I very much need to see what Gruslatic's ledgers are like once I've got this fire going."

I am embarrassed by the cheer that greets me as I ride towards Ufra's army the second morning after our assault on the tower. There are about a thousand, as the two scouts had said, and they raise and shake their spears at me as I approach, horns blowing and battle cries filling the sky, loud enough to set birds in flight from the nearby trees. There's another cheer as I come alongside Ufra, who leaps from the back of her horse onto mine and puts her arms about me. The Master leads a song that's taken up by all of them and we are both stilled by the harmony and power of their voices combined. I cannot help but weep.

Leusla is here, Lodre as well, both wearing their crowns. Their armour, the armour of their horses, is ceremonial, though it's practical enough, and it gladdens me, for they do not mean war by such a display.

"I have missed you, Ufra-wen," Ufra whispers in my ear from behind me, kissing my cheek.

"And I you, Driwna-wen."

The Master whistles for a halt, to rest the horses. "What awaits us at the Spike?" he asks.

"Nokes. The militia and Gruslatic are in the jail below the tower, as is Crejda and her clearks for their part in the slavery."

"Our scouts told us you planned to make the Spike ready for us, that we wouldn't meet resistance."

"You won't. I hoped to save lives by doing so. But things are, sadly, much worse than we thought. I am here to beg you not to enter Farlsgrad. You no longer have such urgent need of it and I would spare your lives."

In the following hours we camp near the border of Farlsgrad and Leusla's Hidzuc lands. They tell me they had planned to salt fields, burn sheds, wagons, everything they could, to stall and weaken the invasion they expected from a Farlsgrad army. They have suffered too long, Ososi and Sathanti, and their chiefs that are here now could not preach caution or retreat, could not ask their people to swallow what they have suffered for fear it would only make Farlsgrad the bolder, greedier. I am glad to hear they had no plans for the nokes, but I hadn't expected they would. What stops them from continuing their ride into the Spike is my news about Litko, about the real reason for the army and the real power behind it.

"We do not doubt Driwna, but she speaks a truth that can hardly be believed for all that." Lodre Canendrigh this is, sitting with Leusla, their manner familiar but restrained before their soldiers and captains who sit with us, eating from their rations.

"I cannot make sense of why a magist would sink to the level of a warlord, would trouble themselves so much over something so fragile, so public as a throne. If this Litko has made miracles to ally Farlsgrad lords to him it must be to some end none of us here can see." The Master this is.

"He does not make himself king?" asks Leusla.

"What need has he of it? The things he can do . . ." The Master must recall the horror of the Almet, the killing of almost all of his tribe there by Scar and Litko.

"A man such as he might choose a bigger kingdom than Farlsgrad," says Ufra.

"He might put Marghoster on the throne," I say, "for he has not announced himself except through his miracles, and those were done quietly. This isn't a man seeking fame, as the Master says. He acts as an assistant to Stroff. Easier to influence others from the corners than to be standing full on to all in a kingdom."

"Driwna, whatever he plans, king or not, we cannot fight him. Not if there were ten thousand of us could we. This show of defiance of ours, it had some purpose; to make Farlsgrad think again. What do they now have to fear with a magist backing them?"

"What would we do otherwise, etza-Ososi?" says Lodre. "It seems to me we are defeated, we are dead, whether we fight or hide. Our course is right."

"Farlsgrad kills all of one kurch. Not all kurch together," says Leusla. "We find Council again, tell them of this Litko."

"She's right," says Lodre, "These soldiers with us cannot defend against a Farlsgrad army, but the Council can bring many more of us together. We can show them what we have done to fight Marghoster and those that have hunted and killed their kin as they have ours. It is all we can do."

The Master shakes his head but says nothing to this.

"You might go deep into the west," he says, "and your families live far from the border to this troubled land. You might take them south, for Ufra has told me what her father told Driwna, that Lorom Haluim might be found in the Hanwo'q Province."

Ufra puts her hand on his arm. "There is wisdom in all ways proposed," she says. "I cannot lead us south in the hope of finding a magist in what travellers say is the greatest forest in all the world, for we abandon our allies in the Sathanti Peaks on whom the ambitions of Marghoster would soon turn. Such a journey would take a year or more with no little risk to our survival from those who would shun our kind as so many in kingdoms about us do. We cannot retreat west either, for would our enemies not just follow us? No, my people must see me taking some measure of revenge, some punishment such as we plan to do. We reach the Spike this evening at a good canter, we will find the Marghoster sheds and lands and begin there, before we go to his own fort. We risk far less than you Sathanti, for we are few, and can make home in any forest."

"If Marghoster is king he will move on our land in seeking to clean his family's name, right the wrong that's ostracised him from court. We must bloody his nose before we flee, for the magist will come and our obedience will not spare us our lands." Lodre this is. He looks to Leusla.

"We wake Sathanti confederacies to roar. Litko cannot walk all roads. They see Hidzuc and Canendrigh and Ilkashun defy Farlsgrad, they remember."

419

The Creed calls for peace. How then can I support their action except to say that they did not break the peace, Litko did? I help the helpless. In that at least I'm comfortable. Can I be both Ososi and Post?

I start up my pipe as we all finish our food. Ufra leans in to me.

"But once that's done, Driwna, where then will we go?"

Chapter 20

Driwna

Their lives are spared and they resent us nevertheless. The sheds of the Brasks and Marghoster are emptied for them and they resent us nevertheless. We watch those sheds burn, those jetties and those boats of Marghoster's, of Gruslatic's. We burn their crops and no others, salt their fields and no others.

At night the Spike is alive with the hollering and rioting of men who cannot accept the Sathanti here, do not care for their suffering, only that they are invading their land. I understand this, for they do not know the plans of their masters, the suffering they have inflicted and will go on to inflict. There are cries for Gruslatic, for what is familiar. Stalls and sheds are smashed, looting in the dark, the usual hypocrisy. But in the days that follow, those merchants who did not wrong the Hidzucs, the Ilkashun, the Ososi and those last few Oskoro form a council at the table where we parleyed those few months ago, beneath which Crejda, Gruslatic, their clearks and militia still howl and cry out their curses, not yet ready to parley again, despite the mounting stink that requires a brazier of incense stay lit at the door to the stair-well down.

The merchants and those who suffered Gruslatic's corruption are quick to point out his gangers, those who would plot to bring him back and along with that the purses and status they had become used to. The gangers' houses are then looted, they are sent naked into the fields to find a life elsewhere. So, Gruslatic's empire is broken.

It is here, in these gatherings, that Cal is afire. He has a knack for finding the right side of someone and I have marvelled at his work these days we have sought to set up this council to share Marghoster's wealth and decide the fate of Gruslatic. They respect me well enough for what I did in bringing back the vans from the Sathanti, and word of the Lindur Twelve has also travelled. They are cowed by the Master of Flowers and his great Flower of Fates, his plant. Some shrink in terror and whisper rhymes of deference and protection, others beg him for alms, and he has given it them and done much to soften the opinion of those fearing escalation of our revenge. Cal it is brings good reason to them, and he would make a fine High Red, a leader every bit as charismatic as Yblas.

We leave the Spike for the Marghoster estate. The handful of merchants, allied with the craftsmen and others of good standing, may do with the place, and their prisoners, as they see fit. I have the cloaks of Crejda and her clearks, their seals as well. The Post will need to begin again there and the reds that helped me are now promoted and will have to thrive on their wits to make a success of it.

It is on the road east to the Marghoster fort that I'm taken ill. My skin peels, the itching enough to make me weep. Not even Cal can cheer me. The Master and Ufra tell me that I have started the season of thorns. I have felt the vine growing in me, changing the shape of my arms, pushing at the skin. I have felt weak and strong even at different times of the day as it knits itself more and more into my body. The fresh skin is hairless, a mustard colour like Ufra's that is less sensitive to the touch. It feels thicker, somehow, like chewed leather, and the sharpest pains are, naturally, where the thorns begin to push through it. I cannot be without my leathers, like Ufra can. Instead I cut away the stitching and make my surcoat looser.

While I struggle with my body's changes, I am made to rest on the wagons on the way to the Marghoster fort. Within three days of the army arriving there all the fields are burned and salted, all the tenants made to load their own wagons and leave. His militia attempt a resistance, thirty soldiers in all, though as they see the army around them, rather than the bandits they had expected now that Marghoster and his levy of soldiers had gone north, they lay down their arms and leave the walls to the Marghoster fort. There's none can really resist an army without themselves having fightbrews, or even daybrews, and no nokes can drink and eat such things and survive long without first the weaning onto them and then the training to manage them. We help ourselves to all we can use before we burn everything else in the fort, everything Marghoster might value that we do not need. I have carried the Marghoster name for a long time. To pull down and burn the Marghoster's herald on our final evening there is a more savage pleasure than I had anticipated. I think of my pa as it happens. I can't help that.

Under Marghoster war banners, hooded and cloaked in his colours, our Sathanti army readies itself to ride the Fifth, one of the main stone roads that link the borders of Farlsgrad to its capital. Others were going north; mercenaries, merchants seeing profits from what the bigger Marghoster army would need, as well as from the nokes from which that army would take too much.

It takes some debate to decide what we should do now revenge has been taken on Marghoster and his lands. It is seven days' ride to Cathrich Valley, the lands of Lord Cathrich, one who has received the miracles of Litko and in return has furnished him provisions and soldiers. Cathrich Valley is near the heart of Farlsgrad, though its capital is further north on the coast. If they have also gone north to Hildmir's lands or to the Gate, we could strike a further blow to Farlsgrad before returning and heading back into the Sathanti.

We ride to the Messenger's Lodge a day north of Marghoster's fort on the Fifth. It is the Post's main stables for our vans and fast riders all over the south-west of Farlsgrad. We find they have had all provisions taken by the forged order of Rogus, releasing at cost anything Marghoster's army would need. There's six reds there and they're wide-eyed at the sight of who it is I'm travelling with.

After we've made camp outside the lodge, we're sat at a fire, the Master, Cal, Bray, Ufra, Leusla, Lodre and I. One of the lodge's reds comes to me as we get in our pipes.

"May I speak with you, Fieldsman?" he says. He gestures that it be done privately.

"You may speak before us all here, I have no secrets from these. What's your name, red?"

"It's Liskre, lady, I mean, Fieldsman." He's young, can't have long got his cloak.

"Your first posting, here?"

"Aye, Fieldsman."

"Are you enjoying it?"

"It's coin. Better than being wi' my brothers down the mines or breaking stone in the Cathrich quarries."

"It is that. You hear the Creed?"

"I read it, Fieldsman, I have my letters, which I'm grateful to the Post for. Makes sense, don't it?"

"It does. What is it you have for me?"

He hands me a letter, Yblas's seal.

"How did you come by this?"

"There are reds all over the Gate and on the Wheel that are loyal to Amaris, that know the Creed and that what you do takes care of 'em." He smiles as he sees me smile. "I can see you're loyal to her an' all. One of ours got this out o' the Gate and down to me just before the army come through o' that spimrag Marghoster. I don't know what that's all about, but it's no good, is it? Our cleark here is Stroff's man, so don't speak too much o' your plans when you're around him. We were told to watch out for you, Fieldsman. That you're needed." With a clasp of arms he's gone, back to the small lodge in the midst of the stables.

The seal's intact. I read the note out.

FD,
   Curic and Ensma are here. Drudha told everything.
   Proud of you. Y warned. We go to Hillfast.
      A.

I cuss, for I don't know what the drudha might have known of Litko, so Amaris may not be aware of the danger. Curic and Ensma took the drudha north before Litko showed me who he truly is.

"Driwna?" Ufra this is, puts her hand on my arm. "You're angry."

"Curic and Ensma may be trapped at Autumn's Gate. Amaris too. She's someone I care a lot about. She was mine and Cal's teacher, made us believe we could make a difference to the world and gave me this seal, this title to prove it. Without her I'd have not been able to do any of the things I've done."

"You won't leave them there," she says.

"I can't. I had hoped to put the Cathrich fort and its fields to burn, as we have Marghoster's, before leaving to go west with you," I say.

"I had hoped that, too." She finds my hand with hers and lifts it to her lips, to kiss my fingertips. She's not looking at me, she's in her thoughts, coming to terms with this moment as I am.

The Master claps his hands together, makes a sound that almost passes for a chuckle. "It is clear. As it must be and as it is meant to be. Driwna, I will try to explain. Yesterday, you, Cal and Bray drilled the Sathanti soldiers. Ufra and I watched you. Cal, you would make them all laugh as they worked. When the laughter died off, all eyes would be on Driwna as you showed them forms for balance and strength. I took Ufra's hand, asked her to close her eyes, then continue watching."

Ufra smiles. "I didn't understand what he meant by it but he shushed me and I followed your voice, Driwna, and the sounds of leather cracking, the panting of the soldiers tiring, Cal's worksong. I heard nothing else. And he knew that I would hear nothing else. All else had gone still. All else."

"The Song waits, Driwna," says the Master. "It waits for us because we are conducting this part of its melody. We shape something bigger here. And yesterday I could not read that silence, could not tell whether it meant we must go west or have more here to do. This letter brings us together in a way, for now I must go north."

"You speak of this letter as though it is fate, not ill fortune." Ufra this is.

"It is not fate, Ufra. We have a choice of how best to lift

426

the Song to the ears of all, and this letter, what is in Driwna's heart, it strengthens our chorus."

"I don't understand why you must go north, Master," I say. "You, of all of us, have most to protect, and no good can come of confronting Litko."

"I have pondered the plans of this magist. He will pursue us still when we run west, as we have to. Scar will still serve him, the only servant he has that can track us. He hunts Ososi and the last of us Oskoro. None have lived to whom he might have revealed why. The Oskoro he has killed all of, bar the handful that have been so loved and welcomed by all of your families and kurches. He killed my daughter, our future Master, and when I sing for all of the Oskoro I sing also of you, Driwna, you who heard her singing for the light and brought her to it. She found a home here." He lays his giant hand against my chest. "Her longing became yours, colouring your breath, drawing you back to her in the mountains like salmon to the spring of their river. There are no more Oskoro after me. None can take the alkaest now. With my passing we will become Ososi. And we can only become that if Scar dies. My song joins with yours, Driwna, to Autumn's Gate."

'The world shall listen, I am sure of it," says Cal.

"If we should take this letter as our guide and go to the Gate, I fear it," I say. "If Litko is there, we cannot fight him. I bring death to my kurch, my mun, all the sooner if he sees me. But to do otherwise is to abandon those I have a duty to."

"It be why your ma an' pa made that sacrifice, miss, sent you to save your Ufra," says Bray, "an' it seems the doin' of it means finishing this Scar, as the Master wants."

"Stroff will see Amaris dead. It might be Yblas is in danger, for all that she's sent him warning. All of us need a man like

427

Yblas running the Post, not Stroff, not Litko." It seems to me then that this might be Litko's plan all along, already being, in appearance, a high reeve to Stroff.

"Driwna, none can fight Litko," says Ufra. "But why must the fight be with him? Is it not also important that the people of Farlsgrad know this Litko, know that a magist means them harm? There may be a way to draw him out of the shadows, stop him from working in the way he would prefer."

"Who would care when he heals the sick? They would fucking rejoice in his alliance with Farlsgrad," I say.

"Would they? Their new king a puppet? Put on the throne but powerless, a mouthpiece for a magist?"

"They still wouldn't care as long as wagons rolled and plants grew and cattle could feed. They are a different people to the Ososi or even Sathanti; they are ruled by kings and lords, woven in place and expectation so firmly they cannot see how to change the pattern of the tapestry that binds them."

"You did," says the Master.

"I had Amaris. I got my letters and learned. Few here have such a chance. The people of Farlsgrad hated us Bridche all our lives anyway. We have always been outsiders." I put my arm around Ufra, hold her as the chill of the night soaks my skin. "I can't let such a wrong as he is doing be. If I cannot put word out to the Post over the Sar, everywhere, that Litko is a magist, that he has overthrown a king's rule, as he surely will, then not only will Farlsgrad suffer, all kings and chiefs would fear that they were next to fall through the inscrutable plans of a man such as he. My heart bids me go north, Ufra, to help Amaris who has asked for me, to help Curic and Ensma, who I have sent there."

"This is the truth of your heart and I would have that before anything. We shall go to Autumn's Gate."

"You'll get nowhere without a Rulger, Marghoster filth."

"Or a fat old man prone to a bit o' weeping," says Bray.

I can't speak to this, for they've answered my dearest wish.

"What would you have us do, Brother Red?" asks Lodre.

"I won't have you come and die with me, Daith-nu Canendrigh, Daith-nu Hidzuc. I wouldn't have these along either but I cannot persuade them otherwise. You are leaders of confederacies that need you more than ever, they cannot lose you all so soon after losing Yicre and Eirakh. We will burn the Cathrich fort, then you must take this army back, prepare your people for the retaliation that will come. Take back the Ososi, the Oskoro. If we can kill Scar then they might live in peace and prosper once more. Protect what we've won for as long as you can."

They look to the Master and Ufra, as they should, for I am no leader of a people.

"She is right," says Ufra. "I belong with her, she is Ufra-wen. My people must not die because of it. Scar must be killed and the duty falls on no other of my kin."

"I tell my soldiers what we do," says Leusla, getting to her feet. "Sillindar follow you, Driwna. He watch." Lodre stands with her and they leave the camp to meet with their captains.

I feel Ufra's attention on my skin, snagging my thoughts. I need to be alone with her. "Walk with me, Driwna-wen."

As we walk away from the fire into a still, clear night they burst out laughing behind us at something Cal's said and it brings a smile to my face.

"Our last days burn brightest, Ufra-wen. Your thorns know this, I think, seeking the sun while they may, for my own thorns are likewise. We go to our end, my wen, and I would have it no other way."

I want to disagree with her, but the world overwhelms my senses more fiercely than it ever did when facing soldiers in battle. I feel these changes in my body speak to that world, a sound below my hearing, a contract, an alliance of milk and blood. I bring Ufra into my arms as though at another's will, an undertow making a puppet of me. We surrender to its unspoken necessity, fighting for breath, falling.

Chapter 21

The Magist

A warm spring day brings out the crowds, perfect for the hangings and the announcement of a new form of rule in Farlsgrad, a senate, no less, one they laughably intend will bring prosperity that not even the lords of Jua, wealthiest of all men alive, could countenance. These are the glass trinkets the Lord Marghoster's speech is cutting to yield the brightest shine, illuminating the many failings and corruptions of King Hildmir; his cronies, his taxes, his immoral wealth.

Order is not yet restored since my soldiers stormed the streets of Autumn's Gate. How can it be while the bodies of Hildmir's militia are still warm outside the South Gate? Our soldiers, so effective in combat, find themselves incapable of a proportionate response to the hostility of the innocent and ignorant who are even now testing their degraded patience in pockets of defiance in the slums and wharfs; filthy warrens of alleys and passageways that isolate and make vulnerable our savage peacekeepers. Such resistance has cost the slums greatly, our soldiers are wonderfully fearsome killers, but the fire of their rebellious ambition is stoked by our brutality and they remain burning as this new order is born. Marghoster must weed them out swiftly in the coming weeks and months.

None here in the main square care much for anything beyond food, fucking and a good hanging, and if it be their king, all the better an excuse to forgo their duties to watch it and pick over the proceedings for weeks afterwards. Beyond the crowd standing in this square, sitting on the roofs of the buildings and hanging from the shutters overlooking the gallows, the merchants guard their sheds while the gangers, the poor and those with vendettas are taking their chances.

The Lord Marghoster stands on the dais that raises up each of the cross-posts in view of all. Behind him King Gardru Hildmir's head is bowed, while the queen looks coldly upon us all. Their children's heads are also in nooses, one daughter shivering with fear, the other daughter weeping quietly, her louder sobs having attracted the fist of one of Marghoster's guards standing behind her. His youngest, his son, has a hood over his head, his britches wet with piss, which caused a roar of delight when it was noticed the moment they put his neck in the noose. All the while they were being prepared their mother spoke to them, words we could not hear, but they obeyed as best they could, hoping their obedience could somehow facilitate their safety.

The king glances at me from time to time. He was useful in his way, but he was losing the people, as Marghoster is currently outlining to the gathered crowd, losing too the support of the guilds and the Post. The Post is the key tool at my disposal. Its promotion here will give me the wealth I need to push its efforts further west and south into Khasgal and deep into the Sathanti Peaks in search of the Ososi that remain. Lorom Haluim has consorted with them and they remain key to finding him, one of the few that remain of Sillindar's so-called Travellers in all the known worlds. One of the few that could lead us to Sillindar itself.

I have taken my place in the line of men standing in the front row before the gallows, our new militia forming a line that separates us from the mob behind, who are cowed into near silence by the demeanour of my soldiers, for these are the most successful of our experiments, the plants having been grafted onto them to great effect. I stand next to Stroff, of course, and along from him are the Lords Cathrich and Stalder, with Marghoster's wife at the end. The lords are in their cere-monial armour, chestplates more a girdle for their bellies than protection. To my right are the line of merchants that join the Post in backing this coup, all hoping to be enriched as founders of the new senate. They too are in their finest robes, though such woollens, furs and jewellery are causing many to sweat and curse under their breaths at this unseasonably fine day.

As I watched King Hildmir, his queen and children get dragged out of their palace here in Autumn's Gate after we overran it, I stopped briefly to admire it. The palace is on a secluded crescent-shaped shelf in the cliff that stands high over the South Gate, commanding a view of the port and ocean that is said to rival the very finest of any palace either side of the Sar. The would-be senators argued about nothing so much as what use the great house might be put to. Marghoster sought my counsel on legislation that might put it into his family's hands. I despise such grasping, particularly when I am proposed to back it up. I must confess that I harbour a desire to have some rooms of my own adjacent to the great stone terraces that overlook the port. It should be a fitting venue for when my allies in the Accord meet here to plan what more we can do to lure Lorom Haluim out.

I went northwest to the Hildmir estate before we came to Autumn's Gate and we routed his soldiers there, as expected. They had no real warning, no time to gather from the settle-ments all over his lands and forests. They mustered a thousand that we engaged in the fields around his castle. It took a few hours at best before we were inside the castle walls and the soldiers were given the freedom to do what victorious soldiers like to do best.

Hildmir was not there, but most of his wealth was. Years of increases in taxes on trade and his people had paid for an opulence none of the other lords had seen since all audiences were held at the Gate, being easier for all to reach via the roads of the Wheel. Such wealth – in herds, in paintings, friezes and sculptures that were artistically lumpen in both conception and execution – was displayed with pride there, galleries in purpose-built halls full of it.

A statue of Gardru Hildmir, last of his line now, stood in the courtyard in front of the main steps into his castle's central tower. It compensated for so much he lacks. When I do not refo into the likenesses of other people, I choose a fairly diminutive appearance to better serve me, and he still does not match up to it. There's a proud belly on thin legs that a lazy life has given him and I found it nowhere on that statue. I saw also a painting of his father, Feidlic, curse of the Marghoster family for his appeasement of the Sathanti army he was fooled into believing would overrun them. It showed a mighty man standing over the obeisant Sathanti warlords he had defeated.

The follies of Kristuc and Lidic before him were similarly glorified, but all of them had drenched Farlsgrad in the blood of their neighbours and their own, the Marghoster army most of all. I had been to this palace many times while refo'd as Stroff. It was a long-anticipated pleasure to see the outrage on Marghoster's face when he confronted how much grander a few successions' worth of taxes can make a life.

To his credit, Yeismic Marghoster felt strongly that the monarchy should be brought down, that a more democratic solution was the key to prosperity. Yet a democracy that favours him is flavouring his mood, especially now such speeches as I am enduring here in the main square at Autumn's Gate have given him a taste of the fame that mortals so often confuse with power.

As Marghoster lays out the charges against Hildmir, the exploitation of his people in pursuit of his wealth, the need for all of Farlsgrad to have a say in governance, he glows with the cheers.

There are others to be hanged today, enemies of the new senate that would harm its formation. Few here know Amaris, and the merchants I line up with will be pleased she can no longer outsmart them. Stroff is almost licking his lips at the thought of seeing her drop. The young Driwna's accomplices are here also for the noose. They completed the remarkable feat of bringing one of our drudhas from the Sathanti mountains all the way here to be interrogated by Amaris. I hadn't met this drudha, I doubt he'll have revealed me to her, though all our other plans will have been shared I'm sure. Amaris shows no sign of recognising me as anything more than High Reeve Litko as she herself waits for the noose.

Finally, his speeches done to a diminishing, impatient cheer, Marghoster stands to the side solemnly, triumphantly. The guards behind each noose step forward and take hold of the boxes on which the doomed are standing. As always, the executioner steps up onto the dais, on the furthest end to Marghoster, and he raises his iron staff to cheers from behind me. They sense history being made and I have always enjoyed the stillness in those moments before the new course irrevocably begins. Here, the staff strikes the dais three times on a piece of iron over a deep hole, made to help the striking rod reverberate theatrically. He makes us wait between each strike. As the third strike is made the guards pull the boxes on which the convicted stand sharply back and the line of Hildmir, the monarchy itself in Farlsgrad, ends with their desperate writhing and the huge roar laced with the vile, imaginative curses of their subjects.

Amaris is dragged up the steps next, followed by three that get both cheers and curses from enemies and sympathisers alike. Marghoster announces them each in turn. This woman, he says of Amaris, had sought to warn Hildmir of the coming coup, sought to keep this good and patriotic crowd in the awful squalor that suited the king. An angry roar greets this accusation. The others alongside her are gangers, long known to do Hildmir's grubby work as enforcers, the last of them earning the crowd's particular ire as a quite brutal tax collector. It is as I'm thinking about who must be invited to the palace that evening that I notice the two of Driwna's crew waiting their turn at the base of the steps look at each other in surprise, then look at Amaris. She gazes up above the crowd, and I am about to turn and look, for she does not seem lost in thought; rather, she is concentrating on something. Then I see her fingers moving, though her wrists are tightly bound behind her. She's signalling to Driwna's accomplices. Then looks at them. Of the two, the older man, Curic his name, turns about so she can see his own signals from his bound hands, the guard next to him oblivious, caught up in the spectacle. When I look back to Amaris she is staring at me, no, at Stroff. She's smiling as the arrow appears in his head, standing proudly from his cheek, flecking me with blood. Then the screaming begins.

Chapter 22

Driwna

We leave the main road of the Fifth to climb up to the west gate of Autumn's Gate. The early chill has melted into a warm day. As we ascend we look down on the main road as it leads into the South Gate, a high stone wall built against the cliff and running down to the sea's edge. Outside it, beyond the ditch and deadland we see the pavilions and tents, the bodies, hear the laughter and cheering of soldiers at camp. The Sar, glittering wide and blue, fills the east, and the wind blowing off it brings more distant shouting from the port itself. A line of wagons snakes back from the South Gate, people trying to leave the port, protect what they own, traders not wishing to get caught up in the chaos of the coup.

Fifty soldiers wearing the green and black of Marghoster are camped at this gate above the Four Stairs, ten or so of whom are discussing the bribes that apply to the vans looking to leave for the plains, many well-dressed families sitting among their possessions, the families of the merchants who would be looking to profit from Marghoster's rule in the coming weeks, reducing their risk should he go against them.

We are in our red cloaks, for the Post has, apparently, supported this coup. I do not even need to show my seal as we approach, since we look field-worn, muddied, unprofitable. We are waved through into the Gate. The Master had fashioned a wooden circlet that will protect the Flower in his braegnloc when covered in a hood until we get into the city, when there can be no more hiding.

There are reds about the gates to the Posthouse and guards at the steps to all the other fine houses here on the Four Stairs.

"Is Administrator Stroff here?" I ask them.

"He's at the hanging. Bastard's made us miss it."

"Everyone's at the hanging, lady; get down there before one of the clearks gives you orders," says another.

"The High Reeve? Litko?"

"He's with him."

We dismount. The horses will be no good in the streets and alleys.

"They hang the king today then?"

"They do, best hurry or you'll miss it. The mid-day's when they'll do it I heard."

"Stable these horses then, they're from the South Cathrich Posthouse."

"You can stable them yer fuckin' self, lady."

The other one that spoke to us leans into him then, whispering. He nods at the words, then steps forward, and I sense Bray and Cal do the same behind me.

"She'll hang, Fieldsman. Save Amaris," he whispers. He turns then to the others standing about at the gate. "Come on, let's have a few of you get these horses fed, watered and stabled."

438

My crew strip down what they ne‹
and check each other's straps.

"I'll prepare your skin and give you my bi‹
down the hill, away from so many," says the Ma‹
speaking to us all, for his skin rubs to protect us from p‹
cuts and spores are peerless.

"We'll split at the square," I say. "Once the Master's hood
comes off, and Ufra's, I don't know how it will go. Cal and
Ufra will get to roofs, Bray will wait at the main lane into
the square. The Master and I will try and get close to the
gallows. Amaris'll be under guard there, as might Curic and
Ensma, who must hang with her I'm sure. We got weapons
and belts for them?"

"Aye, miss," says Bray.

"What else are you carrying, Bray?" I ask. He looks like
a packhorse, big flasks hanging from the loops on his chest
belt along with the rolled-up belts for Curic and Ensma. A
small shield's strapped to his left arm.

"Besides their belts, there's a few things I learned useful
under the Goose for such work among buildings, and oil for
settin' fires is one of 'em. I's not such a light step to be
climbin' about, anyway."

"Give me their belts, you've got enough."

"Grateful to, miss."

"Post lingo once we can all see each other about the square.
Ufra, you'll have to take Cal's lead. Sillindar follow us, unless
he happens to be that fucker Litko by another name."

The whole of the Gate seems to be in the main square and
about it. Cal has been patiently signalling to Amaris from
high on the roof of a three-storey building, finding a vantage
there for the hanging. I can't see Bray or Ufra, but he can.
Cal has signed that Ufra is on a roof to his left and Bray is

...dge of a lane leading out of the square over to our right. They will have sporebags and will be hoping to channel the crowd towards us by putting the bags down left and right. Cal has signed that Amaris will be hanged, Curic and Ensma are also surrounded by guards, waiting their turn for the noose. The Master's blood rises in us; we drank well as we embraced before splitting up.

The Master and I stand at one end of an alley crowded with spectators. Guards block off the far end of the alley next to the dais. This is the closest the Master will get without drawing comment, as all eyes are on the square. We'll use this crowd when it's panicking to hide us, as it'll be the only way Amaris, Curic and Ensma can run.

Cal signs that he sees Stroff before the dais. He cannot see Litko nor waste time signing to Amaris to tell her of Litko's true nature. I doubt she knows yet of Litko's significance anyway. Cal focuses his signing on letting her know where I'm waiting and what we're about to do. I sign to Cal that we must at least kill Stroff if we can, damage Litko's secrecy, force him to find another to ally with. Then there's a hush, the crack of the executioner's iron rod, once, twice, thrice in the silence. I start to push through the crowd. Hildmir and his family drop; there's cheering, feet thumping on floorboards and shouting in the square and buildings around us that edge it as those leaning out of shutters watch the end of Farlsgrad's monarchy.

The air sharpens as I rise on the Master's blood. Cal unshoulders his bow, though he's holding a big sporebag in his right hand. The bodies of Hildmir and his family writhe and fall still amid the shouting and cheering. A couple on the roof near Cal glance at him but think no more of it, perhaps seeing just more guards looking to keep order. I can sense everything now, the smell of the Master behind me is a summer field

440

and before us there are the sour currents of rotting teeth and fish, wet leather, sweat-soaked wool, bacca, as vivid as my sight. I pick out Marghoster's words as I do the whispers of the whores in the rooms above me, the duts crying, the market callers in the streets around us, the bawdy songs coming from broken voices echoing about the lanes here.

Cal signs that he's going to kill Stroff, then cut down Amaris at the rope, the latter a master's shot on any other brew. I sign for the sporebags to go on the executioner's count of one before he shoots.

I can't see Amaris get led up to the noose with the others. I hear the jeering, the crowd in full voice now with the excitement of the sudden change in their history. Marghoster speaks, denouncing her. Cal takes an arrow from his quiver. I look back to the end of the alley and nod to the Master, who removes his hood, cloak and the circlet protecting the Flower. There's a gasp from those around us, a couple of nokes step back from him. He begins deep breathing, his great chest filling, forcing his heart to beat faster, his blood to empower him further. The executioner strikes the dais. Bray and Ufra will take their cue from Cal. Cal throws his sporebag down into the crowd below him, then nocks an arrow. He shoots, the first for Stroff, the second for Amaris. Screaming erupts, choking and coughing following. I'm sorry for those that might die from the spores, but there's no painless way of overcoming the odds and the fuckers stacked against us. I run forward, pushing through the nokes and into the guards at the end of the alley, who form up as they sense something's wrong.

"I need to move the prisoners!" I shout at them. I've got colour, belts and leathers, my red cloak, more than that I'm risen on something finer than any fightbrew. "Amaris cannot escape!" They don't question me, looking about instead for their captain, unable to act on their own initiative.

Cal drops back off the roof as those alongside him shout for the guards, seeing what it is he's done. The chaos drowns them out. Ufra, Bray and Cal's sporebags have forced the crowd together and the instinct of it soon targets our alley as planned. I see the guard who has the keys to the prisoners' chains. I force the guards about me out of the way. "You, the keys; I have to lead these prisoners out of that alley before we lose them in this mob!"

He hesitates. "Now, man!"

"What authority?" says his captain. He's in his ceremonial, his rank on an embroidered epaulette, a Farlsgrad soldier; he won't know me as a red.

"Stroff's. Don't fuck with me, this bitch will escape." He looks at the crowd now surging at the line as Marghoster's fierce, misshapen soldiers start killing to force the mob back. I have only moments before Litko is on us, looking for these guards to help get him out of the alley.

The captain pulls the keys off the guard that's holding them, gives them to me.

"Captain, I'm Marschal Crejda. Come with me."

"Yes, Marschal."

A moment later I'm before the three of them, my heart pounding to see them alive, dreading that Litko will see us now. Amaris keeps her head bowed, the severed rope still about her neck. Curic and Ensma have the sense to do the same.

"Move, you traitorous bastards! Captain, follow behind." I lead them away from the dais, shove the swelling crowd aside with my free hand, this giddy strength pushing men and women into the walls, my spear forcing more of them to press themselves to the stone or run ahead of us. It is a shock for them to see a soldier risen on a brew, never mind this brew. I can't see the Master, he must be beyond the end

442

of the alley. I drag Amaris out into the street beyond, turn right, push her against the wall. The Master stands there. The captain pulls Curic by his shirt into the street, Ensma, chained to him following I test the keys on Amaris's manacles. The captain has only a moment to stare up at the Master before he's pulled close as though in an embrace, run through with a knife. There's a surge of people in full flight now from the alley's mouth, running left and right around us. I find the right key to free Amaris, Curic and Ensma from their manacles. The Master cuts the gag from Amaris. She stares up at him in wonder, tears filling her eyes.

"Oh, Driwna!" she gasps, embracing me but unable to take her eyes off him.

"There's an inn, Amaris, the Second Lady, we're heading there to meet with Ufra, Cal and Bray. I hope you've got us some way of getting out of this port!"

"I have, Driwna, a boat meant to take me to Hillfast before I was arrested. We must head there and ready it after we've met up with those two of your crew."

"We should split up, Driwna," says the Master. "There'll be enough chatter about me that the guards and Scar will surely follow."

"You're right," I say. "The Master and I must head for the Second Lady, meet with the others. You take Ensma and Curic to the boat, they'll protect you." I take up the spare fieldbelts on the ground next to the Master and pass them out.

"Agreed, Fieldsman," says Amaris. "Take a route down to the South Quays from the Lady, then along the front to the north quay. Post has a jetty there, *Efne's Grace* is the boat, a fifty-foot knar, single red sail. I don't know what to say but thank you."

I'm about to tell her of the danger we're in when we hear the shouts of guards from along the alley, a horn sounding to move the nokes swarming about us aside. Amaris can see I've much I wish to say, puts her hands on my shoulders.

"We'll talk later. Sillindar save us," she says. Amaris kisses me before leading Ensma and Curic away. We join the flow of people leaving the alley and running down the cobbled street in the opposite direction. We pass a tavern, a fight underway inside, and it draws some of the crowd around us towards it. We pass dockers' houses shuttered and bolted but for the upstairs, families watching us. The Master is drawing eyes and comment as the crowd thins; it can't be helped, we cannot finish this without him. The street slopes upwards and there are deckhands here in a circle giving a beating to two militia stupid enough not to strip out of Hildmir's colours. There's a moment they think they'll try their luck with us that dies in a breath as they see we're brewed up, as they see the Master and his strange loping run. The street's long, gentle rise brings us to the doorway to the Second Lady Inn. It was further than I remembered from the square, though the run was little trouble on the Master's blood. As we stop outside the inn the Master looks back down the lane, sniffs the air.

"Get in!" he hisses.

The Second Lady, named after Teyr Amondsen I know now, is a regular hole for reds working our shed and berths on the dockside. I've got in my cups a few times here in years past, and I recall we have a nook – a private room for Post sailors and workers – at the back of the building. We have to squeeze through the crowd looking to be served at the kegs, but as soon as the Master ducks through the doorway there's a hush and we get the barkeep's attention.

"Who's in the nook?" I ask, for I'm in my cloak for all that I'm with an Oskoro.

The barkeep's an old man, doesn't flinch at the sight of

444

us. "There's a few in the nook I'd normally say you'd leave alone, but . . ."

"Thank you. There'll be three more looking for us, two are reds, one old, heavy-set, the other tall."

"I'll send 'em through."

We push through some younger deckhands at dice around a narrow table and along a short corridor past a stack of kegs to the door to the nook. There's nine in there, air thick with smoke, cheap bacca, some kannab. Two of the bigger men stand as I walk in.

"Private," says one that's sitting down, boot up on the table. He's cold, meaning he's not on a brew or dayer.

"It is private, for Post, and you're not wearing the red, so you'll have to get out to the main room."

He's about to say more when he's nudged, and all their eyes are drawn to where the Master has entered the room behind me. It silences any further lip and they edge past us, some openly fearful of the Master, the others feeling the heat of me, realising I'm on a fightbrew.

I shut the door behind them. "Fucking gangers."

There's three benches here, a large table. Across the room from the door is an open shutter that looks out onto the lane beyond and a house opposite.

"I'll keep a look out this way," I say, leaning out of the shutters to look about.

"Anyone?"

"Empty." There's something on the air, though, a pinch of something not being right, doors slamming further along the lane.

"You are troubled, Driwna."

"If I flowed with the Song as you do I might read it better."

"We cannot stay long, you feel the storm that follows us."

"What if we don't find Scar?" I say. I look back at him,

standing against the door, eyes closed in concentration.

"He will come. The soldier I killed back there will waggle many tongues, and the moment my flower is mentioned Scar will have no other goal than to find me."

"He fled you in the camp."

"He has this Litko now. I will draw them away from you all when the time comes, Ufra-wen." He looks over at me then, knows that reminding me of Ufra stops any further argument.

"You cannot withstand Litko."

"Only Lorom Haluim could. But we all die, Driwna; all that matters is how we improve the Song."

He steps back from the door. "They have come."

The door opens and Ufra leads Cal and Bray in. They're all breathing heavily. The noise of the inn's main serving room has returned.

"Ufra!" I leave the window, jump over the back of the bench and around the table to embrace her. She hugs me fiercely, then I see Cal's bleeding, a gash on his cheek. Bray's standing in the doorway bent over, hands on his knees, fighting for breath, blood on his head and spattered over his leathers.

"Not sure if we brought trouble to you or not," says Cal.

"There be flappin' gums out there about this big man," says Bray. "We have to move quick as we can." He straightens himself, turns to the door and closes it enough to spy beyond into the serving room.

"You are alive," says Ufra. She pulls Cal into our embrace. He kisses us both; none of us can speak.

"Driwna!" Bray this is. The storm has come. "Two soldiers just come in the way we did. Spears, brewed."

I hear a shutter creak open across the lane from us.

"Masks!" I shout, for I see the air is coloured with the

wisps of spores there. Our training is as ingrained as instinct, pulling the masks from around our necks up onto our faces, tying them tight at the back of our heads.

"Run!" hisses the Master. He leaps across the table to the window a fraction too late; an arrow whips past his nose by an inch, hits the table, a splash of thick oil. He pushes the shutter closed as another arrow hits it. I can smell it, fire.

"We split, front and back," I say. "Head for the north quay, a boat called *Efne's Grace*."

The Master looks up at the ceiling suddenly, sniffs the air. "Scar is here," he says. "Ufra, Driwna, with me."

He opens the door and strides out into the main room, bringing a hush to it. There's steps up to the first floor, behind the row of kegs at the main bar. I follow him up the stairs, Ufra behind me. Bray and Cal walk warily out of the main door to the inn. I glance behind me and see the two soldiers Bray alerted us to, standing at the bar. They look away quickly, but not quickly enough. At least they didn't follow Bray and Cal out.

Just as the Master gets to the top of the stairs he stops, stiffens. I hear the creak of a floorboard. He twists back as Scar jumps at him from a doorway on our left, burying a knife in his shoulder. They fall back against the opposite wall. I leap the final steps between us as Scar stabs again, but the Master jerks away, the knife punching into the wall. Scar grabs the Master by the belt loops at his chest, turns him between us as I get to the top step. Boots on the slate roof; three, four pairs above our heads. Scar knows he's fighting for his life as the Master grapples with him, but his brew is strong, there's no fear as there was in the quarry and he is equally gigantic and fearsome as the Master now. There's no way past them, no way to get at Scar for a moment. The Master grunts as Scar's thumb finds the knife wound and digs in. He twists to give my sword an opening, sensing me there at his back. Scar reads it too quickly, jumping back along the corridor, sucking the blood on his thumb and smiling. Boots on the steps behind us, Ufra turns, dodges spear thrusts, then throws herself down the steps onto the soldier there. There's barely a cry before her sword's in the first of them.

More soldiers drop in from the roof through the window of the room on our left. The Master's thrown a bag of pepper powder at them quicker than I could think to do it. His other hand's in his belts looking for plant to stop the knife wound. I edge past him to face Scar, to cover him while he works on himself. Scar has no sword, just the knife. He's waiting. I can't read his other hand's movements; 'trops or powder I can't tell. I go for my own powders, he's not masked. The soldiers in the room are crying out with the Master's pepper powder, fine as flour and as harmless to us that's on the Master's blood. A shiver in my body I sense is caused by the Master warns me of a soldier charging at me from the room. I raise my sword as he comes at me, but he's barrelled into me, my sword catching and slicing through his tunic as he forces the blade up between us. He's from a mountain camp; grey lumpy skin, blind in one eye, as though patches of his face are dead or dying. Ferocious, with no interest in living, he is giving Scar the time he needs. I headbutt him, twice, smash his nose. I let go of my sword to grab his head, wrench it and snap his neck as Scar lunges at me, puts his knife in my belly, slams me into the wall, joy on his face. But it's gone in a moment for we sense Ufra suddenly, leaping the last of the steps to us. The Master ducks into the room out of her way, to kill the other soldiers in there. Ufra sticks Scar with a spear, his hip, again in his side, under his ribs. I hear her gasp; she's been hit by someone behind her on the stairs, a club to the back of her legs. She turns to defend herself, fight them back. Scar staggers away from me, his panting quickly becoming ragged with the pain of his wounds, hands working through his pouches for something to stop the bleeding and the poison. I press onto my own wound, get in my own pouches. I find and pour salts on it, pull gummed linen from a folded wad of them in a hip pouch. The blood thickens, congealing under the linen. There's a dry, sharp pain like the blade's still stuck in there. The Master walks calmly out of the room, his arms soaked in blood. He puts a hand on my shoulder before stepping past me to face Scar once more. More boots on the roof, cracking tiles as they run.

"You'll die today no matter the cost to me, Scar." Scar does not fear him, comes at him fast. The Master whips a bag from his belt, the action tearing the seal, squeezing and spraying the mix inside it over the corridor and us. My sight is gone the moment it hits my eyes, like ants crawling over them, over my face, but Scar takes most of it. I hear another soldier land in the room at the ledge of the window. I pull out my knife, for my sword's on the floor. I can't see. I step forward into the room. I can think only that he mustn't stop the Master, grappling and fighting with Scar. The soldier inches forwards, sees I cannot use my eyes. I follow the leather of his soles on the boards, the crack of his armour, the iron of his buckles. I put 'trops down; my nose gives me a sense of the bodies on the floor about us, the sound the 'trops make as they land paints the rest. I break another bag of pepper powder. Behind me a crack, the Master or Scar slamming into the wall between us. Again a crack, plaster falling away. Ufra is fighting on the stairs once more. The soldier before me lunges, a leap to avoid the caltrops. I misjudge the wall behind me, closer than I thought, feel him land before me. I thrust with the knife, puncturing a flask on his belt as I fall against him and take his sword's advantage away. He steps back, readying to stab me, but cries out; he's stood on one of the 'trops and his leg buckles, causing him to swing. A sharp blow catches my glove, a blow that might have severed my arm had he remained balanced. He tries to butt me, hits me once, but I move my head, get his ear in my teeth as he tries butting me again, tear it off, his strength gone in the pain of it. I need only that moment to stab him over and over till he goes still. As he falls back Scar crashes through the doorway past me, a piece of the wall with him, onto the 'trops, on his back. He howls, scrambles to his feet, his eyes red and swollen from the mix we were hit with, but the Master's followed him, jumping at him like a huge bear, a frightening power, wrapping his arm around him, taking Scar off his feet in a shower of blood and dust, running and smashing through the window frame. Scar's head cracks on the stone lintel as he's carried out and into the ground a storey below.

"No!" Ufra shouts from the doorway.

"I can't see, need alka!"

She drops to my side, her breath catching with the pain of some wound, with using her hands, unstoppering a small flask and pouring the mix over my eyes, working it in with her thumb.

"Driwna, your hand." I try to flex the hand the soldier had cut. Two fingers are gone. She puts the hilt of her knife in my mouth, to bite on. She splashes on alka; I know what's coming as she cracks the jumpcrick bones and the sparks flare up, a moment's warmth before the pain flashes through me, sealing the wound.

"We must help him, my love," she says, pulling at my arm. The mix on my eyes seems to sink into my head, a cold like ice chips thawing under my eyelids and I can make out daylight again. I take my knife to my leather surcoat, grit my teeth and slice it wider at my gut wound, more room to get a proper press on it over the linen. Ufra's gone downstairs, following the noise and shouting, some of it on the air outside. I hobble down after her. There are bodies at the bottom of the stairs, four in all, blood up the walls, a severed head staring up at me as I descend. I pick up an axe, wince and swap hands, seeing blurred outlines of nokes backing away from me, letting me out of the door into the painful brightness of the blue sky and sun in the street. Ufra runs at two soldiers grappling and holding the Master down on the ground. Scar is on one knee, hardly able to stand, wrapping linen about his head, already black with his blood. The pain of my hand is gone, my gut as well, the Master's blood strong. Ufra's kicked one of them off him. The Master, freed, plunges the claw of his wooden hand into the other's chest, rolls onto him, jerks the hand about inside him. I hear muffled cracking; the soldier goes still instantly. An arrow whips past, then another. Further down the street are three archers, Marschal Latimer behind them, the traitorous bastard.

"Ufra, we have to go, get in the slums; we can't finish Scar here." The Master this is. The nokes about us run inside the Second Lady again after fleeing it when we fought inside. More arrows fly past me as I cower, beginning to move back to him, to get us out of there. Scar stands unsteadily. As I offer the Master my hand, I see Ufra pull a knife from a scabbard on her fieldbelt. A smooth throw, fast as an arrow, the knife slams into Scar's chest. He stares down at the handle. I feel the joy of it, a flush of angry triumph, but see then the soldiers behind him are advancing, trying to get a better line on us now he's standing in between.

"Ufra!" I shout.

She's hobbling towards me as best she can, struggling from a spear wound to her thigh, her one arm held close to her as well, protecting another wound.

"Master, we must run," she says. She pulls at his arm, tears in her eyes from the pain it's causing her. I help her, getting under his other arm.

I have to hope Cal and Bray have made it into the slums, for they are not lying in the street about us.

The Master straightens up once he's on his feet, sees the mess of us, sees Scar turn to face Latimer and the others, trying to sign some command before falling to his knees. Ufra gives the Master her spear. He is still for a moment, looks up at the air around us. Breathes. He can finish Scar, I don't know why he doesn't. He looks at us both.

"Lead us, Driwna." As he says it, I see, from further along the lane, more of their soldiers, Marghoster colours, misshapen heads, some bare-chested, ravaged with plant and mixes. The Master must have smelled them before we could have, the tide turning against us this moment.

We push back through the Second Lady, through the nook and out into the other lane at its rear. There are steps down into an alley off the lane, other alleys cross our paths as we head into the gloom of the slums nearer the dockside. I throw 'trops after me, a nasty poison on them, then lead us south-west. Nokes, standing in twos and threes, watch us from dark doorways, clubs and axes in hand, no doubt protecting what's theirs. Children cower as we pass. There's a flute playing somewhere in the shadows of a parallel lane, gulls crying in the air above us. In the twilight of these lanes the air is thick with fear, madness, fatalism, for the poor have no champions, no influence. The Master halts us under an arch at the back of which is a barred door.

"Be still, both of you." He kneels before Ufra and I, unties

452

our masks and has us drink the strange mix he used on Bray after the battle with the Hidzucs; it is alive with what feels like worms.

"You could have killed him, Master," I say.

"I would have died with him, holding off the soldiers that approached. A good death. But Litko is close, I feel . . . the Song, in these stones, this air. He works it, he seeks us. I could not leave you alone and so wounded to face him. You must get to the boat." He smiles. He works quickly, a salve over the wounds where my fingers were, a delicate precision over my gut wound, my press coming off and something of his going in it, a wax then to seal it. I see Ufra's arm is broken. He tears at his cloak, makes her a sling. The vine at her throat is smashed. I can't imagine the pain that will give her when his blood fades in us. This he applies some sort of oil to, meticulously. Then her thigh, scraping something from the bark of his arm, a mould of some sort, sealing up that wound as well. He ties our masks back up, and as he does so he hums, articulating sounds somewhere within his throat that calm us, drawing our focus from the moment.

There's a shout of "Fire" somewhere nearby, quickly taken up by others, coming from beyond the end of the alley we're moving towards. We smell it then, wood burning, thick smoke billowing up over the rooftops of the hovels about us. I help Ufra to her feet. No time for words, a kiss only before I lead us on.

At the end of the alley a wider lane; droopjoints, inns, more tall, unkempt houses for the dockworkers and deckhands. The lane kinks right, beyond which must be the building that's on fire. All around us people are running out, desperate to form up as they must have done at other times, to get water to fight it.

"Fuck! We can't go that way now." I'm about to look for

another path when I see Amaris, head bowed, running from the direction of the burning house towards us. "Amaris!" I cry, thrilled to find her, for she knows these alleys better than any of us.

She looks up, slows a moment on seeing us, a look of relief on her. "It's you," she says, her voice heavier, perhaps the smoke. Then she picks up, running more quickly at us.

The Master shivers. I feel it, his fear, like nails dragged over my skin. He stares straight at me. "Litko!"

A heartbeat. He leaps past me, putting himself between us. Amaris's hand flickers, glimmers with light. It's him. I don't understand, but the air about us, all my new senses, tell me it's him, Litko, yet he's the very likeness of Amaris.

The Master puts his hand out to grab Litko, stop him, but he slips by it. His glittering fist hits the Master square in his chest, a blow I can feel through my soles, but the Master takes it with a grunt. He grabs the arm that's punched him, holds Litko still, deals him two heavy, fast hooked punches to his head. Amaris's face is collapsed, a strange roiling in the skull, her cheeks, yet it's the Master that screams then, high and loud as a horse, looks back at us both.

"Go!" A shout like thunder, filling the alley and rattling the doors and shutters.

He throws Litko into a wall, but a shimmering curling light spreads around them both. They're locked in a grapple, and for a moment I can see Litko is frantic, genuinely fearing for his life against the giant strength of the Master of Flowers.

"Driwna!" Ufra this is, pulling my arm. She kicks open the door to a droopjoint next to us, drags me after her. I cry out for the Master to follow us. The ground beneath us trembles. We run through the den, the droopers on their cots stirring from their dreams, suddenly speaking as one in a strange language. We almost make it to the shutters over

454

the window at the far side of the joint before a mighty, deafening crack runs through the stone, pealing towards us, the thunder of the world being torn apart. Flagstones erupt around us, the force hurling me towards Ufra, herself thrown through the shutters ahead of us. My belly hits the still, I'm winded utterly, the world's spinning, I feel blood from one of my ears running down my cheek.

Silence.

We're on the ground outside the droopjoint. I look along the alley we had tried to jump into, full of the dust, stone and timber from houses that look as though they have been smashed by trebucks. I cannot hear anything. The Master is gone, I can tell it only now; the difference is on my tongue, in my belly. Ufra twitches. I wriggle forwards into the sewage gutter that was once all that separated this row of buildings from the next. I say Ufra's name though I cannot hear it, I feel it only, my tongue making the shape of it. I'm on my hands and knees. Her arm moves, her hand reaching back to me. I clasp her forearm, lean over her. I tell her I love her, I cannot think of anything more important to say. She is grey with dust, spotted with blood, chips of stone in her head, more have torn her leathers, the skin on her arms. There's a high-pitched whine in my ears now, assuring me I'm not deaf. Ahead of Ufra, across the alley, there's a collapsed wall through which I can see into a workshop, its benches, crates and timbers.

I pick my way over rubble, burn my hand on a small iron stove, itself misshapen as though from heat, torn by the claws of a god. I put my hand on Ufra's back, pat it and weep. For the first time in my life I wish for an end to it all. I am defeated.

Ufra moves, rolls onto her back. I see her cough, though our masks help against the dust. The droopjoint we were in has mostly collapsed, the roof falling in as the walls sheared apart. The two buildings next to it, outside which stood the Master when Litko attacked him, they are just foundations, pieces of wall, the corners, all that still stand. Beyond them, the fire still burns, licks of orange light the dust cloud.

Ufra is speaking. Her mask moving. She's looking about us, looking for him I'm sure. I show her the blood on my cheek, gesture that I can't hear her. She stands, shouts his name, his real name, a name that cannot be contained by a lingo, but the silence persists. She looks down at me. Her eyes are like green fires against the grey dust that coats us both. We cannot sit here, she might be saying. She's holding her arm out to me, a look of hate and defiance in her eyes, and it hardens my will again. I take her arm and we pick our way along the rubble over the sewage gutter. I close my eyes a moment, trying to clear them of tears, see Amaris again, running at the Master. Litko. Not Amaris. So Amaris could yet be alive. Or left for dead.

The fire.

Litko had come from the house, must have set it on fire, but for what other reason than to burn her body? If he can change his appearance, he can use hers to great effect if she is not found.

I pull on Ufra's arm, point to the burning house. "Amaris." I hop past her, slipping, picking my way up the alley. There are bodies here, pieces of them, a more familiar horror to me than the shattering power of a magist. I climb over the ruins of the buildings, I feel the warmth of the fire becoming heat, prickling my skin; the buildings either side have caught, nobody left now to man the bucket lines after Litko used his power. The smoke is chokingly thick. I see movement then, on the ground ahead, just outside the burning shell of the house. Amaris, legs tied to a chair, arms free, pulling herself by inches along, her leathers smouldering, her head blackened, but her. I run to her. Part of the wall falls away next to me, sparks blow over me, burning my head, the flames rushing out at me. I take her arm and pull at her in a frenzy to get us away before we burn alive. I start coughing then, pull my mask away to retch with the smoke. Ufra runs up, cuts the rope binding Amaris to the chair, pulls her up into her arms, clasping them over her chest and walking her backwards. She lays Amaris down twenty feet past the burning house, starts work, dribbling water into her mouth. Amaris is delirious, muttering. The skin on her head is badly burned, her eyes are crusted shut, blistered. She breathes yet; shallow breaths, rattling with muke in her throat.

"Amaris!" I open my pot of slippery elm, an ointment for her burns. Ufra shakes her head, but I continue. I know she is telling me it is a waste, but I will not leave her in such pain.

Ufra flicks open her betony pouch, a generous smear that she puts in Amaris's mouth, over her gums, following it with more water.

Her lips are moving, but I can't hear her. I start shouting at Ufra to tell me what she's saying. She holds a finger to my lips as Amaris continues speaking, a muffled and muted warbling. Ufra is nodding now, takes my hand as she listens and puts it in Amaris's, gestures to me, to let me know that she is speaking of me being there. Amaris, her other hand badly burned, fingers fused to a paw, taps her necklace with it, a steel chain and a small carnelian stone, carved like a rod the size of a dut's finger, capped with steel cups either end. Ufra unclasps the necklace, slips it into her pocket. Amaris gestures behind her, to the burning house. They talk, and I gently dab and spread the elm over her eyes and forehead.

Her hand relaxes in mine, the grip gone. Ufra is no longer talking but lets me finish rubbing in the ointment on my finger, the last of it on Amaris's lips.

As I stopper the pot Ufra puts her finger under my chin, raising it so I am looking at her, so I can read her lips. "*Boat,*" she says. "*Ensma and Curic are dead. Litko.*" She does not know the Post lingo that we might sign to each other. I look back to the house that burns wildly and unstoppably.

I'm sorry.

Ufra points to the ruins of a house to our right. Beyond it are the quays, the dock itself. I lean over to kiss Amaris and then I'm pulled up by Ufra. We climb over the remains of the wall and onto the rubble of tiles and beams, kicking at the half-broken door the far side. It is painfully bright beyond, the open sea before us, whalers, caravels and knars on the quay and lining the jetties. I hear a bit more now, the whining in my ears more a hissing, the sound of the world about me filtered as though through a thick wall. She puts her arm around my shoulders and we walk through the crowds that have gathered around the bodies thrown from the buildings, the burned still crying out and weeping. There are lines forming on the dock front, merchants and their guards trying to protect their lots and stores, shouting for water. Wagons fill the main cobbled run along the front ahead of us. Marghoster militia are everywhere now, green sashes made to cover the shortage of tabards and cloaks in these first hours of his taking power. The gangplanks are guarded, but some people still attempt to leap to the boats, or throw children onto them, fearing another stroke of thunder, fearing the port is being smashed by the army that only the day before had battered their walls and overrun their guard.

458

Yard by yard we shuffle through it all, heads down, making for the north quay and the boat that waits for Amaris.

"The necklace, that is our passage to Hillfast," says Ufra, when I gesture to my ears that I might be able to hear her, though it is more her lips I read, the sounds of her voice being in the right place.

I hear her call, then, her arm leaving my shoulder. I look up, hear the sound of Cal's voice, indistinct but the pitch is his. The nokes around him, before a guild's sheds this is, have given him space. He is putting something in his eyes, something to clear them perhaps. He also is covered with dust, though fewer are as we've moved along the front and seen that the fire and the smashed-down houses were only in that small quarter. I hear whistles, still muffled. More militia are running to the quay where the hundreds are gathering to help fight the fire for all their sakes.

Cal looks up, his sight improved. His shoulders sag, relief on him to see us. He says something and from behind one of the sheds we're standing outside of, Bray comes. Ufra's telling them something I can't hear, points to the ruined houses, miming what's happened.

Where's Amaris, the others? signs Cal.

Dead. The Master. Dead.

He wipes blood from his sword, slams it into its sheath to refresh the poison paste. Bray smiles to see us. Embraces Ufra, embraces me.

Boat, signs Cal.

Yes, I reply.

Cal speaks with Ufra then, signs to me what Amaris said.

Give her the necklace. Remember Creed. His eyes fill, then. *Proud of you. Proud of me.*

Rulger filth. I hold him and kiss him. His chest rattles

459

with dust and spores; he smells of the Master, we all have his blood, and it lifts me.

We walk on, no more than fifty yards, threading a line through the dockside throng. I hear Cal's voice better now, behind me, low. Ufra and Bray are in front of me. Then Ufra turns to look behind us, slows. I'm about to follow her gaze when I see Scar step out in front of us, from the corner of a lane leading up off the dockside. There's a hole in his leather vest where the knife was, but no sign of any wound in his bearing. Litko has healed him. He pushes a deckhand out of the way and the others about us fall back, watching as he stands before us. He has the advantage of a spear. We have no bow. We aren't fit to fight him.

"Followed," says Ufra, downcast. I look behind us. Four of Marghoster's militia, strong with colour, risen, two with bows. The exultation of the Master's blood is waning, burned up by the wounds. They stand behind us, cutting us off.

I ready my axe, though it's in my wrong hand. Ufra and Cal ready their swords. Cal begins humming, for he sings when he works.

"Etza-Ososi!" I hear these words well enough from Scar. Bray turns to Ufra then, as Scar says it, puts his hand on her shoulder to hold her still before she can move to meet his challenge. He looks at me, his head half turned to Cal.

"Here be a song for you, Cal Rulger," says Bray. "You keep alive an' write it, how Miss Driwna give The Weeper back his life an' how he gives it back to her now."

He winks at me then drops his sword and walks forward. Scar lowers his spear ready, unsure of Bray's intent. Bray raises his shield, takes one of the big flasks of oil off his fieldbelt, uncorks it with his teeth. He edges towards Scar, who lunges, a look of disgust on his face. The shield slides the spear past Bray. He flicks the oil over Scar, takes two steps back, but stands his ground between the giant and us. Scar leaps forward, spear down, but Bray's fast enough on the blood, twists, brings the shield across the shaft of the spear, sprays him again with oil before stepping sideways. He barely makes it. But Scar is taunted and presses him. Bray reads him, for Scar's advantage is his body, not his training and not the blood of the Flower of Fates. It has returned Bray to his youth, to match the experience of one of the great campaigners, a survivor of Grey Goose's legendary sortie. He moves as a master around Scar's spear, one flick of the flask, another, on Scar's arms, his surcoat, the spear itself, slowly coating him with oil. Scar is relentless, feints, thrusts, swipes, one hand or both. But Bray keeps in our way and Scar falters, the last splash catching his face and chest. Bray throws the flask down then, emptied. Just a shield.

"I thought you strong! I thought you fast! Who is this Scar!" He shouts this to all watching. "A fat old man, I's beatin' you without sword or spear! You are nothin' but a killer o' children!" He keeps on goading him. I begin to realise what he might be attempting to do, but it will get him killed, and he knew it. Scar jumps at him, a huge leap, knows he has to finish Bray, thinks that Bray is only delaying him, thinks there is some other reason for his defensiveness. He expects Bray to jump back and defend, but Bray throws himself forwards, shield sliding the spear past him one final time, letting go of it as he runs into the huge Ososi. He puts his shield arm through the chest straps of Scar's fieldbelt, pulls his jumpcrick bones from his belt and snaps them against Scar's chest, the oil. The bones crack in two, the spark a flash and the flames shoot up into Scar's face, spreading in an instant, a ripple of blue fire turning yellow. Bray screams briefly as Scar drops his spear, gets Bray's throat and head and breaks his neck. He starts shrieking as the oil burns

461

him alive, still pulling at Bray's arm as his dead weight hangs against him. My breath catches in my throat, the shock of what we're seeing echoing all around us among the nokes that watch. I turn, it's all happening too quickly, for Cal steps away from Ufra and I, sword drawn. He blows a kiss.

"This is goodbye, love. Run, for you must make it to Yblas for all our sakes."

He charges the four behind us. I scream for him but Ufra grabs my belt's shoulder straps and she drags at me. I pull against her, looking to follow Cal as the archers raise their bows, but Ufra's fierce strength pulls me into a run past Scar, who's on the ground now, writhing, his flesh smoking, stinking. Ufra stops over him, lets go of me to stab him in the chest before forcing her sword through his head and leaving it there.

"I'm going back, Ufra, I can't leave him!"

"Don't waste what he has earned!" she cries. "Don't leave me alone." She takes my hand as I stare back at Cal, hear his singing. "Live, Driwna, for him and for me."

She pulls me once more into a run, between wagons, through the crowd that's gathered.

Oh Cal, what have you done, my beautiful man, my love.

Chapter 23

Driwna

The sea and the sky are endless.

There are squalls, a swell that our quarter finds "interesting" but Ufra's belly finds otherwise.

I tell her stories of Cal and she tells me stories of her Ososi, her home. The fishermen of *Efne's Grace* listen when they can and tell us stories of their own, for what sailor doesn't have stories. They speak their own lingo out here, names for the moods of water and wind, the clouds, the gulls, the spouts of whales. They do not hide their disappointment at the shoals they could have farmed if not for Amaris's necklace and the greater duty. They wept as I told them of her dying and they tell us stories of her, of a Post within our Post, of brothers in red who pay the final tally, who lived the Creed before Yblas put it to vellum to send out to all corners of the Post on the day of my promotion to fieldsman. On her necklace they've sworn, for she has earned their loyalty, as she has mine, in ways too various to count.

In oilskin cloaks we huddle as we cut the northerlies to our advantage, days of healing and song, uisge and kannab.

The cold coasts of Hillfast edge into view, the harbour as small and grey as I remember it the last time I was here, leaving for home, mine and Cal's first fightbrews having changed us irrevocably, bringing us for the first time glimpses of what we'd come to know as the Song of the Earth.

My season of thorns is over. Eleven have pushed through. There will be more at the end of summer, as the vine grows, strengthening me, making me feel younger than I have a right to feel. More and more, when we're close, I feel Ufra's moods and she mine. I have sudden moments of great sadness and know it is hers. I feel the heat of her joy and I hope it is because she thinks of me or looks on me. Many times it is so and the feeling redoubles in her. To know the bonds of the Ososi, even the beginnings of them as I do now, makes me all the more angry for their suffering. After all that has happened, it is these days on this boat that have taught me, silently, what Ufra and the Master have endured these last years.

Administrator Heikk runs Hillfast, mainly the Posthouse Epny, but there are many Posthouses along the Mosa Road and north along the coast. We have to assume that I am as wanted here as I am in Farlsgrad by those loyal to him and Litko. With Stroff dead it may well be Heikk that gets the promotion to administrator of Farlsgrad.

We have agreed that they would find me some rolls, an ink and quill, for I must record, albeit briefly, what has befallen Farlsgrad and its king. One of our boat's crew, Agrieu, quiet and stoic during the crossing for one so young, will act as bearer of my missives to Yblas. We will stay with the boat until we can safely be led to him. I give Agrieu Amaris's necklace, for none of his crew have put into this harbour before. She will have allies here I'm sure.

464

We spend the night on the boat, in the hold out of the rain, while Agrieu and the others enjoy a night's ale and food on my coin. We cannot risk Ufra being seen and I will not leave her.

The rain clears the following morning, a grey sky. Agrieu returns to the boat, tells me we will be given directions to Yblas. He returns the necklace, along with some crab meat and eggs for our breakfast.

"Might be you get yourselves in the hold an' ready for the call. I bought these robes an' hoods as you asked, they'll hide you an' your belts enough you'll look like travellers."

"Thank you, Agrieu."

"The crew thanks you for the night on a cot with a full belly. Sillindar follow you."

Back in the hold, in the light of a lantern and the open hatch, we put on our fieldbelts. Ufra's question, her concern, I can feel in my chest.

"You worry about us, Driwna-wen," I say.

"I do," she says. "We put on these belts as though we go to war, not to see an ally. Why do we do this?"

It is easy to say that the fieldbelts are easier to carry worn. "I cannot say. Perhaps it is nothing, perhaps it is the Song."

"It may be, Ufra-wen. I cannot read this air as I can at home, but I have yet to stand on this earth and stone and it might tell me much."

We take a pipe until Agrieu lands on the deck above us. He leans over the hatch.

"There's a horse and wagon, led by an old woman, blue cloak. She'll indicate the way an' you just keep back but in sight of her till then." He helps us and our packs and weapons out of the hatch. Two of his other crew are there and we clasp arms.

"We set off on the tide. Might be we see you again in Farlsgrad, eh?"

"Might be."

They make no fuss of us as we disembark. There's reds at work here, for the Post has its own quays. We're both feeling hot in the robes over our leathers and belts as they are, and it feels like a clumsy measure to avoid anyone recognising us as Ososi, but none seem to. The woman in the blue cloak is easy enough to spot, she's five or so berths down the quayside and leading her horse and wagon along with purpose. She takes a couple of turns off the quay through some lanes leading east out of the harbour and it's as we start a rise into the country along a muddy trail that she takes her pipe out of her mouth and spits to her left, looking up that way a moment before carrying on. As we reach the same point, I see a path heading up the hill to the heights above the harbour.

The trail itself is heavily muddied and the long grass to the sides of it hold the day's rain, soaking our boots and robes.

There is a strong, cold wind up here and the clouds race along above us, some blue sky showing over the ocean. Around us purple daphnes are in bloom. Soon the bluebells and cloudberries will fill these grasses.

I feel a greyness then, like a cloud's passed over my sight.

"Ufra?"

"Aaah," she says, "I am remembering how we picked daphne berries in the Sathanti hills. You felt it."

A memory comes to me then, suddenly, my mun holding me up in her arms to reach a branch for its hazelnuts.

"Hazelnut trees," says Ufra. I look to our right, away from the hill's edge, three or four trees among birches and some apple trees.

"This is good land," she says. "It's been allowed to breathe, be itself."

466

There's a sudden flapping of wings in branches, somewhere in the copse. Sparrows fly out.

I shiver.

"Look," says Ufra, "it's there."

We walk a few yards further and the trees give way to a small meadow, and beneath a steep cliff-face we see a low drystone wall with an iron gate marking off a small garden and cottage; thatched roof, peat smoke rising from the chimney. Four huge apple trees sit to the side of the house, the boughs of the nearest one casting themselves protectively over part of the roof. A man in full leathers and belts sits on a stone bench next to the gate. He picks up his spear and stands as he sees us.

"You're expected," he says as we approach. "Hoods, if you would be so kind."

We pull them back.

"Thank you."

It is a low gate, a latch at a child's height. He opens it for us but otherwise averts his eyes to the field beyond, discouraging a more formal or involved greeting.

Limestone slabs from the hills about make a path to a weathered stable door, the top half open. The shutters too are open and behind them are pale yellow plates of bone, held in a wooden frame. .

"Driwna?" Yblas's voice, from inside.

"My Red."

"Open the door, come in." There is the sound of water boiling in a kettle.

The door opens to this main room, the other side of which, in the corner, is a short hallway that must lead to the bedroom and perhaps a kitchen beyond it, for there were two chimneys at either end of the roof.

He has brown woollens on, wears the crow's skull brooch.

He takes the kettle off the stand over the healthy fire he has going, puts it on a stone at the edge of the hearth. He stands and looks at us. I'd forgotten how tall he is.

"An Ososi. It is an honour to meet you."

"She is the etza-Ososi, my Red, and she is my keep, as they say here. This is Ufra."

Ufra bows her head, awaiting a sense of respect as is Ososi custom.

"You are Ufra-wen, then, Driwna?"

"I am." I shouldn't be surprised that he would know how to address me properly.

He bows before her and she looks up at him immediately. He has recognised the respect given him, for he smiles and bows again in thanks.

"I heard also . . . from Amaris. She wrote to tell me you are known as Brother Red by the south Sathanti peoples."

I would reply, but he's read the missives sent the previous day and I see her name has stilled him the moment he said it, his smile caught and broken by a memory of her.

"I grieve for her also, my Red."

His eyes come back to us. "I grieve for all of us, Fieldsman. But we have done what we can. I will make you both some tea. Take off those robes, it's too warm for them in here, but keep on those belts and leathers."

He takes some wooden cups from a shelf above the hearth before I can ask him why. A table stands near the windows, the ground tea leaves smelling sweetly the moment he opens the box, one of many on the table. He stares out of the window, perhaps lost in thought for a moment. I shiver once more, as does Ufra, memories flickering about me like fireflies. He bows his head, continues with spooning the tea into the cups.

"This cottage is called 'The Old House' by those who

know of it. Each High Red is made the High Red here. We swear our oaths on the bloody shirt of Teyr Amondsen's son, Mosa. The first High Red, Brekeuel, he found the shirt in a small satchel under the floorboards by the window of the bedroom next door. With it were some pure silver pieces, Mount Hope stamped, ten or so, as well as Amondsen's letters, that you've read. The satchel with the shirt you'd find now at the academy; it is safer there. I have put your missives under the floorboards at the window, and returned Amondsen's letters there along with a number of my own."

He takes the cups to the hearth, pours the boiling water from the kettle. His hands are trembling.

"The last thing I think we ought to put with those missives and letters is the necklace, Driwna." He stands with our two cups and tears run down his cheeks as he holds them out.

"Yblas? I don't understand. What's the matter?"

We take our cups and he picks up his own, wipes the tears away.

"We get such a short time. It seems the moment we find the good sense our youth takes too long to discover, we are in a race to make use of it before old age hides it again. Who could have seen Litko for what he is? Who could have known he was the shape-changer of legend, the Masja-Mort of Jua. 'Slipp' is how he is known in the Citadels, a magist who could have been anyone, anywhere. He knows of this house, might know everything of my plans for the Post in the southern Sar." He blows on, then sips his tea.

"You have come to warn me of him, as Amaris warned me of the coup and of Marghoster and Stroff's ambition. I cannot fathom the game he is playing and it's too late to run."

"You must, my Red. We can go south, where you might work to uncover him with your Administrators in Mount Hope, Jua, the Roan Province."

"We cannot. I thought nothing of the change of guard at my gate this morning when I woke. I slept badly, memories so strong and real I felt I was still the child in them and that this house and these grey whiskers and old bones were themselves a dream I feared. He was waiting."

I feel a horror in the pit of my gut then, look at Ufra, who stares past Yblas, through the window. "He's here," she says.

"You were dead the moment you walked off that boat, Fieldsman. We all were."

I follow Ufra's gaze through the pale yellow bone of the window plates to the figure beyond, standing alone in the garden. It does not look much like a man, for it seems to ripple, the limbs look too long, they move strangely. I look back at Yblas.

"My tea has a little extra in it, Fieldsman, and so I'll keep our secrets under the floorboards. We must hope he cannot raise the dead." He looks on us both with pity and drinks his tea down in one.

"Yblas, will you not invite me in?" Litko's voice is stronger, the power more overwhelming, than any man or animal could manage. It is as if we are in a cavern and he is speaking into our ears. I look up at Yblas.

"I couldn't save the Post," I say.

"You already have, Brother Red. You have averted a war and saved the Ososi people from oblivion. All will know of Marghoster's corruption and treachery. Litko will surely have to return to the shadows once more. We just won't live to see it." He clasps our arms in turn. His breathing quickens as the poison begins to work. "May Sillindar carry you home to the arms of your Ososi family, to the Song. I will encourage his ego for a few moments at least. It should be enough for you to hide the necklace, for it is a key to many locks." He walks past us and through the door to the garden. He has given us our final moments alone.

I take off the necklace, look down at the finger of carnelian.

"I'm so sorry, Ufra, sorry we could not have a life together, sorry it was me you found to love."

She steps up to me, puts her forehead against mine. "No, Driwna, do not be sorry. If you think I grieve that this moment has come for us, I would say you have much to learn of the Ososi. But there is no time left to learn it." She laughs then, a bright, colourful joy that brings a smile to me, draws my tears. "Here is where we join the Song, pull it out of the stone and air, make a melody for others to hear in the centuries to come."

She straightens up before me, takes from an inside pocket in her leathers a waxed cotton pocket stitched shut. She cuts it open, takes out two seeds, bright orange.

"The Master hoped I might plant these out west. They are from my father, his alkaest." She cuts them open with her knife, drops two halves in my cup. The immense power of these seeds, undiluted by Ososi blood, will kill us even were we to withstand Litko.

"Any last words I can give your family, Driwna Marghoster?" He is standing alone once more, his strange form casting long shadows across the garden.

"Aye! Fuck you, Litko." I drink the seed down and she does the same.

The feeling of the seeds' work redoubles between us as we sense the heat growing in each other. I run to the other room, hide the necklace as Yblas bid me do, then return to my love. Already we're growing, so fast it's an agony, our vines taking the need for words away as the power of the Flower of Fates fills us. I take my axe out of its loop as she unsheathes her sword. I quiver with the coming storm as it burns and snakes up into my heart, a storm big enough to drown this land. The room brightens unbearably as our eyes see beyond the world of men. It takes my breath, how many truths are hidden from us in our prisons of flesh. Only death follows perfection.

Ufra leads us out of Amondsen's house, its old stones laying bare all their fond memories, the roots that hold them to this great shoulder of land as it burns beneath us. Outside we charge at him, rising into arms of light. Reborn.

Epilogue

665OE

"Nobody's been here in years, Cawn."

"I was the last, Kailen. The thatch is in sore need of repair, isn't it? The years fly and there's always something more important to do than tend to this house, let alone enjoy it."

"I understand that far better than I did before our ride from Epny."

I am the Red, the tenth, as Cawn was the ninth. I swore my oaths to him and to the Post on the bloody shirt of a boy, the name of whom is lost to us. Cawn has passed his responsibility, and the small, strange brooch of the Red onto me, amid much consternation on the part of the Administration and their preferred fieldsmen. It might easily have been otherwise, but I have learned of the lengths he had to go to for the votes in my favour and these are debts I will spend many years repaying.

He is a fascinating man; adept politician; historian, and blessed with a detailed grasp of the many threads of the Post's frontiers and problems. The Post is corrupt. But within it, there's a thread of something, something better.

We open the windows and sweep out this small, cold room and its big hearth. He's not too self-important for such work, nor too old, though he aches with his bones, and his once tall and hale figure is now bowed and frail. He is also humming, a song I have heard somewhere.

473

"What is it you sing?" I ask.

"I've heard vanners sing this hymn for their dead, collecting coin from the purses of those survivors to give to the dead's kin."

"Ah, 'Brother Red'?"

"Yes. They sing it when calling for the final tally. It was once mandated, you know, one of the many good things we did for those who die in our service. It faded along with the Farlsgrad Creed."

"Yes. I had heard this. I would reinstate both."

"Sillindar bless you, for you will need such blessing to overcome the foul nest of snakes we have ruling over the Post now. I used to hear, and even sing, 'Brother Red' as a fieldsman, but they don't sing it before administrators, clearks or reeves. I've not heard it once since I became the Red. It's a song for our rank and file, the lifeblood of this kingdom without borders that you now command."

"Said well, Cawn. And do you sing it now because we are here? I never quite understood the final lines until now. *'You'll find there's a room at the Old House; I'll stand at the window and wait.'*"

He pauses in his sweeping, looks about us. "I still don't understand them, but yes, the hymn seems to speak of this very house."

"How could a song that vanners sing refer to this house when it's known only to the Reds?"

"Well, shall we set this fire, for I have a story that might shed some light on the origin of the hymn and a mystery of our own past. A pipe and a cup of uisge before a good fire is the only way to tell it."

"Sit you down, my brother," I say, "let me set the fire."

*

474

I swept out the room and made up the fire with wood from the copse nearby. We're now covered in soot from the chimney I put a brush up into. I will restore this place, for I feel a great peace here, one I would share with my keep, Araliah, for she's always wished to travel.

Cawn speaks. "I set out from the Spike west, seven or eight winters ago. Fieldsman Seventy-three was out past the Bouskill Lakes, past even the Ilkashun lands, near the borders with Western Farlsgard and Ry'yla. We may yet run the road there through to the far coast. I decided to visit the outposts along the lakes and see how this great undertaking was being accomplished. When I stopped at the borders of the Ilkashun lands I saw one of their kurchpoles. They place these poles all along their borders to mark them out. Great thick trunks of wood they are and each carved bottom to top with the victories and legends of their tribe. Being something of a historian I spent time before this kurchpole. Carved into it, about chest height to me, a depiction of the Spike's main tower caught my eye. With it Ososi and Oskoro."

"Oskoro? In the Sathanti?"

"Quite. A Master of Flowers, the Flower of Fates in his head, was depicted. Also shown was a van and these Ososi and Oskoro in battle against those of the Marghoster banner. The one banner I didn't recognise until I later spoke with Ilkashun elders was that of the Hidzucs, a tribe once on Marghoster's border that must have all been destroyed or exiled in an expansion. But what most surprised me was the further depiction on this carving of Ososi and Ilkashun being led out of a depiction of the mountains, yet in the mountains were carved hideous creatures, all presumably slain. There was lettering of theirs, a Sathanti lingo, that was inscribed under this mural as it ran around the trunk. I made my own sketches of it to show them.

"'Brother Red,' they said, pointing to one of the figures with an Ososi, covered and protected by some great tree as they fought. 'Fieldsman,' they said, 'of the Post.' Her name was Driwna, of a lost Sathanti tribe called Bridche. I'll save you any research you might do; her name is on no records I could find in our archives."

"When was this?" I ask.

"574OE. Just short of a century ago."

"Yblas was the Red but died that year, didn't he?"

"Yes, well, presumed dead. He disappeared. Heikk, of this citadel, became our next Red, as you know. These Sathanti spoke of this Driwna with reverence; she struck a peace accord with the Ilkashun, Hidzucs and Farlsgrad, then went into the mountains and brought out hundreds that had been made slaves by the then Lord Marghoster, who had drudhas experimenting on them, splicing plant into their bodies as the Ososi do. These must have been the creatures depicted, and she must have led a force to kill them all. It's hard to countenance the truth of such tales, but while it seems to suffer from the more obvious exaggerations of history, it lends credence to the stories you hear in Autumn's Gate of the army of monsters that came to kill King Hildmir."

"If the date is true she would have been the first fieldsman by a number of years."

"Yes, Kailen. It burnishes Yblas's reputation further, does it not? And the further west I went, all knew of 'Brother Red', the reason our reds are so well received there. Also, most interestingly, one elder told me that a man this Driwna knew, himself of the Post, was the one who wrote 'Brother Red', travelled all about the Sathanti Peaks and went, he said, to live with the Ososi far to the south in Khasgal's Landing. Again, I could find no record of him."

"I recall now this was the very year of the coup, when

476

Yeismic Marghoster brought down the Hildmir line and instituted the senate there."

"Yes, your memory of lineage and history serves you well. There is a tale here, isn't there?"

"This Driwna seems pitched against it all."

"Lesser reds have been revered. She has been forgotten."

"'On our sisters' silent bones rests this world of men', eh, Cawn?"

"Indeed, my Red."

I raise my cup. "Well, here's to the first fieldsman. She upheld the Creed where so few now do."

"She did. And you must, Kailen. You are a fine, fine student of a man's demeanour and purpose. And you must be to begin to change the demeanour and purpose of the Post itself. The coffers at Candar are so vast and full you would scarce believe it. We have no need of anything yet these administrators drive more expansion, throw coin at any and every venture that would see the Post encircle the known world. But to what end? How many more vaults of gold, silver and jewels, rare and ancient treasures does the Post need? That is no end in itself, for greed has no measure."

He shakes his head, falls into silence. I finish my uisge, stand and help myself to another from the flask at the table. I put my hand on his shoulder.

"I will think on all of this, Cawn. You are right to trust me."

"I believe I am. You give an old man hope. But always, always ask yourself this, 'to what end?'"

Cawn left three hours ago, stepping over the broken gate lying on the overgrown grass verge. He gave a final wave as I stood in the doorway, the wind off the Sar roaring through the giant apple trees protecting the house.

The fire is set for the evening, my bedroll is before it on the flagstones. I take a lantern through the door to the short corridor. Beyond it I see a darkened kitchen with another hearth. Between the living room and the kitchen is a doorway to a smaller room, empty now. As in the hall there are nails where pictures and fancies must once have hung. I go to the shutters that open out onto the same side as the living room, goat-horn plates set in these as well. I hum the tune to "Brother Red", thinking of Cawn's story, though quickly enough my thoughts wander to all the things I must now do as the Red.

I'll stand at the window and wait.

I smile. Was this friend of Driwna's here at some point? This place that only those of us elected the Red supposedly knew of? Was Driwna?

I lean forward to scratch at some dirt on one of the plates set into the window frame. As I do one floorboard creaks and gives a little. I press into the floorboard next to it, under my other boot, and it is solid enough. Pressing again, the loose one does actually feel loose, not nailed down at all, and so, intentional. I look down, then kneel, placing the lantern next to this board. I need my knife to get the edge of it up.

In the hole underneath I find a great treasure.

Glossary

braegnloc – skull
braegn – brain

cyca – code/cypher

daith-ru – Sathanti name for keep/wife
daith-nu – Sathanti name for chief
daith-wa – Sathanti name for drudha
dayer – lighter form of fightbrew
droop – drug
droophouse – drug house
drudha – a soldier/herbalist proficient in mixing
        fightbrews and other potions
dut – child/baby

eyrtza – Ososi word for majesty, mastery or focus

ham – short for hamlet

jumpcrick bones – sparker for lighting a pipe or fire
just – courtroom

keep – spouse
kelahlu – nightsong of the Bridche kurch
King's Common – language
kurch – tribe or clan, also refers to their territory
kurch-fod – laws and legends of a kurch

muke – mucus
mun – mother

noke – "no colour": someone who hasn't "paid the colour"

pabagoy – Sathani/Ilkashun word for parrot

refo – magist magic for shape-changing
roll – document/scroll

sib-brother – brother-in-law
sib-daughter – niece

uilest – death tradition
uisge – alcohol
Umansk – Oskoro/Ososi word for human

MONTHS

Winter
Zemna
Jenna
Fevera

Spring
Marta
Aerla
Moxma

Summer
Iuna
Ulyn
Harud

Autumn
Silma
Crutma
Norva

DAYS

(though not all are referenced)
Sillenday
Halumday
Thegnday
Thesselday
Gjanmerday
Sunsday
Moonsday

Acknowledgements

I'd like to thank all at Orbit for readying this manuscript for the world: my editors Jenni Hill and Priyanka Krishnan along with my copy-editors Joanna Kramer and Saxon Bullock for their fiercely detailed eye on the many weaknesses of my prose. Thanks too to Nazia Khatun my publicist for all her support and Lauren Panepinto for her work on the cover design. A shout-out to Jaime Jones for knocking it out of the park on the art too; it's a privilege to have his work on my covers.

Thank you to Jamie Cowen, my agent and my lighthouse, for his continued guidance and support.

I would like to liberally spread my ongoing thanks and gratitude over Pete Withers-Jones, Steve Warren, The Fantasy Hive and my Bristolcon "fab four" – James "Marschal" Latimer, Mariëlle Ooms-Voges, Jude Hunter and Geoff Matthews.

Special thanks too to the Super Relaxed Fantasy Club – Phil, Kristina and Magnus work amazingly hard for us SFF authors and they've also been a great support in giving me the chance to do some readings as well as to meet and make friends with so many other SFF enthusiasts.

Thank you to all my newsletter subscribers for your

ongoing interest in what I'm doing and the occasional emails you're kind enough to send. It's a privilege to be able to share my news and thoughts with you.

Finally, through what's been a challenging time in our lives, my wife Rhian's love and support is the main reason I have managed to write anything at all. You'll do. My kids are all right too. xxx

extras

www.orbitbooks.net

about the author

Born and raised in Barry, South Wales, **Adrian Selby** studied creative writing at university before embarking on a career in video game production. His debut novel, *Snakewood*, is an epic and inventive fantasy about a company of mercenaries and the assassin trying to destroy them. The follow-up, *The Winter Road*, is another gritty epic fantasy adventure, which remembers that battles leave all kinds of scars. Adrian lives on the south coast of England with his family. You can find him on his website at adrianselby.com.

Find out more about Adrian Selby and other Orbit authors by registering for the free monthly newsletter at www.orbitbooks.net.

if you enjoyed
BROTHER RED
look out for

LEGACY OF ASH
Book One of the Legacy trilogy

by

Matthew Ward

A shadow has fallen over the Tressian Republic.

Ruling families plot against one another with sharp words and sharper knives, heedless of the threat posed by the invading armies of the Hadari Empire.

The Republic faces its darkest hour.
Yet as Tressia falls, heroes rise.

Wind howled along the marcher road. Icy rain swirled behind.

Katya hung low over her horse's neck. Galloping strides jolted weary bones and set the fire in her side blazing anew. Sodden reins sawed at her palms. She blotted out the pain. Closed her ears to the harsh raven-song and ominous thunder. There was only the road, the dark silhouette of Eskavord's rampart, and the anger. Anger at the Council, for forcing her hand. At herself for thinking there'd ever been a chance.

Lightning split grey skies. Katya glanced behind. Josiri was a dark shape, his steed straining to keep pace with hers. That eased the burden. She'd lost so much when the phoenix banner had fallen. But she'd not lose her son.

Nor her daughter.

Eskavord's gate guard scattered without challenge. Had they recognised her, or simply fled the naked steel in her hand? Katya didn't care. The way was open.

In the shadow of jettied houses, sodden men and women loaded sparse possessions onto cart and dray. Children wailed in confusion. Dogs fought for scraps in the gutter. Of course word had reached Eskavord. Grim tidings ever outpaced the good.

You did this.

Katya stifled her conscience and spurred on through the tangled streets of Highgate.

Her horse forced a path through the crowds. The threat of her sword held the desperate at bay. Yesterday, she'd have felt safe within Eskavord's walls. Today, she was a commodity to be traded for survival, if any had the wit to realise the prize within their grasp.

Thankfully, such wits were absent in Eskavord. That, or else no one recognised Katya as the dowager duchess Trelan. The Phoenix of prophecy.

No, not that. Katya was free of that delusion. It had cost too many lives, but she was free of it. She was not the Phoenix whose fires would cleanse the Southshires. She'd believed – Lumestra, *how* she'd believed – but belief alone did not change the world. Only deeds did that, and hers had fallen short.

The cottage came into view. Firestone lanterns shone upon its gable. Elda had kept the faith. Even at the end of the world, friends remained true. Katya slid from the saddle and landed heavily on cobbles. Chainmail's broken links gouged her bloodied flesh.

'Mother?'

Josiri brought his steed to a halt in a spray of water. His hood was back, his blond hair plastered to his scalp.

She shook her head, hand warding away scrutiny. 'It's nothing. Stay here. I'll not be long.'

He nodded. Concern remained, but he knew better than to question. He'd grown into a dependable young man. Obedient. Loyal. Katya wished his father could have seen him thus. The two were so much alike. Josiri would make a fine duke, if he lived to see his seventeenth year.

She sheathed her sword and marched for the front door. Timbers shuddered under her gauntleted fist. 'Elda? Elda! It's me.'

A key turned. The door opened. Elda Savka stood on the threshold, her face sagging with relief. 'My lady. When the rider came from Zanya, I feared the worst.'

'The army is gone.'

Elda paled. 'Lumestra preserve us.'

'The Council emptied the chapterhouses against us.'

'I thought the masters of the orders had sworn to take no side.'

'A knight's promise is not what it was, and the Council nothing if not persuasive.' Katya closed her eyes, lost in the shuddering ground and brash clarions of recent memory. And the screams, most of all. 'One charge, and we were lost.'

'What of Josiri? Taymor?'

'Josiri is with me. My brother is taken. He may already be dead.'

Either way, he was beyond help. 'Is Calenne here?'

'Yes, and ready to travel. I knew you'd come.'

'I have no choice. The Council . . .'

She fell silent as a girl appeared at the head of the staircase, her sapphire eyes alive with suspicion. Barely six years old, and she had the wit to know something was amiss. 'Elda, what's happening?'

'Your mother is here, Calenne,' said Elda. 'You must go with her.'

'Are you coming?'

The first sorrow touched Elda's brow. 'No.'

Calenne descended the stairs, expression still heavy with distrust. Katya stooped to embrace her daughter. She hoped Calenne's thin body stiffened at the cold and wet, and not revulsion for a woman she barely knew. From the first, Katya had thought it necessary to send Calenne away, to live shielded from the Council's sight. So many years lost. All for nothing.

Katya released Calenne from her embrace and turned wearily to Elda. 'Thank you. For everything.'

The other woman forced a wintery smile. 'Take care of her.'

Katya caught a glint of something darker beneath the smile. It lingered in Elda's eyes. A hardness. Another friendship soured by folly? Perhaps. It no longer mattered. 'Until my last breath. Calenne?'

The girl flung her arms around Elda. She said nothing, but the tears on her cheeks told a tale all their own.

Elda pushed her gently away. 'You must go, dear heart.'

A clarion sounded, its brash notes cleaving through the clamour of the storm. An icy hand closed around Katya's heart. She'd run out of time.

Elda met her gaze. Urgency replaced sorrow. 'Go! While you still can!'

Katya stooped and gathered Calenne. The girl's chest shook with thin sobs, but she offered no resistance. With a last glance at Elda, Katya set out into the rain once more. The clarion sounded again as she reached Josiri. His eyes were more watchful than ever, his sword ready in his hands.

'They're here,' he said.

Katya heaved Calenne up to sit in front of her brother. She looked like a doll beside him, every day of the decade that separated them on full display.

'Look after your sister. If we're separated, ride hard for the border.'

His brow furrowed. 'To the Hadari? Mother . . .'

'The Hadari will treat you better than the Council.' He still had so much to learn, and she no more time in which to teach him. 'When enemies are your only recourse, choose the one with the least to gain. Promise me.'

She received a reluctant nod in reply.

Satisfied, Katya clambered into her saddle and spurred west along the broad cobbles of Highgate. They'd expect her to take refuge in Branghall Manor, or at least strip it of anything valuable ahead of the inevitable looting. But the western gateway might still be clear.

The first cry rang out as they rejoined the road. 'She's here!'

A blue-garbed wayfarer cantered through the crowd, rain

scattering from leather pauldrons. Behind, another set a buccina to his lips. A brash rising triad hammered out through the rain and found answer in the streets beyond. The pursuit's vanguard had reached Eskavord. Lightly armoured riders to harry and delay while heavy knights closed the distance. Katya drew her sword and wheeled her horse about. 'Make for the west gate!'

Josiri hesitated, then lashed his horse to motion. 'Yah!'

Katya caught one last glimpse of Calenne's pale, dispassionate face. Then they were gone, and the horseman upon her.

The wayfarer was half her age, little more than a boy and eager for the glory that might earn a knight's crest. Townsfolk scattered from his path. He goaded his horse to the gallop, sword held high in anticipation of the killing blow to come. He'd not yet learned that the first blow seldom mattered as much as the last.

Katya's parry sent a shiver down her arm. The wayfarer's blade scraped clear, the momentum of his charge already carrying him past. Then he was behind, hauling on the reins. The sword came about, the killing stroke aimed at Katya's neck.

Her thrust took the younger man in the chest. Desperate strength drove the blade between his ribs. The hawk of the Tressian Council turned dark as the first blood stained the rider's woollen tabard. Then he slipped from his saddle, sword clanging against cobbles. With one last, defiant glare at the buccinator, Katya turned her steed about, and galloped through the narrow streets after her children.

She caught them at the bridge, where the waters of the Grelyt River fell away into the boiling millrace. They were not alone.

One wayfarer held the narrow bridge, blocking Josiri's

path. A second closed from behind him, sword drawn. A third lay dead on the cobbles, horse already vanished into the rain.

Josiri turned his steed in a circle. He had one arm tight about his sister. The other hand held a bloody sword. The point trembled as it swept back and forth between his foes, daring them to approach.

Katya thrust back her heels. Her steed sprang forward.

Her sword bit into the nearest wayfarer's spine. Heels jerked as he fell back. His steed sprang away into the streets. The corpse, one booted foot tangled in its stirrups, dragged along behind.

Katya rode on past Josiri. Steel clashed, once, twice, and then the last wayfarer was gone. His body tipped over the low stone parapet and into the rushing waters below.

Josiri trotted close, his face studiously calm. Katya knew better. He'd not taken a life before today.

'You're hurt.'

Pain stemmed Katya's denial. A glance revealed rainwater running red across her left hand. She also felt a wound high on her shoulder. The last wayfarer's parting gift, lost in the desperation of the moment.

The clarion came yet again. A dozen wayfarers spurred down the street. A plate-clad knight rode at their head, his destrier caparisoned in silver-flecked black. Not the heraldry of a knightly chapterhouse, but a family of the first rank. His sword – a heavy, fennlander's claymore – rested in its scabbard. A circular shield sat slung across his back.

The greys of the rain-sodden town lost their focus. Katya tightened her grip on the reins. She flexed the fingers of her left hand. They felt distant, as if belonging to someone else. Her shoulder ached, fit company for the dull roar in her side – a memento of the sword-thrust she'd taken on the ridge at Zanya. Weariness crowded in, the faces of the dead close behind.

The world lurched. Katya grasped at the bridle with her good hand. Focus returned at the cost of her sword, which fell onto the narrow roadway.

So that was how the matter lay?

So be it.

'Go,' she breathed. 'See to your sister's safety. I'll hold them.'

Josiri spurred closer, the false calm giving way to horror. 'Mother, no!'

Calenne looked on with impassive eyes.

'I can't ride.' Katya dropped awkwardly from her saddle and stooped to reclaim her sword. The feel of the grips beneath her fingers awoke new determination. 'Leave me.'

'No. We're getting out of here. All of us.' He reached out. 'You can ride with me.'

The tremor beneath his tone revealed the truth. His horse was already weary. What stamina remained would not long serve two riders, let alone three.

Katya glanced down the street. There'd soon be nothing left to argue over. She understood Josiri's reluctance, for it mirrored her own. To face a parting now, with so much unsaid . . .? But a lifetime would not be enough to express her pride, nor to warn against repeating her mistakes. He'd have to find his own way now.

'Do you love me so little that you'd make me beg?' She forced herself to meet his gaze. 'Accept this last gift and remember me well. Go.'

Josiri gave a sharp nod, his lips a pale sliver. His throat bobbed. Then he turned his horse.

Katya dared not watch as her children galloped away, fearful that Josiri would read the gesture as a change of heart.

'Lumestra's light shine for you, my son,' she whispered.

A slap to her horse's haunch sent it whinnying into the oncoming wayfarers. They scattered, fighting for control over startled steeds.

Katya took up position at the bridge's narrow crest, her sword point-down at her feet in challenge. She'd no illusions about holding the wayfarers. It would cost them little effort to ride straight over her, had they the stomach for it. But the tightness of the approach offered a slim chance.

The knight raised a mailed fist. The pursuers halted a dozen yards from the bridge's mouth. Two more padded out from the surrounding alleys. Not horsemen, but the Council's simarka – bronze constructs forged in the likeness of lions and given life by a spark of magic. Prowling statues that hunted the Council's enemies. Katya swore under her breath. Her sword was useless against such creatures. A blacksmith's hammer would have served her better. She'd lost too many friends to those claws to believe otherwise.

'Lady Trelan.' The knight's greeting boomed like thunder. 'The Council demands your surrender.'

'Viktor Akadra.' Katya made no attempt to hide her bitterness. 'Did your father not tell you? I do not recognise the Council's authority.'

The knight dismounted, the hem of his jet-black surcoat trailing in the rain. He removed his helm. Swarthy, chiselled features stared out from beneath a thatch of black hair. A young face, though one already confident far beyond its years.

He'd every reason to be so. Even without the armour, without the entourage of weary wayfarers – without her wounds – Akadra would have been more than her match. He stood a full head taller than she – half a head taller than any man she'd known.

'There has been enough suffering today.' His tone matched his expression perfectly. Calm. Confident. Unyielding. He gestured, and the simarka sat, one to either side. Motionless. Watchful. 'Let's not add to the tally.'

'Then turn around, Lord Akadra. Leave me be.'

Lips parted in something not entirely a smile. 'You will stand before the Council and submit to judgement.'

Katya knew what that meant. The humiliation of a show trial, arraigned as warning to any who'd follow in her foot-steps and dare seek freedom for the Southshires. Then they'd parade her through the streets, her last dignity stripped away long before the gallows took her final breath. She'd lost a husband to that form of justice. She'd not suffer it herself.

'I'll die first.'

'Incorrect.'

Again, that damnable confidence. But her duty was clear. Katya let the anger rise, as she had on the road. Its fire drove back the weariness, the pain, the fear for her children. Those problems belonged to the future, not the moment at hand. She was a daughter of the Southshires, the dowager duchess Trelan. She would not yield. The wound in Katya's side blazed as she surged forward. The alchemy of rage transmuted agony to strength and lent killing weight to the two-handed blow.

Akadra's sword scraped free of its scabbard. Blades clashed with a banshee screech. Lips parted in a snarl of surprise, he gave ground through the hissing rain.

Katya kept pace, right hand clamped over the failing left to give it purpose and guide it true. She hammered at Akadra's guard, summoning forth the lessons of girlhood to the bleak present. The forms of the sword her father had drilled into her until they flowed with the grace of a thrush's song and the power of a mountain river. Those lessons had kept her alive on the ridge at Zanya. They would not fail her now.

The wayfarers made no move to interfere.

But Akadra was done retreating.

Boots planted on the cobbles like the roots of some venerable, weather-worn oak, he checked each strike with grace that betrayed tutelage no less exacting than Katya's own. The claymore blurred across grey skies and battered her longsword aside.

The fire in Katya's veins turned sluggish. Cold and failing flesh sapped her purpose. Too late, she recognised the game Akadra had played. She'd wearied herself on his defences, and all the while her body had betrayed her.

Summoning her last strength, Katya hurled herself forward. A cry born of pain and desperation ripped free of her lips.

Again the claymore blurred to parry. The longsword's tip scraped past the larger blade, ripping into Akadra's cheek. He twisted away with a roar of pain.

Hooves sounded on cobbles. The leading wayfarers spurred forward, swords drawn to avenge their master's humiliation. The simarka, given no leave to advance, simply watched unfolding events with feline curiosity.

Katya's hands tightened on her sword. She'd held longer than she'd believed possible. She hoped Josiri had used the time well. 'Leave her!'

Akadra checked the wayfarers' advance with a single bellow. The left side of his face masked in blood, he turned his attention on Katya once more. He clasped a closed fist to his chest. Darkness gathered about his fingers like living shadow.

Katya's world blurred, its colours swirling away into an unseen void.

Her knee cracked against the cobbles. A hand slipped from her sword, fingers splayed to arrest her fall. Wisps of blood curled through pooling rainwater. She knelt there, gasping for breath, one ineluctable truth screaming for attention.

The rumours about Akadra were true.

The shadow dispersed as Akadra strode closer. The wayfarers had seen none of it, Katya realised – or had at least missed the significance. Otherwise, Akadra would have been as doomed as she. The Council would tolerate much from its loyal sons, but not witchcraft.

Colour flooded back. Akadra's sword dipped to the cobbles. His bloodied face held no triumph. Somehow that was worse.

'It's over.' For the first time, his expression softened. 'This is not the way, Katya. It never was. Surrender. Your wounds will be tended. You'll be treated with honour.'

'Honour?' The word was ash on Katya's tongue. 'Your father knows nothing of honour.'

'It is not my father who makes the offer.' He knelt, one gauntleted hand extended. 'Please. Give me your sword.'

Katya stared down at the cobbles, at her life's blood swirling away into the gutter. Could she trust him? A lifetime of emissaries and missives from the north had bled her people dry to feed a pointless war. Viktor's family was part of that, and so he was part of it. If his promise *was* genuine, he'd no power to keep it. The Council would never let it stand. The shame of the gallows path beckoned.

'You want my sword?' she growled.

Katya rose from her knees, her last effort channelled into one final blow.

Akadra's hand, so lately extended in conciliation, wrenched the sluggish blade from her grasp. He let his own fall alongside. Tugged off balance, Katya fell to her hands and knees. Defenceless. Helpless.

No. Not helpless. Never that.

She forced herself upright. There was no pain. No weariness.

Just calm. Was this how Kevor had felt at the end? Before the creak of the deadman's drop had set her husband swinging? Trembling fingers closed around a dagger's hilt.

'My son will finish what I started.'

The dagger rasped free, Katya's right hand again closing over her left.

'No!' Akadra dived forward. His hands reached for hers, his sudden alarm lending weight to his promises.

Katya rammed the dagger home. Chain links parted. She felt no pain as the blade slipped between her ribs. There was only a sudden giddiness as the last of her burdens fell away into mist.

Josiri held Calenne close through the clamour. Screams. Buccina calls. Galloping hooves. Barked orders. Josiri longed for the thunder's return. Bravery came easier in moments when the angry sky drowned all else.

The church spire passed away to his left. Desperate towns-folk crowded its lychpath, seeking sanctuary behind stone walls. People filled the streets beyond. Some wore council blue, most the sea-grey of Eskavord's guard, and too many the garb of ordinary folk caught in between.

Ravens scattered before Josiri's straining horse. He glanced down at the girl in his charge. His sister she may have been, but Calenne was a stranger. She sat in silence, not a tear on her cheeks. He didn't know how she held herself together so. It was all he could do not to fall apart.

A pair of wayfarers emerged from an alleyway, their approach masked by the booming skies. Howling with courage he didn't feel, Josiri hacked at the nearest. The woman slumped across her horse's neck. Josiri rowelled his mare, leaving the outpaced survivor snarling at the rain.

More wayfarers waited at the next junction, their horses

arrayed in a loose line beneath overhanging eaves. The town wall loomed through the rain. The west gate was so close. Two streets away, no more. A glance behind revealed a wayfarer galloping in pursuit. A pair of simarka loped alongside. Verdigrised claws struck sparks from the cobbles.

To turn back was to be taken, a rat in a trap. The certainty of it left Josiri no room for doubt. Onward was the only course.

'Hold tight to me,' he told Calenne, 'and don't let go.'

Thin arms redoubled their grip. Josiri drove back his heels.

Time slowed, marked out by the pounding of hooves and the beat of a fearful heart. Steel glinted. Horses whinnied as wayfarers hauled on their reins.

'For the Southshires!'

The battle cry fed Josiri's resolve. The widening of the nearest wayfarer's eyes gave him more. They were as afraid of him as he of them. Maybe more, for was his mother not the Phoenix of prophecy?

Time quickened. Josiri's sword blurred. A wayfarer spun away in a bloody spray. And then Josiri was through the line, his horse's greedy stride gobbling the last distance to the west gate. The mare barely slowed at the next corner. Her hooves skidded on the rain-slicked cobbles.

Calenne screamed – not with terror, but in wild joy – and then the danger was past, and the west gate was in sight.

The portcullis was down, its iron teeth sunk deep. A line of tabarded soldiery blocked the roadway and the branching alleyways to either side. Halberds lowered. Shields locked tight together, a flock of white hawk blazons on a wall of rich king's blue. Wayfarers filled the street behind.

Thunder roared, its fury echoing through the hole where Josiri's heart should have been. He'd failed. Perhaps he'd never had a chance.

'Everything will be all right.' He hoped the words sounded more convincing to Calenne than they did to him. 'Mother will come.'

Calenne stared up at him with all the earnestness of youth. 'Mother's already dead.'

Spears pressed in. An officer's voice bellowed orders through the rain. Josiri gazed down into his sister's cold, unblinking eyes, and felt more alone than ever.